NIGHT STALKER

The girl must have a date. She was getting ready now, brushing her hair in front of the dresser mirror, a tight skirt stretched across her saucy little behind. Hair done to her satisfaction, she dropped the brush and pirouetted in front of the looking glass. After a moment, she undid the two top buttons of her sweater, tugging the neckline to a low vee; postured, arching her back, turning slightly from side to side. Another button, the neckline pulled wider, showing the top of a lacy low-cut bra . . .

Progress. The man's lips twisted in a satisfied smirk. Exactly what he had expected. And it was so easy. Eventually, they all did exactly what he wanted . . . anything he wanted . . . one way or another.

The light in her room went out; the window went dark. So let her go . . . for now. He would be seeing her later. He'd be seeing a lot more of her.

SECRET FRIEND

SHARON PORATH

ZEBRA BOOKS
KENSINGTON PUBLISHING CORP.

ZEBRA BOOKS

are published by

Kensington Publishing Corp.
475 Park Avenue South
New York, NY 10016

First printing: September, 1992

Printed in the United States of America

CHAPTER I

Midafternoon was the best time. He went upstairs then, just at 2:30, when school was letting out, and stood at the window, watching. The girls, the young girls, walking along together, heads close, talking and giggling. They couldn't see him, even if they looked up—which they never did—here above them, behind the glass. It gave him a funny feeling, to watch them . . . unseen . . . to know so many details about how they looked. Not that he undressed them with his eyes. Oh, nothing so crude. In fact, he liked the way their clothes were; the starchy blouses with vee'd openings pointing down, the light sweaters that clung across budding breasts; tight sweaters and even tighter skirts, tantalizing with hints of what lay underneath. Tantalizing him.

This was the age when girls needed an older friend, someone who knew all the things they needed to know. Almost like a father . . . or a big brother, showing them the ropes. And the girls were nice to him. At least mostly. Not like women his own age, selfish bitches always making demands. Oh, they pretended to be interested in him, of course; but just because they wanted something. And he knew what. He knew all about them, though he was careful never to show his real feelings. They were just like Mom had always said.

The ones like this, now, they looked up to him. He could single out any one he wanted, and they were always flattered, fascinated . . . and a little bit excited. It was heady stuff for an inexperienced girl; even the cautious ones were so easily impressed by an older man, an older boyfriend. And they believed everything he said. In a rush to be grown up, so anxious to appear sophisticated, they all entered willingly into the secret.

After that it was easy. To cajole a chosen girl into the empty house and give her the glass of wine. "To us!" he always said, and it always worked. Flushed and giggly, a little light-headed, they quickly went beyond protesting. Then his gentle kisses could become deeper, more insistent; his fingers could brush, as though by accident, against a breast, or drop to rest on a thigh. And go even further, button by button, or inch by inch beneath their skirts. Some of them, he was sure, didn't even know what was happening. And if one, occasionally, proved to be more in possession of herself, squirming and whimpering . . . well, that was just part of their game.

His face grew hot now, thinking about it; his breath came fast, clouding the glass of the window as he pressed closer, watching them out of sight. He rubbed damp hands down his trouser legs; rubbed again, in front. Watching the young rounding bodies, the narrow hips swinging. Picking one out like something in a market. It was so easy.

And they never told.

CHAPTER II

"Damnation." Carrie frowned upward through cooling drizzle at the single light in the upstairs dormer. *That wasn't on when I left. I'm sure it wasn't.* Blinking raindrops from her lashes, she turtled her head deeper into the turned-up collar of her jacket, lifted the grocery bag out of the back seat, and slammed the car door hard. But even as she squelched along the soggy driveway toward the kitchen entrance, the momentary irritation gave way to a reluctant grin. *You're getting pretty blasé,* she told herself, *when the only thing that really bothers you about a ghost is that it wastes electricity.*

Hitching the limp brown grocery bag into a more secure position, Carrie rattled through her ring of keys and let herself through the side door into the kitchen. She set the groceries on the counter and shed her wet jacket gratefully, savoring the pleasure she always found in the old-fashioned space. Her own space. Their last apartment had been newer and better equipped, with lots of cabinets, larger closets, and up-to-date appliances. But it had remained somehow aloof, a combination of roof and walls, assembly-line shelter.

The house, now, the house had a feel of welcoming. A kettle-on-the-stove, just-baked bread, warm and homey atmosphere. The sort of place everyone likes to remember growing up in, even when they didn't. She had recognized it, like an old friend, despite the layers of peeling paint and dirty wallpaper. The slowly proceeding work of cleaning and painting felt like bringing something back to life. And, of course, it was a form of therapy. Maybe, she thought, what came back to life was me as much as the house. Maybe it was a reciprocal arrangement. She hummed under her breath, a little off-key, as she rearranged the cabinets to accept more cans and boxes, then folded the grocery bag neatly and tucked it away under the sink for reuse.

Absorbed in minor chores, Carrie completely forgot about the family ghost's latest transgression. It wasn't until she trudged upstairs with an armload of freshly washed towels that she paused, reminded. Across the landing from the tiny linen closet, in her daughter's room, the ceiling lamp burned bravely in the late afternoon dimness. *But Lee Ann didn't leave the light on this morning. I'm sure she didn't.* Carrie had been upstairs at least twice since the teenager left for school; she would have noticed.

In the small front bedroom that her daughter had chosen for herself, nothing else was out of order. At least, no more than was normal for a fourteen-year-old. Carrie surveyed the chaos with resignation; although she insisted on regular cleaning and straightening, the actual activity was subject to Lee Ann's liberal interpretation.

A slight frown furrowed the area between her brows, a habit that by now had resulted in a permanent, quizzical crease. If Lee Ann's other casual habits didn't bother her, why was this business with the lights assuming so much importance? It had begun just a few weeks after they moved in, the desk lamp or overhead light constantly burning, and gentle reminders ignored. More pointed requests elicited Lee Ann's hurt insistence that she "had too turned out the lights."

Lee Ann had even gone so far as to suggest that perhaps someone else had been in the house. *A burglar?* The thought prickled Carrie's neck briefly, with the feeling of violation that would come with such an intrusion. But she brushed the unease aside almost at once, half-annoyed and half-amused at her daughter's transparent ploy.

It was such a minor aggravation, anyway. Carrie could have kidded her daughter about heredity—Matt had never turned off a light either. But she wasn't quite able to bring herself to talk about him so casually. Not yet.

Instead she had begun to blame the ghost, a hypothetical haunt who was afraid of the dark. It was a lame attempt to make her point with humor, edging carefully past touchy teenage sensibility. Lee Ann had picked up on the game gleefully, and "the ghost" became a household scapegoat for everything from dirty dishes to socks lost in the wash. But she still regarded her mother with affronted innocence when it was announced that the family specter had left the lights on again.

Her back to the shadowy hallway and yawning stairwell, Carrie felt the beginnings of a shiver prickle between her shoulder blades. It was definitely getting colder. She reached out and flicked the old-fashioned switch, turning the light off with a decisive snap. Maybe it had been on all morning and she just hadn't noticed. Or . . . could there be something wrong with the wiring—a short circuit? Carrie knew that the mysterious force known as electricity could turn lights *out* capriciously; she had no idea whether it could turn them on.

Don't let it be an electrical problem, she worried; and never noticed that she had, out of old habit, addressed her plea to some unnamed but presumably interested entity. I couldn't raise the money to rewire this place, she explained, in one of the endless conversations she held in her head. I've borrowed as much as I can handle for the repairs I've already made. "I'd rather have a ghost than a wiring problem," she said out loud, firmly. The statement hung there, defiantly, in the chilly air of the empty room. Hoping she wouldn't come to regret the assertion, Carrie turned and went back downstairs, just a little too rapidly.

Lee Ann would be home soon. In the tiny front foyer, at the foot of the stairs, Carrie drifted forward and peered out through the high window in the front door. It had stopped raining, but the wind was rising sharply and tattered clouds scudded across the sky. No sign yet of any children, no cheerful yellow bus disgorging its unruly cargo filled with Friday-afternoon high spirits.

Behind her the living room and dining room were bleak and cheerless in the swimming gray light. Water dripped from a gutter somewhere with dismal metronomic regularity. Carrie rubbed absently at her upper arms and retreated to the cluttered kitchen to plug in the coffeemaker. Chilled and fatigued, she pulled her baggy old sweater from its hook beside the door and sat down at the scarred oak table that she hadn't had time to refinish. So many things to be done. Most of them only required her time and effort—cleaning, patching, painting, and papering. Even minor repairs she could take care of herself. But something major like the roof, the furnace—or the wiring—would impose real financial hardship.

Not for the first time, she wondered if she had done the right thing, buying the house. The lawyer who handled Matt's will had expressed reservations, but she hated to think he'd been right. She'd taken an instant dislike to the unctuous, overgroomed man who'd sat primly in his large leather chair, separated from her by an acre of polished desk and a lifetime of different experiences.

"The estate is not really large, you understand." His professional smile had been condescending. "Still, a house could be an excellent investment, providing that you don't tie up all your funds in it." *Did he really think I was that stupid?* "But I would advise you to wait a while and give it more thought before you make a definite decision. Especially now," he had added, delicately avoiding direct reference to Matt's death, "when you're under a lot of stress."

He was trying to be kind, Carrie told herself wearily; she only winced a little, too numb to work up real resentment at his obviously low opinion of her capabilities.

Matt's estate. Such a grandiose term for their small savings and modest possessions, so slowly and painfully acquired. The insurance money had been the only sum of any real significance. It was a painful irony that, after years of saving and planning together, it had been Matt's death that finally provided the home they'd always wanted.

The insurance money had bought the house, and left a small nest egg which Carrie had designated for Lee Ann, for college. Day-to-day expenses she managed from her part-time secretarial job. But a large unplanned expenditure like rewiring the place could easily upset the precarious balance.

Her thoughts, darkening like the day, were interrupted by a scuffing in the driveway gravel; the door flew open and two giggling teenagers blew in with a gust of cold air. Lee Ann and her friend Penny from down the street had been inseparable since they'd moved in, and Carrie had often blessed the fate that had kindly supplied a neighborhood companion for her only child. Although, in fact, it had been the other way around; in a manner of speaking,

Lee Ann's friend had supplied the neighborhood.

"Hi, Mom."

"Miz Sutton."

"We're going over to Penny's after a while and watch a movie on cable. Her mom says I can have dinner with them and sleep over. Is that okay?"

"Sure, as long as it's all right with Penny's mom."

Evening plans thus disposed of, the two girls turned to more immediate considerations, like an after-school snack. As Lee Ann disappeared behind the open refrigerator door, Carrie congratulated herself for having had the foresight to go to the grocery. Fortified against starvation with brimming glasses of milk and a plate of cookies, the girls vanished upstairs to Lee Ann's room.

Carrie gazed after them with fondness and complacency. Compared to so many of the other kids, these two were refreshingly normal. Lee Ann's usual sunny and sensible disposition was beginning to reassert itself as she recovered from the shock of her father's death. And Penny, a levelheaded and intelligent girl, had been a steadying influence. Active and outgoing, she was a perfect foil for the more retiring Lee Ann; her friendship had been a buffer for the other girl during the first traumatic weeks in a new school and an unfamiliar neighborhood. For that alone Carrie would have loved Penny; she had had so many formless fears for her shy and vulnerable daughter.

Shadows began to thicken in the corners of the kitchen; it was getting dark earlier now, and the gloomy overcast hastened the onset of night. Carrie turned on the light and went to rummage in the freezer for a TV dinner: it wasn't worth cooking a whole meal just for one person. From overhead, the still childish voices were a blur of sound, an excited tangle without intelligible words, ordinary and reassuring.

         *   *   *

"Bobby Rhodes is going to be there. He told Ricky." Penny scooted forward on the edge of the bed. "So why don't you come? A lot of the other kids from school are going."

Lee Ann swiveled away from the little maple desk and pushed her chair backward, teetering on two of its legs, trying to think what to say. These days it seemed to take some kind of special effort to keep her mind on what was going on. It was the eyes, she thought. The constant feeling of being watched, ever since they'd moved in. And not just watched. Something worse, something sicky-feeling. *But it has to be all in my head. Like the dreams. There's nobody around, even, half the time.* I'm just nervous, in a new place—and being alone so much. Like Mom says.

Finally she simply shrugged. "I'm just not all that crazy about skating."

"Since when?" Penny sat straight up, sputtering. "And besides," her friend continued, with a typical adolescent *non sequitur,* "you said you thought Bobby was cute."

Lee Ann shook her head restlessly. "Sure, he's cute. I just don't want to . . . go around with him. That's all. You know . . ."

"No, I don't know." Penny huffed in exasperation. "And anyhow, you don't *have* to go around with him. We're mostly just talking about going skating. What's the big deal?"

Lee Ann shifted miserably on the hard chair. *Maybe there really is something wrong with me . . . if even my very best friend doesn't understand.* Penny tried . . . she really did. But the other kids took everything so seriously; and it just didn't seem all that important anymore.

The silence stretched between them almost as wide

as the chasm between teenager and parent. Lee Ann pulled her arms taut against her sides; the muscles across her shoulders ached, and all her insides felt hollow. *Why can't they just let me alone?* The scream buzzed and resounded inside her head like something battering to get out.

The silence broke with a brittle crash and both girls jumped.

Downstairs, Carrie winced at the noise and hoped it wasn't one of the remaining pieces of her good china. Footsteps pounded down the stairs, heralding the arrival of the culprits.

Lee Ann avoided her mother's eyes as she bent to clink shards into the waste can. "Mom, I'm afraid I broke your plate." *At least I guess I did. I'll get blamed for it anyway*. Her voice was thin, her shoulders hunched defensively.

Beside her, Penny shifted nervously from foot to foot. "It wasn't her fault," she piped up loyally.

Lee Ann shot her friend a look that Carrie couldn't read. "I don't know what happened. I put it on the desk next to my books and it . . . just fell off."

Carrie went forward to view the remains. "No problem," she said thankfully. "It was an old one that didn't match anything." Lee Ann sucked absently at her forefinger.

"Did you cut yourself?"

"Just a teeny scratch. I didn't think it would be as sharp as that."

"Maybe you ought to put something on it." Maternal obligation dictated the suggestion, although Carrie knew what the response would be. "I think there are Band-Aids in the medicine cabinet."

Lee Ann made the expected gesture of rejection. "It's nothing," she said impatiently. "We're going down to Penny's now, okay?"

Gathering up jackets, books, and paraphernalia, they departed in a flurry of cold wind and activity. Drawn in their wake, Carrie stood at the front door and watched them go, colorful figures flickering in and out like strobes through alternating pools of streetlight and shadow.

CHAPTER III

There was someone in the old house again—two people apparently, moving in, unpacking, getting settled. And one of them was a girl. A young girl, doll-like and delicate. The man shifted restlessly, trying to see, trying to focus . . . wanting to get closer, anxious, still uncertain just how it was all going to work. He concentrated, straining like a swimmer against an unseen current. It was all so perfect; almost like a dream. Almost.

She was just the right age. Twelve or thirteen, it was hard to tell. And she was pretty. Under a mop of dark curls, her face was pale, pink and white, with an expression that was wistful, almost sad. She moved nicely, too. Gracefully, threading her way through the jumbled rooms, through the furniture set down just anywhere; even crouched on her heels beside a carton or bending over awkwardly to empty a box, the faded jeans pulled tight across round little haunches. A light knit shirt, bright red, curved around her dainty body like a caress, its collar falling away from the too-prominent collarbones . . . the vulnerable neck.

A girl. Another young girl.

*　　*　　*

With the caprice common to early October, Saturday's weather turned warm and golden. Through windows now clean and glistening, the early sun laid a golden lattice across the littered floor of the dining room. Balancing on her rickety ladder, Carrie scraped determinedly at the last of the horrible wallpaper. A garish mélange of unidentifiable flora, with perhaps a bit of fauna thrown in, it might have been designed expressly to ruin appetites. Descending from her perch, she stretched sore arms and viewed the now-bare plaster with satisfaction. Anything was better than that wallpaper.

The first time they stepped inside the house, she had nudged Lee Ann behind the real-estate agent's back: "If bad taste were a crime, they'd have executed someone for this." Rewarded with a wan smile, she had been reassured about the rightness of her decision to buy a house. New surroundings would be a healthy change for both of them, a symbolic cutting of ties.

The apartment had been full of their old life, like echoes. With the help of her doctor's prescription for sleeping pills, Carrie had managed the nights, but sometimes she'd thought the days were just as bad. Even months after Matt's death, she had caught herself turning reflexively toward an empty place . . . listening unconsciously for steps in the hallway, the sound of a key in the lock. His personal things were packed up, given away. But subtler reminders remained, like the sweet, pungent scent of pipe tobacco that lingered in desk drawers and the back of the closet.

The patterns of life, irretrievably altered, shaped themselves around an absence. Carrie and Lee Ann moved around the apartment like wind-up toys running on parallel tracks, close together but never

17

meeting—carefully bypassing Matt's desk, his chair at the table, his end of the sofa . . . his side of the bed.

In early spring the idea of moving appeared, tentatively, with the first early seedlings. Carrie had examined the thought with mild surprise, and set it aside. But once admitted, the concept began to establish itself, unrolling new possibilities. Objectively, she acknowledged that new surroundings would be a healthy step; emotionally, she clung to the security of the familiar, even while she regarded her own indecision with disdain. Carrie had always thought of herself as a capable and independent woman; it was only that she had grown so accustomed to having someone else to share decisions. The removal of that quiet support added another facet to pain; in the lethargy of grief, she vacillated listlessly over even the smallest daily details.

In the end it was the lawyer's unwitting challenge that had goaded her into action. A house made sense for her and Lee Ann, both financially and emotionally. Like a lodestone, the idea drew her: she presented it to Lee Ann like a gift.

The hunt was on.

On her way back and forth from work, on forays to the grocery, Carrie had found herself taking new interest in her surroundings. Each neighborhood was evaluated; For Sale signs occasioned close scrutiny. The search widened; she made inquiries about schools. Armed with a street map, she ranged farther afield, occasionally stopping dead in the middle of a street, rummaging for a pencil to write down a phone number from a realtor's sign in a yard.

Coaxed to accompany her on some of the expeditions, Lee Ann had been withdrawn and unresponsive, sunk in the apathy that had gripped her since her father's death. Hands in pockets, she wandered aimlessly through empty rooms, as de-

18

tached as though her surroundings meant nothing to her. A procession of houses blurred and ran together: featureless cookie-cutter suburban ranches and too-large, dilapidated older places. Carrie's initial impetus faltered, deflated. Striving for objectivity and achieving cynicism, she prepared to abandon her nebulous ideal. Her pleasant little house on a tree-lined street simply didn't exist; or if it did, it would be priced clear out of her reach.

The heat of summer had descended like a blanket. Carrie began to persuade herself that it was, after all, more sensible to stay in the comfortable air-conditioned apartment, with its professional maintenance, than to take on the risks involved in home ownership. The roof could leak, the gutters rust, the plumbing clog. There could be termites—or worse. Hovering over steaming pots in the cramped apartment kitchen, she had felt suddenly tired and pessimistic. Maybe it really was a crazy idea. The lawyer's objections floated back—if she had to find a full-time job in order to afford a house, would she have the time to devote to cleaning, fixing up, doing yard work? And Lee Ann would be alone more.

Uneasily, Carrie's thoughts turned to concern for her daughter. She had been alone so much. Lee Ann's friends, coached by well-meaning parents, had appeared, scrubbed and solemn, at the funeral service . . . and had retreated immediately afterward with the callous self-absorption of the very young. Lee Ann had hardly seemed to notice. After the first tempests of tears and mutual comforting, she had withdrawn inexorably into a silent passivity that stood like a wall, refusing entry. Carrie had scrupulously refrained from pushing at the child; Lee Ann had to have time to deal with her grief in her own way.

She hoped it had been the right thing to do. With

19

the summer, at last, Lee Ann had begun to emerge from her tight and white-lipped silence. And the mindless ebb and flow of adolescent activity had swept her up again as casually as it had dropped her.

"Damn." Carrie burned her finger on a pot lid, stuck it in her mouth, childishly.

"Put some aloe vera on it." Lee Ann appeared at her elbow, vanished briefly, and reappeared bearing a flat fleshy piece of greenery. "It's the same stuff that's in lots of those creams, only organic."

She split the leaf and squeezed it. Carrie eyed the resulting gelatinous mess with some distaste, but decided not to voice her reservations about its curative power. She couldn't understand the current generation's fascination with folk remedies that had been superseded by medical science. At any rate, the burn wasn't bad enough to require much in the way of treatment, and she didn't want to appear ungrateful for her daughter's rare show of interest. Come to think of it, when did Lee Ann become interested in plants, and where had she gotten this one? Carrie vaguely remembered it having appeared on Lee Ann's desk, but she hadn't ever asked about it.

"Thanks," she said. Maybe it was just her imagination, but the sting of the burn seemed to have lessened. "What did you say this was?"

Lee Ann turned away and began to wrest dishes from the crowded cabinet. With blithe disregard for breakability, she added salad bowls, cutlery, and two glasses to the stack and vanished, clinking, into the dining ell. Her voice had floated back. "Aloe vera. I got it from Penny's mom," she volunteered, forestalling Carrie's next question. "I told you about her."

Had she? Probably so, Carrie acknowledged, trying to remember what had been said. With a rush of the guilt that comes so easily to conscientious

20

parents, she thought how out of touch she was with her daughter's life.

There had been only one thing to do in a situation like that. Bluff. "Penny's the girl you met at the . . . uh . . ."

"At the swimming pool with Debbie," supplied Lee Ann obligingly. "She goes to Hanover, but she's Sandy's cousin," she added, imparting obviously significant information and confusing Carrie completely. "We've been over there a few times, and her family's really neat." Lee Ann reappeared at the kitchen door. "Oh, and . . . there's a house down the street from them that's for sale. I've been meaning to tell you."

In retrospect, Carrie wondered why that announcement hadn't been accompanied by a roll of drums or a clap of thunder. In movies and soap operas, pivotal events were always marked by dramatic organ music: she thought fancifully that such a device would be useful in real life. Instead, you passed through major turning points all unaware, and the decisions that shaped your life were only visible when you looked back at them.

And then it is too late. Carrie shook herself, wondering where that morbid thought had come from. She spread newspapers, pried the lid off a can of paint, and stirred, admiring the mellow creamy color contentedly. The house had been the catalyst she had hoped for. Working together, planning, cleaning, she and Lee Ann had once more achieved a comfortable relationship . . . even a degree of intimacy.

From the start, Lee Ann had taken a proprietary

21

interest in the house. And rightfully so, for without her urging Carrie would never have considered it. At their first quick drive-by, the view had been less than encouraging. The house sat shyly toward the back of a large lot, as if trying to escape attention. So far, it seemed to have succeeded. Virtually invisible behind large trees and a disastrously overgrown hedge, it looked as if it had been abandoned for years. The realtor's sign in the front yard was weathered and leaning, almost obscured by the rampant greenery.

Carrie pulled up to the curb and sat staring in appalled silence. Lee Ann, undaunted, got out of the car and advanced purposefully into the yard, intent on looking into windows. Carrie hung back, feeling intrusive, and surveyed the structure from the sidewalk. Its basic shape was appealing, foursquare and solid beneath a whimsical steep-pitched roof. But the facade was a mess of peeling paint, rusting screens, and sagging shutters. Someone had made a few cursory attempts at maintenance; one broken window was neatly patched with cardboard, and the grass had apparently been mowed sometime within the last month.

"Mom, come on." Lee Ann came dashing back. "There isn't anybody living here. Nobody's going to care if we look around."

Carrie wondered briefly just how often her daughter had been here. With her mother in tow, Lee Ann circled the house, pointing out attractions like a tour guide. "Look, there's a fireplace in the living room."

"Which is probably a fire hazard, if it hasn't long since been closed up." But Carrie crossed the porch and stood beside her daughter to peer through the dusty window. The room was nicely proportioned; except for a tiny foyer at the right, it ran the full width of the house. Behind it was a separate dining room, with what looked like a window seat in a bay.

"If it was cleaned up, the woodwork would be beautiful . . . and look at those doors between the living room and dining room."

"French doors. Yes." Despite her initial dismay, Carrie had begun to see the house's possibilities. Just giving it a coat of paint would do wonders. If the price were right . . . and if it proved to be structurally sound . . .

And Lee Ann was really excited about it, displaying the first genuine enthusiasm she had shown since before Matt died. Pleased that something had elicited that kind of response from her daughter, Carrie made an appointment with the real-estate agent.

The rest, as they say, is history.

Guiding them through the house, the professionally voluble agent had been at a loss for words; she seemed to be running through her sales pitch mentally, discarding large portions of it as she went. Ducking a free-floating web, she brushed fastidiously at the front of her immaculate blouse and launched into what remained of her spiel. "It needs work," she said sincerely, "but it does have a lot of potential. And especially for this neighborhood, the price is very reasonable."

In front of the agent, Lee Ann tried gamely to affect an expression of appropriate gloom. But Carrie could tell that she had already formed a very definite opinion.

Carrie herself had to shake off a persistent tendency to visualize the house as it could be, mentally bypassing major expenditures and hours of work. Primed with information and helpful hints from friends and library books—she always did careful research before making major decisions—Carrie prowled through the house, trying to remember all the things she had to look for, all the questions she

23

had to ask.

The answers, when they came, were suprisingly satisfactory. An inspection for termites and pests was negative; the engineering firm reported no major structural problems. Carrie gulped at the figure on the appraisal, but resolutely submitted the offer she had decided on. To her amazement, it was accepted. Out-of-town owners, heirs to the property, were glad to have the house sold, the estate settled.

Faced with an imminent deadline on their apartment lease, Carrie had been confronted with a staggering number of tasks and very little time in which to do them. The closing was held. Utilities were turned on, repair estimates obtained, workmen supervised. At the apartment—already they had ceased to think of it as home—Lee Ann pitched in with uncharacteristic energy. Together, they packed, selected, discarded. Several times in the process, Carrie ran across some long-forgotten item of Matt's, tucked away at the back of a drawer or on a closet shelf. It troubled her that she didn't cry. Moving numbly under the momentum of events, she had begun finally to sever her ties to the past. Already the apartment looked strange to her, its painful reminders beginning to lose their edge. When she closed the door on the familiar rooms for the last time, it was with a curious mixture of anticipation and depression. She looked forward to their new home, but felt disloyal, too, as though in moving she were somehow leaving Matt behind.

Finally, tired and a bit dazed, she and Lee Ann stood amid a clutter of boxes and baggage in their own home. Carrie wondered abstractedly where she had packed the can opener; Lee Ann, more practical, had suggested take-out Chinese.

It wasn't the ceremonious occasion Carrie had envisioned for their first meal in the new house.

Juggling little white cartons, they stood in the dining-room doorway surveying the disarray, which looked, if possible, even worse by artificial light. A central pile of boxes and cartons bulked raw and immense in the sullen glow of a chandelier that resembled an inverted glass toadstool. The wallpaper, hideous by daylight, at night was unspeakable. The immense floral contortions took on an almost fluorescent quality; changes in the reflected light gave them an uneasy aspect of furtive movement.

"It looks like it's trying to crawl," said Lee Ann, who had a macabre way with a phrase.

She and Carrie had looked at one another and succumbed to a fit of helpless giggles, leaning on one another and gasping for breath. If there was a slight edge of hysteria to the laughter, Carrie simply put it down to fatigue and stress.

The morning crept on toward noon, and the direct sun grew almost hot. Carrie wiped her face as she bent to refill the roller tray. When the door slammed, she jumped, nearly spilling the paint. Footsteps announced Lee Ann's arrival—with an entourage, to judge from the sound. Three heads appeared simultaneously around the edges of the French doors.

"I'm home, Mom," said Lee Ann unnecessarily.

"Hi," said the other two. Carrie suppressed an impulse to smile. From the exalted status conferred by sixteen years and a driver's license, Danny Burnett normally looked upon his younger siblings with a certain disdain. It was only recently that he had nobly resigned himself to Penny's company—particularly on those occasions when Lee Ann was also in evidence.

She looked at him now, sidewise, and he stepped forward, holding a small carton. With a sinking

25

feeling, Carrie noticed that the box had air holes. An ominous scratching sound emanated from it; the cardboard flexed and threatened to give way under the onslaught. It meowed.

"What in the world . . ." Carrie began, and Lee Ann interrupted with an imploring look.

"Oh, Mom, wait till you see—she's so cute." She put the box on the floor and began unwrapping the twine that secured it. Danny knelt beside her, ostensibly to help.

"Our next-door neighbor's cat had kittens," explained Penny, hovering.

With the string unwound, the box collapsed completely, and a ball of multi-colored fluff rolled out, squeaking. Righting itself, the kitten glared at them suspiciously, tongue tip protruding as if in deep concentration. Finding no immediate threat, it bent and began to groom long calico fur with single-minded intensity.

Carrie melted. Crouching, she held out her hand for the little cat to sniff. "What a pretty baby." The kitten licked her finger. Lee Ann looked at her hopefully, and Carrie gave in. "You'll have to go to the store and get some cat food and litter and a pan. And we'll have to line up a vet—she'll need shots."

The three young faces relaxed into pleased grins. "Thanks, Mom," said Lee Ann, relieved. "I'll take care of her."

Carrie had been a mother long enough not to put much stock in that promise, but she didn't suppose one cat would be too much trouble. She patted the kitten, now reposing against Lee Ann's shirtfront and shedding liberally. It looked back at her complacently with large golden eyes, then closed them and went to sleep.

"You'll have to shut her in your room for now," Carrie told her daughter. "I can't have her loose

26

while we're painting. Note the plural: *we're* painting. But you might go to the store first. We need eggs and bread and a few other things."

"The big supermarket down at the shopping center would be the best place to go, then," said Lee Ann practically. "They have pet supplies, too." She looked at Danny inquiringly.

"Dad's car's in the shop, but Mom'll let us use hers," he said with assurance.

"We'll ask her if she needs anything from the store; we can pick stuff up for her at the same time," added Penny craftily.

Lee Ann took the kitten upstairs, with Danny close behind, bearing a bowl of milk like an acolyte. Penny followed with a thick section of newspaper. "Just in case," she explained.

Back downstairs, the three collected a shopping list and left on their errand. Carrie reascended the ladder and began to paint.

She hadn't actually met Penny until the day after they'd moved in. When Lee Ann's friend appeared at the door that morning, Carrie greeted her with reserve and a touch of irritation. Surely even a youngster could see that this was not the time for a visit. But Penny never wanted or expected to be treated like a guest. After a brief observation of the amenities, she set to work beside Lee Ann, emptying cartons and carrying them outside for the trash pickup. Watching the two of them as they unpacked, cleaned cabinets, and washed dishes, Carrie had the bemused impression that she had somehow acquired another child.

She had been similarly impressed upon first meeting Danny. Sent to fetch Penny for some family errand, he knocked at the screen door as Carrie stood precariously at the top of a ladder, painting carefully around the front hallway's hanging light fixture.

"Why not put a plastic bag over that?" he suggested practically. "Then you don't have to worry about dripping paint on the lamp. Or I could take the whole light fixture down for you, if you want me to." At Carrie's look of bewildered ineptitude, he stepped in and took over, almost forgetting his original errand in the process.

Since then his visits had increased in frequency, until he and Penny were in and out almost as regularly as Lee Ann. They mowed and weeded, trimmed shrubs and scraped paint. They sprawled across the front porch, guzzling lemonade and emptying bags of cookies. Lee Ann, though still quiet and self-possessed, began to show signs again of the carefree high spirits that should be typical of her age. And Carrie, normally ill at ease around teenagers other than her own, found herself enjoying the company. It was a genuine pleasure to meet youngsters who could look you in the eye and converse in English.

Was she becoming stodgy, at the ripe old age of thirty-seven? Somehow she couldn't quite view herself as part of the "older generation." But the current crop of high-schoolers seemed incredibly alien, with their bizarre plumage and their self-obsessed secretiveness. They seemed to form an entirely separate culture, cut loose and adrift, analyzed and reported on in shouting headlines and tragic statistics: teenage pregnancy, drug abuse, alcoholism, an alarming suicide rate. Walking near groups of them, listening to their music, their chatter, was like invading a flock of exotic birds, brightly colored and skittish. And fragile, though they didn't have the sense or the experience to know it.

She stepped carefully down from the ladder and sat on the lowest rung, resting. How easily Lee Ann could have slipped away from her into those ranks, skipping school, drinking, and smoking pot. Plenty of the kids who got into deep trouble did so with far less reason than Lee Ann had. After Matt's death, Carrie had watched the girl for telltale signs, but she wasn't sure exactly what she was looking for, or what she would do if she found it. The teachers at school had assured her that Lee Ann was doing quite well, considering. She was attending all her classes, turning in assignments on time; her grades had dropped a little, perhaps, but not much.

The one dissenter had been the counselor at the new school. What was his name . . . Meredith? That was it, Frank Meredith: a lanky, almost disjointed-looking man of about her own age, who had looked at her distractedly over the tops of horn-rimmed glasses and lectured her on her daughter's state of mind.

Not that he had anything new to add. "Lee Ann is very unhappy . . ." *After her father's death, what do you expect?* "In fact, I'd say she's seriously depressed." *That's not exactly a surprise, either.*

The interview had not been proceeding well, and he knew it. Behind the horn-rims, his brown eyes were disconcertingly sharp and intelligent. Finally he took off the glasses, as though removing a mask, and laid them on the desk blotter. His sandy hair was rumpled, and his eyes were tired. "I don't know what more I can say," he told her candidly. "I have to respect Lee Ann's confidence about some of the things she's told me."

Things. What things? Carrie folded her arms across her stomach, where the sandwich she'd had for lunch seemed to have turned to stone. *Everything's been going really well. We haven't been having any*

29

problems. She looked back at him coldly. "Is it her grades? Is she skipping classes or something?"

Now his own eyes turned cold, and his voice was curt. "It isn't as simple as that," he told her stingingly. "I think Lee Ann may have a serious emotional problem; I think you might even consider counseling for her."

The idea had jolted Carrie like a physical slap. It was something no one had suggested before. Not even when Matt died. *Some of these guys don't believe anyone can make it through life without professional help.* She had concealed her resentment, at the time, behind a polite and noncommittal response.

In retrospect, she was willing to allow that his intentions had been good. It was just that he couldn't possibly know her daughter that well, not in such a short time. Lee Ann had only transferred to Hanover in September, when they'd moved. And she seemed to have settled in quite nicely . . . made new friends . . . gotten into new activities. She really was doing so much better.

Carrie blinked away the quick hot tears that still surprised her in unguarded moments. How very much she loved that child! Her inarticulate gratitude for her daughter's well-being would have been a prayer, if she could have brought herself to believe in God again.

When another slam of the door announced the return of the shopping expedition, Carrie had almost finished painting the ceiling. Intent, she took a last few strokes with the roller, then climbed down and stretched her aching arms. The mismatched trio appeared in the doorway and produced the contents of shopping bags for her inspection. Food bowl, litter pan, and an industrial-size bag of kitty litter—"It was a lot cheaper," explained Lee Ann solemnly.

They unloaded the groceries in the kitchen and hurried upstairs to introduce Lee Ann's pet to its new possessions. Remembering that the kitten had been sequestered in her daughter's bedroom, Carrie sincerely hoped that the arrival of the litter pan, at least, was not too late.

Back downstairs a few minutes later, the threesome conscientiously presented themselves, ready to work out their obligation. Danny went off to unstick a painted-shut kitchen window. Carrie doled out rollers and brushes, and opened a new can of paint.

Mellow late-afternoon sun was streaming diagonally through the long back windows by the time they finished. With the palest hint of peach in the ceiling color, echoed by a deeper apricot below, the effect was even better than Carrie had anticipated. The room glowed, and even Danny, their token Philistine, made admiring noises.

Removing coverings from the furniture, Lee Ann caught sight of her spattered face in the mirrored back of the old mahogany sideboard. Ducking closer, she turned her head from side to side, examining the effect. "Now I know what I'd look like with freckles," she observed. Penny moved up beside her and inspected her own face, where natural freckles were augmented with random spatters of a slightly different shade. "I think I got more paint on me than I did on the wall," she agreed, fingering a thick apricot streak in her coppery hair.

In the midst of their cleanup efforts, Carrie became aware of a faint noise from the living room. Only mildly curious, she headed for the French doors, gathering paint-spattered newspapers as she went. Before she reached the opening, a small furry body came hurtling through. Delightedly attacking the crumpled papers, the kitten skidded across the floor and caromed off a still-wet wall, adding yet another color to its mottled coat.

"Oh, God," invoked Carrie fervently.

Utter chaos ensued. Lee Ann stared in uncomprehending horror; Penny made a dive for the galloping cat. "Catch her!" she yelled. The kitten evaded her neatly, stepping in an unattended paint tray in the process. Leaving delicate apricot footprints, the tiny animal departed for the kitchen, where Danny was cleaning brushes in the sink.

A pained bellow announced her arrival, followed by a few relatively minor crashes. Danny emerged from the kitchen, nursing a series of scratches and cradling the panicky kitten in his arms. He took a quick comprehensive look at the scene of the disaster and whistled.

"How did she get out? She was shut in your room," he said to Lee Ann. "She really was," he repeated to Carrie, attempting to forestall a parental explosion. Kitten in custody, the two teens beat a strategic retreat up the stairs. There were sounds of running water from the bathroom.

Penny, ever practical, brought wet rags from the kitchen and began to make inroads into the mess. Paw prints and even puddles were eliminated with surprising ease, and Carrie thought with profound gratitude of the inventor of latex paint. "The floor needed cleaning anyway," she muttered in resignation, joining Penny on her knees.

Sweaty and paint-streaked, hair straggling limply from her bandanna, Carrie contemplated refusing to answer when an unfamiliar voice sounded from the front porch. "Hello?" it said inquiringly.

"Mom," said Penny, scrambling to her feet.

Why me? thought Carrie, and almost said it out loud. She had already heard admiring comments about Penny's mother from Lee Ann. If the woman appeared in a stylish outfit, bandbox fresh and beautifully groomed, Carrie would have to be physically restrained from painting her apricot.

Instead, the tiny dark woman who trailed in behind Penny was clad in blue jeans and scruffy sneakers. "I just came down to repossess the car so Keith could take the kids to the library," she explained apologetically. "I've been housecleaning . . ." She made an abortive gesture at her disheveled hair, then looked more closely at Carrie and grinned, crinkling frankly-forty laugh lines around bright blue eyes. Carrie, relieved, grinned back.

"I'm Barbara, by the way. I've been meaning to come down and introduce myself, but I figured you'd want some time to get settled first."

Carrie made the customary disclaimers about the mess, then offered coffee. Barbara responded with obligatory admiration for the wonders Carrie had done with the place, and accepted.

Behind them, Lee Ann and Danny descended, apprehensively reconnoitering over the banister. Dispatched to return the car to its rightful owner, he departed, casting a protective look backward at Lee Ann. She and Penny finished the cleanup, while regaling the newcomer with the explanation for its necessity. The kitten was produced, clean but damp and bedraggled, for admiration.

In the kitchen, Barbara unselfconsciously grabbed a rag and began wiping up paint smears, while Carrie made coffee, poured milk, and produced cookies from a package she had hidden in the depths of the corner cabinet. By the time all four sat down for their impromptu snack, surfaces throughout the two rooms were gleaming, although Carrie suspected darkly that she would continue to find small apricot footprints in strange places for weeks to come.

33

"What are you going to name her?" asked Barbara, stroking the kitten who, exhausted by her performance, had gone limply to sleep in Lee Ann's lap.

Lee Ann pondered the question seriously. Eyeing the miscreant with an attempt at sternness, Carrie responded instead. "Pandora," she decreed. "The minute you opened that box, I knew we had trouble."

CHAPTER IV

Sleep that night was much too deep and very full of dreams. Her father was in some of them—playing games just like when she was a little kid. Running ahead of her in some frantic game of tag, always just out of reach; and when they played hide 'n' seek she couldn't find him at all. Lee Ann rolled her head against the pillow, bereft once again.

The other dream was darker, more disturbing. She couldn't tell at first who was in it—just a figure, bending over her, so close. Closer than anyone had ever been. Closer than anyone *should* be. Hands, touching her, demanding; insistent. And so real.

Lee Ann whimpered sleepily, recoiled, pulled away . . . and awoke, sweaty and panting, sprawled helplessly across the bed, even the spurious protection of her blankets torn away. *Someone . . . there was someone. Right there. Bending over her, touching her.* Her eyes sprang open, wide, so wide they hurt, and the shadow figure above her resolved itself into ordinary darkness. *No one. There's no one here. There couldn't be.* But still she felt the insidious touch on her body, leaving her hot and cold at the same time—tingly, the way a peppermint tastes.

Shuddering, Lee Ann threw herself toward the foot of the bed, reached for and grasped her blanket.

Huddled into its protection, she gave way to a paroxysm of tears, muffling her sobs with one of its folds.

And the man withdrew, fading quickly into the shadows, delighted with his new daring, with this sudden opportunity. Breathless with his own excitement.

The sun was far higher than she expected when Carrie woke the next morning. Sitting upright, she flexed sore muscles and dismissed a nagging sense of urgency, realizing with gratitude that today there was no real need for hurry. She lay back on the pillows with a sigh. Sleep had finally returned, deep and refreshing, with no more need for pills. Sated, she stared lazily at shifting patterns of honey-colored light that flung themselves across the sloping ceiling. It was going to be a beautiful day. Maybe she should take off, go somewhere with Lee Ann . . . a movie, perhaps? It had been quite a while since they had been anywhere together. Vaguely astonished, she wondered where the last two months had gone; except for work and brief errands, she had hardly been out of the house. She hadn't even found time to take Lee Ann shopping for school clothes.

Of course, kids that age preferred the company of their friends to that of their parents. Lee Ann probably didn't view going someplace with her mother as any kind of a treat. But she had been working hard, in school all day and helping around the house on weekends. Maybe she and Penny would like to go to a movie. And Carrie could have the day free to tackle the kitchen. It would take at least the whole day, probably longer. The worst of the three main downstairs rooms, it looked like a major project, and she had unashamedly put it off.

With plans for the day arranged to her satisfaction, Carrie slipped out of bed and headed for the bathroom, admiring herself for her resolve. As she crossed the upstairs hall, she became aware for the first time of small noises from downstairs. Lee Ann, who normally slept as late as Carrie would let her, must be up already.

Brushing her chin-length chestnut hair, Carrie tucked it behind her ears and regarded her reflection critically. Her face looked pale and puffy, even her mouth drained of its normal tawny rose color. Deep amber eyes looked back at her, but she avoided their painful depths, focusing instead on the delicate lines that had begun to etch themselves at their corners. For a moment she wondered whether she should get dressed and take Lee Ann to church.

"Hypocrite," she mouthed at herself, and wearily decided against it. An unquestioning, if lukewarm, believer, she had dutifully attended Mass with Lee Ann for years. During Matt's illness the habitual observances had become less frequent. And with his death, she had retreated entirely from rituals that held no comfort and no meaning for her. Lee Ann had accepted the change in routine without comment, and it had been almost a year since either of them had been in a church.

Carrie thumped down the stairs and paused in the front hall, enjoying one of those rare, rounded moments of utter contentment. Before her the living room lay in peaceful silence, with soft light reflecting from its pristine ivory walls and lying across the expanse of newly cleaned and polished floor. On either side of the fireplace, small high windows of leaded glass poured rainbow light across the hearth. Oblique light slanted through the dining-room bay, warming the richly colored walls and gleaming on darkly burnished woodwork. In the kitchen, where cool indirect remnants of sun picked out every flaw in the chipped cabinetry and worn linoleum, Carrie's feeling of resolve turned to something like anticipation. Despite the hard work, she found immense satisfaction in the results she was achieving with the house.

At the table, Lee Ann had extracted the comic section from the fat Sunday paper, and sat staring at it, chin in hands. She grumped an unintelligible greeting and brushed her tousled dark hair out of her eyes. The gesture was Matt's. Just for a moment, Carrie's throat clenched like a fist. The girl was so much like her father; and Carrie had not yet arrived at the acceptance that could let her take pleasure in that.

"Good morning to you too." Carrie produced eggs from the small refrigerator and began to break them into a bowl. "Scrambled eggs okay?" With the smallest possible motion of her head, Lee Ann indicated that this would be acceptable. Pandora appeared from nowhere, rubbing indiscriminately against ankles and table legs. Carrie glanced at her daughter, who remained oblivious.

The kitten mewed insistently and tangled its claws in the hem of her bathrobe. Suppressing an acid comment about the responsibilities of pet ownership, Carrie contented herself with a theatrical sigh and opened a can of cat food.

The enticing smell of frying bacon filled the room. Lee Ann roused herself sufficiently to emerge from the newspaper and express a desire for coffee. Surprised, Carrie added another scoop to the paper filter and started the machine.

"I thought you didn't like coffee," she said, and was promptly annoyed with herself. It was the kind of inane remark guaranteed to be taken as challenge or critism by any teenager worth her salt.

To Carrie's relief, her daughter condescended to overlook the gaffe. "I just feel like it today," she responded. "I'm tired."

"You are up early." Carrie examined the girl surreptitiously. Her normally pink-fair skin was pale and there were circles under her eyes—eyes, like Matt's, that were by turns gray or green or blue. And just now they were gray as rain. "Is anything wrong?"

Oh God, if only I could tell you. Lee Ann wavered, haunted, almost ready to throw herself in her mother's arms and cry. *Like a little kid,* she told herself scornfully. *And mom will treat me like one . . . pat me on the head and tell me it was just a bad dream. Because it's just too crazy. Nobody would ever believe it. I'm not sure I believe it.*

The gaze she turned on her mother was practiced, bland and unrevealing. "I just couldn't go to sleep. It was the wind, I think."

"Wind?" said Carrie blankly. The evening had cooled as the sun went down, but the air had lain calm and heavy, with very little breeze.

"I know it sounds dumb. I kept thinking it was going to storm."

Having exhausted the topic, Lee Ann applied herself to a large plate of bacon and eggs. At least she wasn't sick. Carrie sat down across from her daughter and reached for the salt. She herself had slept deeply and dreamlessly, almost at once; she guessed the wind had risen later.

"Why is it I never seem to have time for all the things I need to do?" wailed Carrie. From the top rung of the ladder, she surveyed the chaos of the kitchen.

Below her, at knee level, Lee Ann wielded a paintbrush with more enthusiasm than skill. "Maybe because you plan too many things for one day," was her practical answer, and Carrie had to admit the

39

truth of the observation. Her penchant for making long things-to-do lists was an excellent organizational tool, but it took its toll in frustration. She always found herself adding two things to the bottom of the list for every item she crossed off the top.

It wasn't really a bad day's work. The painting, at least, was complete. Stretching, Carrie declared herself satisfied with their progress, descended from the ladder, and began cleanup. She cast an uneasy look at Lee Ann, who was now absorbedly cleaning paintbrushes in the sink. Were the shadows under her eyes deeper, or was it just the harsh overhead light? The girl must be exhausted. Carrie thrust away a stab of guilt: it had been Lee Ann who'd insisted on working. Carrie had suggested that she call Penny and go out, but the notion had been rejected, forcibly enough to make her wonder if the girls had had a tiff.

She dismissed the idea; if they'd had the inclination, they certainly hadn't had the time. When Penny left last night with her mother, she and Lee Ann had seemed to be on the best of terms.

At lunchtime, Carrie had broached the subject again. Over sandwiches and lemonade, she looked out at the sunny yard through the window. "It's too pretty a day to stay inside," she opined. "Are you sure you don't want to call Penny and go shopping or something?"

Lee Ann had stuck out her lip in an exaggeratedly mulish gesture. "Are you trying to get rid of me?" she asked accusingly. And it seemed to Carrie that she was only half-joking.

Touched by the glimpse of adolescent insecurity, Carrie had hastened to provide reassurance. And all afternoon she had taken pains to express her very real appreciation for her daughter's hard work.

But now Lee Ann, humming over the paint-brushes, seemed to have shaken her earlier glum mood. She scrutinized the walls, with their fresh creamy gloss, and offered the opinion that, on the whole, they had done a pretty good job. Casting a disparaging glance at the litter that still covered every horizontal surface and parts of the floor, she added a disclaimer. "We'd have been finished hours ago if you hadn't decided to paint the insides of the cabinets."

Chastened, Carrie admitted to a tactical error. "I didn't know it would take the paint so long to dry."

"We can't start putting stuff back until we're sure it won't stick," Lee Ann agreed. "But how are you going to cook dinner in this mess? I doubt if you can even find the pans."

Although she was beginning to suspect that the conversation was being maneuvered toward a goal, Carrie bit. "I don't know. What do you want to do?"

Lee Ann gleefully opted for hamburgers from her favorite hangout, and Carrie agreed, more out of weariness than gastronomic anticipation. Did teen-agers appreciate any food that didn't come in a bag or bucket poked at them through a window? She tugged off her spattered bandanna and pulled a comb quickly through her hair. After a cursory inspection in the hall mirror, Carrie decided that drive-up windows had their advantages after all. At least she wouldn't have to go inside a restaurant looking like this.

The sky was lowering and early dark was setting in when Carrie returned, tired and irritated. *I'm the only person I know who can get caught in a traffic jam at a drive-in restaurant.* She hoped Lee Ann wasn't worried. No lights were visible in the front of the house as she drove by and crunched into the gravel driveway. Above the side porch, the kitchen windows were also dark. Loath to try making her way through that room's clutter, Carrie clutched her

41

steaming and aromatic sack and edged around a bank of evergreen shrubbery toward the front door. She elbowed the latch, tugging awkwardly at the sagging screen door and sidling through into the shadowy entry.

At the corner of her eye, something moved in the dark.

Stifling a cry, Carrie recoiled, dropping the sack and reaching for the light switch. Heart thumping, she stood numbly in the cramped entryway, gazing at the mirror that hung on the right-hand wall at the foot of the stairs. You nitwit! she lectured herself. Scared to death of your own reflection.

At least she didn't scream. What would Lee Ann have thought?

For that matter, where was the girl? Carrie scooped up her fallen sack and went to dump it on the dining-room table. She flicked on the overhead lights; the gloom retreated and her overactive imagination went with it.

From above her, somewhere upstairs, came a very small sound. Just the faintest stirring. And an almost inaudible protesting whimper. *Now what?* Carrie frowned, her head lifted, listening. *Lee Ann? Wha was the kid doing up there?*

Carrie climbed the first short flight of steps to the lower landing; from there the stairs turned left and vanished into darkness. It remained dark even when she pressed the light switch. Carrie swore mildly and mentally added light bulbs to her shopping list Never a ghost around when you need one, she thought idiotically. Lights coming on all the time by themselves . . . and they *won't* come on when I *wan* them to.

Carrie listened, but the noise did not come again In the dim illumination from the foyer, she made he way up the stairs and across the hall, groping aroun the doorjamb for the light switch in her own room. A

42

soft overhead glow spilled into the hall and drove a wedge of light through the open door to Lee Ann's room.

Her daughter was asleep, flung bonelessly across her bed, with the kitten huddled in the crook of her elbow. She was quiet now, but her face was taut and unrelaxed, intent on some image in her dream. Carrie hovered uncertainly: should she just let her sleep?

A rising breeze nudged at the ruffled curtains, sharp with the beginnings of the night's damp chill. The room was cold. Carrie moved quietly across the floor, grasped the top of the window sash and pushed; the window resisted briefly, then settled into place with a muffled thump. Lee Ann stirred and muttered, drawing in her arms, curling herself protectively tight. Carrie held her breath guiltily, but Lee Ann didn't wake. The cat rose and arched, stretching stiffly to twice its normal height. It bounded off the bed and padded across the floor, twining itself around her ankles and demanding dinner in a piercing treble.

Back downstairs, Carrie threaded her way through the minefield of the kitchen, scooped cat food obediently, and resisted the minimal temptation of the bag of cooling hamburgers. She would wait for Lee Ann . . . let her sleep for a while. They could always rewarm the hamburgers in the microwave; who knows, it might even improve them. She bustled around the kitchen, picking up dishes, pans, and groceries and replacing them in their respective cabinets.

Just as she was thinking of going back upstairs to wake Lee Ann, the teenager appeared in the doorway. "Guess I fell asleep." She yawned and shuffled forward. "You sure were gone a long time."

"They were really crowded." Carrie edged around her into the dining room, just in time to rescue dinner from Pandora, who had forsaken her catfood in hopes of a hamburger. The kitten departed in haste for the living room, and Carrie gathered up the food, scattered but still securely wrapped.

Lee Ann inspected the interior of the refrigerator intently, blinking as though she wasn't sure exactly what she was looking for. "You sounded so far away when you called me, I thought maybe you'd locked yourself out again."

"Not a chance. After I did it the first time, I've been really careful with my keys." Carrie arranged hamburgers and packets of french fries in the microwave. "Anyway, it wasn't me you heard; I was just now getting ready to come up and get you."

I was awake. I know I was awake. Lee Ann froze, soft drink in her hand, staring at the monolithic white front of the refrigerator. *Someone was calling me . . . wanting me. Oh, God does that mean the rest of it was real, too?*

She felt her mother's eyes on her and shrugged. "I must have been dreaming," she said.

They ate companionably at the old kitchen table amidst a litter of paper and cardboard. Pandora ensconced herself in a chair between them, seizing proffered scraps with delight. Lee Ann stroked her absently. "The kitchen looks really nice, now that you've got everything put away." She searched through the debris for another hamburger.

"Wash your hands. You've been petting the cat," said Carrie automatically.

At the sink, the girl narrowed her eyes critically and squinted at the far wall. "The paint looks fine but that one wall . . . I think the plaster is cracked."

"I know. The paint makes a difference, but it still doesn't look very good, does it? Maybe I could cover it with wallpaper." Carrie stacked extra lettuce and tomato on her hamburger and chewed absently. "On the other hand," she admitted, "I might be better off with antique plaster. I've never hung paper in my life, and I'm not sure I want to start now."

"You could do it," said Lee Ann supportively, then proceeded to ruin the effect. "Penny's mom just papered their upstairs bathroom, and it looks great. Little different-colored flowers all over."

Carrie gritted her teeth and refrained from commenting.

"It really isn't that hard," continued Lee Ann volubly. "I bet I could do it," she volunteered, in an excess of enthusiasm.

Carrie blanched, wondering how difficult it was to get wallpaper paste out of cat fur. Or to get cat fur out of wallpaper paste. She visualized the kitten permanently affixed to a wall somewhere.

"No thanks," she said faintly.

Unwilling to drop the idea, Lee Ann offered a compromise. "Why don't you get Penny's mom to help?" she asked blithely. "She wouldn't mind. She's really nice. I'll ask her if you want me to."

"Oh, I wouldn't want to bother her," protested Carrie stubbornly. She sat up straighter and assumed her best look of competence. "Tell you what," she changed the subject, "if you're really set on wallpaper we'll go look at some sample books this week after school. The store should be able to give us instructions. If other people can do it, so can we."

CHAPTER V

It was just about the right time, after school. The girl—Lee Ann, that was her name—came slowly up the steps and let herself into the silent house. Just inside the door she stood for a second, poised as though for flight. Stood looking around, head cocked in a listening posture. But of course there was no one there. She was alone. All alone in the empty house.

At least that was what she thought.

But he knew better. The man watched, secure in his very private vantage point. He waited, savoring the stirring in his groin, the consummate power of knowing that he could do whatever he wanted . . . exactly what he wanted . . . with no one to stop him. No one to see.

He'd been scared—yes, he had to admit it—that first time, when the obsessive need had driven him here. But it was easier now, with practice. He could move about with impunity, and he could see so perfectly, every detail. This was *real*—not like the long years of daydreaming and wishing and nothing more; all that time when he himself was the one being watched. He was in control now. And he was going to stay that way.

The girl shrugged finally, and moved farther into

the silent rooms, shedding her coat, dropping her books on the table. As graceful as ever, even in the ugly denim, body moving as though she knew what to do with it. In the kitchen, now, getting a snack. Using the phone. Then out again, almost immediately; grabbing up her discarded coat and letting herself out the door, so fast it seemed she had hardly been there at all.

He lingered for a time, savoring this ultimate freedom; roaming silently in the silent house, completely at will, lingering over their belongings, *her* belongings. Schoolbooks and papers, the sensuous shapes of perfume bottles on the dresser. Clothing, from tomboy jeans to delicate lace. Ordinary, childish things. The man smiled to himself, thinking . . . and planning.

The October weather had remained unseasonably mild and azure-gold; through gritty office-standard venetian blinds the sun laid narrow bars across Carrie's desktop. She propped her chin in her hands and wished she were somewhere else. Almost anywhere else. Her job ran to fits of frenetic activity, interspersed with lulls when there was little or nothing to do; and this week had been singularly uneventful. The waste of time was galling, especially now, when there was so much to do at home.

Much of the basic work of cleaning, patching, and painting had been completed—at least downstairs—and now Carrie could begin to visualize the rooms the way she wanted them to look. She pulled a note pad toward her and began to doodle, rearranging rooms without the physical labor of moving furniture.

Always before, the appearance of her home had been a matter of happenstance rather than planning. She and Matt had started out, like their other graduate-student friends, in an old apartment building, with a mattress on the floor, brick-and-plank bookshelves and posters on the walls. Gradually they had acquired other furnishings, replaced the shabbiest of their Salvation Army purchases, painted and refinished. There had been a succession of larger, nicer apartments. An extra bedroom . . . a den . . . then a nursery.

Carrie had secretly pined over the perfection of magazine rooms; but all her ideas, her swatches and clippings, had been squirreled away for the house they would someday have. In the indifferent apartments, she had been too aware of their transience. Even after several years, she could never bring herself to drive a nail and hang a picture on those someone-else's walls.

Now, in her own home, Carrie found herself intimidated by the infinity of choices. The selection of colors, the placement of furniture, the hanging of pictures, had taken on an element of ceremony. Everything must be in its rightful place, carefully chosen. It was important, a ritual of belonging.

Matt, as self-possessed as a cat, and as uninvolved with his surroundings, had never shared her feelings. He'd been indulgent about her little hoard of decorative items gathering dust in the back of the apartment closet. But left to himself he'd have pounded nails and hung everything all everywhere and probably crooked.

Dear Matt. Active and impulsive, in many ways her opposite, he had brought joy and spontaneity to her cautious and well-ordered life. Without him . . . well, what more was there to say? Without him. That was the end of the matter. World without Matt, forever and ever, amen.

The phone at her elbow jangled, bringing her back to the present with an almost physical jerk. Carrie blinked and reached for the receiver. "Hello," she

48

said automatically, then hastily added their standard business identification.

"It's me, Mom," came Lee Ann's voice. "I just got home from school, and I thought I'd see if you want to go look at wallpaper when you get off work. You said we'd do it sometime this week."

"Oh, honey, not tonight. By the time I get home and we have dinner it's so late. And you probably have homework."

Carrie listened in exasperation to the disappointed silence from the other end of the line. What difference would one more day make? Placatingly, she hastened on, "Why don't we make it tomorrow? I'll be off then, and we can go right after school."

"Okay," said Lee Ann dully. "I just thought . . ."

"What?"

"Oh, never mind. It isn't important."

"Maybe we can look for some clothes for you too, while we're out. You need a new winter coat, and we can put one on layaway if you find something you like."

"Okay." A note of animation reentered the girl's voice. "Listen, Mom, I'm going over to the library for a while. I've got to get a book for a report. I'll be back before dinner, though."

"Sure, honey. I'll see you when I get home."

The weather, with seemingly intentional malice, turned bleak and chilly for Carrie's days off. She dawdled through Thursday morning, spending a great deal of time accomplishing very little. In justification, she told herself that it was silly to start a large task that would only be interrupted when she had to pick Lee Ann up from school.

Despite giving herself a comfortable margin of time, Carrie found herself leaving as usual in a last-minute hurry. Parked in a probably illegal spot across from the old, brick school building, she kept the motor running and the heater on. It had really gotten cold. She faced the prospect of their planned shopping trip resolutely, but without enthusiasm.

Bells sounded somewhere within the structure; youngsters began spilling out, seemingly from every opening. Carrie watched the surging crowd idly; she was mildly surprised when Lee Ann appeared accompanied by Danny, rather than Penny. Walking close together, talking intently, they came forward slowly, not seeing her yet. Danny passed his hand caressingly across the back of Lee Ann's neck, lifting her hair away from the collar of her jacket in an intimate and proprietary gesture. They paused facing each other, bright head bent over dark curls. Other students flowed around them; like a well-photographed movie sequence, the crowd seemed to focus Carrie's attention rather than distracting it. She found she was gripping the steering wheel so tightly that her hands ached. Then Lee Ann ducked her head and laughed, and the moment—if it had ever existed—was broken. Lee Ann caught sight of Carrie and quickened her pace, calling a goodbye to Danny over her shoulder as she came. Carrie drew a deep breath and firmly dismissed her sudden unreasonable anxiety.

At the store, she immersed herself with relief in commonplace activity, worrying over an instructional leaflet while Lee Ann browsed seriously amid bins of wallpaper rolls. Together they settled on a delicate but colorful pattern, deep stone blue striped with garlands of fruit and flowers. Carrie bought an extra roll, gloomily expecting to spoil a lot of it. She determined to get the job done tomorrow while Lee Ann was in school; if she was going to make a terrible mess of things, at least there would be no witnesses.

The phone was ringing as they entered the house, laden with parcels. Lee Ann dumped her burden on the couch and darted off to the kitchen to answer it. Carrie closed the front door and leaned against it tiredly. Then frowned, staring absently into the foyer in front of her. There was something . . . not wrong, exactly . . . just something nagging at her attention.

The vague impression focused sharply as memory clicked into place: Sunday night, and the half-glimpsed movement in the mirror. Carrie turned her head slowly and stared at the ornately framed glass, which gave back no reflection of her at all. The angle, she realized, was completely wrong. Instead, from this vantage point, it reflected a point above the landing, just where the staircase vanished into shadow.

Something cold ran down her spine and Carrie stood paralyzed, suddenly dry-mouthed. Whatever she had seen, it had been on the stairway. But Lee Ann had been in her bedroom, asleep. *Could there have been someone else in the house?* Someone standing above her on the darkened landing, watching?

Imagination ran riot, just for a second, before Carrie took a determined grip on herself and turned away. If there had really been a movement on the stairway . . . if it wasn't just her imagination, or a trick of the light . . . then it must have been the cat. Of course, that was it: she had glimpsed Pandora scooting up the stairs to join Lee Ann.

Having talked herself into some semblance of composure, she dropped her coat and packages beside Lee Ann's. From the kitchen, the girl's voice rose excitedly. Carrie smiled; they had had a pleasant afternoon together. Even shopping for school clothes had gone surprisingly smoothly. She had been braced for the usual mother-daughter tug-of-war over style and price, but Lee Ann had shown unusually mature concern for their budget, comparing costs and rejecting the very trendy fashion

51

extremes. Carrie, in turn, had repressed her shudders and compromised on several items she would have preferred to veto.

Her daughter was growing up. There was a twist of pain behind the thought, followed as it always was by the knowledge that Matt would not be here to share these years.

Carrie gulped and blotted at her eyes, determinedly setting aside the depression that could so easily negate the pleasure of the day. She had to make herself focus on the good things that remained in her life. For Lee Ann's sake, if not her own.

In the kitchen, Lee Ann was hanging up the phone. For a second as she turned, the overhead fixture lighted her face harshly, shadowing eyes and cheekbones and touching the corner of her mouth with a faint secretive smile. Carrie held her breath, face to face with the adult stranger her child would become.

Lee Ann stepped forward and the light shifted; she turned her face up with an open and eager expression.

"That was Danny," she said, and rushed on, her words running together in enthusiasm. "The community center is having a Halloween party, and they're helping out, and he wants me to go."

The inevitable question. House rules had been that Lee Ann was not allowed to date until she was sixteen. Carrie drew a breath and prepared herself to stand firm against an onslaught of tears and recriminations. Lee Ann hurried on. "And you too. I mean, his mother's one of the volunteers and they're all going, and she's going to call and ask you too."

"Uh . . . well," said Carrie, cravenly relieved, "I guess if the whole family's going, it's all right."

"It'll be fun, Mom. We're going to wear costumes

and everything. What can I wear?"

Without waiting for an answer, Lee Ann dashed off upstairs to dig in the closets in search of inspiration. Over dinner she maintained an enthusiastic, if one-sided, conversation, discussing and rejecting possibilities. Carrie was certain that every piece of clothing in the house had come under the girl's exacting scrutiny. "There's plenty of time," she pleaded. "We can even make something if you want to." In desperation, she invoked the powerful persuasion of peer approval: "Why not talk to Penny and see what she's going to wear?" Diverted, Lee Ann looked thoughtful and finally nodded.

"Now," reminded Carrie sternly, "about your homework . . ."

Lee Ann grimaced, but drifted upstairs obligingly enough, still contemplating prospects. "Maybe a witch . . ."

Carrie sat morosely at the kitchen table, her cup of coffee cooling amidst a clutter of wallpaper rolls and paperhanging equipment. She read the instruction leaflet for the third time. It didn't make any more sense now than it had before.

Out of nowhere, Pandora appeared and levitated to the tabletop to browse for crumbs. When her critical inspection turned up nothing edible, she gave up on the prospect of food and settled for affection. Purring loudly, she butted between Carrie and the pamphlet and began to turn round and round between her arms. Carrie inhaled cat fur and sneezed. The doorbell rang.

Fumbling in her pocket for a tissue, Carrie dumped Dora unceremoniously on the floor and headed for the front hall. No one was immediately visible on the porch; Carrie stood on tiptoe to peer through the high glass panes of the door. On the sisal doormat stood Barbara Burnett, burdened with a large canvas totebag and huddled in a thick sweater against the morning chill.

"Hi," she said, stepping into the foyer and waving the bag with an explanatory air. "Lee Ann told Penny that you were going to be wallpapering today. And she seemed to think you could use help."

"She has no faith," said Carrie aggrievedly. "But she's probably right."

"If you're insulted, you can kick me out," offered Barbara. "But it really will be easier if you have somebody to help. Especially if you've never papered before."

"I never have. I'm sure I could do it . . ." Carrie smiled awkwardly. "But it would be nice to have some help."

Barbara smiled back. Peeling off her sweater, she followed Carrie through the living and dining rooms. "Keith was home this morning, so I dumped the kids with him. I'll have to be back this afternoon, since he has an evening class. But if we're only doing one wall, that should be no problem."

"He's a teacher?"

"Professor of psychology. Down at the university." Dropping the canvas bag on a chair, Barbara began to produce unfamiliar and utilitarian-looking objects. "I brought some stuff I thought we could use." She stepped back to inspect the wall, and almost stepped on Pandora, who was treading a convoluted pattern around their legs.

"I had better shut her up someplace," said Carrie, snapping her fingers to attract the now elusive cat. She hurried up the stairs, gently pushed Pandora through the bathroom door and shut it firmly, ignoring indignant howls. "You're going to stay put this time," she told the little animal. "After that last performance." On the way back downstairs, with a gesture that had become almost automatic, she

54

reached out and turned off the light in Lee Ann's room.

In just a few hours, Carrie stood in front of the freshly papered wall, admiring their handiwork. "It looks even better than I expected," she said. "I really appreciate the help, Barbara—I couldn't have done this by myself."

An unintelligible mumble of acknowledgment came from behind and above, where Barbara was perched on a ladder, applying a narrow strip of matching paper to the soffit above the cabinets. The task finished to her satisfaction, she backed down the ladder and began to wash sticky hands in the sink, smiling at Carrie over her shoulder. "It does look nice, doesn't it? I like the pattern."

"Lee Ann picked it out. I wasn't really sure about the whole idea—the stuff that had been in the dining room was enough to give wallpaper a bad name."

Barbara laughed. "Old Mrs. Markwell was never known for the elegance of her decor: I think her ideas about home interiors stopped dead sometime in the 'thirties."

"From the looks of the place when we bought it, I suspect her cleaning efforts did too."

"It was pretty bad, wasn't it? She couldn't keep it up well the last few years she was here; and then she broke her hip and had to go in a nursing home, and the place was vacant for so long."

"Well, in a way it was lucky for us. I love this place, and we never could have afforded it if it had been in better condition."

"I'm glad it worked out that way." Barbara turned away and began to gather up paraphernalia. "It's such an attractive little house—I hated to see it get so run down."

Cleanup accomplished, they moved the table and

chairs back against the wall. Carrie burrowed in the refrigerator. "Lunch," she explained succinctly. "It's the least I can do after you worked all morning helping me. Do you have time?"

"I think so. By the way, did Lee Ann tell you about the Halloween party?"

"I don't think she talked about anything *else* last night. For a kid who decided last year that she was much too old and sophisticated for Halloween, she sure regressed in a hurry."

"Ack!" replied Barbara, balancing a bowl of salad and making an intricate maneuver to avoid stepping on Pandora.

"Where did you come from?" Carrie confronted the cat, who gazed at her blandly and did not reply. "I shut you in the bathroom."

Barbara made it to the table with salad and bowl intact. "Cats can squeeze through knotholes, I think."

"The door was shut tight. I'm sure it was."

"Well, these older houses have settled over the years; lots of times, the doorways are a little out of kilter, or the doors have sagged a bit, and they just don't latch properly."

"I guess so," said Carrie uncertainly. *But this time it was a different door. This time she was shut in the bathroom. Not Lee Ann's bedroom.* She set out the makings for sandwiches and sat down at the table. Pandora, all innocence, hopped into her lap and settled down contentedly.

"Anyway," continued Barbara, "about Halloween. I wanted to ask if you'd come, too. I need a few more adult volunteers, and it'll be a nice chance for you to meet a few people."

Not quite sure what she was getting herself into, Carrie nevertheless made the obligatory response. "Sure, I'll be glad to help," she said, with a feeling of doom. "Is it on Halloween night?"

"This year it is, since it's a Saturday. Usually it's just the closest weekend." Barbara began building an impressive sandwich. "It started out as a party for the little kids, and then we included the bigger ones . . . they have a room to themselves with different games and music for dancing. And now we have games and a bake sale and stuff for the adults, too. It raises some money for the community center, and everybody has a lot of fun. I'd be glad if you would come . . . and I think you'd enjoy it."

"What do you want me to do?"

"There's not that much work involved, really. I'm in charge of activities for the little kids, and I need a few adults to help watch them . . . make sure everybody gets a chance to bob for apples and play all the games . . . hand out treats . . . that kind of thing." Pandora stood up and stretched, peering over the edge of the table hopefully. Barbara extended a scrap of lunchmeat and the kitten took it daintily.

"Am I supposed to wear a costume?"

"Almost everybody does. We give prizes to the best ones in each age group." Barbara looked sidewise at Carrie's dubious expression and laughed. "If you can't find anything to wear, you can always borrow from us: our house is the unofficial costume bank. A bunch of the kids will be coming over to raid the attic, and I can find you something if you want."

"Maybe I'll come as the ghost," said Carrie.

Barbara looked at her quizzically; Carrie smiled and shook her head helplessly. "Family joke," she said.

CHAPTER VI

Lee Ann was late coming home from school. Carrie gravitated nervously to the front window for the third time, peering across the lawn toward the street. The late afternoon sun laid long shadows across the lawn. In noisy groups and giggling pairs, the neighborhood children had come and gone, drifting homeward. Maybe Lee Ann had missed her bus. Or decided to walk.

In the kitchen, Carrie distracted herself with thoughts of dinner. If she had all the ingredients, there was time to make lasagna—one of Lee Ann's favorites. Investigating the refrigerator for ricotta, Carrie was relieved to hear the front door creak open. "Mom?" came a tentative voice.

"I'm in the kitchen," she yelled back. "Come and look."

Lee Ann appeared in the doorway and drooped against the frame with a load of books in her arms. "I didn't know if you'd be home or not," she said.

"I usually try to be here when you get home," said Carrie, puzzled. "Unless I'm working."

Her daughter advanced into the room and dumped her books on the table.

"I got the wallpaper done today," Carrie pointed out.

58

Lee Ann looked around without enthusiasm. "It looks nice," she said apathetically.

Disappointed at the lack of response, Carrie looked more closely at her daughter. "You're kind of late today, honey. Is anything wrong?"

"No. I just stayed at school for a while. Talking to Mr. Meredith. He said . . ."

Meredith? That overbearing counselor? Carrie frowned. "Mr. Meredith? What did he want? Are you having some problems in school?"

Lee Ann frowned back. "Why do you right away assume I'm having problems in school? My grades are perfectly okay, aren't they?"

"Far as I know, sure." Carrie's tone was conciliatory. "It's just . . . he's the counselor, isn't he? So it made me wonder if you were having a problem."

"No," answered Lee Ann. Her voice rose and cracked slightly. "I'm not having a problem in school." *My problem's at home, but it sure won't do me any good to talk to you about it. All you ever do is jump on me. Like now. Mr. Meredith tells me I need to talk to you, but you won't even give me a chance.*

It wasn't like Lee Ann to be so defensive over a simple question. *Did something happen to upset her today?* Carrie's maternal antennae began to quiver. *With Meredith, maybe? Wasn't there something wrong about this guy, having young students in his office after hours?*

"Um," she said delicately. "Is there something else wrong? Something we ought to talk about?"

Lee Ann shook her head obstinately. "We were just talking, that's all. Mr. Meredith is a nice guy. We're friends."

Carrie swallowed, trying to bring her suspicious mind under control. "Okay—I wasn't fussing at you. You just looked kind of upset. And I was worried when you were late. That's all." Carrie hastened to change the subject. "Lasagna for dinner. It'll be ready in about an hour."

Over steaming and aromatic plates of lasagna and garlic bread, Lee Ann regained some of her usual good spirits. "Did Penny's mom help with the wallpaper? Penny asked her, and she said she would."

Carrie nodded, her mouth full of lasagna.

"Did she ask you about the Halloween party? Are you going to go?"

"Yes and yes. We'll have to do something about costumes for both of us, I guess."

Lee Ann helped herself to another slice of garlic bread and applied butter with a lavish hand. "I'd like to do something really glamorous," she said. "Like a fairy-tale princess. Maybe Cinderella. Don't you have *any* old dresses we could make a ball gown out of?"

"Not really," admitted Carrie meekly. "We never went to fancy parties and dances much. I guess we led a dull life."

Lee Ann sighed gustily. "Well, that's what I'd *really* like. I guess I'll have to borrow something from Penny. She says they have lots of stuff."

"And I'll find something for me," Carrie assured her, with the baseless optimism of someone who was planning to put off looking as long as possible.

Lee Ann screamed. It just came out, shrill and piercing, before she was even completely awake. *There—at the window. Trying to get in.* She scrabbled upright, backed against the headboard of the bed, tugging at the blankets with nerveless fingers. And screamed again.

From the hall, her mother came dashing, hair and eyes wild. "Lee Ann, what . . .?"

"There! At the window." One thin arm flung out in a trembling gesture.

Carrie turned, involuntarily, to look. Turned back, immediately, with that patronizing maternal smile. "There's nothing there, sweetheart. You had a bad dream."

"No." Lee Ann shook her head as though she could shake off creeping uncertainty. "There was someone there. Trying to get in."

"Honey, you were dreaming. Someone would have to climb up on our roof. . . ." Her mother strode purposefully toward the window and stood looking out.

"There was someone there. There was!" Lee Ann's voice thinned with self-doubt. It sounded so crazy.

At the low dormer, Carrie shivered, shrugging deeper into her heavy robe. It was so cold in the room. As cold as if the window *had* been opened. She leaned closer to the dark glass and peered sideways along the eaves. The roof here was steep-pitched, but not completely inaccessible; especially with the low porch roof just below. Could there really have been someone out there?- Carrie leaned still farther forward; cheek against the cold windowpane, looking for movement, listening for rustling in the shrubs below. But there was nothing, and she hadn't really expected it.

She shivered again and turned back to her daughter. "It was just a dream, Lee Ann," she said firmly. "You know sometimes dreams can seem very real."

The man melted into the shadows, knowing quite well that they would never see him. He almost laughed and had to smother it, not sure whether they might hear. It was so easy, coming and going as he pleased, completely untouchable. Almost enough to

61

make it worthwhile, the long time with all his emotions, all his *wanting*, shut up inside. Almost worthwhile, because it had been a good time for learning; and he had learned, oh, he had learned. What people wanted, and how to give it to them. How much they would believe. How to make them believe.

Now he could put it all to use . . . to get what he wanted. And no one would ever know.

Carrie woke the next morning to dank gray gloom and the sound of teeming rain on the roof. The whole house was cold now. It's your own fault, she told herself sternly. You should have lit the furnace a long time ago. The serviceman who'd cleaned and checked the heating system had showed her how, but Carrie had put it off, shying away nervously from the unfamiliar and risky-seeming task. Perhaps she could ask Danny. Or maybe she should call the serviceman back?

In disgust, she pushed aside the thought. *It's my house, and my furnace. If a man can light the stupid thing, so can I.* Sitting up in bed, she huddled into a thick robe and groped for her slippers. No sound came from Lee Ann's room as she drifted past quietly.

Downstairs, Carrie found the flashlight immediately in a sideboard drawer; a more protracted search through kitchen cabinets unearthed live batteries. Armed with extra light and half a box of matches, she groped her way down the sagging basement stairs. The square space below was damp, with a single tiny rivulet snaking across the uneven floor to a central drain. Small high windows looked out at shrubbery instead of sky, admitting only a vague, shifting green light. At the foot of the stairs, an unshielded bulb shed a pale circle of light.

Carrie made her way across the room to where the old gravity furnace bulked, like some bizarre dinosaur. With the flashlight propped on a convenient box, she knelt and tugged loose the resisting cover plate, turned the gas valve to "On" and struck a match. The tiny reassuring flicker of the pilot light appeared obediently. With pleasure, Carrie watched its bright blue dance for a moment; then she replaced the cover, thumping it into place with the heel of her hand.

She stood up, brushing at the skirt of her bathrobe, belatedly listening to noises from upstairs. Had Lee Ann called her? Above the faint murmurings of the furnace the summons was repeated, now unmistakable. "Mom? Mo-om!"

Carrie gathered flashlight and matches and headed for the stairs. Above her, light footsteps padded rapidly through the dining room. Lee Ann's thin voice rose again, shrilly, jagging across the morning silence. "Mommy!"

Tripping over the hem of her long robe, Carrie hurried up the stairs and burst through the door into the kitchen. Lee Ann appeared in the doorway, eyes wide and frightened. "Mommy? Mommy, where were you?"

Carrie dropped the flashlight on the counter and caught her breath. "I'm right here," she said irritably. "Where did you think I was?"

"I didn't know," wailed Lee Ann. "I just woke up and you were gone!"

Carrie stared. "For Pete's sake, Lee Ann. I just went downstairs to light the furnace. Why the big panic?"

Lee Ann looked down, watching her hands intently as they twisted the sash of her bathrobe into intricate macramé. "I don't know," she muttered. "I just . . ." Her jaw clamped tight over the unfinished explanation and she shrugged, the unsatisfactory

63

and slightly insolent ending to so many conversations.

The unsettling rush of adrenaline drained away, and Carrie forced herself to put aside her exasperation. "Well," she said briskly, "I'm here, and I'm ready for breakfast. How about pancakes?"

"Fine." Lee Ann clipped off the word with relief and barricaded herself behind the refrigerator door, passing eggs and milk around its edge.

Carrie stood at the griddle of the wide, old-fashioned range, watching pancakes with one eye and Lee Ann with the other. The girl fidgeted around the room, meticulously adjusting the placement of plates and silverware on the table, pulling the fringed cafe curtains closed across the streaming window. At the side door, she pressed her face close to the glass and gazed out morosely at the sodden landscape. *I don't think I can stand to be cooped up here all day.*

"Do you think it'll rain for long?" she appealed. "I thought maybe we could go out today . . . do some shopping . . . or go to a movie."

"Doesn't look like a very good day for it," was the practical rejoinder. "We've already gotten most of your school clothes, and I don't think there's anything else we need badly enough to be worth going out in this weather."

I really need to get out of here. Lee Ann rested her hand on the ornate old doorknob and twisted it listlessly; her breath steamed against the cold glass. *What's crazy is, I'm afraid to leave Mom. Something's going to happen, and I don't know what, and I don't want something to happen to* her *now too.*

"If there's a movie you want to see, why don't you call Penny and get her to go with you?"

Lee Ann twitched one shoulder in an ambiguous gesture.

64

"Or she might like to go shopping with you."

Her daughter's back was stonily resistant. Carrie gave up and turned her attention back to breakfast, flipping pancakes dexterously onto a waiting plate. "Get the syrup, will you?"

A stack of pancakes, orange juice, and a tall glass of milk seemed to restore Lee Ann's normal composure. She extended a finger, sticky with syrup, to Pandora, who sniffed, licked, and sneezed with an air of disgust.

"She'd probably really prefer catfood," said Carrie. "Why don't you open a can for her while I clear the table?"

At the sink, she continued conversationally, "The Halloween party is only a couple of weeks away. Didn't Penny ask you to come over so you could work on your costumes together? That might be something you could do today, since you haven't found anything you like yet. Her mom said they have an attic full of old stuff."

"I just don't feel like it," said Lee Ann finally.

"You and Penny haven't had a fight, have you?"

"No. I just don't feel like going over to her house today, that's all."

Carrie stacked the last of the dishes in the drain rack to dry. "But I thought you wanted to get out of the house."

"You don't understand." Lee Ann sighed expressively.

"No," said Carrie in bafflement. "I guess I don't."

On Monday Carrie arrived home from work to find Lee Ann sitting on the steps, huddled around a lapful of books. "Hi," she said, surprised. "Did you forget your key?"

"No. I was just waiting for you."

"Is something wrong? You look upset."

Lee Ann jerked her head toward the house. "I got home and the light was on in my room again, and . . . I just didn't want to go in."

Carrie threw a glance sidewise at the dormer window, bright in the gathering dusk.

"And before you start blaming me," Lee Ann continued vehemently, "I didn't leave it on. I know I didn't!"

This wasn't a family joke anymore. "You were scared." Carrie sat down on the cold concrete step beside her daughter.

Lee Ann gave her mother a narrow look, trying to decide whether the words were sympathetic or derisive.

For once, Carrie read her daughter correctly. "I'm not making fun of you," she said earnestly. "I've been a little nervous myself a few times."

The edges of Lee Ann's colorful notebook were rumpled and dog-eared where she picked at them. Her voice was very even, almost casual. "Do you think somebody's been getting into the house? Like a burglar or something?"

Carrie cocked her head thoughtfully, even though she'd already considered and discarded the idea. "Doesn't seem likely," she said. "I don't think a burglar would want to turn the lights on. And besides, it's happened a few times when I was here . . . times I'm pretty sure the lights came on by themselves."

Her daughter stuck her nose in the air with a look of superiority. "I told you all along it wasn't me."

Carrie nodded. "At first I thought one of us was being absentminded . . ."

"Meaning me." Lee Ann looked sour.

"Well, it was usually the light in your room," Carrie said reasonably. "But I know there were some times when you didn't leave it on. I'm sure of that. So I'm going to call an electrician and have someone

66

come and check it out. We may have a problem with the wiring."

Lee Ann's look of surprise was closely followed by one of relief. "I didn't think of that. Do you think that's what it is?"

"If it isn't you or me, then it must be the wiring," Carrie answered, with an assurance that she didn't really feel.

The electrician who came on Thursday shook his head in bewilderment. "The wiring may not be up to the latest standards . . . but there isn't anything really wrong with it. I've been over this place from top to bottom, and everything checks out fine."

Carrie looked at him helplessly, feeling foolish. "I know it sounds dumb," she said. "And it's not as though it's a really big problem. Just the light in that one room, like I told you on the phone."

"Well, let's have a closer look up there," he said kindly, and plodded back up the stairs. In Lee Ann's room, Carrie watched anxiously as he pulled the light fixture away from the ceiling and probed at the wires. "Nothing," he reported, replacing the glass shield.

"Tell you what," he said finally, with the attitude of a physician offering a placebo to a hypochondriac patient. "I can put in a new switch for you, if you want me to. There doesn't seem to be anything wrong with the old one, you understand; but lots of people like the modern, silent ones better anyhow."

Producing a screwdriver and attacking the wall plate, he continued comfortingly, "Look, I've got kids of my own. They're always leaving lights on, doors open—you name it. You can talk yourself blue in the face, and it doesn't help. They just don't think."

67

"Mmmm," said Carrie noncommittally. Why was it always so cold in here? The heat duct was open; by rights, the upstairs should be warmer than the rest of the house. Her own room was always pleasant. Maybe they should leave this room for storage and move Lee Ann to the back bedroom before winter arrived.

She moved around aimlessly, squaring up piles of books and papers on the desk and picking up a sweater draped over the back of the chair. Considering the usual habits of its teenage occupant, the room was surprisingly neat.

"There!" announced the electrician, closing his tool case with a snap. "I'll just go down and turn your power back on." Carrie smoothed the bedspread, which was slightly askew, and turned to follow; as she did, her foot brushed an object on the floor. Half hidden under the bedskirt lay a small framed photograph of Matt and Lee Ann together— one of the last—taken during a trip the summer before last.

It was the little things like this, all unexpected, that hurt so much. Carrie turned it over and over in her hands, remembering.

Matt. And Lee Ann. Always Lee Ann, who had been "Daddy's girl" right from the start. The images flooded back, vivid and painful . . . Lee Ann as a toddler, bouncing on Matt's knee . . . boosted high to ride on his shoulders. And later, the two faces so startlingly similar, the twin understanding smiles that flashed between them. Carrie could summon it back so easily; but the memories were always silent and frozen like snapshots. Even Matt, so alive and vital, was still forever on a square of film in a dime store frame.

Downstairs, the electrician coughed a reminder. She placed the little photo on the bedside table and went heavily down the stairs.

68

* * *

She was pottering aimlessly in the kitchen when there was a sharp rap at the door, which opened to admit a gust of wind, Barbara, one child, and several dead leaves. With a breezy "Hello," her friend dropped into a chair and hoisted the toddler onto her lap. Carrie examined him surreptitiously and tried to decide which one it was before offering an appropriate greeting. With five kids in the Burnett family, she still hadn't quite sorted them out. She finally settled on a course of caution.

"Hi," she said.

The child, who appeared to be about two, eyed her with equal caution and said nothing. Barbara produced the ubiquitous canvas tote bag and rummaged. "I brought a couple of things for you to try on. There's a really elaborate flapper costume, all fringe and feathers. One of my friends gave it to me years ago, and I don't think it's been worn since." She eyed Carrie analytically. "It ought to be just about the right size for you."

"It sounds cute," said Carrie, who hated the word cute. "I just feel kind of dumb and self-conscious about dressing up in a costume. Even for Halloween."

"You don't have to if you don't want to," said Barbara comfortingly. "But," she reminded, "everybody else will be in costume. You'll be more conspicuous if you're the only one who isn't."

"True," sighed Carrie, and capitulated. The flapper costume was a delight: a short sheath of black taffeta, completely covered with row after row of slinky fringe. A marabou boa completed the outfit.

"All you'll need is some net stockings and black shoes. Maybe a headband. And a long cigarette holder."

"It's a lot nicer than anything I could have come

69

up with. I really appreciate your finding it for me. But you didn't have to go to the trouble of delivering it, too; you should have called me to come and get it."

"I was on my way to the library anyway," Barbara explained. "I guess I should be grateful that the kids read, but I wish their reading matter included the little date cards in the back pocket. I've paid so many overdue fines this year that they're planning to name the new wing after me."

She paused for breath and accepted a proffered cup of coffee. "And I needed to get to the costumes before the kids did. A bunch of them are coming over tomorrow after school to make decorations for the party and rummage in the attic for old clothes. Do you think Lee Ann would like to come?"

Caught off guard, Carrie hesitated. "Um . . . I don't know," she said . "I'll have to ask her. It's nice of you to invite her," she added politely.

Barbara looked at her sharply. "Listen, I'm being a shameless meddler . . . but is Lee Ann mad at Penny about something? They've been such good friends, but lately Penny says Lee Ann is sort of avoiding her. And she doesn't know why: they haven't had an argument or anything. Do you have any idea what happened?"

"Not a clue," said Carrie, and decided that that covered the situation as a whole. She was ashamed to admit that in her concern about Lee Ann's dejection she hadn't spared much thought for Penny's feelings.

"Well, I didn't really expect that you would. They don't tell us old fogeys much, do they?" Barbara spooned sugar into her cup and stirred, gazing thoughtfully into the swirling liquid.

"Has she said anything to Danny about it? Maybe he could find out."

Barbara shook her head. "He already tried. He said he thought Lee Ann was going to cry, but she

70

wouldn't talk about it. Danny thinks she's really depressed and unhappy about something, but he doesn't know what to do about it.

"I'm not sure what I think *we* can do about it, either. They're at the stage where they're touchy about privacy. Penny would be furious at me for just talking about her problems, much less actually doing anything."

"I know." Carrie wondered how much of her own worry she could share with her friend. Never a terribly voluble person, since Matt's death she had grasped furtively at the occasional support of adult conversation. But she had, with a curious self-imposed discipline, rationed herself to undemanding, essentially meaningless interchanges, fearful of putting too much pressure on tenuous friendships.

She sighed and admitted, tentatively, "I think the problem may be more Lee Ann's than Penny's. She's been awfully moody lately. I keep telling myself it's a normal phase, but I'm starting to get worried about her."

"It's a difficult age," Barbara nodded. "And of course, losing her father, then moving . . . she's bound to be pretty unsettled." She looked at Carrie squarely, with real sympathy, not with the avid predatory interest of so many other acquaintances. Condolence callers had circled Carrie like buzzards when Matt died, but most of them had vanished immediately afterward, in search of a new sensation.

"She went through something like this when Matt died . . ." *When Matt died.* She could say it now, a bald statement of fact, without grief pinching her throat. It had taken so long to gain that little detachment. Too long.

"She was at such a vulnerable age. I expected . . . I don't know what I expected. Kids her age can get so completely derailed by such little things." Carrie stared fixedly at the spoon in her hand, turning it over and over. "But Lee Ann seemed to handle it pretty well. As well as you could expect. She was withdrawn and depressed for a long time; but that's perfectly normal. And lately she seemed to be getting over it, going out and doing things with her friends."

But she did it all without me. The one real crisis in her life, and I was too tied up in my own grief to pay any attention. Sure, I went through the motions, I watched for signs of any severe disturbance. But it would have taken something big and splashy to get my attention, wouldn't it?

"You don't get over something like that all at once, though," Barbara interrupted her thoughts. "Maybe this is some kind of delayed reaction."

Carrie's shoulders slumped. *Why couldn't it be just normal adolescent temperament? Like with everyone else's kids?* "The guidance counselor at school said she was depressed," she confessed.

"Frank Meredith?" Barbara said. "He and Keith were at school together. He's very good with the kids."

Carrie snorted. "He may be good with the kids, but he's not much with parents. He was pushing me to get her into counseling, but he couldn't even give me a good reason why."

"Maybe he's taking it too seriously," Barbara admitted, "but you can understand why he's so cautious. After last year . . ."

"I wasn't here last year." Carrie tilted an eyebrow inquiringly.

Haggard lines sketched themselves on Barbara's face, adding extra years. "One of the girls at school committed suicide," she explained softly. "She was kind of a wild lonely kid, and Frank had been working with her: it was really a shock."

"Oh God, how awful." Carrie softened her previous estimation of the man. Maybe she was lucky that Lee Ann had a counselor who cared so much.

"Anyway, if Frank thinks she needs counseling, it might be a good idea. His intuition is usually pretty good."

Carrie floundered, a moment of panic followed by a surge of resentment. Just as she'd got her life back under control again, was it slipping away from her in another direction? *Damn it, there's nothing* wrong *with Lee Ann.*

"Of course, it's entirely possible that the girls have just had a fight," she suggested coolly. "It's normal for kids this age to be moody; and their friendships tend to blow hot and cold, too. If we just leave them alone, they'll probably make up before the week is out."

Barbara, sensitive to Carrie's feelings, or perhaps just easily sidetracked, agreed. "You're probably right. But I'm not being underhanded in inviting Lee Ann to their little get-together: Penny said she would like her to come, but she hasn't been able to talk to her."

Ashamed of her defensiveness, Carrie hastened to make amends. "Penny's such a nice girl, and she's good for Lee Ann. But I can't push. You understand," she finished helplessly, fluttering.

"It would only make her dig in her heels and refuse. Oh, I know."

Having disposed of a topic that the average child psychologist could milk for a book or two, the two women sat musing separately, sipping from the steaming cups. The baby, whom Carrie had now identified as Jeremy, by his curls, dabbled his fingers in his mother's saucer.

"Well," said Barbara, mopping at the child and gathering up her belongings simultaneously, "I guess I'll be off. Do you want me to yell up to Lee Ann and ask her?"

"Oh, she isn't home. Yet. I was expecting her any minute." Suddenly reminded of the latening hour and darkening sky, Carrie stammered in confusion. Where *was* her daughter?

"It isn't really that late," Barbara said serenely. "It just seems that way these days when it starts getting dark so early. I just assumed Lee Ann was home when I saw the light in her room." She headed for the door. "Anyway, the invitation stands. Tell her we'd really like her to come."

Carrie nodded dumbly. The door closed and the silence closed in again, more insistent for having been kept at bay. *I will not—I absolutely will not— go back upstairs and turn off that damn light.* And this time the thought had an edge of fear.

The front door opened and closed quietly, as though Lee Ann were hoping to enter unnoticed. Somewhere, faintly, a car door slammed. Had someone brought her home? Wiping her hands on a dishtowel, Carrie hurried out through the dining room.

"Lee Ann? I was starting to get worried about you."

Poised at the foot of the stairs, Lee Ann turned reluctantly, visibly arranging her face into the expressionless mask that served her as a shield.

The quiet shutting-out was more difficult to handle than outright rebellion. Marshaling her memories of Child Psych 101, Carrie groped for the right combination of firmness and understanding. Or, she admitted to herself, just a way to maintain discipline without setting off an explosion.

"I know there are things you want to do after school, with the other kids. And that's okay," she said carefully. "But when you're going to be this late, you have to call and let me know."

There! That was pretty good, she congratulated herself. She moved forward slightly and looked at

Lee Ann for a reaction. The girl shifted impatiently and said nothing; in the swimming shadows, her face was impossible to read.

Exasperated, Carrie continued past the point of caution. "I just don't want you out walking around when it's getting dark. It isn't safe." Then, remembering the faint sounds of the car, she probed, "Or did someone bring you home?"

Lee Ann appeared to consider a multitude of possible responses. "Why?" she stalled.

Why? Because I'm your mother, and I'm responsible for your welfare—that's why! On edge, Carrie choked back the impulse to scream and grasped for self-control.

"I thought I heard a car," she replied mildly.

Lee Ann eyed her warily, testing which way the wind blew. "Danny brought me," she admitted finally.

Distracted from the original issue, Carrie mulled over a new concern. *Were the two of them getting a bit too . . . involved? Kids that age . . . how much time were they really spending together?* Rediscovering the dishtowel still hanging damply from her hand, she examined it critically, picking at a loose thread. "Are you, ah . . . seeing a lot of him?" she asked tentatively. "I mean, he's a very nice boy, but . . ."

It earned her the eye-rolling "Why me?" look used universally by teenagers to keep adults in their places. "For Pete's sake, Mom," snapped Lee Ann, "you say you don't want me walking home late, and then you act like I did something wrong in getting a ride."

There was probably a flaw in that logic somewhere, but Carrie couldn't put her finger on it right away. Accepting the impasse for the moment, she changed the subject to dinner and sent Lee Ann upstairs to wash before setting the table.

75

In the kitchen, Carrie dashed to the rescue of a pot of vegetables that were just beginning to scorch. She went through the rest of the dinner preparations mechanically, thoughts anxiously circling and returning, but came to no conclusion. With the guilt that is immediately recognized by every working mother, she worried about Lee Ann's lack of supervision. The girl was alone much of the afternoon on the three days that Carrie worked. And lately she had begun coming in late after school even on the days when Carrie was at home.

And Carrie had—stupidly?—accepted her explanations at face value. *Was this how it started, with kids who got in trouble? With parents who were too trusting, or just too preoccupied, to ask questions? For that matter, what good were questions? If the kids were up to something, they'd lie about it, wouldn't they?* Carrie paused, hotpad dangling forgotten from one hand. At least Lee Ann hadn't lied to her. Evaded, perhaps. But she had given an honest answer when Carrie had questioned her directly. *That was a good sign, wasn't it? Wasn't it?*

Feeling somewhat better, Carrie began to ferry steaming dishes into the dining room. Perhaps over the meal they could have a good talk and get things straightened out. "Dinner's ready!" she called, in the general direction of the stairwell.

Her good intentions were forgotten almost immediately. Footsteps dragged slowly across the living room, and an ashen-faced Lee Ann appeared at the French doors. "Mom . . ." Her voice quavered. "Why . . . ?" Voice breaking now, she gave up the attempt at speech and simply gestured, advancing to lay a small object gently on the table. It was the tiny photo of herself and Matt—the one from her bedside table.

Carrie stared, uncomprehending. "What's the matter? I don't understand."

76

Lee Ann dropped limply into a chair and snuffled, nose reddening and spots of color reappearing on her cheeks. "Why did you put that in my room?" she demanded, wavering between tears and anger.

"Honey, I didn't." Carrie reached for the little photo and turned it over. "It was on the floor, half under the bed. I just picked it up and put it on the table." It was half an explanation; unless pressed, Carrie didn't plan to explain *why* she had been in Lee Ann's room. She had already resolved not to mention the electrician's visit and disconcerting diagnosis.

Privacy, however, was not Lee Ann's immediate concern. "But how did it get there?" she asked pointedly. "It isn't mine. I put all my . . . my stuff away. You know I did!"

It was true. After Matt's death, Lee Ann had gathered up her photos and reminders of her father and packed them all away. For weeks her bulletin board and the frame of her dresser mirror had maintained a sterile look of desertion, before the usual teenage memorabilia had begun creeping back to replace the pictures of Matt. Stricken, Carrie reached for the snapshot and shoved it into a sideboard drawer, out of sight.

"I'm sorry, Lee Ann," she said reasonably. "It was probably in one of your cartons when we moved; and it just fell out somewhere along the line and got kicked under the bed."

Lee Ann made an abrupt, half-formed movement. "Mother, you don't understand. It isn't *mine!* I had some of the pictures we took at the park, but they were on my bulletin board." Her voice, not quite under control, rose in desperation. "I didn't *have* anything in a frame."

Dumbfounded, Carrie opened her mouth and shut it again. So much for rational explanations. "Are you sure?" she asked lamely, more for her own reassurance than from any real disbelief.

Lee Ann managed a faint look of resentment. "Of course I'm sure," she said emphatically. Then the facade of adolescent independence cracked. She covered her mouth with her hands and began to sob.

"Where did it come from? Mommy . . . where did it come from?"

CHAPTER VII

Carrie bent protectively to enfold Lee Ann. *When they're little, you can solve all their problems with a hug. Why does it have to get so much harder when they grow up?*

Drawing a jerky breath, the girl drew away self-consciously, reached for a paper napkin and blew her nose. Carrie, whose back had begun to hurt, straightened gratefully but with slight regret. "Well, I guess we'll just have to blame it on the ghost," she said lightly—and knew it was a mistake as soon as the words were out of her mouth. *Damn!* How utterly insipid and patronizing she sounded. She could remember how, as an adolescent, she had hated adults who talked to her that way.

Lee Ann hunched her shoulders and stared at the table miserably. Carrie looked down at the top of her head, wondering what to do next. Although her first instinct was to protect her child, she had to admit that so far her efforts had met with spectacular failure. Look, she told herself firmly, you expect honesty from Lee Ann; then you have to be honest with her in return. If it kills you.

She touched the girl lightly on the arm. "I'm sorry, Lee Ann. That was a stupid thing to say. I was just . . . I'm a little upset about it. Because I don't

79

know what to tell you. If the picture isn't yours, then it must have been Dad's. There was so much stuff of his—pipes and photos and personal things—and I just threw it all into boxes, because I didn't want to look at it. I don't know how the picture got into your room, but I'm sure there's a reasonable explanation."

Dark head cocked, Lee Ann looked at her sideways; it was impossible to tell whether she accepted the hollow reassurance. "Okay," she said slowly, "I guess you're right." And added, heartbreakingly, "I was a little upset, too."

Over dinner, by common consent, they avoided sensitive subjects. Carrie remembered to extend the proxy invitation to the Burnetts' Friday costume rummage. "It sounds like fun. And you don't have a costume yet," she finished. Then stopped, restraining herself from any further urging.

Lee Ann speared a piece of broccoli with her fork and examined it critically. "Maybe I will. Danny said they had a lot of neat stuff." She popped the broccoli in her mouth and made a face. "Yuck. That stuff tastes worse than usual." She finished dinner in silence, frowning at her plate and pushing the food around with her fork. Several times Carrie caught her staring into space with a puzzled expression, as though trying to remember something that eluded her. It was not until much later that she understood the direction Lee Ann's thoughts had taken and wondered if there was anything she might have done to forestall it.

The next afternoon, Lee Ann appeared quite promptly after school, once again with Penny and Danny in tow. Carrie, standing on a dining-room chair while changing a light bulb and wishing she could replace the entire ugly chandelier, almost lost her precarious balance in surprise.

"Hi!" they chorused, and Penny beamed at her. "Can Lee Ann come over and eat dinner with us? My mom says it's okay."

"If it's all right with your mother it's all right with me. You're going to be working on costumes, too, aren't you?"

"Yeah, and making decorations. We do this every year, and we have cider and doughnuts. It's almost like having another Halloween party."

"I'm going to change clothes," Lee Ann broke in. She looked at Penny significantly and made a slight beckoning movement with her head. "Come with me." Danny, left behind, stood fidgeting in the doorway. Rocking backward on his heels, he peered after them toward the stairwell, then turned and rested both hands on the mantel, ducking his head between his arms and staring into the cold fireplace. Twice he shifted and cleared his throat nervously. But Carrie, intent on maneuvering a delicate old glass globe back into place over the new lightbulb, paid little attention.

"There!" She descended from the chair and looked at Danny, slightly puzzled at the lack of conversation from the normally talkative and self-possessed teenager. "Would you like some hot chocolate or something?"

"Uh, we'll have a snack at home, I think. Thanks." He looked at her and seemed to be about to add something when the girls came pounding back downstairs. They surrounded him like a whirlwind and swept him toward the door.

After a lackluster dinner of leftovers, Carrie settled herself back at the dining-room table with calculator, pencil, and several month's bank statements. She looked at the checkbook sullenly, suspecting that it

81

had been up to its usual sinister machinations behind her back. Setting her mouth firmly, she went to work, using one hand to fend off Pandora, who was fascinated by all the little scraps of paper.

It was almost ten o'clock when she finished, the checkbook balanced and a neat pile of payment envelopes waiting to be mailed. About time for Lee Ann to be home. As if in answer to her thought, footsteps scraped across the porch and there were faint sounds at the front door. Carrie gathered up bank statements and calculator, and opened the sideboard drawer. "Oh!" She stopped, dismayed. The little photo of Matt and Lee Ann stared up at her, where it had been tucked away and forgotten. Across the face of the picture the glass was splintered in an ugly diagonal crack.

Carrie's face prickled with a hot rush of adrenaline. Of course it was her fault; in her haste she must have thrown the photo into the drawer too roughly. But she couldn't let Lee Ann see it. Guiltily, she moved the photo to the next drawer down and tucked it behind the bank statements, out of sight.

Where was Lee Ann anyway? She hadn't come in. Carrie listened, but the noises on the porch were not repeated. Puzzled, she crossed the living room to the front windows, leaning across the couch to move the curtain aside. And drew back immediately, cheeks scalding. Of course. Danny must have walked Lee Ann home; the two dark forms on the shadowed porch were oblivious to the movement at the window, clinging together, his head bent to her upturned face. Carrie tiptoed back to the kitchen. When the door opened, she was rattling the cocoa pan ostentatiously.

"Mom?"

Lee Ann poked her head around the kitchen door, cheeks pink. *With cold?*

"Are you making hot chocolate? We had a great

82

time. And I found a terrific costume—wait till you see!''

She bounded off upstairs, leaving her mother staring abstractedly into the cocoa. Dully, Carrie examined her mixed emotions. Did all parents feel this way when they were first confronted by their children's maturing impulses? She had always prided herself on being a modern, enlightened parent. And anyway, it wasn't as though the kids had done anything *wrong*. She drew a deep breath, calming herself, and poured the steaming cocoa into heavy mugs.

The girl moved across the room, completely unselfconscious, pulling the clinging sweater over her head, setting her hair abristle with its static electricity. Steadying herself on the dresser, she wriggled out of the heavy jeans, hips emerging from their grasp like a snake shedding skin. Reaching behind, she unclasped the almost-unnecessary bra.

Over the head now went a fluff of pastel fabric—a dance dress of some sort, delicate and lacy. A brief struggle with a zipper; wispy folds briefly muffled the outline of her body, then settled into place with breathtaking effect. Above a full and flowing skirt, her body emerged like a flower, swathed in some pink satiny stuff. Tiny glittery straps seemed to be the only things holding up the overlarge top; its neckline draped so deeply that the edges of her nipples showed, rosy above the paler pink.

So perfect. Just so perfect. The man bent slightly, shifted unobtrusively, easing the constriction of his clothes, the bursting pressure against the seams at his crotch. Sometimes he had to remind himself to be patient, to discipline himself. The anticipation was part of it all: the subtle pleasures of watching, maneuvering, manipulating her into doing whatever he wanted. And it was so easy.

The girl had gone now, back downstairs and out of sight. But it didn't matter. She'd be back. The man let out pent breath, overwhelmed by the rush of sensation, by the heady knowledge of his own power . . . and of his plans.

"Ta-dah! Look, Mom!" Lee Ann pirouetted in the doorway, in a froth of pink and spangles. "Isn't it pretty? It's an old evening gown that belonged to Penny's mom."

Carrie gaped. Accustomed to seeing her daughter in jeans and enveloping sweaters, she hadn't quite realized what a very nice figure the girl had. And the long dress, with its clinging, low-cut bodice, had been expertly cut to make the most of even meager curves.

With the survival instinct common to teenage girls, Lee Ann correctly interpreted her mother's look. Tugging at the gown's thin pink shoulder straps, she rearranged the neckline upward. "I think we'll have to adjust the top a little," she said appeasingly—a suggestion with which Carrie agreed wholeheartedly.

A week later, hair piled high in an extravaganza of curls and ribbons, décolletage adjusted to her mother's minimum standards of decency, Cinderella departed for the ball. Accompanied by Penny, who was dressed as a black cat in leotard and whiskers, she swept out the door to where a dazed-looking Danny waited behind the wheel of his mother's small sedan.

That had been almost an hour ago. Now Carrie stood in front of the mirror in the steamy bathroom, applying eye-liner and wishing she hadn't agreed to attend the silly party. Matt had loved Halloween, getting into the spirit of the holiday with imagination and gusto. He always found some excuse to dress up, even if it was only for the benefit of the neighborhood kids who rang the bell to collect their treats. How strange it felt to be going to a party without him. Carrie's throat tightened; she would not cry! She gulped cold water, blinked rapidly, and blotted at her eyes, trying to avoid smearing the just-applied makeup.

Clad only in lacy black underwear, she padded across the hall, feeling as self-conscious as though she were not alone in the silent house. In her own room, she grabbed the skimpy black slink of a dress, slid it over her head and smoothed the cool fabric over her hips. That's not much of an improvement over underwear, she thought, turning before the long mirror and attempting simultaneously to pull up on the neckline and down on the skirt.

Giving up the attempt, she settled for camouflage, donning black lace stockings and flinging the feather boa around her shoulders. Enhanced by the unaccustomed makeup, her face looked rosier, her eyes enormous. *Not bad for an old lady.* She smiled shyly at her reflection and turned to go, high-heeled shoes tapping busily across the bare hardwood floor.

Passing the door to her daughter's bedroom, Carrie averted her eyes from the chaos, which was even worse than usual. Lee Ann and Penny had spent much of the afternoon closeted together, experimenting with hairstyles and inexpertly applying cosmetics, engaged in endless debate over the merits of various accessories. Shoes, stockings, and jewelry lay scattered across every horizontal surface, amid a jumble of jars and tubes, ribbons and hair rollers. A fashion magazine lay face down next to one of Lee Ann's treasured old volumes of fairy tales. And the overhead light was on. Again. In the center of the bed, Pandora raised her head, twitched one ear, and yawned. Cold air eddied, ran like ghostly fingers up Carrie's arms and across her bare shoulders; she shivered, vulnerable in the scanty costume, in the raw exposing glare. Reaching one arm just far enough to flick the switch, Carrie turned off the light and plunged down the stairs, leaving her house to the possession of darkness.

At the community center, the parking lot was already overflowing, and costumed figures were drifting toward the brightly lit building. Carrie nosed into a parking spot almost a block away, then emerged from the car to a deserted street, where huge old trees, so colorful in the daytime, turned the sidewalk into a tunnel of darkness. She clutched her coat around her and began to walk.

When a tall figure loomed out of the darkness at her elbow, it seemed so entirely appropriate that Carrie didn't even jump. It was, after all, Halloween—a night when strange things are *supposed* to happen. She moved aside slightly, but without apprehension, like an actress who knows the script is on her side; and the man swept off an enormous plumed hat and made her a courtly bow. Of course—just another neighborhood resident heading for the party. Impulsively, she pulled her coat open like wings and responded with quite a creditable curtsy. Then, feeling like Alice stepping through the looking glass, she accepted his offered arm and they walked toward the community center together.

The door was flung open by a very short ghost; the cavalier stepped back and let her precede him into a hallway eerily aglow with ultraviolet light, festooned with streamers and echoing with hollow recorded peals of maniacal laughter. The muffled thump of rock music identified the teen party, somewhere off to her left; from the right came the delighted shrieks of smaller children. Involuntarily, Carrie shrank just a little closer to her masked escort.

Who broke his mysterious silence for the first time. "That's me," he said.

"What?"

"The laughter. It's a new touch this year. We recorded it in Keith's basement last week. What do you think of it?"

Wondering what the correct response was for a question like that, she opted for candor. "It sounds . . . very insane."

"Good," he said, looking pleased.

They were swept apart as a horde of small children jostled by, closely followed by a cackling green-faced witch. The children raced on excitedly, but the witch came—literally—to a screeching halt.

"I see you've met Frank," said the apparition prosaically.

Carrie looked again and recognized Barbara. "Not exactly," she admitted.

Then . . . *Frank? Oh no, surely not.* Carrie dwindled with embarrassment, looking over her shoulder at the caped figure who now looked all too familiar. Of course, he was an old school friend of Keith Burnett's, wasn't he? And if he worked at the school, it was logical that he should live in the neighborhood.

"Carrie Sutton . . . Frank Meredith," confirmed Barbara, who had obviously forgotten Carrie's tale about her earlier run-in with the school guidance counselor.

Is there a hint of mockery in his smile? No; to give him credit, his look of pleasure seemed quite genuine.

87

Carrie realized that she was scowling and quickly arranged her own features into an expression more appropriate to social introductions. Frank removed his huge hat in an expansive gesture, flung back his satin-lined cape and made another elaborate bow. It was really very impressive.

"Let me take your coat," offered Barbara. "We'll ride herd on the kids for a while; then I'll get someone to take over, and we'll join the grownups and introduce you around."

Carrie handed over her coat obediently, rearranging the feather boa and tugging discreetly at the bodice of the dress under its concealment. "You look terrific," said Barbara with satisfaction, and shoved the coat at Frank, who was hovering appreciatively. "Want to look in on the big kids first?" Without waiting for an answer, she trotted off down the left-hand corridor. With a quick, uncertain smile at Frank, Carrie retreated after her.

She was right behind as her hostess tugged open one of a pair of heavy double doors and motioned her through. The door thunked shut behind them and Barbara disappeared, her black costume swallowed up in the shadows before she had moved even a few feet away. Carrie stood still, disoriented, while her eyes accustomed themselves to the gloom.

Lee Ann reveled in the darkness, velvety and secretive, as intense as a gathering storm; crackling with the fierce energy of the strobe's lightning flickers. She moved with it, with the raw rock music that throbbed and snarled, bass rhythm pounding like a pulse . . . pressing against Danny, then whirling away, abandoning herself to the dance's teasing, too-adult movements. Around them the music swirled and eddied, setting vibrations thrumming in the floor; rhythmic, sensual, hypnotic. Lee Ann could feel it in her bones, her teeth, the sudden thudding of her heart—the rush and tumble of her blood.

Her partner looked up and faltered to a halt. Surprised, she stood still, following the direction of his gaze to the hallway door that had opened. *Mom! A surge of consternation—What will she think? What is she going to do?—* was swallowed up by outrage. *Why can't she let me alone?*

The width of the dance floor was between them. Lee Ann grasped Danny's hand and tugged, slipping farther back into the shadows. Half in embarrassment and half in fury, she broadcast a silent blast at her mother: *Go away! You don't belong here.* Drumbeats took up the rhythm of her rage; the volume of the music rose to towering proportions, hammering at the walls. The other dancers massed between them like a wall, closing ranks, shutting out the adult intruder, who shrank away and retreated. Lee Ann turned back to Danny with a smug cat-smile, moving closer and closer, giving herself up to the music as it rose to frenzied climax.

Carrie dipped her head, away from the dizzying lights, from the dancers illuminated in jerky freeze-frame motion. Misshapen shadows pulled free from the surrounding darkness and flung themselves, capering, across the walls. Her slight ill-at-ease feeling tightened with a premonition of real dread. None of the costumed figures before her were familiar: strange masked faces gazed at her blandly, silently, a collection of grotesques from a Fellini film. In the intermittent bursts of light, they seemed to loom ever closer, slipping sickeningly in and out of vision.

Carrie took a step backward, prey to sudden unreasoning panic. *There's something wrong. Something . . .* She held her breath as though it could be snatched away from her, clapped hands over her ears, shut her eyes; shut it all out, denying. *Something terrible.* The music rose in intensity. At the point where noise became pressure, it leaned on her like a weight.

A hand touched her arm. Carrie jerked and would have screamed if she had been able to draw breath. Barbara motioned and drew her into the hall; behind them the music surged triumphantly, hurling itself against the muffling doors.

Carrie propped herself against the hard tiled wall, shaking, grateful for the sturdy reality as much as for the support. Desperately, she drew at the lighter, cooler air, struggling against a gray film of nausea.

Gradually, the crushing panic receded, fading like a dream in daylight, leaving her feeling no more than foolish. Barbara gave her a measuring look, but made no comment, for which Carrie was grateful. As long as no one said anything, she could pretend that it hadn't happened . . . it wasn't real.

The other woman turned away, glaring balefully at the closed doors. "Well, we're not going to find them in *there* without a flashlight," she said. Her tone was cheerful, almost normal. Almost. Maybe it was only Carrie's imagination that detected a faint echo of her own distress.

Barbara's mobile face gave no hint of undue concern. "Frank and Keith are going to be splitting chaperon duty," she assured Carrie. "They're the only people I could find who claim to actually *like* teenagers. Frank even says he doesn't mind the music . . . but I think he's just being macho."

She flashed Carrie a grin that was now Halloween impish. "Let's leave it to them, shall we? It's about time to face our stint with the *little* hellions." Barbara turned away in a flutter and swirl of black witchrobes, and Carrie collected herself and followed, closely as though for safety.

*　　*　　*

Across the square central hallway, Barbara led her toward a second large room where, to judge from the sounds, small children were engaged in either games or hostilities. Barbara waded into it, knee-deep in small bobbing bodies. "Aren't they cute?" she asked fatuously. Carrie plunged bravely after her, and soon relaxed enough to be able to agree. One small dimpled girl, in a yarn wig, looked disconcertingly like the Cabbage Patch doll clutched in her arms— right down to a matching layer of dirt, collected, Carrie suspected, at the party. Jeremy Burnett, curly head protruding only slightly from an immense padded orange pumpkin, marched past stolidly on sturdy green-clad legs. His five-year-old brother Jason, garbed as a lion, watched her gravely with huge dark eyes from the depths of a shaggy fake-fur mane. Having chased and caught the tail of his costume, he inserted the limp tassel in the corner of his mouth and chewed meditatively.

For a couple of hours, Carrie and Barbara supervised games, awarded prizes, handed out refreshments, and separated combatants. When reinforcements arrived for the next supervisory shift, Carrie was flushed, breathless, and disheveled—and having a wonderful time. Almost reluctantly, she followed Barbara through the double doors into the relatively cool and dimly lit hall.

When a lanky form detached itself from the darkness and greeted them with Frank's unmistakable voice, Carrie realized belatedly that she had failed to retrieve the marabou boa, discarded as an impediment in the course of a rowdy game. With an effort, she stifled her impulse to dive back through the swinging doors and joined the small crowd of adults who had gathered in the hallway. Barbara bounded away and reappeared to produce Keith for inspection: a fair-haired, nondescript-looking man whose amiably distracted expression concealed a razor-sharp intellect.

The level of noise, which had waxed as the evening waned, made further introductions futile. Carrie smiled and nodded and resolved to sort everyone out later. Frank produced a paper cup of spiced cider; out from behind the concealing horn-rims and officious manner, out from behind the authoritarian desk, he was really rather nice. She sipped gratefully as she was swept along with the group into another room teeming with costumed figures. These at least were her size; and amid the brightly colored regalia, she soon spotted several costumes that made her own seem demure by comparison. A harem dancer billowed by, diaphanous veils fluttering around what looked like a bikini constructed of coins. Even allowing for inflation, it could hardly have contained more than thirty-nine cents worth of change.

Barbara reached out like a fisherman with a net, and snagged a chunky figure from the crowd that streamed by. "This is our Gypsy fortuneteller," she announced. "Marge Copeland . . . Carrie Sutton." Marge, swathed in a miscellany of brilliantly colored skirts and shawls, was almost perfectly square. Clanking with gaudy jewelry, toothy smile revealing a matching hint of gleaming metal, she looked like something that ought to be up on blocks in the front yard. At least until she spoke, in a low, pleasant, cultivated voice. "Hello, Carrie. Happy to meet you." Despite her tiny stature, her handclasp seemed to envelop Carrie in warmth.

"You're the one whose daughter is Penny's friend." Marge cocked her head, birdlike, retaining her grasp on Carrie's hand as though she had forgotten it. The bright smile faltered, clouded over by a faint look of puzzlement. She pulled Carrie's hand toward her, holding it almost against her body, and leaned forward. "You must take care for her," she said, calmly but forcefully. Confused, Carrie shot her an insincere smile and made a discreet attempt to reclaim her hand. The Gypsy's face tightened along with her grip; with visible effort, she searched for words, as though presenting a difficult concept to a foreign listener. Finally, failing to improve on the original, she repeated it with precise emphasis. "Take very good care for her." Clasping Carrie's hand in both of hers, she folded the fingers inward as if she were closing them around an object; then she released her with a reassuring pat, and trundled off toward the corner tent to resume the role of fortuneteller.

Or had she ever stepped out of character at all? Carrie gazed after her for a moment, unnerved. Then normal practicality reasserted itself; dismissing the peculiar little episode as just an adult version of a Halloween prank, she turned back to Barbara and her friends. Among them, she stood quietly against the wall, watching the swirling crowd and listening to the conversations that ebbed and flowed around her. Soon she would quietly make her excuses and leave. Or so she told herself.

Instead, she found herself being drawn beyond polite social exchanges into interesting, sometimes heated, discussions. A plump blonde in a ballerina costume offered an outrageous opinion on a current political issue, seemingly for the pleasure of hearing the howls of protest that arose. A balding man in a nondescript toga engaged Carrie in amicable debate about changes in the local school system. Frank, leaning his rangy frame against a wall, spoke seldom, but his occasional comments were thoughtful and penetrating.

When next she looked at the clock, Carrie was

shocked at how much time had passed. Keith and Barbara had slipped away and now reappeared, each draped with a small sleepy form; Robin, their ten-year-old, followed under her own power, heavy-eyed but protesting. With a guilty jolt, Carrie realized that it was past midnight. *Now who's Cinderella at the ball?* She had given Lee Ann a twelve o'clock curfew, fully expecting to be home before her daughter arrived. And here it was she who had lost track of time and stayed too late.

Too late. The words coiled unpleasantly in her mind, and she shivered despite herself, even as she regarded her own overactive imagination with disgust. Nuts! she told herself succinctly. Plenty of fourteen-year-olds baby sit in other peoples' houses until two and three o'clock in the morning. Why am I getting the jitters over Lee Ann being home by herself for half an hour around midnight?

Frank, as though sensitive to her mood, looked at her with eyebrows raised. She smiled at him wryly and shrugged. "At midnight I turn back into a parent."

Carrie rounded the corner, driving just a little faster than she should. She had left the party with Keith and Barbara, after helping them sort out coats, costumes, and various belongings. Frank, evidently a family favorite, scooped up the sleepy and peevish Robin and had jollied her into reluctant laughter by the time they all reached Keith's battered station wagon. He really was good with the kids.

Then, despite Carrie's protests, he had insisted on walking her to her car. In the sheltering darkness under the trees, she faced him and awkwardly extended her hand in a gesture that was both link and barrier. Although she was unable to see the expression on his face, she was sure there was a note of

94

mockery in the exaggerated gallantry with which he bent and kissed it. As she pulled the car away from the curb, she looked back in the rearview mirror and raised a hand in a tentative gesture. But his cloaked form had already vanished back into the shadows.

Barbara Burnett's car was parked in front of the house, and lights were on. Danny had brought the girls back on time, then—more or less. As she felt her rigid shoulders relax, Carrie realized how tense she had been. Clasping her keys in cold fingers, she crunched across the driveway to the front porch, where Lee Ann had left the light on for her. What a strange reversal: the teenage daughter waiting up, leaving lights on for Mom. Carrie thought briefly of new friends, new possibilities . . . and wondered if it might happen again.

As she closed the front door behind her, there was a quick flutter of movement from the dimly lamp lit living room; young voices picked up a lively conversation. Lee Ann, huddled into a borrowed shawl, perched beside Danny on the couch, chattering brightly about the party. But where was Penny? It was not until Carrie saw Lee Ann furtively pull up a shoulder strap under cover of the shawl that she realized Penny wasn't there. And why.

Obviously, the two had dropped their unwitting chaperon at the Burnett's first. And now, instead of worrying about curfew violations, Carrie had to worry about how *early* they had come home.

Something in her face must have changed then; the conversation trailed off into uneasy silence. Danny touched Lee Ann's hand gently and rose to leave, looking at the floor and muttering an indistinct goodbye. Lee Ann accompanied him to the door; in the foyer she gathered dignity about her with the shawl and faced her mother.

Buffeted by conflicting emotions, Carrie resisted her immediate impulse, which was to scream—or sit down and cry. She forced herself to speak calmly, although even to herself her voice sounded strained. "I think we need to talk, but let's do it in the morning, okay?"

Lee Ann dipped her head in a gesture that might have meant anything, then fled up the stairs. Carrie turned out the lights and locked the door before following slowly. Upstairs, the hallway was cold.

CHAPTER VIII

So the girl—Lee Ann—had a boyfriend now. And the mother didn't like it a bit. Jealous, perhaps?

The man moved restlessly, a few steps forward, a few steps back, prowling the small and featureless room; a predator, waiting to be released. But the only release now was inside his head, in the images, the remembering. Watching the two of them, awkwardly side by side on the old sofa, in the low lamplight, the boy slobbering over her with clumsy kisses and experimental adolescent fumblings; the top of her dress pulled down and the pale gleam of her breasts, the nipples hardening under his hands. And she liked it. He knew she did.

The man's own hands began to tremble.

She smiled at first when she felt it . . . *Mom?* Tucking her in like a little kid. Just the same, the touch was comforting. Wrapped in dreamy lassitude, Lee Ann smiled again and drifted back to sleep.

Then came sluggishly awake, edgily, peevish. The blankets were moving down, away from her chin, taking away the cuddly warmth. *She's not getting me up. It isn't time to get up yet.* Lee Ann scrabbled at the covers with fingers still weak and clumsy with sleep. And felt the hands . . . sly and secretive, smoothing across the fabric of her nightgown, undoing the ribbons at the throat. Big hands, coarse and damp, under her gown now, on her skin. On her breasts, brushing her nipples, coaxing them upright, drawing unexpected responses from her unwilling flesh.

Her eyes burst open. She stiffened, arms flailing, mouth stretched wide around a scream that was too big to emerge. Another touch, now, light and hot, on her thigh; fumbling with the hem of her gown, drawing it up.

Her breath came hard now, ragged and harsh like sobs, and she thrashed, feet kicking free of the tangling blankets. One lashing hand struck the wooden headboard, hard, with a hollow thud.

Dimly through ringing ears, she heard her mother's sleepy query: "Lee Ann?"

And the scream tore free. Lee Ann threw herself against the headboard, curled as small as possible, clutching spasmodically at her pillow. She gasped, haltingly, dragging at the painful air; and screamed again, as though she might not be able to stop.

"Lee Ann! My God, Lee Ann." Her mother's weight sagged the edge of the bed, her mother's warm hands patted, arms encircled and held. "Lee Ann, honey, what's wrong?"

It was cold, so cold. Even the blankets, drawn back up to enfold her, didn't seem to help. Lee Ann shuddered. "There was somebody," she choked. "Right here. By my bed."

Her mother's arms tightened comfortingly; but before she opened her mouth, Lee Ann knew that she wasn't going to understand. Not at all.

"Honey, it was a dream." Carrie rocked gently, warm cheek pressed against her daughter's hair, so that Lee Ann could feel the words as well as hear them, feel the movements of her mother's speech against her temple. Saying exactly what Lee Ann knew she would say. "There's no one here."

The adamant embrace was suddenly stifling. Lee Ann surged upright, pulling away. "I wasn't dreaming. There was someone here. There *was!* He touched me!"

Guilty conscience? The unspoken thought swam upward from Carrie's subconscious, and her face went rigid, though Lee Ann wasn't quite sure why. But her voice when she spoke was perfectly controlled. "Honey, there's no one here. You can see there isn't." She reached out and snapped on the little bedside lamp, creating illumination where communication failed.

"But there was! There really was." Out of reflex, not really thinking, Lee Ann's eyes turned to the window.

Carrie sighed, thrust away sleep-short exasperation, and went to perform the examining-the-window charade. At a casual glance, it was fully closed, even locked; but the old wooden windows were warped, and the rotating thumb latch had completely missed the mating piece of the outer sash. The ineffectual bit of hardware was in the right position, but the window wasn't locked.

Sunday morning Carrie was awakened by the phone; she pulled herself up out of sodden sleep and reached for the bedside extension. Ten, according to the digital clock, although it felt much earlier. Frank's voice, disgustingly cheerful, sounded in her ear. "A bunch of us are going back over to the community center this afternoon to clean up. We could use some extra help, so I'm supposed to inveigle you with my vaunted charm."

Carrie felt faintly irritated. It wasn't her party, after all; she had been an invited guest. "Uh . . . when?"

she stalled.

"About two. I'll pick you up if you can come."
Silence followed as she tried to think of some graceful
excuse; Frank threw in his final inducement. "Just
think, it's a chance to see me in another of my many
guises."

Carrie laughed. A sense of humor was one of the
last things she would have expected from this man.
"I can hardly wait," she said drily. But she hung up
feeling more anticipatory than she had felt in
months, and in the shower she almost gave way to an
impulse to sing.

Like a grotesque shadow cast by an inoffensive
object, her distorted fears of the previous night
dwindled to insignificance when she confronted
them objectively. What, after all, was really wrong?
Loud rock music and a moment of claustro-
phobia . . a slightly dotty neighbor with a strange
sense of humor . . . a young girl kissing her boyfriend good night. Not to mention Lee Ann's middle-
of-the-night burglary scare. Maybe both of them were
having nightmares. They were both tired and under a
lot of stress, after all.

After breakfast, in a burst of energy, she tidied the
house and began to vacuum the downstairs rooms.
Pandora, who had been sleeping in a corner of the
sofa, rose to face the roaring machine belligerently,
spat, and departed for the relative quiet of the
upstairs. Carrie continued cleaning contentedly.

It was almost noon when she turned the vacuum
off, and heard the first faint stirrings from Lee Ann's
room. The girl came drifting down the stairs in a
bathrobe and fuzzy slippers, cat cradled in her arms.
With her dark hair tumbled around her pale face, she
looked far younger even than her fourteen years. And
her face today was paler than usual.

Something inside Carrie twisted, and she retreated
cravenly from the confrontation that last night had

seemed inevitable.

Briskly, she led the way into the kitchen, obscuring her thoughts with activity. "Are you okay, honey? You don't look like you feel well."

"I'm all right." Lee Ann drooped over the kitchen table and Carrie poured her a glass of orange juice.

"You probably didn't get enough sleep . . . being out late, and then having bad dreams on top of it. You have terrible circles under your eyes." Carrie separated strips of bacon and wrapped them in a paper towel for the microwave. "Why don't you try to take a nap this afternoon? I'm going to be gone for a while, helping Barbara clean up over at the community center." She didn't mention Frank.

"I know. Danny and Penny are going, too. They asked me to come, but I don't know if I will or not."

The apparent lack of interest would have been reassuring if it hadn't rung slightly false. Carrie retrieved the cooked bacon, began scrambling eggs, and changed the subject.

"Well, if you do come over with them, I'll see you there. And even if you don't, cleanup is still the order of the day. Your bedroom is a disaster."

After breakfast Lee Ann washed her dishes without being reminded and returned upstairs, ostensibly to clean her room. She was still closeted there with Pandora when Frank arrived. Carrie, who had been dithering in the living room, watching for him, hurried into the foyer and called up the stairs. "Lee Ann, I'm leaving now. I'll see you around suppertime. Okay?"

An answering "Okay" floated down the stairs like an echo. Carrie paused briefly to inspect her flushed face in the mirror, grabbed her coat, and let herself out before Frank could come to the door. Hoping that Lee Ann wasn't watching from the window above them, she hurried down the front walk, throwing the coat around her shoulders as she went. "Well, you've got yourself another willing worker," she said brightly, and winced inwardly at the brittle tone of her own voice. Frank ushered her toward the curb; once past the tangled evergreen hedge that enclosed the yard, she began to relax.

In the car Carrie turned to look back at the house, shading her eyes against the high sun. No face looked after them; nothing moved at the dormer window. She settled herself against the cracking vinyl upholstery, faced Frank as he slid under the steering wheel, and searched for another opening remark—one that wouldn't sound brainlessly inane. "Thank you for coming to pick me up." *There. Simple, polite, and honest.* Perhaps her social skills were way out of practice, but that was no reason to resort to the coy, artificial chitchat she had always abhorred.

"Thank you for volunteering."

"I didn't volunteer."

"Details." He turned the ignition key, and the car wheezed twice, pitifully, then coughed and started. "Actually, it was part of an insidious plot to see you again."

"In one of my other guises?"

Frank made a muffled choking sound and concentrated on shifting gears, easing the car away from the curb. "Yes, and may I say you look just as delightful today as you did by moonlight."

"There was no moon last night."

Frank looked wounded. "But if there had been, you would have," he retorted, mangling syntax beyond recognition. "Is there no poetry in your soul, woman?"

Lacking a suitable response, Carrie laughed and let the conversation drop. Beside her, Frank hummed under his breath contentedly, and they drove the rest of the way in surprisingly comfortable silence.

At the community center, it became obvious that

the cleanup brigade was just an excuse for another party. Carrie recognized many of the people from the night before; coming and going with brooms and garbage bags, they kept spirited conversations echoing in the high-ceilinged rooms. She spotted Barbara, who waved and beckoned. "Hi, Carrie! Thanks for coming. Frank, you're just the man we need to take down the streamers; nobody else can reach them."

They were absorbed into the activity so quickly that Carrie had little time to feel self-conscious. Frank braced himself on a rickety stepladder and began to detach the highest of the crepe paper decorations. The plump blonde who had been a ballerina last night was now clad in jeans and sweatshirt; she gave Carrie a friendly smile and a garbage bag. "Remember me? Louise Hilyard. If you'll help Barbara gather up the big stuff, I can get started sweeping the floor."

Carrie obediently began to circle the room, picking up discarded paper plates and cups, crumpled napkins, and other less identifiable debris. Looking up from her own struggle with an overstuffed bag, Barbara smiled. "It was nice of you to come help, Carrie. I hope you enjoyed the party enough to make it worthwhile doing some of the work."

"You know, I really did. It was the first party I've been to since Matt died, and I thought I would be uncomfortable, but I wasn't."

"I'm glad," said Barbara sincerely. "We've got a super bunch of people, and I thought you'd enjoy meeting them."

"You were right; I did. Louise seems like a really nice person. I enjoyed talking to her and her husband—Mark, is it?"

Barbara nodded affirmatively. "He's a part-time instructor at the university. Friend of Keith's. He and Louise haven't been married very long." She picked

103

up still another handful of wadded paper, straining the capacity of her bag to the limit.

"And the Gypsy fortuneteller—Marge—who is she? What does she do?"

"Quite a character, isn't she? Marge worked for the post office for years, and now she's semiretired. I think she still does volunteer work at the library."

"She must make a good fortuneteller," ventured Carrie. "She almost had me taking her seriously."

"Oh, did you get a reading from her?"

"No, it was when you introduced us. She made some cryptic remark . . . something about taking care." Carrie shrugged, embarrassed without knowing why. "I'm sure it must have been a joke; there wouldn't be any reason for her to want to scare me."

Frank appeared at Carrie's elbow and peered quizzically over a massive armful of discarded orange and black crepe paper. "Who scared whom?" he asked, sternly but grammatically.

"Oh, it wasn't anything. The fortuneteller, Marge, said something kind of peculiar to me, and I was asking Barbara about her. That's all."

Frank looked at her thoughtfully. "Where are the garbage bags?" he asked.

Barbara laughed and produced another bag, holding it while Frank dumped his burden. "What exactly did she say to you?" she pursued.

"It was about Lee Ann, actually; she asked about 'Penny's friend.' And she told me to be careful . . . to take care of her." Carrie laughed deprecatingly. "This is silly. Three adults standing around seriously discussing a Halloween party fortuneteller."

"Well, I don't know how you feel about that sort of stuff, but Marge does take it seriously. It's not just a Halloween stunt; she's been giving readings in her home for years."

At Carrie's unbelieving look, Barbara hastened on. "Don't get me wrong; she's not a crackpot. Marge is well educated, and maybe smarter than any of the rest of us."

"That doesn't mean she can't have a screw loose." Carrie blurted out, then stopped, aghast at her impulsive retort. She shook her head in quick negation. "I'm sorry. I didn't mean to sound insulting; I just can't really believe that kind of stuff."

"It's okay," said Barbara comfortingly. "I know it sounds crazy. But Marge is entirely sincere. She won't take money for readings, even though she could use it; she says it isn't ethical."

"If she'd given you the standard carnival spiel about meeting someone tall, dark and handsome, you'd have wanted to believe her," said Frank flippantly, with an exaggeratedly meaningful glance. "Instead she told you something unpleasant, and you *don't* want to believe *that*. In an inverted sort of way, it gives her more credibility."

Putting aside her initial reaction, Carrie examined the idea. *The trouble is, I think I do believe her. I don't want to, but I do.* She almost opened her mouth to say so, then thought better of it. *If I start trying to explain, they'll think I'm the one who's crazy.*

Louise swept by in the wake of a huge broom, and the conversation, to Carrie's relief, dwindled to a halt. Frank drifted off, bearing trash bags for disposal, and Barbara scanned the room, assessing progress.

"I think that's about all we can do in here for now. Let's leave it to Lou and her broom, and we'll go see how Penny and the other kids are doing cleaning up their part."

In the bright morning light, the scarred double doors of the teen room were completely unremarkable. One side stood wide, propped by a heavy trash

105

container. In Barbara's wake, Carrie hesitated almos[t] imperceptibly, then stepped through into a spac[e] now sunlit, peaceful, and utterly ordinary. Dus[t] motes surged in the spill of light from the hig[h] windows, and last night's streamers hung limp an[d] dispirited from the ceiling. Other decorations ha[d] been taken down, and the expected trash had largel[y] disappeared. Light young voices rang in the hollo[w] stillness; two unfamiliar girls busily stuffed larg[e] plastic bags, and across the room Penny piloted [a] pushbroom with abandon.

Barbara leaned against the wall and regarde[d] the evidence of youthful energy with admiratio[n.] "You guys have done a great job; it looks lik[e] you're almost through already," she said. "We ca[n] get Danny to take down the streamers. Is he he[re] yet?"

The closest of the two girls shook her head blankl[y,] dark tail of hair switching. "Haven't seen him,["] responded the other, a thin little figure with a shar[p] face framed by a riot of brown curls. Penny pause[d,] leaning on the broom. "I think he was going to pic[k] up Lee Ann," she volunteered. "But it seems like h[e] should have been here by now."

Carrie's brow creased in an involuntary frow[n,] hastily erased as Barbara turned to her.

"Well, we'll get one of the other guys. Carrie, wh[y] don't you see if Frank's finished in the other room[?"]

As if her suggestion had been a conjuration, Fran[k] appeared in the doorway. "I think we're all done i[n] there," he reported, waving lazily in the gener[al] direction of the corridor. "What do you want us to d[o] now?"

"How about taking down the streamers in her[e.] I'll check on the adult party room, and I think we'[ll] be finished." Barbara cocked her head as if i[n] thought. "Then why don't you two pick up Lee An[n] and come over for a potluck dinner? Nothing fanc[y,]

I'll make a big pot of spaghetti and throw some garlic bread in the oven. It would make a nice way to wind up the weekend.''

Carrie opened her mouth to make a polite refusal, but Frank interrupted her smoothly. "We'd love to," he said, ignoring her silent outraged gestures. "I'll get some salad stuff on the way over.''

"Great!" Barbara flashed them a delighted grin, in which Carrie thought she detected a slight conspiratorial element. "Bring the guitar, too. I'll see if Louise and Mark want to come." Barbara receded rapidly down the hall, talking over her shoulder as she went, and Carrie turned to Frank, uncertain whether to be angry or amused.

He looked down at her, pleasant homely face arranged in a furrowed expression of worry that would rival a basset hound's. "You don't really mind, do you?" he asked plaintively. "It'll be fun."

An hour later they rattled to a stop in front of her house, behind a car which Carrie identified, with a sinking feeling, as Barbara Burnett's. Frank draped himself over the seatback and began to rearrange groceries and guitar case to make room for a passenger in the back seat. "Don't bother," she told him tightly. "Lee Ann can just ride down with Danny."

Frank grunted something unintelligible and eased himself gingerly back into the front seat. All clownishness set aside, he looked at her soberly. "I gathered from Barbara that Lee Ann and Danny are seeing one another. Are you upset about it?"

His deep-set brown eyes were kind and concerned. *Part of his professional stock in trade?* But Carrie, to her own surprise, swallowed a self-reliant rebuff and gave way to the impulse to confide.

"I've got nothing against Danny: he seems like a real nice kid. But Lee Ann isn't even fifteen yet. She's not allowed to have regular dates; they only go out in groups, like last night." Her voice trailed off lamely. "I just get worried sometimes . . . with me working . . . that she doesn't get enough supervision." Carrie leaned her forehead against the cold glass of the window. "Darn it," she burst out, "I don't approve of her having him in the house when I'm gone."

"Have you tried telling her not to?" asked Frank reasonably.

"We always had a rule that she didn't bring friends home when I wasn't there unless she asked me first. But it kind of went out the window when we moved here; I was so glad for her to be coming out of her shell and making friends." Carrie shook her head helplessly. "And now, I just don't know how to handle it. I can bring the rule back up, but how do I enforce it? And if they're . . . I mean . . ." Carrie fumbled for words, grateful for the fading light that hid her hot face. "They could always just go somewhere else," she finished lamely.

Frank whistled softly through his teeth. "'Tis a puzzlement," he quoted.

"I . . . look, I'm sorry to be laying my problems on you." *He's certainly easy to talk to. No wonder the kids like him. But I'm not one of his impressionable high-school kids.* Carrie strove for a tone of lightness. "Come on in for a minute. I want to change my shirt and we'll collect Lee Ann and Danny. Then we'll go make salad for the thundering herd; and I want to hear you play that guitar."

The teens were at the kitchen table with mugs of cocoa, all innocence. Carrie swallowed irritation at Lee Ann's too-sweet smile, and was mildly, childishly gratified at the utter shock on the girl's face when Frank followed her into the kitchen.

At the Burnett's they walked into a scene of

organized chaos. It was one of those households, it seemed, where everyone gathered in the kitchen and "helped." Louise and Barbara hovered over steaming vats at the stove; Keith presided at the counter, preparing large loaves of garlic bread for the oven. In the adjoining dining area, Mark Hilyard sat with Jeremy on his lap, entertaining the two smallest children, while Penny and several friends stacked plates and silverware on the long refectory table.

With the arrival of Danny and an oddly silent Lee Ann, the adolescent population was judged to have reached critical mass. Table setting completed, they were excused—and strongly encouraged—to gather downstairs in the basement game room.

The adults were absorbed into the bustle without comment. Frank set his parcel on the center island and began to extract lettuce and vegetables with the air of a magician conjuring a rabbit from a hat. Obviously familiar with the layout of the kitchen, he delved in the cabinet for a stainless steel bowl the size of a small washtub and began to shred lettuce. At Carrie's request, he also produced a cutting board and paring knife; she took up a station across the island from him and began slicing tomatoes.

Fragments of several conversations floated past, as enticing as the spicy aroma of tomato sauce and garlic, and as difficult to grasp. Carrie gave up trying to follow any one discussion and simply listened, bemused, to the bantering exchanges. By the time they all converged at the table, the talk had turned to an in-depth analysis of the previous night's party.

The annual event had begun, apparently, as an alternative to trick-or-treat excursions for the neighborhood children. "When we had all that furor over sickies giving kids tainted candy," Barbara explained for Carrie's benefit.

"Trick or treat is nothing but petty extortion

anyway," grumped Mark, affecting an air of exaggerated misanthropy. "I've never understood why adults didn't stamp it out years ago."

Behind him, Penny appeared in the vanguard of teenagers and younger children. "It's just for fun," she defended. "What's wrong with dressing up and asking for treats?" The others nodded supportively and flowed around her, heading for the stove.

"Of course it's harmless," added Louise. "The kids these days don't really mean that they'll play tricks on you if you don't give them something."

"That was the original meaning, though. That's where 'trick or treat' came from," insisted Mark stubbornly.

"Actually, the original meaning of Halloween goes back a lot further than that," interrupted Barbara, smoothly forestalling a family argument.

Mark swung his attention to her. "Well, sure, everybody knows it's the eve of All Saints' Day. But I can't see what that has to do with costumes and pranks and treats."

Keith cleared his throat and assumed a professor-ish demeanor. "The costumes and pranks are probably a debased form of an even older observance," he lectured. "Halloween was originally a pagan festival that marked the turning point of the year: from summer and light to winter and darkness. And it was a commemoration of the dead."

In the crowd of young people across the room, someone dropped a spoon.

"I'm not talking horror-movie stuff, you understand. To followers of the old religions, it was a sacred observance—the night when the veil between the worlds was thinnest, and you paid honor to those who had gone before."

Carrie glanced sidewise nervously, to where Lee Ann stood motionless among the jostling teenagers, face taut and intent. Barbara followed the direction of her gaze; across the table, Keith moved slightly as though someone had kicked him. The brief and embarrassed pause that ensued was broken almost immediately as everyone began to talk at once.

Lee Ann dropped her eyes. Staring fixedly at the plate in her hands, she moved away with Danny at her elbow, drifting back toward the basement stairs.

CHAPTER IX

In the week that followed, Frank called twice. Each time Carrie refused his invitation, though she couldn't explain why, even to herself. And she maintained a perverse hope that he would try again.

The days grew gradually shorter and grayer. Carrie intensified her work on the house, as though she shared nature's imperative need to prepare for the coming of winter. Chinks were caulked, storm windows washed and installed. The furnace burbled away cheerfully, turning itself on and off reliably and with increasing frequency. The chimney was cleaned and inspected, and firewood was ordered.

It was spitting snow the day the truck arrived; she and Lee Ann and Danny worked steadily for almost an hour, stacking the short logs in the sheltered lee of the small side porch.

In the mysterious manner of teenagers, relationships seemed to have been restored without question, rifts healed without a scar. Or at least without explanation to parents. Carrie simply watched and was grateful as Lee Ann began once more to appear promptly after school, often with Penny, Danny, or both in tow. Carrie, in turn, restricted her errands to mornings, and came home as soon as possible on the days when she worked.

"I'll just take a few of these inside and put them in your log basket." Danny hefted the last pieces of wood and trudged up the steps. Lee Ann darted ahead of him to open the door.

In the kitchen, Carrie draped her damp jacket over a chair and kicked off her wet shoes. She poured milk into a pan, added cocoa, and stood absently warming her hands at the stove. A faint whiff of smoke drifted by, acrid and faintly sweet. Had Danny gotten a fire lit already?

She poked her head around the dining-room door, framing an appreciative remark. Lee Ann, on the floor in front of the fireplace, was talking rapidly, gesturing excitedly, cheeks pink. Beside her, Danny bent close, though not for the reason Carrie would have expected. His voice rose slightly, and he banged his fist against the floor in emphatic punctuation. Lee Ann recoiled and shook her head, looking more subdued.

Carrie drew back into the kitchen and busied herself for a moment arranging mugs and doughnuts on the table before returning to the doorway. "You guys want to come and have cocoa?"

She walked slowly through the dining room, half her attention on her own overfull cup. "Or we could have it in here . . ." *In front of the fire.* But there was no fire. Behind the two teenagers the grate was cold and black, the logs still stacked neatly in the hearth basket.

"I could have sworn I smelled smoke. I thought maybe you'd lit a fire." Lee Ann flicked a glance at Danny, with an expression that was gone before Carrie could identify it. Then the two on the floor looked up politely, faces blandly unreadable.

"No . . ."

"We didn't know if you'd want us to."

*   *   *

Throughout the downstairs rooms now, new curtains were in place; the furniture was arranged to Carrie's satisfaction, with wood pieces polished or refinished, and mismatched upholstery disguised with slipcovers or brightened with colorful pillows. Despite a gray and dismal afternoon, the living room was warm and cheerful; the only blot on its serenity was a large cardboard box which sat amid a sea of newspaper in the middle of the rug.

Also sitting in the middle of the floor, Barbara extracted Pandora from the box. Holding off the cat with one hand, she groped for more newspaper with the other, and continued wrapping and repacking unused items from Carrie's cherished hoard. "It's perfect, Carrie," she continued an interrupted conversation. "The pictures and stuff make a really big difference."

Carrie nursed her thumb, still throbbing from its most recent encounter with the business end of a hammer, and agreed. With her treasured paintings, prints, and favorite objects now in place, the rooms looked complete. Someone lived here.

She had planned it as her own private ceremony: the final taking of possession. Alone, she had brought the box downstairs and investigated it with pleasure, sorting not only objects but memories. The glass candlesticks that had been a wedding present . . . inexpensive posters that had brightened their first student housing quarters, the delicate dancing figure she and Matt bought at an art fair. All wrapped in layers of newspapers and tissue, still smelling faintly of Matt's pipe tobacco. Carrie unwrapped and sorted and sometimes wiped at her eyes, streaking her face with the dust of past years.

By midafternoon she had made little progress. Her choices were laid out on the floor, first in this arrangement, then that. She held a print at arm's length, trying to visualize it hanging in place above

114

the mantel. Or perhaps the wall above the couch?

She had been kneeling amid the debris in helpless indecision when Lee Ann came home from school, this time accompanied by Barbara as well as Penny.

"Hi, Mom. What are you doing?"

"At the moment . . . making a mess." Carrie rose stiffly and began to rake crumpled packing into a neater pile with the side of her foot.

Barbara smiled apologetically. "I gave the girls a ride home from school, since it was starting to drizzle, and Lee Ann asked us in."

"I'm going to make cocoa," explained Lee Ann, "and Penny and I are going to work on our book reports together."

"Sounds good." Carrie stretched and rubbed her aching back. "I needed a break, and I'm not getting anything done anyway."

The girls clattered away toward the kitchen, shedding jackets and schoolbooks as they went. Carrie shrugged ruefully at Barbara. "I've been unpacking and trying to find places to put things. I hate having stuff still in boxes after almost four months."

Barbara nodded with understanding, but no great sympathy. "I've still got stuff in boxes, and it's been eight *years*. I figure if I haven't missed it by now I don't really need it."

She bent and picked up a small watercolor from the heap on the floor: a cloudy, impressionistic autumn scene, evocative of wood smoke and wet leaves. "Ohh . . . beautiful." She smiled at Carrie in delight. "Where are you going to put this?"

The discussion that followed ranged through the living room and dining room, continued over cocoa and cookies, and ended by providing more assistance than Carrie really wanted. Together, the four of them maneuvered a heavy framed print into the position of honor above the fireplace. Barbara arranged delicate candlesticks at one end of the mantel, three glass paperweights at the other. Penny and Lee Ann carried off the dancer figurine and two small ceramic pieces for the dining-room sideboard.

Now Lee Ann stood in the middle of the living room, head cocked to one side. "It looks like something out of a magazine, Mom."

"It really does," agreed Penny.

"Depends on what magazine you have in mind," retorted Carrie wryly. But despite her disclaimer she was pleased with their results. "Thanks for the help, you two. But now it's time to get started on those book reports."

It was then, as she and Barbara finished their cleanup, that Carrie had her inspiration. "I've been thinking," she said, an utter untruth since the thought had just now occurred to her, "that I might have a few people over one evening, now that the place is in better shape. You and Keith, of course; and do you think Louise and Mark would like to come?"

Before Carrie could finish a "what-have-I-gotten-myself-into" thought, Barbara looked up from her seat on the floor and smiled. "That would be fun," she accepted blithely. "And why don't you ask Frank, too?"

Carrie wondered darkly if that was what her subconscious had had in mind all along. Frank's invitations had presented her with a quandary, and this was a near-perfect solution. "Sure," she said. "That's a good idea."

"And Lee Ann can go over and spend the evening with Penny and Danny, if she wants to."

In her uncharacteristically impetuous invitation, Carrie hadn't given any thought to Lee Ann. The girl *would* be bored amidst all the adults. "That would be great," she said. "She'll enjoy it a lot more than being here with us."

116

*   *   *

With her home pronounced ready for company,
with invitations issued and accepted, Carrie flung
herself into nervous preparation. After two layers of
stark white paint and a thorough scrubbing of the
dingy old light fixture, the windowless upstairs hall
became substantially brighter. For one entire day,
Carrie worked in the bathroom, with after-school
assistance from Lee Ann, provided despite her
mother's protests about the dismayingly small space.

"See," she said triumphantly, "if I stand in the
bathtub, I can work over here, and I'm not in the
way."

Carrie sighed, blew a lock of hair out of her eyes
and resisted an impulse to urge her daughter to go
somewhere else. Together, they scrubbed the soap-
scummed tile, spackled old plaster, and applied fresh
white enamel to the trim. Avoiding each other's
elbows as best they could, they applied pretty floral
wallpaper.

"Looks good," pronounced Lee Ann. "I told you
we could have it ready in time for the party." She
fished in the bathtub for the wallpaper strip that was
soaking there, folded it into a less unwieldy size and
handed it to Carrie, who was perched precariously on
a rickety stepladder in the corner. "And so what if the
bedrooms are still kind of messy? We'll just close the
doors."

"If they'll stay closed," answered Carrie abstractedly, smoothing the wallpaper panel into place.
"Which reminds me: why don't we move you into
that back bedroom across the hall? Your room is
chilly and drafty now, and it's going to be downright
cold later on."

"No!" Lee Ann's voice was overloud in the tiny
room.

Carrie jumped, banged her head on the sloping

117

ceiling, and looked down in surprise. "It was only a suggestion. You don't have to jump down my throat."

"I didn't mean to," Lee Ann muttered, and busied herself with the next strip of wallpaper. "I just don't want to move. I like my room."

"Well, it's up to you. I'm just afraid you may be uncomfortable." Carrie shrugged, turned her attention back to the wall, and changed the subject. "Barbara said you could spend the evening at their house Saturday. You might even plan to sleep over, if you want to."

There was no response. Silence spun out, broken only by faint splashing sounds as Lee Ann fished another wallpaper strip from the tub and folded it meticulously. Her face was unreadable.

Carrie twisted, rocking the unsteady ladder, and reached down for the paper. Water dripped down her arms and pattered on the newspapers that covered the floor. "I figured you'd just be bored if you stayed here," she continued, striving to keep the wheedling tone out of her explanation. "It's only some of my friends coming over, not like it was a real party, anyhow."

Lee Ann's shrug was eloquent. *Why do I have to leave so she can have a few friends over? Am I in her way . . . is that it?* She leaned over to pull the stopper from the tub drain, and watched intently as the water swirled away.

Carrie made a face of exasperation at the unresponsive wall. What was the matter with the child? She smoothed wallpaper with unnecessary force and made determined conversation.

"This is going to look really nice. We might think about wallpaper like this for your room. It would be pretty, with white curtains and maybe a pink bedspread. I've been thinking about painting that old dresser white, and we could get a wicker dressing

118

table later—maybe for Christmas." She cast a quick glance over her shoulder for a reaction. "Do you think you'd like that?"

"I guess." Lee Ann rose awkwardly, wiping damp hands on the seat of her jeans, and began to gather the sticky newspapers that covered the floor. Still without meeting her mother's eyes, she carried her armful away down the stairs.

Dusk was gathering in the corners by the time Carrie finished her own part of the cleanup. Lee Ann had retreated to her room; her radio, playing softly, murmured unintelligibly behind the closed door. Clutching tools and folded stepladder, Carrie made her way to the basement, passing quickly through the feeble circle of light at the base of the stairs and bumping blindly across the uneven floor in the dimness beyond. It was almost fully dark in the far corner storage area; Carrie banged her shin on something and swore. Resting the ladder against her hip, she groped for the ceiling fixture's pull-chain.

Bright new light fell around her like a tent, and prickling unease came with it. The brilliance that should have been comforting and reassuring instead made the darkness worse by contrast. At the edges of vision, the shadows withdrew furtively and coalesced into a swarming blackness where anything might hide. Dazzled in the shower of cold light, Carrie froze, isolated and vulnerable as a rabbit transfixed by onrushing headlights. She slitted her eyes like a cat, protectively, as though she could achieve a cat's night vision. Did something move, there in the corner? Carrie jerked her head around, fast enough to dizzy her, but not quite fast enough to see. *What is it? Who's there?* Her heart accelerated mindlessly, bumping heavily against her ribs, and each breath came with difficulty in her tightening chest.

Nobody's there, you idiot. Carrie hauled firmly at the reins of galloping imagination. *This is silly.* But modern rationality paled before primitive fear, and the casual ease of electric light seemed small and fragile shelter against the looming darkness. Carrie held her breath, waiting, muscles fiercely taut, poised for flight. When the furnace came on with a breathy *whoomp* she jumped convulsively.

In a scatter of panic, Carrie heaped paperhanging paraphernalia on the shelves and gave the ladder a halfhearted shove toward its accustomed corner. It took all the self-control she could muster to tug the chain pull again; as shadows reclaimed the storage corner, she fixed her eyes on the stairway light and fled the basement with more haste than dignity.

By the end of the week the house—except for the bedrooms—was as immaculate as it would ever be, and entirely ready for company. Carrie's first attempt at entertaining on her own went off surprisingly well, despite all her nervous intimations of disaster. Everyone ate heartily, which was the highest praise any cook could expect. They lingered over the wine which was Frank's contribution; and when Carrie began to clear the table, they followed her, like members of the family, to rinse and stack their dishes. Finally declaring her kitchen too small for Burnett-style entertaining, Carrie gave up on the chores and joined the others for dessert and coffee in the greater comfort of the living room.

Now, with six people taking up every available seating surface and part of the floor, the room seemed much smaller than usual. Surrounded by the warmth of friendship and conversation, Carrie was reminded of her early married years, when friends and fellow students had gathered in cramped apartments for cheap meals and earnest, heated discussions. For once, the memory was pleasantly nostalgic and almost without pain. She leaned back comfortably in the corner of the sofa, enjoying the renascence of talk and laughter.

It was almost midnight when Louise stirred and began to search under the chair for her shoes. "I hate to break this up, but we have to get up early tomorrow: Mark has to sing at church." She padded across the room, collected her coat from the bentwood rack and bent to engulf Carrie in an enthusiastic hug. "Thanks for asking us! This was so much fun, and dinner was terrific."

Barbara prodded her husband. "We should be going too," she pointed out. "You know Jeremy will get one or both of us up disgustingly early." From his comfortable position on the hearth rug beside Pandora, Keith grunted acknowledgement but showed little inclination to follow through with actual movement.

"It'll take at least five minutes or a good swift kick to get him moving," observed Barbara cheerfully. "I may as well help you clear up a bit before we go." Over Carrie's protests, she began to gather plates and cups, insisting "I hate to go off and leave a mess for someone else to clean up." Not to be outdone, Frank uncurled his lanky frame from the floor and followed her toward the kitchen, helpfully bearing one overlooked glass.

Carrie ran hot water into the chipped sink and began to rinse sticky plates. Frank retrieved a cup from the stack on the table, poured the last of the coffee and leaned against the counter beside her. "Thank you for asking me," he said quietly.

"I'm glad you came. I really enjoyed having everybody." Carrie's response was politely correct but also entirely sincere. He was a warm and comfortable presence, easy to be with; and she found herself increasingly drawn to him. In the dining room, Barbara could be heard clinking silverware busily. Carrie held a dessert plate under the stream of

121

water and rubbed fiercely at a nonexistent spot.

From the corner of her eye she could see Frank scowling morosely into his coffee cup. "What I mean is . . . I wasn't sure whether you weren't ready to go out with anyone . . . or you just didn't want to see me."

"Oh, Frank." Carrie turned impulsively to face him, flinging water from her dripping hands.

The look on his face lightened perceptibly, even as he brushed at his dampened shirt front. Moving closer, he reached behind her with a long arm and snagged a dishtowel from the counter. Carrie dried her hands, drawing out the moment, wretchedly aware of him and not at all sure what she wanted to do about it.

Across the room the side door flew open and a gust of cold air hit her like a slap.

"So that's why you were so anxious to get rid of me," said Lee Ann in a calm hard voice. The door slammed sharply behind her with a rattle of cold glass. Carrie recoiled, the metal edge of the counter top pressing knifelike against her spine.

Her daughter's voice rose raggedly. "Just what are you up to with *him?" And what has he been telling you about me? The one grownup I could really talk to . . . one I thought I could trust. And all the time he's been running back to you, I bet.*

Carrie's face scalded, her flare of outrage jumbled with anguished half-understanding of Lee Ann's pain; she choked back quick hot words and only moved her head in dumb denial. Drawn by the sound of voices, Barbara appeared in the dining-room doorway and stopped as though she had encountered some invisible obstacle.

"You didn't care about Daddy. You couldn't have if you're already looking for somebody else." *And he's my friend. Why did you have to pick my friend?*

At Carrie's side, Frank drew a breath in sharply

122

"Oh, Lee Ann . . ." Carrie's stunned protest emerged through a humiliating knot of tears, and was swept away.

"And you don't care about me. You're always trying to get rid of me . . . telling me to go places . . . get out of the house." *Maybe you both only pretended to care about me. Maybe neither one of you ever really cared.* Lee Ann's eyes, too, were brimming. "Would you feel better if I died too?" Her voice soared to an insane pitch.

And stopped.

Everything stopped, motion as well as sound.

Carrie's ears clogged, as though with an abrupt change in altitude or pressure. Her surroundings receded; Frank and Barbara and Lee Ann all drawn away to some place unreachably far and disconnected. The homely surroundings of the kitchen looked suddenly, subtly wrong, like a familiar room seen in mirror-reverse. And it was cold. *So cold.* In bell-jar isolation, Carrie held her breath, superstitiously resisting pervasion by that vile and oppressive air.

Behind her, something stirred, shattering the heavy silence with a rattling like that of bones. Frank's cup, still with an inch of cold coffee in the bottom, jittered in its saucer. All of them watched as it lifted from the counter, spun across the room, and dashed itself violently to pieces against the wall.

Carrie gripped the edge of the counter hard and drew a deep breath, uncertain whether it would emerge as a sigh or a scream. She heard Frank whistle softly through his teeth.

Lee Ann backed up, encountered the wall, and continued moving as though she could push her way through it. A muffled whimper emerged between the white-knuckled hands pressed against her mouth.

From the doorway, Barbara watched consideringly, as though it were not at all uncommon to see a

123

cup fly through the air by itself. Of course, in a household with several small children, it probably wasn't.

It was she who broke the paralysis, moving into the room and stooping to collect the shards of china. "We broke a cup," she explained calmly to Keith, who appeared belatedly, drawn by the crash.

White to the lips, Lee Ann tore a paper towel from the roll and squatted beside Barbara, mopping spattered coffee and trying vainly to restore a normalcy that had shattered with the cup.

"I didn't do it," she said thinly. "I wasn't anywhere near it."

"No," comforted Barbara. "We saw it. It wasn't your fault.

"Not really," she added cryptically.

It was a subdued group that gathered around the wreckage of the party in Carrie's dining room.

Barbara had gone upstairs with a gray-faced Lee Ann; Frank drew Keith aside for a brief explanation under the pretext of making more coffee.

Now Barbara slipped quietly through the French doors. "She's asleep."

"Did she say anything? What did she say?" To her own ears, Carrie's voice sounded tense and strident.

"I don't think she knows what to say. She doesn't understand this either, and she's scared to death."

"She's not the only one," said Carrie wryly.

Frank reached across and covered her hand with his; Carrie grasped it gratefully. "I saw it myself, and I still can't believe it." She summoned an unconvincing grin. "You read about stuff like this in tabloid newspapers—haunted houses where things go flying around."

Barbara nodded sagely. "A poltergeist."

124

"A what?"

"Poltergeist. It's German for 'noisy ghost.'"

Carrie gave her a horrified look. "You can't really mean my house is haunted."

"No," said Keith firmly. "It's not the same thing at all." He cleared his throat and settled back to lecture. "Poltergeist activity is actually fairly common, and it has nothing to do with ghosts. Instead, it seems to be linked to the presence of an adolescent child."

"Lee Ann." Carrie frowned. "But, Keith, she didn't throw that cup. All three of us were there, and we saw it move—by itself!"

"Eminent scientists and other trained observers have been fooled by sleight-of-hand tricks," observed Keith reasonably. Barbara straightened in her chair and opened her mouth to object; Keith raised a hand to forestall her, then hurried on. "But I'm not saying that's what happened here. The theory is that there's a lot of undirected energy in any adolescent; under stress, it can be focused so strongly that it may actually affect material objects."

"You mean that somehow Lee Ann can move things just by thinking about it."

Keith nodded.

Carrie looked around her at the ring of somber faces and began to marshal objections. "If she was the one who did it, then why was she so frightened? That was no act—she was white as a sheet!"

"She doesn't necessarily *know* she did it. It's not something that's under her control."

Propping her elbows on the table, Carrie grasped the hair at her temples with both hands. "I just can't believe it," she said plaintively. "This kind of stuff isn't possible."

"We all saw it, Carrie." Barbara poured more coffee into her cooling cup.

"There's such a thing as collective hallucination."

Frank's mouth twitched. "I don't think collective

125

hallucinations have ever been known to break up the china."

The laughter that followed was disproportionate to the feeble joke, but it effectively dissolved the tension that had built around the table. Barbara passed the coffee pot around, and they all busied themselves for some moments with sugar, cream, and more general conversation.

Then Carrie leaned forward and set her cup on the table with an emphatic thump. "Okay," she said. "So my daughter has just thrown a coffee cup across the room without touching it. But I still don't understand how she did it. Or why."

"*Nobody* really understands how it works," said Frank gently. "But we all know that the subconscious mind can be responsible for some pretty strange things. Think about it: psychosomatic illness means that the mind is making the body sick . . . producing physical symptoms with a non-physical cause. We accept that easily enough because it's a familiar idea, because doctors and scientists have studied it and made it respectable."

He leaned forward and tapped his cupped fingers on the tabletop for emphasis. "If you accept the idea that the mind can affect the body, it's a fairly logical extension to think that the mind might also affect things *outside* the body."

Carrie looked at him stubbornly, harking back to the challenge of their first conversation. "Well, then, what are we saying? That Lee Ann is . . . disturbed?"

"No." Barbara jumped in immediately, comfortingly. "She's been through a very difficult time; she's still grieving."

Frank looked less certain. He paused, choosing words carefully. "I'd be surprised if there wasn't also some buried anger—anger at her father for leaving her." He tactfully ignored Carrie's startled look.

"And most of all," added Barbara thoughtfully,

126

"she's growing up ... going through a lot of upheaval, both physically and emotionally. Supposedly that's why poltergeist phenomena occur in a household with an adolescent child: it's an outlet for this immense turmoil of energy and emotions."

"Exactly," nodded Keith. "Although in fact, a poltergeist isn't *always* linked to an adolescent." He took a sip of cold coffee and made a face. "One psychologist reported poltergeist-type phenomena that occurred around one of his adult patients. His analysis caused a real furor at the time: he was one of the first to come right out and say that the phenomena were related to sexual repression or frustration."

He set the coffee cup on the table and looked at it reproachfully. "Of course, he was a Freudian."

And everyone laughed—including Carrie.

CHAPTER X

In the next few days, a flurry of activity in the office distracted Carrie from all other considerations. She came home tired, threw hodgepodge dinners together, and gave short shrift to everything except the most vital chores. Lee Ann was subdued and unobtrusive, staying out as much as possible with Penny and Danny, and spending most of her time at home closeted in her room.

In relentless daylight, the happenings of the weekend had dimmed and dwindled. Like pain, fear lost its power as it passed into memory—able to be recalled, but not relived. The house was primly silent and inoffensive, as if to distance itself from any blame for the anxieties of its occupants. Lights stayed off, doors stayed closed, crockery remained intact. And Carrie tiptoed through it all, trying to pretend that life was normal.

When Frank called at the end of the week, she was almost surprised. "Why yes, everything's fine." She glanced guiltily across the room to where Lee Ann sat at the kitchen table. It would be the one night her daughter remained downstairs to do her homework. Lee Ann looked up from her books and watched narrowly. Carrie turned her back and muttered into the phone, knowing her face reflected her confusion.

"I called," said the disembodied voice from the handset, "to find out if you two have plans for Thanksgiving. Keith and Barbara always include me in with their family, and they asked me to bring you this year, if you want to come. Lee Ann, too, of course."

At the table, Lee Ann had returned her gaze to her homework, but Carrie suspected that her attention remained focused on the conversation. "Uh, I don't know. I hadn't thought about it," she stalled. In the polite silence from the other end of the line, her thoughts circled miserably. *Lee Ann will have a fit. But darn it, I've got a right to lead my own life.*

At length she asked meekly, "Could I call you tomorrow? Would you mind?"

"This is better than an outright refusal," came the optimistic response. "I must be making headway."

Carrie laughed. "I think you could say that," she answered drily. "I'll talk to you tomorrow. And . . . thanks."

She hung up and turned to face Lee Ann, who was elaborately engrossed in a math problem. "We've been invited to Thanksgiving dinner at the Burnetts'," she said.

"Oh. Was that Barbara?"

It was Carrie's turn to be elaborately engrossed, this time in dinner preparations. "Do you want to go?" she threw over her shoulder, peering intently into the nearest cabinet with no idea of what she was looking for.

"I guess. We're out of school, and I'll probably be down there anyway. We're out Friday, too, and Penny and Danny and I were thinking about going to a movie or something."

Acknowledging the necessity of barter, Carrie nodded acceptingly. "I may get started on my Christmas shopping then. Although the stores will be awfully crowded."

* * *

She called Frank at work the next day, with an acceptance and stumbling apology. "I hope you don't think I'm terribly rude. I felt like I had to consult Lee Ann; and I wanted to try and do it without another big explosion."

"I understand, Carrie, and it's okay."

She took a deep breath and rushed on, suddenly a bit ashamed of the compromise idea that had seemed so inspired the night before. "Would you mind terribly if we just met you at the Burnetts'? There's really no reason why you should have to call for us, when we're just down the street."

"If that's what you want, it's all right." His tone was neutral, but she could sense the underlying disappointment.

"Please don't think I'm giving you the brush off, Frank. I'm trying hard to consider your feelings as well as Lee Ann's."

"What about your feelings?" He echoed the voice of her more assertive self, and in almost the same words: "You're entitled to a life of your own."

"I know. It just . . . isn't easy."

"I'm sure it isn't," he said heavily. "But I want to keep seeing you."

Carrie smiled at the phone and admitted, finally, what some part of her mind had decided much earlier. "I'd like that, too, Frank. I enjoy your company. I'm just trying to find some sort of balance that will let everyone be comfortable."

"We could sneak around," he suggested gravely, and Carrie laughed.

"I may take you up on that."

The girl—Lee Ann—must have a date. She was getting ready now, brushing her hair in front of the

130

dresser mirror, poised on long coltish legs, a tight skirt stretched across the saucy little behind. Hair done to her satisfaction, she dropped the brush and revolved in front of the mirror, watching the effect with some satisfaction. After a moment she undid the two top buttons of her sweater, tugging the neckline to a low vee; postured, arching her back, turning slightly from side to side. Another button, the neckline pulled wider, showing the top of a low-cut bra and the eager swell of creamy flesh above its lace.

Her full lips softened briefly in a lazy pout, a parody of fashion-model style, then twisted in a grimace as she put out a mocking tongue at her pink-faced reflection. The girl snatched up her purse and turned to go; but she refastened only one button of the sweater.

Progress. The man's lips twisted in a satisfied reminiscent smirk. Exactly what he had expected. And it was so easy. Eventually, they all did exactly what he wanted . . . anything he wanted . . . one way or another.

So let her go . . . for now. He would be seeing her later. A lot more of her.

Carrie dithered nervously between closet and dresser that Thursday, rejecting three or four outfits before settling on a lacy pale blue sweater and gray wool slacks as the right note between casual and dressy. At the bathroom mirror, she applied makeup with a little more care than usual. Around her the house felt quiet and benevolent; the lights in Lee Ann's room were off, and Pandora lay somnolent in the middle of the bed. "I'll bring you some turkey," promised Carrie giddily, on her way down the stairs.

The wind whirled briskly around her as she scuffed

through the crisp leaves, holding her coat bunched shut at the neck and swinging a heavily laden tote bag. Along the street, the lawns swam in thick golden light, and the sky was an almost impossible blue.

At the Burnetts', the door swung open before she could knock. Ten-year-old Robin, flushed with her responsibilities as hostess, took Carrie's coat and directed her to the kitchen. "That's where everybody is."

Keith greeted her with a hug and a steaming cup. "My famous spiced cider," he explained. "To take the chill off."

Carrie produced foil-wrapped loaves from her bag. "*My* famous cranberry nut bread," she retaliated. "I brought one for you, too, Frank." She raised her head shyly to his light kiss. Barbara, at the oven, smiled approvingly and saluted them with the turkey baster.

Frank scooped up something that lay on the kitchen counter and deposited it in her hands. "I brought you something, too," he said.

"A book?" Carrie asked witlessly. She turned it over, dubiously examining the lurid cover illustration.

"Don't judge it by its cover," advised Frank tritely. "It's about occult phenomena, including poltergeists, and it's really a very authoritative work—by the psychologist Keith was talking about the other night."

Carrie nodded dutifully and tucked the book into her bag before Lee Ann could see it. Then, putting unpleasant thoughts out of her mind for the moment, she let herself be absorbed into the kitchen bustle. At the stove, she hovered in the redolent steam, mashing potatoes at Barbara's direction, removing casseroles from the oven. "If you want parsley for the potatoes," said Barbara at her elbow, "there's a bunch drying in the pantry."

"You grow your own herbs?"

Barbara nodded. "They're better fresh; and I like growing things I can use."

"That's right: you gave Lee Ann that funny 'burn plant.'"

"Aloe vera. They're really handy plants. I always keep one in the kitchen."

Carrie stepped into the old-fashioned pantry and gaped at the ceiling, festooned with drying bunches of greenery like an herb garden turned upside-down. *Okay, which one is the parsley? I should recognize* parsley, *even if I don't know a lot of these others.* Absently, she rubbed a leaf between her fingers, savoring the rich spicy aroma. *Oregano. And that's sage. And rosemary, there, the one with the needle-like leaves. But where's the parsley?* Carrie pinched the leaf of a likely-looking candidate and recoiled at the sharp, acrid smell. *I don't know what that is, but it sure isn't for cooking! Something medicinal, like the aloe? I'll have to ask Barbara.*

But when she stepped back into the kitchen, bearing a sprig of parsley like a prize, it was to find Barbara busily engaged, leaning over the open oven and poking the huge turkey with a long fork. "This is about ready," she announced. "Tell the guys to start setting the table, would you? And somebody needs to call the kids." In the ensuing bustle, Carrie promptly forgot the puzzling little plant, even though its unpleasant odor lingered faintly on her hands.

The smaller children were served and seated at a low table in the corner. Jeremy, under foot, was scooped up and deposited in his high chair. Footsteps on the stairs announced the arrival of the teenagers, and Carrie braced herself as Lee Ann swept like an arctic cold front into the warmth of the kitchen. Her color high, eyes glinting frost-gray, she raked Frank and her mother with a look of ice and venom.

As the three teenagers filled their plates and disappeared to the downstairs game room, Keith whistled silently and cast Carrie a look of sympathy. "I think I'd almost rather have her chucking coffee cups at my head," he said.

Frank stood beside Carrie, staring at the wall above her head with furrowed concentration. Whatever he saw there seemed to surprise him. "I'm dense," he announced, and waited for someone to contradict him. No one did. "If it makes you feel better, Carrie, she's partly mad at me. I should have seen it before."

Everyone looked at him. "Of course," said Keith soothingly. "She would resent any man in her mother's life right now. It's a betrayal . . . replacing her father." His words were pedantic, but his tone was very kind. Carrie swallowed hard and avoided Frank's eyes.

"Besides that," said Frank impatiently, "I was *her* friend first."

Barbara's eyes rounded with understanding. "You were talking to her at school, weren't you? She told Penny."

"Right." Frank nodded emphatically.

"She may even have a little crush on you."

Frank glowered at her, embarrassed.

"Well, it would be perfectly natural," she continued, unperturbed.

"Um," said Keith, mulling over the new idea. "That would explain the violence of Lee Ann's feelings. If she saw this as losing a friend. Or having her confidence betrayed."

Carrie concentrated on maintaining her tenuous grip on composure. "Well, maybe I can understand her behavior better now. But I still don't know what to do about it."

134

Keith sighed. "I think time and patience may be the only answers, Carrie. And you will have to be firm: you can't let her dictate your behavior. She still needs to have limits . . . all kids do."

"And if it gets any worse," added Frank apologetically, "I still think you should consider counseling." He ignored Carrie's stubborn glare, and lowered his head confidingly until their foreheads almost touched. "Whatever you do, though, . . ." he said plaintively, "don't let her talk you into giving me up."

Everyone laughed, then, dissolving tension; Carrie blushed, appreciating the benediction of their shared understanding. Someone handed her a glass of wine, Frank pulled out her chair, and they all joined hands around the table as Keith said a brief and unfamiliar blessing. Carrie was oddly comforted by the gesture; under the combination of another glass of wine and the concern of her friends, the crystalline knot in her stomach began to dissolve.

Around the laden table, they talked and laughed, bolstering her with inconsequential conversation. Keith settled happily to carving the turkey, after what seemed to be traditional and obligatory pleas of ineptitude. A parade of fragrant, steaming bowls was passed from hand to hand. When Frank raised a glass with the toast "Good friends!" Carrie blinked and looked steadily at her wineglass, taken aback by the sudden maudlin sting of tears behind her eyes. This was something she needed, something she could finally accept: the warmth and caring—the love—of good friends. And of one in particular.

Later, replete, they gathered around the fireplace in the big comfortable living room. Keith laid logs and kindling randomly in the grate and started a fire, to Carrie's great admiration, with surprisingly few matches and no profanity. Frank produced his guitar from somewhere behind the couch and ran his

135

fingers across the strings, turning the keys at the top of the neck and adjusting the tuning. Huddled against a large cushion at the end of the couch, Carrie listened in pleasure to the ebb and flow of discussion and song.

Around midnight, she began to yawn and Frank put away his guitar. "Let me drive you home," he invited. "Not that a brisk walk in the cold wouldn't be good for both of us, but I'm feeling decadent."

While he rummaged in the hall closet for their coats, Barbara went off to check on the younger set. "The kids are watching a movie downstairs," she reported. "If Lee Ann can stay till it's over, Danny and Penny can walk her home."

Carrie nodded assent, stifled another yawn and hugged Barbara affectionately. "This has been so nice. Thanks for letting me come."

Frank's old car lurched and shuddered down the street and died with seeming gratitude in front of her house. At the front door, Carrie manipulated the key with fingers that were beginning to numb, swung the door ajar, and turned to him: "I would ask you to come in," she said uncomfortably, "But I think it might be better not to. Not right now."

He nodded easily; and Carrie, reassured, stepped closer, a little awkward. The kiss that began so tentatively lasted far longer than either of them expected, and left Carrie, at least, more shaken than she cared to admit. Despite the warmth that rose in her, she shivered, body and emotions beginning to come painfully back to life. When Frank left, after a time, she went slowly up the stairs to prepare for bed and listen for Lee Ann to come in.

At some point in the night, Carrie sat bolt upright in bed, disoriented, straining her eyes against the darkness and her ears against the thudding of her own pulse.

She'd heard . . . something. But what? A hoarse and muddy whisper, half-heard and only half-remembered. In her dream, an insistent summons, seductive and frighteningly powerful. But that was only a dream.

This was real. She was *awake*, aware with intense clarity, pressing her hand for reassurance against the harsh wool of the blanket, feeling almost with relief the atavistic prickle of gooseflesh as her skin crept with cold. *Someone had called her.*

Lee Ann? *I was waiting for her.* Carrie rubbed her eyes, disoriented with sleep, and glanced at the digital clock that cast a greenish firefly glow across the nightstand. 3:16. Lee Ann had been home for hours.

Carrie frowned into the darkness. "Lee Ann?" she called softly.

No answer. But was there another sound? From the hall . . . or from Lee Ann's room?

Carrie reached for the robe that lay across the foot of the bed and struggled into it. Across the hall, her daughter's room was dark and cold. A rising wind pushed relentlessly at the front window, rattling the panes and setting the ruffled curtains into restless motion. Carrie padded toward the bed and tugged at the tangled blankets, drawing them up around the sleeper. Lee Ann roused and muttered. Tensing away from her mother's hands, she surged upright, bedclothes clutched against her chest, eyes blank.

"What?" she said.

Carrie patted her, made soothing motions. "It's all right, honey. Go back to sleep."

"Mommy?" Lee Ann turned her head, very slowly. "Is it time to get up?"

"No, honey, it's the middle of the night. You must

137

have had a dream." Carrie sat on the side of the bed and smoothed her daughter's hair. "Go back to sleep."

Lee Ann lay back obediently, and was asleep at once—if she had ever wakened at all. Still Carrie lingered, all too wide awake. Because now she remembered what the voice in her dream had called—not her name, but Lee Ann's.

CHAPTER XI

Carrie sat at the old kitchen table, musing over her second cup of coffee and reading the front page of the morning paper for the third time. Almost at her feet, Pandora basked in the warm draft of air from the floor register. A faint stir of sound sifted down from overhead; Carrie looked at the ceiling apprehensively and began to gather her thoughts for the upcoming confrontation. She reminded herself optimistically that Lee Ann was usually good-natured and reasonable; it ought to be possible for them to discuss things calmly and rationally. A long quiet talk would be good for both of them.

Upstairs, the bathroom door slammed, hard. *So much for calm and rational.* Carrie winced and revised her hopeful plans. They had to come to some kind of understanding; but now, with both of them edgy and short of sleep, was not the time.

She dug her fists into her eyes and yawned. Bedroom slippers flapped across the dining-room floor, and Lee Ann appeared in the doorway, heavy-eyed and petulant, wielding silence like a weapon. No, thought Carrie resignedly, definitely not a good time for a talk.

Lee Ann moved back and forth across the kitchen, assembling breakfast and ignoring her mother.

Carrie read the front page of the paper again. Across the table, Lee Ann dropped her laden plate to the table, seemingly from a height of several inches. Elaborately oblivious to Carrie's startled frown, she slid into a chair and barricaded herself behind the comics section. The rest of breakfast was punctuated by emphatic thumps and rattles of mug and silverware, as Lee Ann strove to make her displeasure heard as well as felt.

Carrie remained resolutely silent, preserving a facade of composure as long as possible. But when Lee Ann's final show of temper shattered a glass and sent orange juice spraying across the table, adult restraint shattered with it. Carrie shot upright and brought the flat of her hand down hard against the table. Belatedly, she hoped she had found a spot where there was no broken glass. "Damn it, Lee Ann!" she snapped. "This has got to stop!"

Lee Ann looked back at her, wide-eyed. The morning paper drifted unnoticed to the floor. Carrie crumpled a paper napkin and dropped it into the puddle of juice, leaving more extensive cleanup for later. First things first. "You do not," she began again, "run my life. And I will not put up with these childish temper tantrums whenever you don't agree with me or don't like what I do."

The apprehension in Lee Ann's eyes gave way to obstinate resentment. "You could at least *wait*. You could *wait* before you start trying to . . . to change everything."

"I don't understand what your *problem* is. Lee Ann, I loved your father just as much as you did; and I miss him just as much. You can't really think that I don't."

More clearly than words, Lee Ann's frozen countenance conveyed her disbelief. Appalled, Carrie lashed out, hurling words like stones. "Lee Ann, your father is dead, and nothing we can do will

140

change that. But *I'm* alive. *You're* alive. You still have your friends; you like to go places and do things with other people. So why is it wrong for me?"

"It's different," came the nearly inaudible answer. Lee Ann's face went, if anything, a shade paler, and her voice took on a note almost of desperation. "You were his wife. You should be the one . . ."

Her words ended on a choked-off sob. *Why can't you understand? Why can't you see?* Face pinched, pallid as a waxwork, she began to shiver. And Carrie realized suddenly how cold the room had become.

The chill coalesced in the air, pressing in on them, deadening sound. Carrie gulped, dry-mouthed, against the pressure, hearing only the pulse that beat in her ears, picking up tempo at a frightening pace. The kitchen *warped* around her, floor receding into distance, walls and ceiling meeting at impossible angles. Her own hands on the table looked far away and unfamiliar. A small drop of blood gathered sluggishly in one palm; she watched in fascination as it formed a viscous black-red bead, then closed her hand slowly as though to contain it.

A rough sound came dully through the thickness in her ears, scratching at the surface of the cold. Carrie raised her head as though against some terrible weight, afraid of what she was going to see. Across the table, Lee Ann huddled in her chair, eyes wide with shock. Painful as an unuttered scream, the tension swelled and thinned, stretched to its limits . . . and burst.

Sound and movement flooded back. And the third chair at the table, unoccupied, lurched backward, jerkily, an inch or two at a time, grating on the worn linoleum. Carrie had the wild and hysterical notion that something unseen was sitting down to breakfast with them, before the chair tipped crazily and crashed to the floor. Lee Ann shot her mother a look of entreaty, quickly engulfed by malicious satisfaction. Then she fled out of the room and up the stairs, leaving chaos in her wake.

Carrie stood numbly at the table, rubbing absently at the cut on her hand. From some secret place, Pandora emerged, crouching low, fur abristle, puffed like a blowfish to twice her normal size.

"Poor baby." Carrie bent and wiggled her fingers, making cat-attracting noises. She scooped up the tiny animal and cuddled her, finding some comfort of her own in the process.

By the time Lee Ann reappeared, bathed, dressed, and bundled into a heavy quilted coat, the kitchen was restored to normal, broken glass cleared away, dishes done, and all furnishings upright. With Pandora and another cup of coffee on the table in front of her, Carrie was finishing the morning paper, sitting defiantly in the errant chair.

"Where are you going?"

Lee Ann, ever the chameleon, surprised Carrie by answering sweetly. "Burnetts.'"

"When do you think you'll be back?"

"I don't know for sure. We may go to the mall."

"You and Penny and Danny?"

"We were talking about doing some Christmas shopping." Lee Ann hitched up her shoulder bag and headed for the side door, prattling on. "We might even go to a movie with some of the other kids later. There's a new one at the Village that everybody says is really good. So don't expect me for dinner, okay?"

"Don't be too late."

The door shut firmly between them, and Lee Ann's footsteps faded rapidly away down the gravel drive. Carrie put down the newspaper and sat for a few minutes with her head in her hands. Then she went upstairs and retrieved Frank's book from the bedside table. Still in her old housecoat, she curled up comfortably in a chair and began to read. It was hours later before she put the book down and dropped her head against the back of the chair, thinking.

"It happened again," she explained.

Barbara, sitting across from her in the big country kitchen, listened without interruption to her account of the morning's tribulations.

". . . so I finally sat down and read the book Frank lent me." Carrie cupped her cold hands around the warm coffee mug in front of her. "About poltergeists. It's by a psychologist."

"I know the one."

"It said a lot of the same things you did, the other night. About undirected energy, and frustration. And it made me realize how much pain and anger Lee Ann must have bottled up inside—to cause things like this." Her voice caught, raggedly. "I'm really worried about her. This may not be supernatural, but it sure isn't *normal*." She took a sip of the hot coffee, hoping to dissolve the lump in her throat. "I don't know what do to."

"Usually when teenagers have some sort of outburst, it's a way of getting attention—or maybe asking for help."

"I'm beginning to believe Frank was right: that she *needs* help. A counselor . . . or maybe even a psychiatrist. But I'm worried about what her reaction would be if I suggested it. I'm afraid it might just make things worse.

"That's why I thought I'd talk to Keith. It's his field, and he might know someone who could . . . talk to her informally."

Barbara nodded reassuringly. "I'm sure he'll have some ideas. And he'll be glad to help." She went to set her mug in the sink. "I also think we should call Frank." At Carrie's look of consternation, she raised a hand, forestalling objections. "Lee Ann has talked to him. He probably knows more about what's going on in her head than anybody else. And this is serious enough that I think he might overcome his ethical objections and tell us about it."

Frank responded to a dinner invitation with typical bachelor enthusiasm. "We need someone to help eat leftovers, anyway," Barbara explained to Carrie, "and you and Frank and Keith can talk."

Swept along despite her own uncertainty, Carrie donned a spare apron and began to help make salad. She was slicing tomatoes at the sink when Frank came in, closely followed by Keith and Penny. Just Penny.

The dinner conversation that evening was intense, though not exactly what Carrie had had in mind. Keith, at the head of the table, was looking un-accustomedly severe. The smaller children had eaten in subdued silence and escaped to the TV room. A red-eyed Penny sat slumped in her chair, pushing pieces of turkey around with a fork. "I don't know where they went," she said again. "Lee Ann was just really upset, and she wanted to talk to Danny. They didn't need me hanging around."

Carrie twisted her fingers together. "It's getting dark," she said. "And they aren't back yet."

Everyone understood. Even Penny. "I told them," she wailed. "I was afraid they were going to get in trouble."

"Well," said her father succinctly, "you were right."

"They haven't done anything *bad*. Honest!" She turned to Barbara, apparently in appeal to the more lenient of the two parents. "Danny's only trying to help. We were both trying to help."

The adults around the table frowned at each other.

144

"What do you mean?" at least two of them asked simultaneously.

Penny fidgeted and looked on the verge of tears. "I'm not supposed to tell."

"Oh, God." Carrie pressed both hands against her mouth, fighting her own tears, full of unformed fears and imagined terrors.

Beside her, Frank cleared his throat and spoke reluctantly. "Because she was scared, you mean?"

The room was absolutely still, so quiet that Carrie understood parenthetically how a silence could be termed deafening. It positively roared. Or perhaps the sound was only in her head.

Surprise and shock chased themselves across Penny's face, finally followed by a look of relief. "Right." She nodded at Frank gratefully. "And she needed us."

"Scared?" Carrie gave them both an uncomprehending look. "Of what?"

"The house," said Frank slowly. "Or something in it." He glanced at Carrie hesitantly. "Or maybe herself."

It had begun more than a month ago, according to Penny. "You remember when she was acting so funny, and I thought she was mad at me? It was a couple of weeks before she'd talk to me—or Danny either. Because she thought she was going crazy."

Carrie made a smothered sound and Frank leaned over and squeezed her shoulder gently. "Because of the things that were happening in the house?" he prodded Penny.

The girl nodded, absolved of the burden of secrecy by his shared knowledge. "All these strange things had started happening. Like in a haunted house: noises at night and lights that came on by themselves and doors that wouldn't stay shut. But nobody seemed to pay much attention—or think there was anything strange—except her." Carrie winced, unable to look at Frank. Penny fixed her eyes on the table and plowed on determinedly. "And it was mostly around her. It was the light in her room, and the door to her room. And sometimes her things were moved around."

"She never *said* anything." Carrie's voice was hardly above a whisper. "We kidded about the lights sometimes; but she never said anything about the other things . . ."

Penny took a gulp of milk and addressed Carrie pleadingly. "You seemed to think she was just leaving the lights on or not shutting the door tight, and she started thinking maybe she *was* doing it. And not remembering. She was scared that there was something terrible wrong with her." Penny drained the glass and looked around at them defiantly. "But there isn't. You may think I'm crazy, too, but I was there once, when a plate with some cookies jumped off the desk and broke. It didn't just *fall* off; it went up in the air and flew clear across the room. And nobody touched it. I was *there*. I *saw* it."

Carrie closed her eyes and clasped her hands together tightly. "I believe you," she said.

The rest of them nodded soberly. "Did she tell you about the nightmares?" asked Frank.

"Just that she was having really terrible dreams. They made her even more sure that there was something wrong with her." Penny glanced at the window, where darkness lurked like something out of the human subconscious. "Anyhow, she was acting funny at school—sitting by herself at lunch and not talking to anybody."

Frank nodded again. "That was about when I started talking to her," he said.

"And she stopped taking the bus and started hanging around, you know, staying at school or going to the library or the mall or someplace. Because she didn't want to go home by herself. We

146

couldn't figure it out. At first we thought she was mad at us. But she talked to Danny sometimes, and she seemed to feel better when we were around. Even then it was like she was very sad and depressed."

"She went to the Halloween party."

Penny nodded. "For a while I didn't think she would. She seemed real glad when Danny asked her, but then—for about a week—she would hardly even talk to us. It was so weird." She shrugged. "Finally— I guess it was about a week before Halloween— Danny had the car and it was really cold, and he got her to let him drive her home. They went for a ride, and she broke down and told him what was going on. Then the next day at school they told me."

Carrie steepled her hands together and pressed them hard against her burning eyes. She had to try her voice twice before she got it working. "You all have been trying to protect her."

"She seemed to feel a lot better just telling us. Because we didn't think she was crazy, see? We just started going places together after school—or she came home with us. And when she had to be home, one of us stayed with her."

Penny directed an appealing look at her father, who dismissed her with a bemused gesture. Poised on the verge of flight, she added one final plea. "Look, Danny and Lee Ann really . . . like each other. But they're not dumb. They wouldn't do anything . . . stupid. It's just, sometimes they want to be by themselves. Without being hassled. That's all."

The teenager bolted down the stairs to the recreation room, and silence surged backward in her wake. Carrie shook her head, stunned. "I never realized it was that bad. I never realized . . ."

Barbara reached out impulsively and took her hand; Frank took the other. Badly shaken, Carrie let herself cling briefly to the comfort of contact and the warmth of their small circle.

147

*　　*　　*

When the missing pair walked in a few minutes later, it was positively anticlimactic. Looking by turns sheepish and defiant they faced the adult tribunal across the width of the table and the even wider gulf of years.

Barbara was the first to break the paralytic silence. "Why don't you guys get yourselves some leftovers and go eat downstairs?" she suggested.

One pair of eyes widened in amazement; the other narrowed in suspicion. But both teens seized on the reprieve, loaded plates from the stove, and fled.

"Well, it looks like we've been presented with two problems for the price of one," said Barbara briskly. She and Carrie had filled the men in on the events of the morning as they cleared the table and made more coffee.

Now Barbara flourished the pot inquiringly. "The question is: what are we going to do now?"

"Become caffeine addicts, I suspect," answered Frank unhelpfully, holding out his cup.

"A distinct possibility," acceded Barbara, pouring. "Carrie?"

Carrie pushed her mug across the table. "Fill 'er up," she said glumly, and sipped at the steaming beverage.

"We'll talk to Danny, Carrie." Barbara replenished the sugar bowl and set it in the middle of the table.

"I'm not sure how much good it will do." Depressed, Carrie huddled over her coffee cup for warmth. "Damn it," she burst out, "I hate feeling like a dirty-minded, suspicious old woman. They're just kids, after all."

"And kids just like them get in trouble every day."

Carrie sighed. "I know. But from what Penny says, Danny has been a really important support for Lee

148

Ann. And I don't know what will happen if we threaten to take that away."

"We're not, really. We're just making it clear that they have to obey your rules."

"I'm not sure Lee Ann will see it that way." Carrie drooped dejectedly, resting her chin in her hands.

Keith looked at her sympathetically. "Do you still want me to get someone to talk to her? Maybe it would help." Frank patted her shoulder encouragingly, but refrained for once from offering an opinion.

"I don't know," said Carrie unhappily. "This is getting so complicated." She gazed into her mug as though searching for answers in the steam. "I'm afraid anything I do will just make matters worse."

Barbara nodded and pursued the thought for her. "If she's already afraid that she's losing her mind, introducing her to an analyst would only make her certain of it."

"Exactly." Carrie nodded vehemently. "Keith, thanks, but let's not do anything about it right now. Or about Danny either. Okay?"

Keith and Barbara nodded in unison. "It's your decision, Carrie. But if you need help, just let us know. We'll do anything we can."

"I already know I need help," admitted Carrie wryly. "I'm just not sure whether I need it from a psychiatrist . . . or a priest."

CHAPTER XII

When the chill on the front porch began to numb her feet and creep up her legs, Carrie gave up on propriety and invited Frank inside. Listening for Lee Ann's return from the Burnetts', where she and the other two teenagers had been absorbed in video games, they nevertheless sat close together before the fireplace, holding hands, thawing gradually, and only occasionally talking.

After one particularly memorable pause in the conversation, Carrie leaned back breathlessly. "Maybe I should go ahead and let her start dating," she said, apropos of nothing at all.

Sidetracked, Frank tried gamely to gather his thoughts. "Huh?" he asked intelligently.

"She'll be fifteen soon—next month, in fact. Lots of her friends are already dating. Maybe I should just relax the rules and hope for the best. After all, they say kids tend to act out your expectations. So maybe if I do something to let her know that I love her and trust her . . . maybe it will make a difference."

"Hmm." Frank sat back and gave at least the appearance of deep cogitation. "It might help, at that. And under the circumstances, I don't see how it could hurt. At the very least, it would remove the necessity for sneaking."

"Exactly." Carrie propped her chin on her knees and gazed pensively at the fire. "Although I don't like being inconsistent: I don't want Lee Ann to get the idea that all she has to do is disobey a rule often enough and I'll change it." She glanced at Frank for a reaction, then reminded herself with irritation that it wasn't *his* problem. "But I have to do something," she continued, more emphatically than necessary. "Just sitting around ignoring the problem isn't going to make it go away."

Frank shifted to face her, dragging his long legs into an uncomfortable-looking tailor posture and propping his elbows on his knees. "You've got good reasons for changing the rules this time," he said thoughtfully. "As you pointed out earlier, this is not exactly a normal situation. Lee Ann needs support; and she's at the age where she wants it more from her friends than her mother. So far, her relationship with Danny—and Penny—has probably helped more than it's hurt. At least it's kept her from being too scared."

"Right. Now she's doing better . . . and I'm the one who's scared."

Somewhat later, warmed more thoroughly than the fireplace alone warranted, Carrie let Frank out the side door and went quietly upstairs. She pummeled a pile of pillows into submission and lay propped up with a book on her lap, not reading. When the front door opened and Lee Ann's footsteps mingled with the faint night sounds of the house, Carrie reached furtively for the bedside lamp and turned it out.

It was the hands, again, that woke Lee Ann, sometime in the middle of the night, in the darkness. Hands

151

drawing the blanket away. Hands at her shoulders, pushing the modest flannel gown away. Brushing lightly, lightly, across her breasts, brushing again until the tender flesh swelled to their touch. Teasing her nipples hard and upright, tracing them with circles that froze and burned, burned like her own shame at her body's response.

For a long time Lee Ann lay paralyzed, eyes squeezed shut, head turned as far as possible into the pillow, away from . . . what? From a dream? A nightmare? But this wasn't a dream. It wasn't. It was real, and it changed everything. It changed *her*.

The man's hands shifted now, warm and caressing, moving down the length of her body, her legs. Drawing the hem of her gown up, slowly, gently, all the way to her waist. Lee Ann's face went hot in the darkness and she pressed her legs together, pressed her head hard into the pillow. On the inside of her thigh now, on that very sensitive flesh, a touch that almost tickled, and she shivered with cold and fear and delicious sensation. His hands moved upward, probing, invading, and her breath came fast and ragged . . . but she didn't scream.

The next morning began one of the few remaining glorious last-of-autumn days. Carrie sat contentedly at the kitchen table, finishing coffee and newspaper. At her elbow Pandora lay inert on the discarded front-page section, raising her head only now and then for Carrie's absent-minded caress.

Her head was lifted now, in splendid simulation of alertness at the sound of slippered footsteps in the dining room behind them. Lee Ann shuffled across the room to the refrigerator, running her hand down the little cat's back in passing, smoothing the rumpled calico fur.

"I thought Pandora wasn't allowed on the table,"

she said.

"She's not," Carrie shot back flippantly. "She's on the newspaper." It was an opening too perfect to be missed. "Anyhow," she went on, "it's my rule, and I can break it if I want to."

Lee Ann poured orange juice and sipped, standing in front of the open refrigerator and eyeing its contents without enthusiasm.

"Speaking of rules," Carrie continued, "we need to discuss the matter of your social life." Obviously suspecting the direction of the conversation, Lee Ann flicked her mother a wary glance; she set the butter on the counter and popped slices of whole wheat bread into the toaster.

"Your dad and I had always said you couldn't start dating until you were sixteen; but a lot of things have changed since then. And I think you're mature enough now for an occasional date."

Lee Ann's eyes widened, despite a valiant attempt to keep her face inscrutable. "Honest?" she asked, as though expecting the permission to be snatched away.

Carrie nodded affirmation. "Not every weekend," she cautioned, "and you're not going to stay out real late, but I think it would be okay for you and Danny to go to a movie or something once in a while by yourselves."

"Oh, that would be great!" Lee Ann swiveled away from the counter, her face open and luminous with delight. For a moment, Carrie thought her grown-up daughter would propel herself across the room for an ecstatic hug. Then the old toaster twanged its metallic announcement, and the girl turned away, catching slices of toast deftly and spreading butter with meticulous precision. "One thing hasn't changed, though," Carrie continued. "I expect you to tell me where you're going and who you're going with."

"Sure, Mom. I always do."

"Like yesterday?"

Lee Ann looked at her cautiously, trying out an air of wide-eyed innocence. "It wasn't totally definite, but I told you where I was going."

"But not who with—with whom."

The girl sighed and gave up pretense. "I never said Penny was going with us. You just took it for granted."

"I took it for granted that you were obeying the rules."

The cheek that Carrie could see turned pink. Lee Ann broke eggs into a bowl, added milk, and attacked them with a whisk. "We didn't do anything wrong, Mom. I needed to talk to Danny, and I didn't want a whole lot of people around. That's all."

Carrie was silent for a moment. "It might be good if you and I could talk sometimes, too," she said tentatively. "Instead of just getting mad and yelling."

Her daughter nodded somberly, and Carrie forced herself to go on. "I know you're upset about my seeing Frank. But it doesn't mean that I didn't love your father. I've simply had to accept that he's dead and that we have to get on with our lives without him."

Maybe you didn't love him enough. Maybe that's it . . . I just loved him more than you did. With intense concentration, Lee Ann poured the egg mixture into a skillet and stirred. *And look what happened. Maybe loving somebody too much isn't a good idea. It might be better just not to care. Just take what happens and go on . . . like Mom.* She blinked twice, hard; the fingers that held the spatula were white as bone with the tension of their grip. Carrie reached out in a spontaneous gesture of comfort, and aborted it in midmovement as her daughter straightened, unchildlike resignation hardening her face.

But Lee Ann's response, when it came, was

154

surprisingly innocuous. "Are you going to get married again?"

"Maybe. Someday. But I'm not planning anything like that yet. And if I do, I'll certainly discuss it with you first. Right now, I mostly need some friends around . . . people to talk to . . . the same as you."

Lee Ann moved listlessly between stove and counter, spooning scrambled eggs onto her plate and pouring more juice.

Carrie prodded. "We may even be talking about a lot of the same things. I've been just as concerned as you are about some of the things that have happened around here."

Halfway between counter and table, Lee Ann paused, her face like a creature's that looked out of a cage.

"Like what?" she whispered.

"The coffee cup that . . . broke. The chair, yesterday. And the lights."

Lee Ann lowered herself into a chair, very carefully, as though something inside her might spill. "You know I didn't do any of those things. I really didn't."

"I understand." Carrie poured herself a cup of coffee and sat down across from her daughter. "But it doesn't mean we're going crazy, either." She noticed her daughter's almost imperceptible recoil and leaned forward urgently. For once, she simply *had* to get through to the girl.

"Apparently this kind of stuff happens a lot more than you would think; I can even remember reading about it in the papers a few times." Lee Ann looked skeptical, and Carrie plowed on determinedly.

"I don't know if I can explain it exactly; Barbara and Frank have been trying to explain it to me. Things happen, usually when someone in the house has a lot of strong feelings bottled up. And they get so powerful that they can actually move a chair—or break a coffee cup—when they finally explode."

Hope glinted like a spark in the back of the girl's eyes and just as quickly turned to ash. "But how?" she asked.

"I don't know," admitted Carrie. "I don't think anyone does. But there are lots of things about the human mind that we don't understand."

Emotions rippled like water across Lee Ann's mobile face. "Okay," she sighed finally. "You're still saying I did it. You're just not sure how."

"*Who* did it isn't important. What matters is that there's a natural explanation. It's not something to be scared of."

Lee Ann's smile was bleak, with a puzzling hint of condescension. "I'm not scared," she reassured her mother. "Not anymore."

The teenager's reaction seemed to serve as a barometer, accurately predicting the lull that followed. The house remained quiet and inoffensive through a succession of dreary days, as blazing autumn faded quietly into December and killing frosts turned the yard gray with a foretaste of official winter.

On the morning of Lee Ann's birthday, Carrie presented her with a fluffy pink sweater—and a stack of pancakes playfully decorated with a bright red candle. Her daughter came home from school that day with cheeks as pink as the sweater, wearing a tiny gold pin in the shape of a cat that had been a gift from Danny.

Practicing urbane adulthood in suit and tie, Danny called for Lee Ann on their first official date the next weekend; Carrie saw them off to a school dance with a mixture of sadness and relief. When Frank asked her out to dinner a few days later, she accepted with only momentary hesitation. Mention-

156

ing it to Lee Ann that evening took far longer.

Carrie prepared Lee Ann's favorite—lasagna—as a premature peace offering; over steaming plates, she dropped the information very casually, into the conversation. Lee Ann's mouth thinned and whitened, but she continued to eat for some seconds without comment, as distant as though the table between them were the surface of a continent. "Is that," she asked finally, "why you started letting me date? So you could too?"

The unexpected response struck Carrie like a blow in the dark. "Of course not!" she retorted, too quickly. She braced herself for the expected tempest, and was genuinely startled to see pain, rather than anger, on Lee Ann's face. "Honey," she began more gently, "I let you start dating because I thought this was a good time to allow it. It doesn't have anything to do with Frank and me. I wish you weren't so unhappy about our going out, but I don't need your permission to do that."

For once Lee Ann was the one reluctant to pursue the point. Chin propped on hand, she responded with an all-purpose shrug and an elaborate and world-weary sigh. Minutes wore on with no further comment. Carrie pushed pieces of lasagna around on her plate with absorption. Finally Lee Ann pushed back her chair and began to gather up dishes.

"That was good lasagna," she threw over her shoulder as she headed for the kitchen.

Carrie smiled. "Glad you liked it." She gathered up her own dishes and began to run hot water into the dishpan, content with the shaky beginnings of peace.

Almost a week later, dressed in sweatshirt, jeans, and bandanna, Carrie paused on the threshold of Lee Ann's room, with a stepladder, several rolls of

157

wallpaper, and an expression of resignation.

It has potential . . . but that's about all it has.
Despite the charm of its low, sloping ceiling and
windowed dormer, the room had always been
depressing—painted woodwork chipped and yel-
lowed, wallpaper peeling in layers reminiscent of
geological strata. And a full weekend of work had
only made matters worse. In the merciless north
light, old gray plaster was indecently exposed,
piebald with fresh splotches of white spackle. Debris
littered the floor like storm-wrack, and tatters of
steamed-off wallpaper formed drifts in the corners.
Displaced furniture huddled in the middle of the
room as if in fear.

Lee Ann lived placidly amid the mess, her bed an
island, and only the top two drawers of her dresser
accessible. In her after-school hours, she had given
the woodwork two coats of fresh enamel, which now
gleamed white against the dead gray of plaster.

Carrie, with a much lower tolerance for upheaval,
averted her eyes from Lee Ann's "nest" in the middle
of the room. Moving carefully in her narrow
workspace, she marked and measured, drew wallpaper out from the roll, and cut the first strip of paper
for the complex shape of the front dormer.

By noon, the work was half-done; pretty pastel-
flowered paper covered the dormered front and half
of one side wall. The room had already undergone an
amazing transformation—if viewed selectively. Carrie descended the ladder with a sense of release; on the
way downstairs, she began to hum. In the sunlit,
pleasant kitchen, she assembled a sandwich, heated
leftover coffee in the microwave, and sat warming her
hands on the mug. *That room is always so cold.*
Storm windows would help, but they were expensive.
She wondered if the budget would stretch to new,
heavier curtains—perhaps some of those with the
insulating lining. And carpeting—later. Or just a

158

larger, thicker rug in some cheerful color.

She sat idling over the morning paper for a time, washed the dishes, swept the kitchen floor, and went to get the mail. It wasn't until she caught herself paging seriously through a sporting-goods catalogue that she realized she was deliberately killing time. "Back to work," she told herself sternly, marching briskly through the living room and more slowly up the stairs.

It seemed only a short time later when the front door opened and a confusion of voices and footfalls sounded in the foyer, sorting themselves out gradually as they came closer. Danny, Penny, and Lee Ann jostled for space in the doorway; from somewhere behind them, in the hallway, Barbara's presence was evidenced only by her voice.

Carrie ignored them long enough to finish trimming the last strip of wallpaper in the corner. "You can come in if you can find a place to stand," she invited generously. "Don't step in the water tray."

Lee Ann tiptoed gingerly over the protective expanse of sticky newspapers and looked around happily. "It looks great, Mom!"

"Well, it's getting there." Carrie straightened up and rubbed her back wearily. "Why don't you guys have a snack while I clean up in here; then you can help move the furniture back."

The three youngsters clamored away down the stairs, leaving Barbara hovering in the hall. "It looks like you could use some help," she offered cheerfully. But she lingered hesitantly in the doorway before stepping through. Then, amid the stacked and jumbled furniture, she bobbed in and out of sight, picking up newspaper and wiping the floor. Carrie went off to dump sticky tools in the bathtub; at the chipped basin, she sluiced warm water over her grimy arms and face.

159

"That's all we really need to do right now, Barbara," she called. "I'm going to wash up: why don't you go on down and join the kids?" Carrie pulled off her protective bandanna, tugging sharply at nape hairs tangled in the knot. "Ouch!" She grimaced and dropped the crumpled kerchief in the general vicinity of the clothes hamper.

In the mirror she could see Barbara, across the landing, leaning silently against the door frame of Lee Ann's bedroom. Carrie pulled her old pink comb quickly through her hair. "You didn't have to wait for me," she told her friend. "Let's go get some cookies before the kids eat them all."

Barbara looked at her oddly and straightened, seemingly with an effort. Her face was pensive and perhaps a little pale.

"Barbara? Are you all right?" Carrie's concern was genuine, but she let herself be reassured by the other woman's quick denying headshake.

"I'm fine," came the prompt reply. "At least I hope I am." Barbara quirked a one-sided smile and led the way down the stairs. "This time of year, I don't have time to get sick."

In the big warm kitchen, around the table cluttered with schoolbooks and teenage paraphernalia, her friend's normal color soon returned, along with her habitual ebullience. Carrie poured cocoa, commandeered a few of the chocolate-chip cookies, and dropped into a chair, already beginning a mental list of things remaining to be done.

Abstracted, she didn't hear Lee Ann's question until it was repeated. She blinked, swallowed her mouthful of cookie and gathered straying thoughts. "What?" she said.

Lee Ann sighed. "I said, what do you want us to do next? Move the furniture back?"

"Oh. Yes. Unroll the rug first, but leave the curtains down so I can wash them. You can decide

160

MORE PASSION AND ADVENTURE AWAIT... YOUR TRIP TO A BIG ADVENTUROUS WORLD BEGINS WHEN YOU ACCEPT YOUR FIRST 4 NOVELS ABSOLUTELY *FREE* (AN $18.00 VALUE)

Accept your Free gift and start to experience more of the passion and adventure you like in a historical romance novel. Each Zebra novel is filled with proud men, spirited women and tempestuous love that you'll remember long after you turn the last page.

Zebra Historical Romances are the finest novels of their kind. They are written by authors who really know how to weave tales of romance and adventure in the historical settings you love. You'll feel like you've actually gone back in time with the thrilling stories that each Zebra novel offers.

GET YOUR FREE GIFT WITH THE START OF YOUR HOME SUBSCRIPTION

Our readers tell us that these books sell out very fast in book stores and often they miss the newest titles. So Zebra has made arrangements for you to receive the four newest novels published each month.

You'll be guaranteed that you'll never miss a title, and home delivery is so convenient. And to show you just how easy it is to get Zebra Historical Romances, we'll send you your first 4 books absolutely FREE! Our gift to you just for trying our home subscription service.

BIG SAVINGS AND FREE HOME DELIVERY

Each month, you'll receive the four newest titles as soon as they are published. You'll probably receive them even before the bookstores do. What's more, you may preview these exciting novels free for 10 days. If you like them as much as we think you will, just pay the low preferred subscriber's price of just $3.75 each. *You'll save $3.00 each month off the publisher's price.* AND, your savings are even greater because there are never any shipping, handling or other hidden charges—FREE Home Delivery. Of course you can return any shipment within 10 days for full credit, no questions asked. There is no minimum number of books you must buy.

4 FREE BOOKS

TO GET YOUR 4 FREE BOOKS WORTH $18.00 — MAIL IN THE FREE BOOK CERTIFICATE T O D A Y

Fill in the Free Book Certificate below, and we'll send your FREE BOOKS to you as soon as we receive it.

If the certificate is missing below, write to: Zebra Home Subscription Service, Inc., P.O. Box 5214, 120 Brighton Road, Clifton, New Jersey 07015-5214.

FREE BOOK CERTIFICATE

4 FREE BOOKS

ZEBRA HOME SUBSCRIPTION SERVICE, INC.

YES! Please start my subscription to Zebra Historical Romances and send me my first 4 books absolutely FREE. I understand that each month I may preview four new Zebra Historical Romances free for 10 days. If I'm not satisfied with them, I may return the four books within 10 days and owe nothing. Otherwise, I will pay the low preferred subscriber's price of just $3.75 each; a total of $15.00, *a savings off the publisher's price of $3.00.* I may return any shipment and I may cancel this subscription at any time. There is no obligation to buy any shipment and there are no shipping, handling or other hidden charges. Regardless of what I decide, the four free books are mine to keep.

NAME

ADDRESS _____ APT

CITY _____ STATE ___ ZIP

TELEPHONE
( )

SIGNATURE _____ (if under 18, parent or guardian must sign)

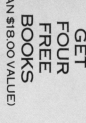

GET
FOUR
FREE
BOOKS
(AN $18.00 VALUE)

ZEBRA HOME SUBSCRIPTION
SERVICE, INC.
P.O. Box 5214
120 BRIGHTON ROAD
CLIFTON, NEW JERSEY 07015-5214

where you want everything, but I think maybe you should put the bed against the inside wall, away from the windows." As Lee Ann nodded agreeably, Carrie identified her last thing-to-be-done item and pounced on it triumphantly. "While you're at it, empty the dresser drawers and we'll carry it down to the basement. We've got enough enamel left, and I'm going to paint it white to match the woodwork."

Leaving crumbs on the table and glasses in the sink, the teenagers trooped off upstairs to attack their task. The military metaphor was particularly appropriate; overhead, heavy footfalls, shouted commands, and generic noise resounded like the soundtrack from a war movie. Carrie stiffened and glanced anxiously at the ceiling after one particularly horrendous scraping sound was followed by a loud crash. When no one came dashing downstairs to report a casualty, either human or furniture, she allowed herself to relax.

Across the table, Barbara reached for another cookie and grinned. "At least it's natural causes this time," she said.

Carrie looked at her, puzzled.

"Moving the furniture."

"Oh." Carrie grinned too, reluctantly, and consoled herself with the last cookie.

"Seriously," continued Barbara, "how are things going?"

Carrie swallowed a bite of cookie and considered. "Well," she said, "it's been a lot more peaceful. But I'm not sure what that means."

Barbara quirked an eyebrow questioningly, and waited.

"After all the furor, I should be grateful for some peace and quiet," said Carrie apologetically. "Instead, it's making me nervous—like waiting for the other shoe to drop."

"But nothing else has happened?"

161

"No, thank goodness."

"What about Lee Ann? Would she tell you if anything had happened to scare her?"

"I think so. I don't know." Carrie fluttered, confused, then firmly gathered herself together. "Why?" she asked. "Is there something going on that I don't know about?"

Barbara shook her head, but a tiny frown marred her forehead. "Penny's been a little upset, that's all. Danny and Lee Ann have been going around together and leaving her out, and she feels bad about it. But she also says Lee Ann is acting different."

"Different how?"

"She can't quite describe it. More grown up . . . like she isn't interested in the same things anymore. Penny says they still sit together at school—go places together and talk—but it seems like Lee Ann's mind isn't on what they're doing. She always seems to be thinking about something else."

'What does Danny say?"

"Not much. He recites details of where they went, with whom, and what they did. But that's all I can get out of him; and I wouldn't be surprised if there were things he isn't telling."

Carrie made a deprecating gesture. "I wonder if Penny's a little jealous. It's natural for the two of them to want to be by themselves sometimes, but it's got to be hard for her to accept."

Barbara nodded. "I told her that, and she understands. But she still says she thinks there's something wrong."

"Well, it sounds like a bad case of puppy love to me." Carrie shrugged as if her gesture could throw off the problem. "At least"—she grimaced—"I *hope* that's all it is."

Three sets of footsteps thumped down the stairs and headed back to the kitchen. "Open the door, Mom," panted Lee Ann, hefting an empty dresser drawer. "We'll take these downstairs, and then we'll be done." The teens plodded heavily toward the basement, then bounded lightly back into the kitchen, freed of their burdens.

"You have to come see," urged Lee Ann breathlessly. "The room looks so nice!" Upstairs, she stepped blithely over the threshold and turned an impromptu pirouette in the center of her room. "Isn't it great?" Indeed it was, they all agreed sincerely. Even with the curtains down, and the bed heaped with the erstwhile contents of dresser drawers, the room looked fresh and inviting, dainty and feminine.

So why are we all just standing here in the doorway? Like no one wants to go into that room. No one but Lee Ann. The thought skittered through Carrie's mind and almost as rapidly was gone. Penny and Danny stepped forward, lifted the little dresser, and lurched back into the hallway and down the stairs.

"Are you going to paint the mirror, too?" Lee Ann raised one corner of the frame experimentally.

"Yes, but let me take it downstairs. It's pretty heavy."

Clutching the mirror awkwardly and fending off Lee Ann's helping motions, Carrie backtracked down the stairs and into the kitchen. Out of breath, she relinquished her load to Danny, who uncomplainingly made his third trip to the basement.

Barbara was coming down the stairs as she returned to the living room. "There are times," Carrie observed, "when I wish I'd bought a ranch house."

Resident of a home of similar vintage and design, Barbara nodded in weary recognition. Then, making noises about dinner and her disruption of Carrie's schedule, she collected her children and retreated into the early dusk.

Silence settled in their wake. Carrie resumed her chores, cleaning wallpaper tools, preparing their own evening meal, and prodding Lee Ann about homework. It was much later, at the end of the day, that she dropped her dirty jeans into the clothes hamper, and bent to pick up the forgotten red bandanna from the floor.

The nape-knot had been undone. And the tangled strands of hair were gone.

CHAPTER XIII

Even in the basement's dim light, the footprints were clearly visible—tiny smudges all across the top of the freshly enameled dresser. Carrie glared at Pandora, smoothed a new coat of white across the telltale marks, and picked a cat hair out of the sticky gleaming surface.

"What is it with you and paint?" she muttered. The little cat, who had wisely retreated to the top of the storage shelves, slitted her eyes, and produced a bubbling purr.

It had taken till Saturday morning to get around to painting the dresser, and Carrie had almost finished when the phone rang. Absorbed, she'd ignored its peremptory summons. As the mother of a teenager, she knew the phone was never for her, anyway.

But Lee Ann's voice had followed up the phone's strident ringing with a vocal summons. "Mo-om! It's for you," she'd bellowed, sounding surprised and mildly affronted.

Carrie had returned Frank's affable greeting with pleasure and had put her stamp of approval on their dinner plans for that evening. Now, back in the shadowy environs of the basement, she repaired cat-damage and resumed her earlier preoccupation.

This business with her bandanna had disturbed her deeply, cracking cool-headed logic like a weed insinuating itself through concrete. Unlike the other things that had happened in the house, this was sly and secretive. Unlike the random explosions of poltergeist energy, this was . . . personal.

The scarf had been knotted—tightly knotted. It couldn't have come undone by itself. Had someone—*Barbara. It had to be Barbara*— deliberately taken that tiny tangle of hair? And if so, why? With a dim half-remembrance of some horror film or ghost story of her childhood, Carrie was certain she *knew* why.

Didn't witches need a physical link in order to wreak harm on a victim? Like in that movie, when they stole the guy's glove—or was it a tie? They made voodoo dolls with wax and fingernail parings. Or locks of hair.

This is crazy. Carrie bent over and picked up a dirty paper towel from the litter on the floor. *We're talking about real life, not a movie. Things like that don't really happen.* She wiped absently at her hand, where a drizzle of white enamel from the forgotten paintbrush was creeping slowly down her wrist. *Sure. And coffee mugs don't really fly across the room by themselves.*

Her skin prickled all over, as atavistic impulse tried to raise hackles that no longer existed. Could somebody, somehow, have engineered the things that had been happening in her house? Was a human intruder to blame for the lights that wouldn't stay off . . . the doors that wouldn't stay closed? What about the other things—the coffee mug, the chair that moved? *There are drugs,* her mind whispered. *Hallucinogens.*

But why? There's no *reason* for anything like that. At the gritty old gray washtub, Carrie rinsed her brush in an icy trickle of rusty water. *So maybe I'm crazy.* She examined the thought soberly. *I mean really mentally ill. I've been under as much strain as Lee Ann, after all. I've started jumping at shadows and imagining things. And now I'm getting paranoid, isn't that the word? When you feel like people are out to get you? That even your friends are conspiring against you?*

She shut off the water, shook the brush, and laid it on the dusty edge of the tub to dry. Barbara was one person who had been a friend when she really needed one. From the vantage of the laundry tub she faced the clenching possibility of genuine loss. The Burnetts had been so nice. *But why?*

They were the only people in the neighborhood who had gone out of their way to be helpful. *Because they want something?*

Carrie rubbed at her temples, where a very real headache was beginning to take shape. How could she possibly think anything as crazy as this?

Crazy. *Crazy.* The word scalded her accusingly. But it wasn't just her. Lee Ann had had so many of the same kind of experiences. *We can't both be going crazy. Not in exactly the same way, at the same time. These things are really happening. I may not understand it, but that doesn't mean it isn't* real.

Pandora, still perched on the shelves, leaned forward with a consoling *prrut* and Carrie jumped. "Don't you move," she cautioned. "You've done enough damage for one day."

The cat, as usual, ignored the injunction. She gathered all four feet under her, waggled her hindquarters, and launched. Barely clearing the newly painted dresser, she landed in a graceless skid on the smooth concrete floor and vanished up the stairs. Bereft even of feline companionship, Carrie thrust away her depressing thoughts and hurried through the cleanup chores.

She then emerged from the dark confines of the basement into the kitchen's matter-of-fact and cheerful brightness. Under the weight of sun and scrutiny, ramshackle suspicion collapsed abruptly. *What in the world is the matter with me?* Carrie regarded her quandary of the morning in bleak amazement. And gave herself her own prompt answer. She was too tired, had too much to do, was spending too much time alone. And the upcoming holidays were supposedly the worst time for depression. Disgusted, she gave symbolic bootstraps a healthy tug. *Okay, so weird things have been happening in the house. But we know the explanation, and we've started working this out.*

Get with it, kid, she exhorted silently. You've been on your own too long. Now it's time to rejoin the rest of the world. You're lucky to have friends like the Burnetts . . . and Frank.

Pleased with her renewed objectivity, Carrie rewarded herself with the most pleasant of her appointed weekend tasks. She piled favorite records on the stereo, propped a battered cookbook against a canister, and began her traditional holiday baking, accompanied by baroque chamber music. Lee Ann soon drifted downstairs, following her nose to the source of wafting spicy-sweet scents.

"What's that?" she asked.

"Vivaldi."

"Looks more like chocolate chip." She helped herself to a still-warm cookie. "Are you going to make regular Christmas cookies, too?"

"If you can find the cookie cutters. I haven't seen them since we moved in."

"I'm pretty sure they're in a box with some old pans and stuff, upstairs. I'll go look." Lee Ann went bounding away, poised adolescent transformed in an instant into exhilarated child.

Much later, every available inch of tabletop and counter surface was covered with cookies, and Carrie, Lee Ann, and the kitchen were covered with flour.

Lee Ann laughed and brushed her hands on her jeans. "I'm a mess," she said happily.

"So am I. I should have worn an apron."

"You don't *have* an apron."

"Maybe that's why I didn't wear one." Carrie laughed too, adult restraint also giving way to childish high spirits. Then she looked at the clock. "Whoops! We've got to get this place cleaned up; Frank's coming by around seven, and I still have a lot of things to do."

Lee Ann's face changed only slightly. She produced broom and dustpan from the pantry and began sweeping cheerfully enough. "Why don't you just stack the dishes in the sink? I'll do them later—and put the cookies away."

"Would you, honey? That would be great." Carrie cleared the table, took a second look at the clock, and bolted for the stairs, wondering if she had any nice clothes that didn't need ironing.

A fast shower sluiced away flour and sugar and the remains of white paint; a pink silk blouse and gray wool skirt emerged from the closet in suitable condition, and one pair of hose seemed to have miraculously avoided runs. Carrie applied a light touch of powder and pink lipstick, dabbed on perfume. When Frank rang the bell, she descended the stairs looking calm and serene, but feeling as though she had run a hundred-yard dash.

His look of quiet pleasure made it worthwhile. For a moment, it even seemed he would speak—before he was overwhelmed by an onslaught from Lee Ann. Appearing to have buried old enmities, she came dancing up to them energetically, drawing them to the kitchen. "You've got to see," she said. "We've been making cookies all afternoon. Some of them are for you!"

Frank duly admired the products of their labors, accepted a clumsily wrapped foil package with

169

eloquent expressions of gratitude, and frowned at Carrie. "I hope you haven't spoiled your appetite," he said severely.

"Where are you going, and what time will you be back?" interrupted Lee Ann, practicing role reversal with a malicious grin.

"Francesca's over in Clarion Heights," Frank answered meekly. He cocked an inquiring eyebrow at Carrie. "You said you like Italian?" At her nod, he turned back to Lee Ann. "And I'll have your mother in by midnight. Okay?"

"Okay," she affirmed, and busied herself at the sink. "Have a good time!"

The silence of the house was too large for her, too demanding. It swallowed the familiar chatter of the television, until the characters on the screen looked distant and meaningless, buzzing like flies against their glass confines. Lee Ann sighed and switched off the set, watching its comfortable presence dwindle into a single glowing dot. It was dark now, and all the windows had turned to mirrors, black and opaque, giving back nothing to her glance.

Around the first floor she checked and rechecked the locks, pulled the curtains, turned out lights. *Not that it does any good. Some things you can't lock out.* It was an understanding no one else seemed to have. She hugged the knowledge to herself, secretly, as though in possession of something stolen.

Upstairs she crossed the landing, very quietly, into her mother's room, opened drawers, searching . . . ignoring utilitarian cottons, jeans, and sweaters . . . running her fingers luxuriously through a small cache of scented silks and satins. *There. At the bottom of the stack. Where she won't notice.* Carefully, Lee Ann extracted her choice—a sleek gown of lace and nylon, black, completely unlike

170

anything she owned. *Mom doesn't wear this kind of stuff anymore anyway. Or maybe she does. Just not at home.*

She slipped back into her own room, furtively, feeling her pent breath quicken and deepen . . . feeling her heart begin to accelerate. *But of course there was no one to hear her . . . no one to see her. Yet.* Slowly, dreamlike, she discarded bulky clothes, pulled clinging satiny folds over her head. Back arched, she shook her dark curls free and shivered as they brushed her bare shoulders.

Almost midnight. *The witching hour, don't they call it?* Lee Ann smiled to herself and curled catlike between the cold sheets, waiting for her body's heat to warm them. Waited for sleep. And for whatever would come after that.

The restaurant glittered, tiny strands of bubbling lights woven into silken greenery and reflected in glasses of garnet wine. Somewhere above them, hidden speakers warbled background music, cheerfully managing Christmas carols along with the usual Italian repertoire. Carrie watched her own hands, toying with the stem of her glass; for the first time, she had removed her wedding ring. She wondered if Frank had noticed. Somehow, she thought he had.

They talked sporadically, about anything and everything: friends and families, feelings and philosophies. He was divorced, amicably enough, with no children. His one brother lived out west someplace, and his mother was retired in Florida. In turn, Carrie found herself talking almost easily about her parents' deaths—and the utter desolation of losing Matt.

"I've learned to appreciate friends even more now," she said. And suddenly realized that she faced a source for answering some of her earlier questions. "The Burnetts, especially, have been wonderful." Faintly ashamed, she led him on. "Have you known them a long time?"

Frank nodded, turning his wineglass in long fingers. "Keith and I were roommates in college. We didn't see too much of each other after that: he went on to grad school, and I was married and going to school nights. But after I was divorced, he and Barbara looked me up. They've got a nice group of friends—an almost family kind of thing, so it doesn't matter if you're married or single. And they don't keep trying to pair you up with somebody."

Carrie raised an eyebrow in mock skepticism.

"Well, they *don't*," he insisted indignantly. "This was *my* idea."

She smiled and sipped at her wine, eyes lowered demurely. His mundane recitation had put the last nail in the coffin of suspicion. So, she told herself sternly, they're just nice people, and maybe they take in strays sometimes. Who are you to complain about that?

Calmed and heartened, she turned the conversation to other topics, and they lingered over the wine, hands lying close on the tabletop, touching, and eventually twining together in warmth and reassurance.

When they walked out into the parking lot, it was into an icy reality. The temperature had dropped at least ten degrees, and a brisk wind scudded dry leaves and discarded papers across the glazed asphalt. In the opaque privacy of the icy car, Frank uttered what may have been incantations under his breath, then coaxed the cold engine into life. Staring fixedly at the dashboard and nursing the accelerator with practiced dexterity, he cleared his throat. "Would you . . . ah . . . like to come back to my place for a while? I can fix coffee—or tea or something—and

172

there are the cookies . . .''

She had known that would come. Carrie hugged her coat around her, waiting for the reluctant engine to give up some warmth. "Not tonight, Frank. Not yet." She looked straight ahead at the frosted windshield, wondering if she had answered a question he hadn't asked.

It seemed not. He shifted awkwardly, bulky coat restrictive in the small space. Keeping one cautious foot on the accelerator, he rested his hands on her shoulders and kissed her carefully on the forehead. "Another time?" he asked gently.

Carrie swallowed and nodded. "Another time," she said.

It was late when Carrie woke the next morning. She rolled over in cocooned warmth, stretched indolently and smiled at the clock. Sounds from the kitchen below indicated that Lee Ann was already up. Carrie sighed and emerged into the chilly day. She took her time showering and dressing, and went downstairs slowly, hoping that her pleasant evening wouldn't be spoiled in retrospect by an early morning confrontation.

Lee Ann, at the stove, waved a spatula in casual greeting. "Scrambled eggs?"

Carrie inspected the pan unobtrusively. "Sounds good," she approved. The cooking contents looked, for once, surprisingly palatable; although Carrie, in her relief, would have eaten almost anything that was offered.

"You can start the bacon," offered Lee Ann. "I'll get juice." She spooned puffy golden eggs onto a plate. "Did you have a good time?"

Carrie nodded behind her back. "Um-hmm."

"What time was it when you got home?"

"A little after midnight, I think. Not too late."

Carrie arranged strips of bacon on a paper towel, laid it in the microwave, and punched buttons intently.

"I thought it was later than that. I was awake till after midnight." Lee Ann's tone bore only the slightest edge, but Carrie, long used to interpreting her daughter's moods, was instantly alert.

"Was everything okay here?" She frowned. The girl had an absolute knack for making her feel guilty. "Maybe we should have asked Penny to sleep over. Or you could have gone there. You know you could always call the Burnetts if you're scared or anything."

"I wasn't scared." Lee Ann contorted her face indignantly. The microwave pinged its signal, and she extracted the paper-wrapped bundle of bacon, dumping crisp slices onto the platter beside the eggs. "I told you . . . I'm all over the nightmares. In fact, I kind of like being alone sometimes."

The year dropped toward its nadir in a dreary succession of short gray days. At the office, Carrie worked full-time, engulfed in the annual preholiday rush. At home, evenings fell into a pleasant routine, addressing cards at the kitchen table or baking while Lee Ann sat across from her companionably, doing homework. Frank called almost nightly, and she looked forward to their long rambling conversations, which Lee Ann magnanimously ignored.

Despite herself, Carrie faced the holidays with some semblance of anticipation. Last year, in the paralysis of grief, she had ignored Christmas as much as possible, resentful of its false-faced and hollow intrusion. This year, she was determined, it would be better. If not for herself, then for Lee Ann.

In a determined departure from the patterns of previous years, Carrie discarded the tiny artificial evergreen that had graced their holidays in the

174

apartment, and proposed to Lee Ann that this year they buy a "real" tree. Carried away by holiday spirit, she even called Barbara and invited the entire Burnett family for a tree-trimming party, with cocoa and carols, the Saturday before Christmas. The invitation was accepted with alacrity, and Barbara reciprocated—or, as she insisted, retaliated—with an invitation to Christmas dinner at their house. Both events, of course, grew to include Frank. This year *was* going to be better.

The week before Christmas, she and Lee Ann, with Danny along for encouragement and muscle, made their pilgrimage to select a tree. Sprawled across a local shopping center's parking lot, the sales area was a pine-scented maze, like a forest with price tags. Danny led them to the low-cost clearing and helped select a small but shapely tree from the bewildering array. Holding it upright for Lee Ann's approval, he perused it sharply. "Do you think it'll fit in the car?" he asked.

"Oh, dear." The trunk of her cheap foreign car would barely hold a few sacks of groceries. Carrie sucked at her lower lip in dismay. "I never thought of that."

In these days of fuel conservation and downsized cars, it was apparently a common problem. When the burly lot attendant approached, it was with holiday greetings and a length of twine. "We'll just tie it on top, ma'am. It'll be fine . . . as long as you're not going far."

Carrie paid for the purchase, assuring him that she was not intending extensive travel, and set off for home, crouching low and peering at the road through feathery green branches. "I feel like Birnam Wood," she joked, and the teenagers looked at her blankly. The classics, apparently, still evoked the same rousing disinterest that had been common when she was younger.

175

Once safely home, they stood their purchase in a bucket on the porch, while Danny assembled the spidery pieces of a red and green metal stand. Carrie took herself off to the kitchen to make cocoa, leaving the teens to move furniture and bring the tree inside.

Finally the little evergreen stood braced before the front windows, spindly base wrapped in a sheet, ready for its transformation into a seasonal symbol whose origins had been forgotten. The youngsters sat sprawled on the displaced couch, admiring their handiwork, sipping hot chocolate, and holding hands openly.

Finally Carrie rose and began gathering up the sticky cups. "Thanks for the help, Danny," she said over her shoulder.

"No problem." He stood up politely, taking his cue to leave. "I'll see you tomorrow," he said, presumably including both mother and daughter; but his eyes never left Lee Ann. He moved toward the doorway, shrugging on his coat, and Lee Ann drifted after him. From the kitchen, Carrie heard their light voices lapse into a silence that thickened and grew; she was on the verge of a throat-clearing intrusion when the front door opened and closed and Lee Ann went scampering up the stairs to shut herself in her room.

The house, that Saturday, was alarmingly full, with Carrie and Lee Ann, Burnetts large and small, and one Meredith, large. The effect was like that of a Gypsy campground—bright and exuberant, a tumult of color and music and voices.

Once her mind was made up, Carrie had gone all out for nostalgia. In the fireplace, Frank had kindled the obligatory log fire, which crackled amiably, almost overheating the small living room. The doorway to the dining room was hung with mis-

176

tletoe, and in the room beyond, cider, eggnog, and fruitcake were laid out on the sideboard, amid branches of greenery and bright red candles.

With the teens at the table stringing popcorn, and the smaller children cutting and pasting ragged paper chains, the kitchen was a Norman Rockwell vignette. No doubt the famous painter would have omitted the popcorn on the floor and the lavish smears of paste everywhere, but then art should never be slavish about imitating life.

After a time, they all gathered around the tree, watching as the children wove its festive cocoon. Danny hung strands of rainbow lights, and Penny and Lee Ann draped shimmering garland, all with a precision sure to amaze any mother who ever faced a teenager's room. Perfect shining glass balls and painted wooden figures were lovingly placed, democratically sharing the dark branches with the clumsier beauty of childhood handmades. Robin solemnly bossed the placement of their ramshackle red and green chain, while Jason gravitated toward the glitter of store-bought decorations with magpie fascination. Even two-year-old Jeremy took part, indulged with selected ornaments of unbreakable ribbon-wound foam.

Finally Lee Ann unwound tissue wrappings from the golden treetop star and handed it to Danny, mutely conferring on him the privilege of adding the crowning touch. With poised awareness of her role as hostess, she offered Penny the honor of lighting the tree. Someone touched the switch to darken the room, and they all paused in appreciative silence, watching as tiny multicolored bulbs sprang into brilliance, bubbling on and off, sending reflections darting across the myriad gleaming surfaces.

"It's beautiful," breathed Robin, who was never silent for long. In the finest holiday spirit, she seized a reluctant smaller brother in a sticky hug. The flickering light bathed their rapt faces in angelic rose and gold, alternately shifting to demoniac hues of blue or green.

Frank cleared his throat and began a familiar favorite carol, which was picked up immediately by the youngsters; Carrie joined in hesitantly, then Barbara in her uncertain soprano. Keith bayed in the background. It was all quite unutterably hokey.

No one ever remembers more than one, or at most two, verses of a Christmas carol; so after an enthusiastic chorus, the singing stuttered to a halt. Danny turned the lights back on, Carrie poured eggnog, and Frank waylaid a pink-cheeked Barbara under the mistletoe. Even Keith, normally so reserved, was caught up in the spirit; meeting Lee Ann in the same doorway, he surrounded her with a bearlike hug and bestowed a quick kiss that left her flushed and giggling. An exuberant Jason began piping a nursery-school rendition of "Rudolf, the Red-Nosed Reindeer." Midway through he forgot the words; but with a trouper's determination, he began again from the beginning . . . and then again—until someone distracted him with a cookie.

Returning to the living room with a plate of fruitcake, Frank folded himself into a chair beside the fireplace. Lee Ann, curled up on the hearth rug, actually spoke to him, much to Carrie's surprise. Frank didn't appear surprised at all—or perhaps he just hid it well—as he bent his head to listen carefully, his manner entirely without adult condescension. Carrie, watching, was grateful that at least one of her problems might work itself out. Barbara's right, he's good with the kids, she reflected; and then, He'd make a good father. The thought was completely inadvertent, of course, and almost immediately quashed.

After a time someone started another carol, and they began working their way through as many

178

songs as they could remember—or at least the first verses thereof. Feigning disaffection, the teenagers departed for the Burnetts' house to watch a TV movie, taking a large slab of fruitcake with them for sustenance. Jason finished his latest cookie and launched an attack on "Jingle Bells."

The evening wound down, carols interspersed with coffee and conversation. When the fire burned low and the children began to bicker, Barbara bundled the remaining members of her family off for home and bed. In the foyer, Frank and Carrie stood side by side and watched them out of sight.

"I guess I'd better be going too," he said, with a significant lack of conviction and an inquiring look.

Carrie dipped her head in reluctant affirmation. "Lee Ann will be back soon," she explained. "Danny's supposed to walk her home right after the movie's over."

He nodded acceptance, drawing her into a comfortable, undemanding embrace. And it was, after all, quite some time before he left.

CHAPTER XIV

Two days before Christmas, Carrie let herself in the front door, threw her coat over the bentwood rack in the corner, and collapsed on the couch in the living room.

"Mom?" Lee Ann's voice floated in from the kitchen, closely followed by Lee Ann herself. "You were late, so I started dinner."

"Why, honey, thank you." Despite her fatigue, Carrie came bolt upright and started through the dining room, sniffing anxiously for the smell of burning. Lee Ann viewed the smoke alarm as a sort of kitchen timer, invaluable for letting her know when things were done. "Why don't I take over now?"

"Okay." Lee Ann handed over a dripping wooden spoon and retired from the stove without visible reluctance. "I'll set the table." She opened cabinet doors and began to extract dishes, clattering back and forth to the table. "Do you have to work tomorrow?"

Carrie lifted pot lids and began to stir. "No, I'm off till Monday. And I'll be back on my regular schedule then, three days a week."

"A bunch of us are going to go ice-skating, if that's okay. At the rink on the plaza. And maybe over to Debbie's for hot chocolate afterward."

"Sure, I guess so." The ice rink had been brand

new when she and Matt were students. Carrie remembered her own skating dates, coming in flushed and tingling with the cold, standing sock-footed on the heat registers, close together, warmed as much by each other as by the mugs of cocoa they consumed. She swallowed hard, blinked, and poked blindly at the boiling potatoes, far more fiercely than the inoffensive vegetables warranted.

Lee Ann looked at her curiously. "I'll be back in time for dinner," she promised.

Christmas Eve dawned brittle and colorless, under a sky gone white with cold. Carrie drew her housecoat around her shoulders, groped for her warm slippers and yawned. She had slept deeply, gratefully; half-rousing automatically at six and rolling over with inarticulate pleasure for another few hours' rest. Now she ran fingers through her hair, tightened the sash of her robe, and shuffled off to the bathroom. The silent low-ceilinged upstairs spaces reshaped themselves around her presence, enfolding her like a cocoon.

She emerged slowly, warmly dressed in sweater and jeans, and dawdled down the stairs, feeling the temperature drop as she descended. When she ventured out on the porch for the newspaper, her breath hung cloudily before her, smudging the crystalline air. Scanning the headlines absentmind-edly, she headed through the living room toward the kitchen. Under foot, something crunched.

Carrie looked at the broken ornament for several seconds without understanding, while the cold began to claim her hands and feet. This was the worst yet. It's not fair! she wailed silently, childishly. Everything has been fine. We've been getting along so well!

But she couldn't deny the evidence of her own eyes.

Across the hardwood floor, area rugs were rucked and scattered, strewn with delicate glass globes, bits of torn garland, and tatters of paper chain. One of the foam balls lay denuded, its brilliant red ribbon unwound and trailing. *The poltergeist—was that what they called it? It has to be. But Lee Ann isn't even up yet!* The cold intensified as Carrie's skin prickled into gooseflesh.

Something rustled.

In the wan sunlight from the front window, the decorated Christmas tree shivered and swayed, whispering like a forest glade teeming with unseen life. The newspaper slid from her hand into a huddled heap, and Carrie locked her knees to keep from following it to the floor.

Then the evergreen branches parted, almost at eye level, and a small pointed feline face peered at her inquiringly.

Carrie closed her eyes, inhaled a steadying breath, and blew it out with gusty indignation. "Get down from there!" Snatching up a section of newspaper, she folded it to authoritative thickness and brought it down against her open palm with a satisfying *thwack*.

Pandora withdrew her head with uncatlike haste and scrambled downward in a hail of shredded tinsel and pine needles. The tree rocked alarmingly. Another ornament dropped to the floor and rolled crazily across the wooden boards, drawing Carrie's eyes like a decoy. In an instant, the kitten plopped to the floor and raced for the stairs, displaying a fine feline instinct for self-preservation. From Lee Ann's room, within seconds, came distant sounds of thrashing and sleepy indignation, as the errant animal landed in the middle of the bed—and its occupant. Carrie grinned despite herself, then began to pick up the debris before her daughter saw it.

*   *   *

From its rude beginning, the day slumped back into somnolence. After restoring order to the living room, Carrie slouched pleasantly at the kitchen table to have her equanimity completely restored by coffee and the morning paper.

With the intuition peculiar to teenagers, and often mistaken for common sense by unqualified observers, Lee Ann asked no questions and offered no comments. After a field hand's breakfast, she gave her room a cursory cleaning and departed for the ice rink with Penny and Danny. Left to herself, Carrie stacked records on the stereo, wrapped final packages, and baked another batch of cookies for the Burnett kids.

That evening, sitting cross-legged on the floor by the fireplace, she and Lee Ann opened their presents. It was a long-standing family custom, established by her own parents to avoid too-early wakenings on Christmas morning, continued in the spirit of romance when she and Matt were first married, then perpetuated in self-defense after they became parents themselves.

Over the last few days, a modest stack of shiny packages had appeared, scattered invitingly beneath the tree. At the last minute, the wicker dressing table, a not-very-well-kept secret, had been carried downstairs and adorned with an impressive red bow, while Lee Ann obligingly lingered in her room.

At Carrie's call, she'd come pelting down the stairs and paused at the doorway, eyes widening theatrically, though with genuine appreciation. "You *did* get it! Oh, Mom!" She ran her fingers ecstatically over the intricate wicker arabesques, and admired herself in the dainty oval mirror. "It's the best Christmas present ever!" she cried extravagantly.

Now, with a plate of Christmas cookies and a glass of eggnog at hand for sustenance, Lee Ann delved gleefully amid the gift-wrapped boxes under the tree. Lifting packages with exaggerated ceremony, she read each tag aloud as if the name on it were a surprise. "Mom!" she discovered, and handed over a box with crooked wrapping adorned by a gold satin bow, only slightly the worse for a few feline teeth marks. "And this one's for me!"

They made another ceremony of the unwrapping, removing tape and folding paper with the thrifty pretext of saving it for next year. Carrie smoothed appreciatively a new pair of gray leather gloves, then admired the melting pastels of a soft wool scarf. Lee Ann exclaimed over a trendy blouse and hugely enveloping sweater, but reserved her greatest ecstasy for the much-wanted designer jeans. "Usually I think it's stupid to pay more for clothes just because they have a special label," she said in explanation of her request, "but these really are better quality. And the fit is *great!*"

In the spirit of the day, even Pandora was not forgotten. A catnip mouse, wrapped as carefully as any other gift, was opened by Lee Ann with enthusiastic feline assistance. Dora sniffed appreciatively along the toy's lumpy length, then pounced, batting it back and forth between scything paws in a rousing but one-sided game of cat and mouse. Lee Ann dropped to her hands and knees and joined in, mimicking the lightning crisscross passes that ought to send cats sprawling, but never do. Carrie retreated to a chair, out of the way. By the time the two combatants tired of the game, she was fairly certain that the tears in her eyes were only from laughter.

The Burnetts' kitchen, next day, was likewise a scene of controlled chaos—but at least it was in

184

someone else's house. A tidal wave of children hit Carrie about the knees, all talking at once, all insisting that their holiday loot be examined and admired. The teenagers surged back and forth between stove and counters, alternately helping and getting in the way.

A ransom of homemade cookies bought off the smallest members of the besieging horde, who departed for other regions, squabbling amiably. The second batch was handed over to the teens; thus persuaded that starvation was not imminent, they gathered up Lee Ann and evaporated into the basement family room. Peace—or some semblance thereof—descended upon the kitchen.

It lasted only until Frank arrived. Carrie was setting the table when he was escorted in, steered by Jason and Robin like an ocean liner bullied by tugboats. With one arm he held Jeremy perched on his hip; with the other he juggled a large bag that bulged with mysterious parcels. "Help," he said plaintively.

Barbara laughed. "Out!" she intoned in dire incantation. "Until dinner's ready!" She waved her wooden spoon like a magic wand and the children obligingly disappeared, trailing giggles behind them.

Laughter returned, later, around the big table, as bowls were passed and blessings uttered. Robin and Jason chattered blithely, vying for attention; the teenagers spoke to each in cryptic code; and the adults regaled each other with stories of Christmases past. In his highchair, Jeremy pursued his private interests, doing things to his carrots that would have appalled the most hardened botanist.

The table was cleared, dessert served; and Frank's presents had been bestowed on all deserving children. The teenagers drifted away to the basement recreation room, and the smaller children began to

185

droop, like tight-coiled watch springs winding down. One by one they were taken away to bed, leaving the adults to linger over coffee and liqueurs as, around them, the house settled into rest and silence.

After a time Frank cleared his throat. Releasing Carrie's hand, he delved once more into his bag and produced a box of chocolates for Barbara. "I waited until they'd gone to bed," he explained, with an expression of cunning. A larger square box, clumsily wrapped in golden foil, he set before Carrie.

"Oh, Frank," she said faintly, lifting the object inside from its swathes of tissue. At her side, Barbara leaned forward with a wordless sigh of appreciation. A miniature carousel gleamed between Carrie's hands—a fantasy of bright colors and gilded wood, and porcelain animals poised forever in joyous leaps. Frank touched a lever somewhere underneath and the antique mechanism whirred into life, revolving decorously and chiming the fragile melody of an old-fashioned waltz.

Carrie shook her head in wonderment. "I don't know what to say." Wavering uncertainly between laughter and tears, she touched the tiny flag that flew bravely from the crest of the merry-go-round canopy.

Frank smiled at her gently. "The look on your face is enough," he said.

"It snowed," complained Lee Ann the next morning, rubbing at her breath on the window and scowling at the glittering blanket as though at some personal affront. "Penny and I were going to go to the mall today."

"Right after Christmas is a great time for shopping," agreed Carrie. "At least for those rare souls who have any money left." She raised an eyebrow inquiringly, and Lee Ann grimaced.

186

"I'm broke. But Penny got some money from her grandmother for Christmas, and I was just going to go along with her." Lee Ann shifted restlessly, twining her fingers in the slender gold chain bracelet that had been her present from Danny—Carrie had been relieved that it wasn't a sweetheart ring.

Lee Ann dropped the curtain back into place. "Why couldn't it have done this earlier? It would have been perfect for Christmas." In her voice was a not-quite whine.

Carrie examined the drifts at the edge of the porch with a critical eye. "It isn't too deep. You and Penny could walk over to the park and go sledding."

"That might be fun," considered Lee Ann, probably weighing the possibility of getting Danny to go too. "Her mom would make us take the little kids with us, though, I bet." She wavered indecisively, turning the bracelet round and round on her thin wrist.

"You could call Penny and see what she wants to do. Or just go over there for a while."

The tumbled dark head drooped against the window again. "Mostly I just want to get out of the house," said Lee Ann, who had, to Carrie's certain knowledge, been out of the house every day that week.

Carrie bit back a scream of exasperation and resorted to other tactics. "While you're making up your mind, I'm going to fix us some brunch." You could always rely on food to distract a teenager. "What's this?" She twisted her neck for a better look at the box that lay abandoned on the dining-room table. The top proclaimed its contents in garish colors. "Incense?"

Lee Ann made an impatient face. "That's not what's in it. Penny just used that box. It's a candle."

"A candle?" That wasn't much more logical than incense.

187

Lee Ann looked at her pityingly. "Uh-huh. A scented candle. It's pink, so it goes with my room." She pushed aside paper towels that had been tucked around the box's contents. "See? Her mom made it. It's got dried herbs and stuff in the wax, so it gives off a nice smell when it burns."

She held it out—a tall rosy pillar with delicate leaves and flowers faintly visible beneath the translucent surface. The odor, though not the usual floral perfume, was light and woodsy-pleasant. Carrie touched the pale waxen surface with one finger, lightly. "That was nice," she said automatically, and wiped her hand on her pant leg without even noticing that she did so. From inside herself somewhere, she extracted a meaningless smile. "Why don't we put it where everyone can see it? On the mantel, maybe. Or in the dining room: it could be a centerpiece."

Lee Ann drew her brows down ominously. "It's my candle. They gave it to me—for my room."

Carrie shrugged helplessly. "It was only a suggestion."

The week ran slowly down to year's end. Outdoors the weather flip-flopped into an unseasonable thaw, the snow dwindling into dirty leprous patches. Cold rain dropped slowly out of the sodden sky, turning the yards to mud and sending trickles of icy brown water snaking along the gutters. Carrie's spirits sagged, holiday cheer turned unaccountably dumb and brooding. She told herself it was only the weather.

Certainly nothing else was wrong. The days were peaceful, the nights uninterrupted. But anxiety trailed at her heels as she prepared for work each morning, quietly so as not to wake Lee Ann. She let

188

herself out of the sleeping house with a guilty sense of abandonment, and in the evening paused on the doorstep to brace herself. But nothing happened. Nothing at all.

New Year's Eve, and the girl must be getting ready for a date. Freshly bathed, swathed in a heavy bathrobe, she moved around the bedroom in matter-of-fact fashion; but her eyes were dreamy, and her mouth curved in a secret smile. Looking forward to the evening. Getting ready.

Standing beside the bed, she loosened the sash, dropped the robe across the coverlet and stood naked—breathtaking in the gentle rounding of breasts and curve of waist, the flat tummy, and the childish delta, as yet only lightly furred.

She moved, then, too soon, too abruptly, pulling on panties, pretty shiny nylon. Then the bra, tiny crescents of lace, so tiny, barely covering the little tits. Catching sight of herself in the mirror, the girl stopped; completely immobile, arms crossed, hands resting on opposite shoulders. Riveted, she watched herself in the silvered glass, as though the image were a stranger. Very slowly, her hands moved forward and down, sliding the straps off her shoulders, caressing her upper arms. Downward still, pushing the lacy fabric away, cupping her own breasts. Her lips parted, breath coming faster; her thumbs circled tentatively, experimentally, bringing the tender buds of her nipples to urgent bloom. Eyes closed, she let her head droop backward and sat down very hard on the side of the bed.

Getting ready. The man smiled at his own wit and drew himself away silently. It was still very early, too early. But he could wait. He had all the time in the world. He could come back later . . . when she was even more ready.

In contrast with the quiet week, New Year's Eve was a night of frenetic activity and alcoholic gaiety . . . all of it somewhere else. In the Hilyards' tiny living room, the last evening of the year was passed sedately, with the promised "few friends" and a gentle flow of conversation, music, and laughter. A small TV set in one corner marked the time, flickering with images of traditional Times Square revelry; but the sound was turned low, and no one paid much attention.

Tired from the extra seasonal demands of her job and the added round of holiday activities, Carrie had almost hoped for an excuse to decline Louise's invitation, issued jointly to her and Frank. She had broached the subject of the party to Lee Ann almost apologetically. "Your dad and I never went out on New Year's Eve," she explained, "and if you don't want me to go, I won't."

Lee Ann regarded her mother with an almost comical expression of stupefaction. *"Everyone* goes out on New Year's Eve," she sputtered. "And besides," she added, assuming the teenager's rightful role as family social arbiter, "the Hilyards came to *your* party."

Mildly stupefied herself, Carrie acknowledged that she was predestined to attend the party and then phoned Frank to accept. Over dinner that evening with studied nonchalance, Lee Ann suggested "Since you're not going to be home, maybe I'll go over to the Burnetts' for New Year's Eve." She assumed her very best look of self-conscious virtue. "I know you wouldn't want me to go out anywhere in a car."

"You're right." Carrie recognized manipulation when she saw it, but decided not to do anything about it right then. "I don't really want you to be by yourself, so going to the Burnetts' is a good idea. Have you told them about it?"

"No, but I'm sure it will be all right."

Lee Ann's confidence was borne out by Penny's enthusiastic endorsement and a more sedate invitation from Barbara. "We're going to Mark and Louise's, too," she said. "And the kids are going to have pizza and watch a rented movie. Danny can walk Lee Ann home—or she can sleep over, for that matter."

With that assurance, Carrie left for the party in reasonable spirits, jauntily returning Lee Ann's offhand wave and openly taking Frank's arm as they walked across the yard. The temperature had been dropping steadily all day, and the air was so cold it glittered. Underfoot the ground rang like something hard and hollow, and tussocks of thin brown grass broke with small crisp sounds. Frank's car squatted in the driveway like a toad, dragged unwilling from garaged hibernation. "It started," offered Frank reassuringly. "And by now the heater's almost warmed up."

Carrie settled herself on the cracked vinyl seat with reservations which proved well founded; the heater hissed with apparent derision and gave forth intermittent blasts that were only slightly warmer than the outside air. Fortunately, it wasn't far to the Hilyards' house, and after being at the party for an hour or so, Carrie realized her feet were almost thawed. She sipped gratefully at a cup of hot spiced cider and listened absently to the group chatting at her elbow. They were alternately debating the possibilities of cold nuclear fusion and the merits of two opposing ball teams.

The door swung open, directly into the small

191

living room. More guests came in, puffing and stamping, remarking on the cold as though to be sure no one else had overlooked it. Keith and Barbara came, laughing and nodding, through the crowd toward Carrie. Behind them, Marge emerged from an old black coat, looking like a molting crow. "How are things?" she croaked.

"Fine. Everything's fine." Carrie smiled at her brightly. "It's a nice party." She began to edge away, but Frank was at her elbow, doling out more cider. Barbara, at her other side, reached across for a cup. They all smiled at her benignly. Their teeth were very white. Carrie stood still, hemmed in by the relentless circle of her friends.

The rest of the party blurred at the edges like an old photograph; conversations flowed around her, as unintelligible as a record played at the wrong speed. Carrie drifted, fidgety and out of sorts, feeling the beginning of a cold that had nothing to do with the weather.

On her own front porch, later, she rested her head against Frank's shoulder; but even under his warmth the ice refused to melt. Eyes open, she examined the coarse weave of his coat, feeling the rough wool harsh against her cheek . . . feeling little else. When he tipped her face up, she accepted his kiss passively, eyes lowered, shuttering herself against his questioning look.

"It's late" was all he said. "You must be tired." And she nodded in relief, squeezing his hand with what warmth she could muster as she slipped away toward the warmth and familiarity of the house.

Above her something stirred in the silent darkness.

Carrie stood stone-still in the open door, *listening.* Paralyzing cold seeped slowly into the foyer around her in the long seconds before the sounds came again. White-lipped, wide-eyed, she turned her head to Frank in mute appeal, and sagged gratefully against

192

him as he nodded. Thank God, he heard it too!

They shuffled in the narrow doorway like a pair of comedians doing a routine, Frank intent on entering, Carrie in front of him loath to move. Shepherding her forward, he shut the front door just as light blossomed about them, at the top of the stairs.

Carrie shut her eyes, swallowed drily, and reminded herself to breathe. Frank found the light switch and the foyer around them brightened into life. Footsteps came across the landing and down the stairs. Two sets of footsteps.

Lee Ann descended slowly, deliberately, her face defiantly expressionless. She was clad in a pair of old and too-tight jeans, with every evidence of having dressed hastily: her feet were bare, and despite her slender build, it was obvious that she wore nothing beneath the soft cotton sweater.

Danny came quietly down behind her, eyes fixed on the stair treads as though the footing were treacherous. Lee Ann slid her arm around his waist in a proprietary gesture, and gave her mother a sly and victorious smile.

It seemed to Carrie that the bright light in the foyer dimmed . . . or that the darkness had begun to encroach on it. Danny dropped a quick hug around Lee Ann's shoulders, sidled past them, and was gone, cold air eddying in his wake. No one spoke. Lee Ann turned with great deliberateness and went back up the stairs.

The tiny entry hall still seemed unbearably crowded. Carrie held herself carefully motionless, rigid shoulders aching under the weight of her heavy coat. She wished irritably that Frank would go away; it was too much to have to fight the desire to throw herself into his arms and cry.

As though he sensed her misery, he moved nearer and put his hands gently on her shoulders. "It isn't the end of the world," he said. Carrie, in no mood for sensible advice, braced herself against both his touch and his sympathy.

The hands on her shoulders tightened for a second before falling away. His lips brushed her hair lightly. "I'll call you tomorrow," she heard; then the door opened and closed, and she was alone.

At the top of the stairs, the hallway was silent; Carrie could hear water running behind the closed bathroom door. She stepped forward, into the triangle of light from Lee Ann's open door. The bed was tumbled, and the room was permeated with the sweet outdoorsy smell of herbs. On the bedside table, the roseate candle had burned very low.

CHAPTER XV

Bright late-morning sun lay like a mantle across the yard outside, giving the new year a cheerful start, and making Carrie's mood blacker by contrast.

I trusted you, she raged silently, and you've just proven that I shouldn't have.

Coffee swirled in a miniature maelstrom around her spoon as she stirred violently; even after a long and sleepless night, she was still uncertain about the best approach to take with her daughter. What could she possibly say at this point? Should she say anything at all? Carrie dropped the spoon beside her mug with a despairing rattle. Would anything she could say or do make a difference anyway?

When Lee Ann came downstairs it was nearly noon and Carrie was still undecided. She made French toast in grim and punitive silence, stealing glances at Lee Ann's face without really knowing what she expected to see there. Shame? Guilt? Remorse? What she actually saw—and should have expected—was nothing. Lee Ann sipped orange juice nonchalantly and pretended to read the paper.

Carrie turned her eyes upward and wished that she believed in some heavenly source from which inspiration—or at least moral outrage—might come. But all she saw was the brownish crack that spiderwebbed across the corner of the ceiling above the stove. She sighed and deposited a plate of French toast in front of her daughter.

"I don't want to spoil your breakfast," she said, "but I think we're about to have a fight."

"Over Danny?"

"Over your conduct." Carrie turned and tossed the spatula in the sink with a resounding clang. "I let you start dating because I thought you were mature enough. I trusted you."

"I'm mature enough to make my own decisions."

"And it was a terrific decision you just made, wasn't it? You've been dating for less than a month; you've only *known* Danny since October!"

"September. And what's the big deal, anyway? Times have changed, Mom . . . things are different now."

"Not *that* different."

"I'm not going to get pregnant, if that's what's bothering you."

Carrie reached blindly for something to hold on to, came up with her breakfast mug. "It's more than just that, Lee Ann," she stalled. Automatically she took a swig of cooling bitter coffee and made a face. "There's a little matter of self-respect involved."

Her daughter raised an ironic eyebrow; despite her own relative innocence, Carrie had to will herself not to blush. She groped urgently for words that would be meaningful to the teenager, and was surprised that she couldn't find any. Did every generation, no matter how liberated, go through this with its children?

"It's your body, that's what I'm trying to say. Maybe you have the right to make decisions about it . . . but they have to be *your* decisions. Not someone else's. You don't owe anyone else any rights over your body. That's all."

196

Lee Ann looked thoughtful, but unimpressed.

Carrie began to get a definite sinking feeling. Her better judgment told her to quit while communications were still open; but a final feeble salvo emerged nevertheless, in a voice that sounded exactly like her own mother's, twenty years ago. "If Danny really loved you, he wouldn't try to pressure you into things."

Lee Ann looked back at her coolly. "He didn't."

Using mindless work as a refuge from her own treadmill thoughts, Carrie shuttled back and forth through a house that closed over her like an imprisoning hand. Lee Ann had left, not mentioning where she was going, although Carrie was fairly certain she knew.

Her daughter was slipping away from her.

She has to grow up sometime.

But Lee Ann is only fifteen. Barely fifteen. That's too young.

Or does every mother say that?

Lee Ann had always been so quiet and shy; not at all the type to get into the usual adolescent scrapes . . . or any other kind of trouble. Had she really changed that much, or was she still under some terrible strain?

How would I know? Would she tell me? She was scared before, and where did she go for help? To Penny and Danny.

Carrie remembered her bizarre experience at the Halloween dance—her sense of a completely alien culture, closing ranks against the intruder in their midst. In the intermittent flicker of the strobe lights, she had caught a glimpse of something primitive and tribal lurking where civilized and unseeing adulthood had not yet overlaid it.

Nonsense. The brisk and sensible reply came from

197

some everyday part of her mind. *It's natural for teenagers to have their own little in-crowd. And it's perfectly normal for a young girl to prefer her friends to her mother.*

A tiny furrow stitched itself like pain between her eyes. *So my teenage daughter is sleeping with her boyfriend. This should not exactly come as a shock— not to someone who grew up in the sixties.*

She's just so young, that's all. So very young.

Carrie leaned heavily against the wall and stared unseeing into her daughter's room. Lee Ann was drifting away from her . . . but what was she drifting *toward?*

Around her the house was cold and silent; the afternoon was graying, getting colder. Crouched uncomfortably on the hearth rug, Carrie twisted newspaper strips into tight knots and jammed them into place beneath a carefully structured pile of logs and kindling. Finally, satisfied, she applied a match to several exposed edges of paper and sat back on her heels to watch the advancing flames.

Cross-legged before the fireplace, she watched tiny spears of fire probe amid the kindling. The rolls of newspaper curled and blackened, falling away to the bottom of the grate, but the twigs and logs remained untouched. Determined, Carrie crumpled more newspaper, stuck it beneath the logs, set it burning, and dropped the match before it singed her fingers.

The first tiny pieces of kindling gave way to the flames, and wisps of woodsmoke began to drift upward. She watched, delighted, as the burning paper dropped away to ash, and the edges of the logs began to char and redden. Absently, she fanned away the smoke that crept in tendrils across the hearth. A line of pallid flame crawled slowly between the logs;

198

at the back of the fireplace something popped with a burst of sparks.

Carrie's eyes began to water as she set the mesh screen in place and moved away. Other people's fires weren't this smoky. A hazy scrim now filled the room around her. Frowning, she tugged open one of the front windows, wincing at the sudden chill. The smoke, now thicker, billowed and surged. In the dining room the smoke alarm emitted a tentative *cheep*.

With a similar noise of dismay, Carrie bolted through the French doors and banged them shut behind her just as the smoke alarm burst into frenzied and full-throated warning. Pandora, beneath the table, bristled and fled, bounding across the dining room and into the kitchen. On tiptoe atop a dining-room chair, Carrie scrabbled at the smoke alarm, cringing beneath the furious assault of sound. She pulled away the cover, tugged the battery loose from its connecting wires, and relaxed gratefully in the sudden silence.

Ears still ringing, she armed herself with a pitcher of water from the kitchen and sidled through the glass-paned door, dousing arms and shirtfront in the process. The logs in the fireplace had kindled, perversely, to a small but satisfactory blaze, and the room was filled now with acrid gray smoke. Carrie tossed the contents of the pitcher directly at the thin yellow heart of the fire; steam hissed and roiled and added itself to the already opaque air.

What happened next was—surely—a product of her streaming eyes and the seething smoke. Beside her, in the thickened atmosphere, a single space began to clear. The haze of smoke and steam gave way as though to a physical presence . . . and a roughly man-sized shape stood imprinted in the fog like a shadow in reverse.

199

No! Carrie squeezed her eyes shut, hard, and opened them to the same uncompromising vision. *It's a trick of the light. Or the smoke. Or something.* She flailed with her arms, fanning smoky tendrils into restless motion, but that one clear pillar of space, remained, its outlines unwavering. *There's nothing there.* But her heart stuttered and thumped, pulse battering at her ears like a fist striking a shuttered door.

It isn't real. Of course it isn't. Carrie blinked and dabbed at her eyes, trying to rub away the image. But it remained, whatever it was, and her flesh crawled with the notion that it looked back at her.

Almost without volition, her feet carried her backward. She recoiled against the fireplace mantel; and was startled into a shaken, bleated cry when a voice spoke almost at her elbow.

"Carrie?" Frank hovered briefly at the window, then bolted away across the porch. "Carrie!" The front door rattled and flew inward and Carrie ran across the room to him.

After a moment of utter, though pleasant, confusion, Carrie disentangled herself and stepped away, flushed and even more disheveled than before.

"Are you okay?"

Carrie swallowed hard against an irrational rush of tears and nodded mutely. Frank's hands tightened on her shoulders. "I came up on the porch and smelled smoke. . . ."

Unable to stop herself, Carrie began to shiver. Frank looked at her hard, then to her relief turned his attention beyond her to the living room. He sneezed. "Traditionally, the haunted house gets burned to the ground at the end of the story, but I think in this case it's a bit premature."

Carrie laughed shakily, but remained where she was when he crossed the room and knelt at the fireplace. "I was trying to light a fire," she explained, striving to match his light note. "But I guess I'm not Girl Scout material."

Frank examined the fireplace tools critically, selected the poker, and began to probe awkwardly inside the fireplace opening. Something gave, with a raspy screech of rusty metal, and the hanging smoky pall began to swirl in new currents and eddies. Frank sat back on his heels and coughed. "You forgot to open the damper, that's all." He levered the logs apart and began to scatter the last smoldering remnants. "The fire's pretty much out, and the smoke should clear soon. No real harm done."

"Just when I start feeling really self-sufficient, something like this happens." Carrie glowered at the dank mess on the hearth. Frank looked at her thoughtfully, and she flushed. "I just feel so stupid," she continued apologetically. "I never even thought about the damper. Anyway, Frank, your timing was terrific. Thanks."

He unwound his long frame from the hearth rug, returned the poker to its rack, and smiled at Carrie as she stood huddled into herself against the chill. "I think we can close the windows now. You look cold." He tugged the resisting sashes into place and secured the old brass locks, then turned to Carrie, who hadn't moved.

"What else is wrong, Carrie?" he asked gently. "You looked absolutely terrified when I came in. And it wasn't the fire that did it."

Carrie opened her mouth and closed it again, struggling visibly. "I thought I saw something," she said finally, faintly.

She swallowed and gestured, angular with nerves and exasperation. "Oh, Frank, this is stupid. I'm just a little jumpy. And I scared myself, that's all—like a little kid who just watched a horror movie."

201

Frank narrowed his eyes and made a noncommittal sound. Then he moved abruptly, as though coming to a sudden decision. "Look, Carrie, get a jacket and let's walk down to the Burnetts'. We can talk there, and it will give the smoke time to clear."

Carrie opened her mouth to protest, unwilling without any real reason. But she considered the alternative and changed her mind. Frank waited while she ran upstairs for a coat, then followed her outside and slammed the door behind them.

With Keith and several of the children gone, the Burnetts' big yellow house lay in unaccustomed silence. Barbara moved around the kitchen, making coffee and listening to their disjointed recital.

"You actually saw something in the living room?" She set mugs and a plate of doughnuts on the table.

"Not exactly," Carrie elucidated. "It was more like something I *didn't* see."

"A feeling?"

"No, it was really there. Or rather it wasn't."

"You saw something that wasn't there," said Barbara patiently.

"No, it was what she *didn't* see that wasn't there," supplied Frank helpfully.

Barbara flopped onto a chair and began to laugh. Even Carrie smiled, restored somewhat by coffee, doughnuts, and calm acceptance.

"There was . . . something," she began again. "In the smoke. It sounds so stupid . . ." Her voice trailed off, but at Frank's encouraging nod she gathered her breath and plunged on. "There was an empty space: a sort of *negative* place in the smoke. Like there was something there. Something I couldn't see."

"Hmmm." Barbara picked up her coffee cup and sipped absently.

202

"You two must think I'm crazy," mourned Carrie, propping her elbows on the table and clutching her head with both hands. "Right at the moment, *I* think I'm crazy. I don't believe in ghosties and ghoulies and long-leggity beasties and things that go bump in the night." She crossed her arms on the table and looked down at them stubbornly. "It was smoky and my eyes were watering and I was already . . . jumpy. I just scared myself. That's all. The smoke formed a funny pattern for a minute, and my imagination did the rest."

Barbara looked at her evenly. "Jumpy or not," she said, "I don't think you're the type to see things that aren't there."

Carrie's throat closed in a sudden knot, her nose prickled and she realized that despite her best efforts she was going to cry. Frank patted her awkwardly on the back, Barbara supplied a box of tissues, and they waited patiently until her tears had dried to gulps and snuffling.

"Somehow," said Frank portentously, "I suspect this is just the tip of the iceberg." He folded his hands behind his head and leaned back comfortably in the chair. "Carrie, you're not the type to get this badly rattled over a wisp of smoke. What else is wrong?"

Carrie sniffed, blew her nose, and gave up. "It's all of it together," she began, not particularly coherently. "Remember the stuff Penny was telling us—about odd things happening in the house and scaring Lee Ann? The lights coming on by themselves, doors that won't stay shut?" She met Barbara's accepting glance, then glared defiance at Frank, beside her. "Well, it isn't just in her head. I can't believe that anymore."

Both of the others were quiet as Carrie rushed on, adding her own experiences: the movement glimpsed when nothing was there . . . the photograph that appeared and then self-destructed . . . the cold in Lee Ann's room. And the dreams.

"It wasn't all that bad at first." She paused, trying to read reaction in their faces. "Even the flying coffee cups and moving chairs . . . they're all things that can have perfectly natural explanations. That's what I've been telling myself. But when you put it all together, it's just . . . too much."

When they nodded soberly, she almost began to cry again, in sheer relief. Frank extended an arm along the back of her chair, and she leaned her head back, just for a second taking comfort from the touch.

Barbara rested her chin in her hands and looked thoughtful. "Well, the poltergeist theory doesn't hold up anymore, does it?"

"What do you mean?"

"Most of this stuff is classic, textbook poltergeist—objects moved, lights turned on and off. And Lee Ann seems to be the catalyst, for obvious reasons: adolescent upheaval, grief at her father's death, and now jealousy over Frank. But your little-man-who-wasn't-there—in the smoke—"

"Who may very well have been my imagination."

"—isn't at all typical of a poltergeist." Barbara finished her coffee and set the cup down.

"You're right." Carrie's eyes widened with sudden revelation. "Like you say, Lee Ann is supposed to be causing all that. But this time she wasn't even home!"

"And when you saw someone—or something—on the stairway; she was asleep then, right?"

Carrie looked inward on a welter of images, on feelings she had so carefully suppressed. "There's something really wrong here, isn't there?" she asked finally; knowing that it wasn't really a question. "Something a lot more than just misdirected adolescent energy."

204

Barbara's face showed her agreement; Frank's most definitely did not. "Let's not get carried away," he broke in, determinedly rational. "The poltergeist theory still fits the facts better than anything else."

Carrie turned on him. "But it doesn't explain what happened today. No matter what, you can't blame Lee Ann for that!'"

He looked at her, eyebrows raised. "But there isn't any other explanation. Unless you think your house is haunted?"

It was the first time the word had been uttered. Carrie wriggled uncomfortably on the hard kitchen chair. "I don't believe in ghosts," she said stubbornly.

"Well," he countered, "if you discard the poltergeist theory, a ghost is what you have left. And I don't believe in them either."

"There are some other possibilities here," Barbara hastened to intervene. "Frank, you can accept the idea that there are things around us we can't perceive with our senses. I mean, you know radio waves exist, yet you can't see them . . . we know there are sounds at pitches we can't hear . . . colors out of our range of vision."

"Sure," Frank answered rebelliously. "But those are natural phenomena. It's not the same thing as . . . as ghosts and demons."

"A ghost may *be* a natural phenomenon. There's a theory that strong human emotions can make a sort of imprint on the atmosphere of a place, like a recording." She smiled at him, too sweetly. "Not that different from the idea that strong human emotions can move objects."

Somewhat later, in the Burnetts' comfortable, slightly shabby living room, Carrie sat, knees on chin, staring thoughtfully into a cheerful fire. She now knew far more about ghosts than she had ever

205

wanted to know. A welter of books on the subject lay scattered across the hearth rug around her, and Frank, in a chair at her side, was thumbing through still another volume.

There were, it seemed, a number of different theories about hauntings, and Barbara had explained them all, with side excursions courtesy of Frank.

"The classical ghost story seems to grow out of religious beliefs," she had begun. "You have a soul or spirit that survives bodily death, but remains earthbound for some reason."

"They're supposed to go to heaven or hell," quipped Frank irreverently, "but some people just have no sense of direction."

Barbara ignored him loftily. "Around the turn of the century, people began taking a more scientific approach. When they gathered and evaluated reports, they found that ghost stories seemed to fall into several different categories." She leaned over, sorting through an untidy heap of books, and handed Carrie an impressive-looking volume. "This is by one of the founders of the Society for Psychical Research. It's about apparitions of living people."

Carrie looked dubious. "You mean you can be a ghost without even being dead?"

"Maybe 'ghost' isn't quite the right word," laughed Barbara. "But there have been a lot of cases like that: someone who's in an accident appears to a close friend or relative, or a soldier is seen by his wife just at the moment he's wounded in battle. They're not dead, and don't even have to be sick or injured; sometimes it's just people who're under severe stress, appearing to someone close to them. There have even been people who claimed they could do it voluntarily."

Carrie flipped pages at random; the book looked

almost boring enough to be taken seriously.

"Then there's the instant replay," Frank chimed in; and for just a second Barbara looked almost as blank as Carrie. "The one you were talking about," he prompted her.

"Oh, yes. It's a relatively recent theory." She rummaged through the books on the rug for a suitably authoritative volume. "And perhaps a bit more scientific," she added, watching Frank for signs of acceptance. "The idea is that very intense feelings can leave a permanent impression in a place. Like the magnetic pulse of a tape or radio signals in the air, imperceptible until they're played back by the right receiver."

"Lee Ann," said Carrie.

They looked at her.

"The right receiver," she said impatiently.

Barbara nodded, and even Frank looked thoughtful. "And you're picking up some things too, but maybe not as much."

Carrie picked meditatively at a thread on the hearth rug. "I could live with that," she said slowly. "It's not . . . personal. You can't be afraid of a tape recording."

With a resigned air, Frank turned the discussion from the theoretical to the practical. "So what do we do about it?"

"One logical step would be to find out more about the house and its history—the people who've lived there. . . ."

"And died there?"

"And died there, yes." Barbara nodded firmly. "Maybe that will tell us what—or who—is still hanging around."

Carrie winced. But Frank, by now, was intrigued by the intellectual puzzle. "The library would have some records," he mused. "And the local genea-

207

logical society. Probably there are other places, too."

"I think I can find out some stuff from Marge. She worked at the post office for years, and she knew everybody in the area.

"For that matter," Barbara turned from Frank to Carrie, eyes narrowed in thought, "why don't we ask Marge to come over and look around your house? I told you, remember, she's . . . a sensitive. If anyone can tell you what's in your house, she can."

CHAPTER XVI

There was one other person who could have told Carrie what was in the house. Lee Ann came up the front walkway now, across the frozen lawn, half in anticipation, half in dread. There was a light in the dormer window, her window. It looked down on her like eyes, blazing with loving—and voracious—welcome.

Her mother's car was in the driveway. She tiptoed across the porch and opened the front door, very quietly, listening to the silence. No one home. *Out with Frank somewhere, I bet.* Her mouth thinned. *Hypocrites, both of them.* She really couldn't take much more of her mother's lectures. Even her friends were getting into the act now. Penny, with her silly fears. *She's proved I can't trust her anymore.* And Danny, quieter but still worried, watching her . . . always watching her.

She fled up the stairs to her room, trying to stay a step ahead of her thoughts. *Why can't they just let me alone? All of them.* But not completely alone. That wasn't really what she wanted either. And she wasn't even sure who *they* were.

Lee Ann threw herself on the bed, petulant. All of them, expecting something from her. Wanting something from her. And she knew what it was.

When darkness began to gather at the windows, she looked up and smiled.

Wrapped in concealing shadow, the man gathered himself, with an effort of will like physical exertion. In his own place, unseen, he pressed his hands against another pane of cold glass, and smiled in response.

Carrie walked home hand in hand with Frank, wearing renewed confidence like a borrowed cloak. But like the emperor's clothes in the fairy tale, complacency began to disappear when she looked at things objectively. And by nightfall it had vanished entirely.

A haunted house. She glared at her own face, floating wraithlike in the bathroom mirror. The idea had seemed at least relatively logical when Barbara had explained it; but now it dwindled to impossibility under the harsh fluorescents. *Ghosts clanking chains in the hall? Sure. Bats in the belfry, more like.* She wryly stuck out her tongue at her shocked reflection.

I just can't believe this. Damn it, I feel like a cover story from a supermarket tabloid!

Frank didn't believe it either. Not really. Oh, he was polite, but he was still certain that Lee Ann was behind it all—the disturbed adolescent of the psychology textbooks.

There was no sound from the teenager's bedroom; only the glow of light under the door showed that she was home. Carrie shut her own door, weary to the bone; but sleep eluded her for a long time.

By now he probably thinks I'm disturbed too. And maybe he's right. Maybe I just imagined it . . . that thing in the smoke.

She shivered and drew the covers up further around her neck. *No, darn it! I saw it. I really saw it. It wasn't my imagination. And Lee Ann didn't have a thing to do with it.*

So Barbara must be right. *My house is haunted.*

Carrie lay still, listening to the darkness, watching the shadow-patterns that formed and re-formed above her on the low ceiling. But what she was really seeing was a hazy pattern materializing in her head.

Or was there, just possibly, another answer to her quandary? A human answer. *In the movies, there would be a sinister villain, trying to drive us out and take possession of a treasure hidden in the house.*

Right.

But still, Barbara seems to know so much about this. Strange things start happening in my house, and she always has a nice neat answer.

The bedside clock whirred softly and informed her that it was now past 1:00 A.M. *Appropriate. I feel like part of the script for a late-night movie.* Giving up on sleep for the moment, Carrie pummeled the pillow into a soft heap at her back, pulled herself into an upright position, and tried to pull her scattered thought processes together.

Barbara. With her peculiar herbs. Her handmade candles. Her calm acceptance of fortunetellers . . . psychics . . . ghosts.

Barbara. Who had, quite surely, taken that lock of Carrie's hair from the bandanna knot.

But why? What was she trying to do? And what possible reason could she have? It was all totally insane.

What echoed in her head then could have been the voice of every day's headlines: *Insanity doesn't need a reason.*

*   *   *

211

"I just can't quite believe it," said Carrie for at least the eighteenth time.

And Frank, who had kept count, gave her another patient response. "I understand. I can't quite bring myself to believe in ghosts either." He set his coffee cup down and fixed her with a quizzical look. "But I thought you were sold on the idea."

"I was. I am." Carrie contemplated internal turmoil with dismay. "I think." A week of constant fretting had only left her more confused than ever.

The state of mind was apparently contagious; Frank looked appropriately bewildered.

Carrie gazed back at him bleakly. *It's not so much whether I believe in ghosts . . . but whether I believe in Barbara.* She opened her mouth, closed it again, wavering, wondering how much she could say to him in confidence. *After all, he is a good friend of theirs.*

"Darn it, Frank," she burst out miserably. "I don't know what to think . . . about anything."

"Why don't you tell me about it? What you're worrying about. Maybe I can help." His smile was gentle, calm, and solid enough to lean on.

Carrie closed her eyes, hoping to hide the weak humiliating tears. *I shouldn't need someone to lean on. I should be able to handle this all by myself.*

But I can't.

Or maybe I don't want to.

"It bothers me that Barbara knows so much about this." The words emerged, almost without volition, before Carrie could talk herself out of it.

"Well," he said offhandedly, "Barbara's one of those people who read everything they can get their hands on—and remembers a lot of it. And it's an interesting subject."

Carrie tried to read his face and failed. "What I guess I'm saying," she continued stubbornly, "is that I don't know how she fits into this."

212

Frank leaned back, carefully expressionless. "I'm not sure I understand."

The statement lay on the table between them like a challenge. *What am I doing?* Carrie's hands knotted into fists, curled, uncurled. *The only people who've helped—who've cared—and I may be driving them away. Driving him away.*

But she had to know. "Whatever's going on, Barbara seems to be in the middle," she explained haltingly, watching him, groping her way on. "No matter how weird it is, she always has an explanation." Once started, the words gained their own momentum; they came tumbling over one another in a torrent, only semicoherent, unstoppable. "There are those strange herbs of hers. Even one she gave Lee Ann. And the candle . . . in the bedroom . . . with her and Danny."

Frank's face flickered, but not, apparently, with anger. Disgust, perhaps? *Compassion for this poor neurotic female?* Carrie leaned forward, feeling the table edge sharp against her forearms, paying no attention to the discomfort. "Frank, she took a lock of my hair."

His eyes widened this time, almost imperceptibly, but it was enough. He understood. Carrie sat back, rubbing absently at her arms and wondering what she had set in motion.

"Um," said Frank. He ran a hand up the back of his neck with a dazed expression. "So what are you saying—that she's trying to hurt you somehow?"

"I don't know. I realize it doesn't make sense." Her tone was soft and appeasing.

"Of course it doesn't," he sputtered. "For God's sake, Carrie, this is paranoia! I've know Barbara for twenty years, and she's one of the warmest, most caring, *decent* people I've ever met."

"I agree, it doesn't make sense. But nothing about this makes sense. And I can believe in a crazy person a

213

whole lot easier than I can believe in ghosts or poltergeists."

"But Barbara's your friend! What has she ever done to hurt you? Or to make you think she would?"

"Maybe it's not what she's done. Maybe it's what she *is*."

Barbara really took it very well.

They had arrived at her house in a confused tumble of expostulations from Carrie and explanations from Frank, which Barbara sorted out placidly.

"If you're not too sick of coffee?" She waved the carafe inquiringly and began to make coffee as though it were quite routine to have the Inquisition appear in her kitchen.

With the brew gurgling contentedly in the background, she plunked herself down at the long plank table across from Carrie. "You're right," she said, "I'm a witch."

There seemed to be nothing to say to that. Carrie didn't even try. *So I was right all along.* The thought numbed her. Arms crossed defensively, she sat rigid, utterly at a loss. *This can't be happening. This can't really be happening.*

The coffeemaker stopped.

Carrie closed her eyes. *I can't believe this.* But her feeling of imminent danger drained away abruptly. She crossed the room on unsteady legs and helped herself to coffee.

"Just exactly what is going *on* here?" she demanded crossly.

"It's not something to be afraid of, Carrie." Barbara poured coffee for herself and Frank; Carrie shook her head at an offer of doughnuts. Were they really standing here calmly, having a snack and discussing witchcraft? Shouldn't they be sticking pins in dolls or something?

"First of all, let's discard the horror-movie clichés. Okay?" Barbara settled herself on a tall stool at the center island across from Carrie. "Witches don't have any strange supernatural powers, and we're no wickeder or more evil than anybody else."

Carrie tried hard to keep skepticism out of her expression, but her voice emerged hard and challenging. "So what does witchcraft mean, then?"

"The word itself derives from the old English 'wicce,' which just means 'wise one.' Early witches were village healers and leaders of the native religions—priests and priestesses."

"You mean it was a religion?"

"Still is," said Barbara matter-of-factly. "It's a survival, or maybe a revival, of the very early religions . . . religions that venerated the earth as lifegiver and sustainer—and revered a divinity that was everywhere."

"That all sounds very innocent." Carrie unhappily heard the sarcasm in her voice, but she remained resigned to the necessity of proceeding. She had already gone too far . . . yet it wasn't far enough. What about magic and spells?" she flung out. Even if I don't believe in all that, maybe you do!"

Her final accusation thudded into the silence like a thrown rock—shattering, maybe fatal: "What did you do with that lock of my hair?"

Her breathing sounded ragged. Carrie gripped the edge of the countertop behind her, wondering if she had the strength to run. And if she did, where would she go?

Finally Barbara stood up, slowly, as though approaching a frightened animal. "I'll show you," she said.

It took all of the trust Carrie possessed—and most of the courage—to follow her up the stairs. Barbara ushered her into a tiny room tucked under the eaves, and up to a low table that stood against the wall. The

215

top was strewn with a profusion of gaily colored candles; the fragile curl of Carrie's hair lay intertwined with Lee Ann's darker strands, sheltered in an aromatic wreath of evergreen sprigs.

It wasn't quite what Carrie had expected.

Almost an hour later, Carrie sat with her back propped against the wall of the bare little room listening to the end of a long and rambling explanation. Frank, who had poked his head in before entering, sat beside her just inside the door looking very neutral.

"We think of magic as a natural force," Barbara waved her hands expressively. "Maybe something we all were in touch with at one time, the way some farmers still can sense changes in the weather, or dowsers can find water." Her face was intent and earnest. "We don't pretend to really understand it but it isn't anything good or evil. Like electricity, it's just a power that can be used to do what you want."

This isn't real, Carrie thought again, wearily. But her thoughts turned toward hope as a sunflower turns to the light. "And you were trying to use it to protect me? Us?"

Barbara, sitting cross-legged on a colorful hooked rug, nodded emphatically. "Sure. When things started happening and Lee Ann started getting scared, Penny did a kind of blessing for the house, but it didn't seem to help. I thought maybe they were just being dramatic . . . until that first time I went into Lee Ann's room. I don't mind telling you it gave me the creeps."

"So you took that bit of hair from my bandanna."

"And Penny got some out of Lee Ann's brush." Barbara swept her own hair back from her eyes. "It gave us a stronger link, you see. Something physical . . . a part of the person. It's easier that way."

Carrie swallowed and nodded dazedly.

"I guess I should have told you before." Barbara smiled apologetically, cast a comradely glance at Frank. "It never occurred to me that you'd be afraid of us."

Beside Carrie, Frank dropped his eyes shut with a resigned sigh, and something inside Carrie turned to stone. "Us?" she echoed faintly.

"Oh, he's one too," said Barbara cheerfully. "Didn't he tell you?"

CHAPTER XVII

Frank walked her home, fisted hands jammed deep into his pockets, watching her sidewise, trying to gauge her reaction. Carrie kept her face very still, giving nothing away. *Not to give him the satisfaction.*

"I'm sorry I didn't tell you," he said finally. "It's one of those things . . . you don't know where to start."

Carrie only shook her head, unable to find her own words; not even certain what it was she wanted to say. *I feel like such a fool. I thought I had my eyes wide open, and I still walked right into this.*

Barbara's explanation had been all very innocent. *But if it's so innocent, why didn't he tell me? What did he have to hide?* Carrie watched the gray sidewalk moving past beneath her feet, its uneven surface— heaved by frost, cracked by time and weeds— crumbling at the edges. Like her life. *What else is there about him I don't know? What else is there that I ought to know?*

Numb, she shuttered her disturbing thoughts behind a mask of poise, closing him out. *If he can hide things, so can I.* On the front porch, she kept her eyes fixed on the doormat, fumbled with the keys, ignoring his awkward gesture that started as an embrace and ended as a pat on the shoulder.

"I'll call you," he finally said.

Sleep that night was very long in coming. Carrie sat huddled in bed, sleepless, her mind tossing up involuntary images, alternately heartening and horrifying. The day's conversation with Barbara was supposed to have allayed her fears; instead it had opened the door on new terrors.

So Frank was in this, too. And had been very carefully concealing his involvement. *Why?* If it was all as innocent as Barbara had said, why hadn't he told her?

She had asked herself that same question over and over and each time had come up with much the same answer.

Lee Ann. It all focused on Lee Ann.

Barbara and Penny were making friends with her before we ever moved here. Giving her that strange plant . . . aloe, was it? And then it just happened that there was a vacant house right down the block from them—the only *decent house I saw all summer long. Could they somehow have maneuvered that? Surely it wasn't possible.* But then neither were flying teacups.

A car passed with a shushing sound, headlights glancing off the front window and sending a sweep of brightness like a searchlight across the dormered ceiling.

And as soon as we moved in, there was Danny. Such a nice kid, so friendly. Getting close to them . . . getting close to Lee Ann . . . getting her into bed.

Could that be it . . . what they wanted? A taste of nausea rose in Carrie's throat as she forced herself to examine the thought.

Because Frank had also had contact with **Lee Ann**

as soon as they moved. He'd been so caring and concerned. Gaining her confidence. Talking to her alone in his office, after hours.

Even Keith must know, must be a part of it. *So good with the kids.* Both of them, so good with the kids.

Oh, God, it isn't possible! Carrie pulled her knees up and hugged the blankets tight against her chest, wishing it were as easy to maintain her grasp on reality. Lee Ann knew better; she knew about things like that. Carrie had talked to her, and they even taught about it in school. Besides, the girl was fifteen—not like a little kid, who could be talked into anything.

But she had changed so much.

There are drugs. The whisper ran through her mind. *That's what hallucinogens are—drugs for altering someone's mind!*

Carrie groaned and buried her head in her arms, black thoughts swooping and flittering around her like bats disturbed in their cave. A suspicion that she had tried to bury now raised itself up and refused to stay dead.

There was the business of the candle, for one thing. The candle that had been handmade . . . by Barbara. What kind of herbs had been used in it? And what effect did they have as they burned?

Could someone be giving Lee Ann drugs? It would explain so much. *Could someone have given me drugs—something to cause the things I've seen?*

Someone. Barbara? Keith? Maybe even Penny or Danny. Or Frank.

Something inside Carrie knotted, twisted until she thought she would scream. She sat forward, laying her cheek against blanketed knees.

Oh God, this can't be happening. These people are my friends. And this is one time in my life when I really need them.

Could it all have been a sham? All of it? All of them? Penny's friendship, Danny's . . . Barbara's welcoming openness . . . Keith's quiet, helpful support.

And Frank. Who had appeared out of the Halloween darkness so opportunely—as if he had been waiting for her. Frank, who had also been so kind and so friendly. Who had seemed so interested and attentive. *Seemed.*

Frank. Whose last little protégé had committed suicide.

Carrie squeezed her eyes shut against the dark, but it was even darker inside her head.

In the next room, Lee Ann swam upward slowly through layers of dream and darkness. Eyes shut, she woke cradled in languor, rapt, weak with a trembling, melting sensation that left her limp and gasping. Like someone on the edge of a precipice . . . or someone who has just stepped over.

Dazed, she lay passive, waiting, coming sluggishly back to full awareness . . . of her nightgown rucked and twisted, of the coarse lace rasping across her breasts, of the hot wetness at her honeyed center. Compelled, she ran her hands over the unfamiliar landscape of her changing body, feeling its new responses, hot and eager. Unwilling responses that lingered and left her shaken to the depths.

Beside her the mattress sagged, and the old bedstead creaked mockingly; but when she reached out, her outflung hand encountered only the icy sheets.

Eyes still closed, she began to cry.

"What about Saturday? Barbara set it up tentatively with Marge, and she says Lee Ann can stay over with Penny." Frank lounged in the kitchen doorway, hands in pockets, watching her with hangdog appeal. He had been waiting on the doorstep when she'd arrived home from work, looking as transparently harmless as was possible for a healthy six-footer. Carrie had hesitated just for a second before asking him in, but if he'd noticed he hadn't commented. Now she looked at him blankly.

"You remember," he prodded. "Barbara was going to get Marge to come and see what she could tell us about your house. It's what I came to ask you about the other day," he added, "when we . . . um . . . got sidetracked."

Carrie froze in the act of opening a package of hamburger. He sounded so normal. How could he sound so normal?

"Anyhow, I think it would still be a good idea." Frank actually scuffed his foot on the linoleum, prodding with his toe at a crack. "She might be able to give us a lead—a name, a date—something we could track down. And we'd all feel better if we could finally get a handle on this thing."

Carrie closed her eyes on the bright, normal kitchen and looked again at blackness. *What am I inviting into my house? What have I invited into my life?*

"Carrie?" Frank's voice, coming from limitless distance, held only gentleness and concern.

This is insane. They're your friends, and they're trying to help.

Inside her, something sank away, fathomless. "I can't," she whispered dully. *I can't take the chance. It isn't just me; I'd be gambling for Lee Ann as well.*

"Honey? What's the matter?"

Even in her distress, Carrie noted the endearment and filed it away for future examination. "I can't," she said more firmly.

"Why?" He moved as though to touch her, but she

222

slipped aside, head turned away, pretending not to notice.

Because I'm scared! She screamed silently, neck muscles straining, the sound so real in her head that it seemed he *must* hear it.

"Carrie?"

She shook her head wordlessly. What was there possibly to say?

"Honey, I don't pretend to have any easy answers for you. I wish I did. But I'll do anything I can to help." He reached out to cover her hand with his own, very lightly, but pulled back almost at once. "You don't have to be all by yourself anymore . . . unless you want to."

His eyes, when she could bring herself to meet them, were puzzled and a little hurt. Was he that good an actor? *Am I that good a judge?*

Under her hands, the countertop bulked smooth and worn. A few feet away, Frank's face looked equally worn, open and full of a fatigue that matched her own. Surely that was real. Surely he was real.

Damn it, she thought, I need somebody to trust. One hand rubbed at her forehead, at the deepening crease between her brows. *I only wish it could be him.*

"I'm scared," she said finally, simply.

"Of course you are."

"Of you."

Frank stood very still . . . mercifully, because Carrie was certain she would scream if he moved.

"You can't really mean that."

"For God's sake, Frank, you tell me you're practicing witchcraft, and you expect me to take it as if you were practicing piano! Ghosts and poltergeists . . . curses and spells . . ."

"We never said anything about curses."

"No, of course not, it's all sweetness and light, isn't it?" Her lip curled scornfully.

"No." He dropped the word heavily, as though it

223

were a burden. "Nothing is all sweetness and light Certainly not in a religion that's been persecuted almost out of existence."

"Religion!" Carrie propped her hands on her hips combatively. *Might as well have it all out in the open.* Nothing between them could ever be the same again anyway. "How can anyone call *witchcraft a* religion?"

"Barbara tried to explain it to you. Couldn't you a least be open-minded enough to listen?"

"Oh, she made it all sound very harmless. But I've read about so many other things—devil worship, sex cults, drugs . . . child abuse . . ." Her voice quavered despite herself.

"You've read about it *where?* The checkout line a the grocery store?" He ran a hand through his hair in exasperation. "Have you ever read a *real* book on the subject? Sociology or anthropology? Even pop culture?" Suppressed anger boiled to the surface in sarcasm. "Or are you waiting for them to make i into a movie?"

Stung, Carrie recoiled. "All I know is that this craziness only started when we moved here . . . and then all of you turned up so neatly. And you had such nice neat answers for everything. It doesn't make sense unless you're involved somehow."

"Of course we're involved. We're trying to help you, damn it!"

"But why? Why should you go out of your way for me?"

His taut shoulders relaxed abruptly, and his face drooped into sadness. "I thought you were reason enough," he said quietly.

The unexpected gentleness left Carrie unnerved *Why don't I just stop this? It would be so easy to believe what he says. Believe they're all my friends Because what have they really done? What have the ever really done to hurt us?*

Aghast at her own weakening, she forced herself to display defiance. "I was reason enough? Or was it Lee Ann? You've all been very interested in her right from the start, haven't you?" His eyes widened, and she wondered if she had struck a nerve. "What do you want with my daughter?"

Silence. Frank's face was as immobile as granite, and almost as unyielding. It may also have been a shade paler.

Now I've done it. Carrie felt as if she'd spit out something noisome—like in the fairy tale, when toads leapt from the princess's mouth as she spoke. Her own venomous words were almost visible; if she looked, she might see them hopping around the kitchen floor.

Finally Frank stirred, and the effect was like that of a stone carving coming to life.

"First of all," he grated, "what Barbara told you about our beliefs and their origins was true. The crap about curses and devil worship and black Masses didn't start until newer religions came to power and began ruthlessly exterminating anybody who didn't agree with them. That's history, lady," he added nastily. "And I, for one, can't help but wonder why you reject the idea of a beneficent nature religion, then willingly swallow some crazy remnants of medieval superstition."

Carrie's mouth flew open, but Frank bulldozed straight over her, flailing his arms. "Secondly, we have nothing to do with what's happening in your house! Do you really think one of us threw that cup? Or moved a chair at the breakfast table? Did I somehow manage to rearrange the smoke from the fireplace? Honest to God, Carrie . . ." Sputtering, he stopped for breath and further ammunition.

"But what about magic?" Carrie, determined, wrested the conversation back to her argument. "What about spells?"

225

"If I could do things like that with magic, I'd go on the stage." He stared at her bitterly and returned to his original attack. "As for your daughter, I'm her friend. We all are. And we tried to be there when she needed us. That's all."

"But the way she's acting . . . drifting further and further away from me, getting so involved with all of you. And Danny, at least, has certainly taken advantage of that!"

"What do you think—we put an evil spell on her?"

"Why not? You believe in them, don't you? For that matter, I might believe in them, after some of the things I've seen!"

"Damn it, woman, if I'd put a spell on you, it would have been a love spell!" His voice was a low growl, and he looked bitter. "But I didn't—as you can very plainly tell!"

Would have been. Just for a moment, Carrie turned the words over in her head, mourning so many things that might have been. But she held herself rigidly away from him, keeping her grasp on anger and fear.

Frank slammed both fists down on the table, hard, and Carrie jumped. "What does it take to get through to you?" He leaned across the old oak surface toward her, his voice rising in outrage. "You know what your problem is? You're a bigot!"

Carrie, for once, was speechless.

"You don't know the first thing about wicca, and you don't want to know. But you immediately believe the worst, just because it's something you don't understand." In full cry now, he drew himself upright. "Maybe you're the one with the problem: have you ever heard of a persecution complex? Why are you so willing to believe people are trying to hurt you . . . and so unwilling to believe anyone would try to help?"

He realized that she had ceased to argue and

226

moderated his voice. "Carrie, this is my religion, and I won't let you persecute me because you don't understand it—and aren't willing to learn."

Slinging his coat across his arm, he let himself out the side door. And the kitchen was suddenly very empty.

CHAPTER XVIII

For days after that, Carrie waited for something to happen, but nothing did. The house lay prim and silent, as if it knew it had overstepped its bounds. She saw nothing of Barbara; and whenever the phone rang, it was always for Lee Ann.

On her day off, she went to the library. After last week's explosion of fear and self-righteous hostility, her characteristic honesty had taken over, driving her to independent sources for more information. She browsed the shelves, thumbing through thick historical tomes and slick modern books, finding a surprising number that echoed Barbara's innocuous explanation of modern witchcraft.

Looked at objectively, their beliefs weren't that much stranger than many mainstream religions. *If I tried to explain Church doctrines to someone who'd never even heard of Christianity, how crazy would I sound?*

At the office on Monday, she addressed a postcard and scrawled two words across its face: "I'm sorry." But she couldn't bring herself to drop it in the mail.

The weekend came, bringing weather as bleak as Carrie's thoughts. Lee Ann stayed away as much as possible, probably with Penny and Danny. Carrie wondered how much she knew—or guessed—about her confrontations with Barbara and Frank.

Now a cold wind was rising, as the day rapidly grayed toward evening. Saturday night. Alone. The trees outside seemed to crowd closer to the windows; Carrie drew the curtains and wished that she could as easily shut out the darkness that had taken over her life. Not for the first time, she found herself dreading the approach of night.

Upstairs she lay awake for a long time, listening for Lee Ann . . . for noises at the front door . . . to the long silence . . . then to footsteps on the stairs. Listening for other noises in the silent house. It was very late before she slept.

Her dreams were fitful and tangled, with images that beckoned just beyond her reach, important answers that lay just past the edge of understanding. Carrie twisted fretfully, restlessly, stretching every sense toward something vital—something that she *must* reach. Gasping, she broke through a final barrier—only to wake once again in the relentless cold of her room, feeling the dream slip from her grasp and dwindle into meaninglessness.

Heart pounding with the unrewarded effort, she lay still, eyes wide, staring at the shadows that gathered in the corners at the peak of the dormered ceiling. Reasonless tears pooled in her eyes and slipped down the sides of her face into her hair. Time drifted loosely in the darkness; it took a while for Carrie to realize that the sounds outside her door were real, not just an echo from her dream.

She sat up slowly, willing the old bedstead not to creak. At the edges of vision, the clock flickered a greenish reminder: 3:15. From the hallway the noise came again, a formless padding just barely perceptible against the background of normal night sounds. Lee Ann?

229

Carrie leaned forward, intent, peering at the half-open door as though her eyes could tell her what her ears were hearing. In the next room her daughter stirred and muttered. Whoever was walking in the hallway, it wasn't Lee Ann.

What now? Carrie huddled, indecisive, clutching the blanket in front of her like a shield. She *reached*, again, as in her dream, straining with eyes and ears against the breath-held waiting silence. When the furtive movement came again, she was uncertain which sense had perceived it.

Was *this* what her daughter had gone through for all these months? This helpless dread? This paralyzing certainty that someone—or something—moved in the darkness?

Lee Ann. Her daughter was alone now, perhaps awake and frightened. Carrie threw back the covers decisively and slipped out of bed; drawing her heavy robe around her, she moved quietly on bare feet toward the door. Beyond, the hall lay in thin translucent darkness, edged with the deeper bulk of shadows. Carrie blinked and stared, steadying herself against the reassuring solidity of the door frame. Was there one shadow that didn't belong—a darkness more opaque, more real, than the rest? Something moved, just at the edge of her vision, and Carrie gasped, flinging her head around with an abruptness that dizzied her. In the next doorway a pale figure stood. Lee Ann, face moon-white in a tangle of dark hair, barefoot in yellow flannel pajamas. "What?" she asked querulously.

The girl turned her head slowly from side to side, scanning the hallway with eyes that were blank and unseeing. "What?" she asked again, as though in response to some half-heard summons.

Carrie shifted nervously. "It's nothing, honey," she said reassuringly. "Go back to bed."

Blinking owlishly, Lee Ann turned toward her . . .

and began to fade from sight. Carrie watched, dry-mouthed and unbelieving, as the darkness between them surged and roiled, obscuring the pale figure in gathering shadow. Faintly, through the black scrim, she could see movement, as Lee Ann flung out her hands in a spasmodic gesture of denial.

Barely at arm's length, something groped its way into existence, drawing the shadows around it like a garment . . . struggling toward its final shape.

"Mommy?" The sound was more a whimper than a scream, muffled like the cry of a child who does not expect to be comforted.

Carrie jerked convulsively, chest heaving, her lungs dragging at the thin warped air. *Lee Ann!* She took a single step forward, out of the illusory shelter of her doorway, into the unclean, seething cold. "It's all right, honey," she said, but her voice wavered, shrill and unconvincing. "Lee Ann, go back to bed. Go back in your room."

Only a few feet away, Carrie sensed, rather than saw, movement in Lee Ann's doorway. Between them, the blackness contorted and coalesced into tenuous semblance of a human figure. In another second, would it extend arms? If it turned, would it have a face?

"Mommy!" Lee Ann's cry was faint and despairing.

Carrie threw her arms across her eyes and thrust blindly toward her daughter, making herself as small as possible, pressing herself hard against the wall. Her shoulder bumped painfully against the frame of Lee Ann's door and she stumbled, suddenly unsupported, into the open entry.

"Lee Ann?" With what seemed like the last of her strength, Carrie grasped her daughter's shoulders gently. Under the soft flannel the girl's bones felt thin and fragile as twigs; Lee Ann's eyes were wide and ash-dead with shock. Behind them, the hallway was empty.

"You saw him too, Mommy. Didn't you?"

Carrie's face felt like something carved; she worked to shape words with lips and tongue that were dry and wooden. "It was a dream, Lee Ann. You had a nightmare."

"No." The girl resisted the gentle pressure that was coaxing her back to bed. "It wasn't a dream. That's what you always say, but this time you saw him too. I know you did."

Carrie squeezed her eyes shut, wishing it were as easy to close out the image that lingered in her mind. Numb and exhausted, she surrendered to truth. "Yes," she said quietly. "I saw him too."

It didn't occur to her to wonder why they both assumed their visitor was male.

Neither she nor Lee Ann slept much in the hours of the night that remained. Tucked back in her tumbled bed, the girl tossed and thrashed restlessly, while Carrie curled up uncomfortably in an overstuffed chair dragged in from her own room. At breakfast they both were heavy-eyed and silent, pushing food around without eating, surreptitiously feeding their bacon to Pandora.

When Lee Ann went upstairs to dress, Carrie cradled her head in her hands and examined her options, which were pitifully few. Finally she reached for the phonebook. I can't think of anything else I haven't tried, she thought with resignation, and began to dial.

"Church?" said Lee Ann later when Carrie broached the subject. She gave her mother an incredulous stare above the plate she was drying. "We haven't been to church in . . . forever. Why do you suddenly want to go now?"

"I just think it might be a good idea." Carrie fished another plate out of the dishpan and handed it to her.

232

"After last night." She took the dried plate back and added it to the stack in the cabinet next to the sink. "We have to do something," she said.

"Like what?" Lee Ann's nostrils flared like a frightened animal's. "You really think going to Mass will help? Daddy never went to church; and you haven't been for years."

"I was thinking of talking to the priest, too."

No! Lee Ann whirled to face her mother and almost dropped a cup. "You can't do that!" she blurted out.

Carrie took the cup and put it safely away. "Why?" she asked. "I mean, I know it's weird; but I'm pretty sure the Church has some prayers or something that would help."

You don't understand. You don't understand at all. And I can't explain it to you . . . even if I thought you'd listen. Lee Ann looked at her mother helplessly, groping for some argument that could forestall her plan. "He'll think you're crazy. You know he will."

"It's worth trying, that's all." Carrie dried the next dish herself and sighed. "We can't go on living like this."

"Well, I'm not going. I have to do my homework for tomorrow, and I was supposed to go over to Penny's later on."

"Okay." Carrie shrugged and dropped the subject. It would probably be easier to handle it herself, without a rebellious teenager in tow.

In the end it didn't seem to matter. Carrie tiptoed into the quiet sanctuary of the church and slipped into a place at the back. Kneeling in prayer for the first time in many years, she tried to reestablish the age-old connection. But the ceremony paced itself before her like a play, and she could find in it neither meaning nor solace.

It was with a sense of futility that she presented herself for her appointment at the rectory afterward. Father Dennison, a pleasant-faced middle-aged man, offered her coffee in his study and nodded kind encouragement as she stumbled through her story.

"Umm," he said, in obvious bemusement. He tented his hands in a gesture that might have been prayerful and looked at her over the top of his glasses. "I must confess that you have me at a bit of a loss, Mrs. Sutton. Please understand, I want very much to help. But I'm not sure I understand what you want of me."

"I'm not completely sure myself." Carrie smiled uncertainly, wishing she could tell what he was really thinking. "I believe the Church used to have a ritual, a blessing or something, to cast out a . . . an evil spirit."

She watched his face closely, trying to judge his response. *An evil spirit. God, it sounds so crazy. Lee Ann was right; this isn't going to do a bit of good. I'll be lucky if he doesn't call the men in the white coats.*

"You're talking about exorcism?" The clergyman's eyebrows shot upward so far that they might have disappeared in his hairline if it had not receded so much. "Umm," he said again, taking off his glasses and wiping them vigorously. "The ritual does exist, but it's almost never used. In fact, many in the Church consider it a medieval remnant. In thirty years as a priest, I have never heard of it being performed."

Carrie looked down at her hands, which were twisting in her lap as though they had a life of their own. "Then there isn't any chance you can help us?"

He replaced the glasses and leaned back in his chair. "If we were to ask for an exorcism, there would have to be a thorough investigation, you understand . . . in order to get permission from the bishop."

His look was hesitant and apologetic. "That usually involves a consultation with a psychiatrist, in order to rule out . . . ah . . . natural causes."

"Are you saying, then, that I should take my daughter to a shrink first?"

"I suggest it, Mrs. Sutton, in order to spare your daughter any undue attention or embarrassment. Particularly since she has undergone such a recent trauma." Father Dennison spread his hands as though displaying her options on his desktop. "It's my understanding, in cases such as this, that . . . ah . . . an illness is most often found to be the answer."

"I see." Carrie nodded acceptance, telling herself that this was approximately what she had expected. So why did she find herself fighting the urge to burst into tears? "Thank you, Father. It was nice of you to talk to me."

He ushered her out with obvious relief and empty assurances that she could come and see him anytime. "I'll offer some prayers for both of you," he said.

Carrie went down the steps without looking back, and didn't cry until she reached her car.

Lee Ann was gone when she came home, and the house was depressing and echo-empty. Lovingly chosen colors had turned drab and the pretty wallpaper only looked inane. The hearth stank of ashes, and dust and bad dreams had gathered in all the corners.

Carrie made herself a sandwich, looked at it with distaste, and put it back in the refrigerator uneaten. She leaned on the counter, wondering if she could stand another cup of coffee, unable to summon enough interest to fix one. The phone rang several times before it could penetrate her lethargy.

"Hi," said a familiar voice, with a tentative inflection that turned the syllable into a question.

Carrie clutched the telephone like a talisman. "Frank," she got out; and then her throat closed with a knot of relief and remorse. *He knew I needed him. Somehow he knew.* Maybe there was something to this psychic stuff after all.

He demolished the thought almost before she had formulated it. "Lee Ann told Penny . . . about last night," he explained prosaically. "And Penny told Barbara, and Barbara told me."

Carrie's head spun. The explanations and apologies she had experimented with went out of her mind. "There was someone in the hall," she blurted. "Or some*thing*." Her voice came out high and childish. "I *saw* it. I really saw it. Lee Ann and I both did." She pressed her free hand against her eyes, fighting tears of weakness.

"Do you want me to come over?" he asked.

She nodded dumbly and choked some sort of affirmative.

"I'll hurry."

Outdoors it was as gray as ever, but the house seemed brighter. Across the table, Frank was energetically polishing off an impressive sandwich, closely watched by a hopeful Pandora. Carrie poured coffee, holding her hands as steady as possible. "I'm sorry about the other day," she began. "Some of the things I said . . ."

Frank dismissed her apology with an offhand gesture and reached for his mug. "Tell me what happened," he invited calmly.

The coffee was cold by the time she finished. "I know you don't believe in ghosts; I never did either. But it's better than thinking my daughter is . . . mentally disturbed." She shot him a furrowed look, anxious that he understand. "And I really can't imagine how Lee Ann could have caused this, anyhow."

236

Frank leaned back and pursed his lips in a soundless whistle. "Neither can I," he admitted, though there was a note of caution in his voice, and his face was furrowed with thoughts he didn't share.

"I've got to do something, Frank. I can't go on like this." She dropped her eyes to her hands and her voice almost to inaudibility. "I even went to a priest," she said.

Frank gave her a sober comprehending look, recognizing the desperation that had prompted her action. Then his mouth quirked irrepressibly. "I'll bet I can guess what he said."

Carrie grinned back, very faintly. "He was ready to throw a net over me," she agreed. The grin quickly faded under the weight of humiliating memory, and she looked down again. "I need help, Frank." Her voice dwindled, almost out of control. "Please."

Warm hands enveloped her cold ones where they lay on the table. "We'll do what we can," he comforted.

We. Surprising how just one syllable could hold so much reassurance. So much promise. Carrie tried it out in her own mouth. "Where do we start? What do we do?"

"Let's start with what we originally planned. Get Marge to come in, and see what she can tell us. Once we know more about what we're dealing with, we'll have a better idea of what to do."

It made as much sense as anything else. With the first faint stirrings of hope, Carrie agreed. But what followed, like many facts, stubbornly refused to fit the theory.

CHAPTER XIX

Carrie turned from the living-room window and retraced her path back to the kitchen. No sign of them yet.

I still can't believe I'm doing this. But she held on firmly to one simple, persuasive thought: *It can't hurt.* She repeated it over and over, like a protective spell of her own—Barbara's phrase.

The other woman had been so genuinely concerned, so hurt by Carrie's fears. Her conversation had constantly circled back to that. "We don't expect you to share our beliefs, Carrie. Or even understand them. What's important right now is that we *are* your friends. You may not believe we can help . . . but *please* believe that we're not trying to hurt you."

And Carrie had shakily accepted the reassurance. Besides, she thought wryly, what other choices do I have? Anyone else will think I'm crazy!

But still she waited with every nerve shrieking, and experienced a moment of sheer panic when the doorbell rang.

Around Barbara and Frank, the small front hallway assumed claustrophobic proportions, seeming filled to capacity with people and icy air. They jostled, smiling reassuringly, unwinding scarves and removing coats while exclaiming about the cold, voicing amazement at the wind-chill factor. Carrie looked past them both.

To where Marge came trundling across the threshold, as implacable as a tank—and almost as heavily armed. Her bulging tote bag made a solid *thunk* as she set it on the floor by her feet.

What do you say to a visiting witch? Carrie's nerves, sandpaper-raw with strain, tightened another notch to the verge of hysteria. *Something very polite, of course.* At a loss for the etiquette of exorcism, Carrie grasped at social niceties as she might have clutched the wheel of a skidding car. "Let me take your coat. Won't you sit down? Would you like a cup of coffee—or tea, perhaps?"

"Tea would be nice." Marge nodded agreeably. Carrie garbled something incomprehensible and bolted for the kitchen.

How in hell did I get into this? At the sink, she ran water and sipped slowly, clutching the glass with both hands. Frank loomed behind her. A silent and supportive presence, he patted her shoulder awkwardly and laid out all the wrong utensils for the serving tray.

She half expected a dormouse to emerge from the teapot during the mad party that ensued.

"My, the house looks nice," said Marge, looking around vapidly through thick spectacles. "Barbara said you had done wonders with it." Her short square figure was ensconced at one end of the couch, and she was sipping tea genteelly. The swollen tote bag crouched at her feet like an inanimate beige familiar.

Carrie uttered polite inanities and eyed the unrevealing canvas surface with trepidation. *A crystal ball? Jars of herbs or potions? Eye of newt and toe of frog?*

"A tape recorder."

Marge dropped the flat statement, like a stone, into the running babble of conversation, and Carrie jumped guiltily.

"No, I don't read minds." Marge blinked benignly, her eyes magnified like an owl's behind the thick lenses. "But you were looking at my bag; and people always wonder what kind of arcane paraphernalia I've got with me."

"Well, don't tease, Marge," interjected Barbara. "Tell her what's in the bag."

"Actually," said Marge good-humoredly, "the tape recorder is about as arcane as it gets." She bent over and rummaged in the canvas depths, extracting a small portable recorder that she handed to Frank, and a stack of books that she piled on the nearest end table. "I also brought a few books to lend you—things that may help shed a little light on what's going on."

"I can certainly use that." Carrie flashed her a brief but genuine grin, which almost immediately began to crumble at the edges. "I didn't really know what to expect," she explained. "Barbara said you're a psychic, but I don't know exactly what that means . . . or what you're going to do."

"All it means—at least to me—is that I seem able to get information through some means other than the physical senses. The scientific term is ESP: extrasensory perception. It's nothing terrible or weird," she added, with a hint of defensiveness. "In fact, some people refer to it as a sixth sense; they think it's something we all have, or had in the past. You've probably had brushes with it yourself."

Carrie suppressed a dubious expression; then wondered with wry amusement why she bothered. *How do you hide your feelings from a psychic?* And then, *It must be awful to live with one.*

Barbara leaned forward and set her coffee cup on

240

the floor beside her chair. "Think about it, Carrie. Haven't you ever had a feeling or hunch that turned out to be right? Like thinking about someone you haven't seen in ages, and then running into them. Or knowing who's on the phone before you answer it."

"But that's not ESP."

"Oh yes it is." Marge nodded emphatically. "Most people call it coincidence and let it drop. But by definition, ESP is anything you know without knowing *how* you know it."

Carrie looked crestfallen. "Somehow I always thought psychic powers would be more . . . dramatic than just knowing who's on the phone."

Marge laughed at her wistful tone, but Carrie, chewing at her lower lip, was already worrying at another concept.

"Okay, so you've got this 'extra' sense. But how do you use it? What do you do?"

"It's hard to describe. I try to put everything out of my mind—make it blank. Then I just sort of . . . open myself up. Not straining, like you might with your eyes or ears, but just trying to be . . . open . . . receptive."

"Like in a séance?"

"Spiritualists!" Marge sniffed. "Channeling peace-and-love messages from their Indian spirit guide or somebody's dear departed Aunt Maude!"

"And 'channeling' lots of money out of the suckers' wallets," noted Frank, in disgust.

Barbara quashed them with a look. "Let's not get on that soapbox now, or we'll be here all night." She turned to Carrie. "What they're saying is that it isn't necessary to sit around a table holding hands in the dark."

"Although it would be fun," added Frank, irrepressibly.

Carrie's head swiveled between them in bewilderment. "What *do* we do, then?"

"Nothing outrageous or flamboyant," Marge assured her. "I'm going to walk through the house, that's all, and see what impressions I get."

"Where does the tape recorder come in?"

"It's a control. I'll tell whatever I feel, and Frank will record it as we go along."

Carrie looked puzzled.

"Keeps her honest," Frank teased. "You've probably noticed that most psychics get a whole lot more accurate after the fact. You'll have hordes of people claiming they foresaw a disaster or predicted the results of an election. But damn few of them can prove they were on record *before* it happened."

"That's not the same thing."

"True. But no matter how careful we are, or how honest Marge is"—he tipped his head toward her in acknowledgment—"we tend to remember things the way we *think* they happened or the way they *should* have happened. Not to mention that memories change and fade with time. It's just the way the human mind works. The tape recorder, on the other hand, is always accurate."

It should have been ludicrous. Four intelligent adults stomping around, hunting ghosts with a tape recorder. Marge's foursquare figure led the way, with Frank at her heels flourishing a microphone. Barbara drifted along in their wake, hands in the pockets of her denim skirt, looking around her with as much interest as if she were visiting a museum.

Carrie, bringing up the rear, felt vaguely disappointed, as though they were cheating . . . or at least cutting corners to an unacceptable degree. This sort of endeavor properly required a dark night, with a thunderstorm raging, and candlelight flickering along the tapestried corridors of an ancestral mansion. *No wonder ghosts have been reduced to mere recordings of their former selves. What self-respecting specter would be caught dead haunting a little clapboard cottage in broad daylight?*

The intrepid band descended first to the basement, at Marge's insistence. Holding hard to the reassurance of scientific theory—*You can't be afraid of a tape recording*—Carrie stood on the bottom step and watched as Marge turned her face up to the cobwebbed ceiling and closed her eyes. In the pallid light, her face was clear and trackless, a blank slate. "No," she said finally. "Nothing."

"Nothing" was the refrain as they proceeded up the stairs to the kitchen, and through the dining room. In the living room, near the fireplace, Marge paused, with an intent listening air. "Smoke." She frowned. "Nothing really unusual. Just more of a sense of people . . . activity. The people in the house probably always gathered around the fireplace."

By now the light was thin and gray; a host of shadows crowded them on the stairs, then drew back to stand watchfully around the edges of the upper hallway. "Nothing," reported Marge after a moment. She poked her head briefly into the bathroom and shook her head. "I'm beginning to feel like a failure," she grumbled, her exasperation only partially feigned.

Reluctantly, Carrie opened the door to the back bedroom—their "junk room," where anything not currently in use tended to migrate. "It's a mess," she said apologetically, but everyone else was politely oblivious. Marge was looking around with actual enthusiasm. "There ought to be *something* here," she muttered, half to herself. "Bedrooms are always . . ."

The remainder of her comment was lost as she

threaded her way through the disorder and hauled at a dusty rocking chair. "Maybe it will help if I get more relaxed," she said, moving a pile of *National Geographics* from the seat to the floor. Settling her bulk firmly in the creaking chair, Marge rested her head against the carved back, face lax and open, breathing slowly and deeply. After a time, without any outward change that Carrie could identify, the serene and untenanted expression hardened into a patina of strain. Finally the look of effort crumpled into a frown, and Marge stirred and opened her eyes. "I don't feel anything here, either," she admitted. "I don't understand it."

Nothing. Carrie ignored Frank's half-grin of apology and embarrassment. Nothing, she thought, swallowing hard against a taste like rising sickness. We're standing around playing stupid charades because I don't want to face the fact that my daughter is mentally ill. And maybe I am too.

Carrie followed the rest of them across the hall, then stood leaning, numb and dispossessed, against the doorframe of her own room. Marge, looking grimly determined, took up her station in the room's dilapidated armchair, shoved haphazardly into the front dormer to create a quiet sitting nook. It crossed Carrie's mind to wonder if she would ever savor her favorite reading spot in just the same way again. Gradually the psychic's hands opened and lay still on the chair arms, and her head sank back against the worn upholstery.

This time it took longer. Carrie stood rigid, listening to her own heart, a dainty imperceptible ticking that picked up speed and force as the minutes dragged by. Marge's head moved slowly from side to side, eyes closed, like some blind thing scanning the room with its other senses. Carrie could almost *see* the tension that surrounded her like the dish of a radar antenna. When the other woman's eyes snapped open, she jumped.

"Depression," murmured Marge. She frowned and closed her eyes again. "Someone . . . a woman . . . I can't tell who." Her voice pulled and dredged, digging up something deeply buried. "There were a lot of tears. A child . . . the woman's child . . . not dead, but very troubled."

Frank pressed forward with the tape recorder. "Can you see them? Who they are?"

"No. There's nothing visual; nothing really . . . identifying. Just feelings . . . and they're pretty vague."

Sure are, thought Carrie resentfully. Your Halloween gypsy act was better.

In what seemed to be typical behavior, Marge opened her eyes and mouth simultaneously. "A lot of good *that* is," she grumped, echoing Carrie's thought with disarming honesty. "Doesn't tell us a thing!"

"You could have been picking up Carrie's feelings," hypothesized Frank.

"Or this might have been Mrs. Markwell's room," ventured Barbara helpfully. "Did she have problems with any of her kids? I don't know anything about the owners before her."

Marge flattened them with a look. "It doesn't matter," she said. "What we're looking for is something that could explain Carrie's problems with the house, and this isn't it."

Surprised by the other woman's no-nonsense attitude, Carrie took a new grasp on her own composure. She rubbed abstractedly at her forehead, where a mild headache was beginning to form.

"Your daughter's room next?" asked Marge.

Lee Ann's room. The last place. *If we don't find something there, then what?*

Just inside the doorway, Marge stood immobile,

245

gathering herself. In the low, dying light, her face had a ghastly drowned look. Eyes half-closed, she drifted through the soft shadows, fingers trailing lightly along the edge of the old dresser, moving across the mirror's wavery glass. At the foot of the bed she stopped, head bent, lips moving, leaning on the low bedpost.

Something? Frank shifted nervously where he stood against the wall. Behind him, Carrie stepped reluctantly across the threshold, folding her arms protectively across her chest. *If there's anything wrong in the house, it must be here.*

Marge bent further, fingers clenched on the footrail of the bed. Her stertorous breathing resounded against the low ceiling. *Something?* They waited. But when Marge raised her head it was in a gesture of negation. "I don't get anything helpful here, either," she said slowly.

Despair buzzed bee-like in Carrie's ears, muffling the medium's voice. She closed her eyes, just for a moment, shuttering herself against the bitter disappointment, against the others' glances of uneasy sympathy. *There* isn't *anything wrong with me. There* isn't *anything wrong with Lee Ann. It's something here. Something in the house.* The room was abnormally silent. With an effort, she unwound her arms, releasing herself from the shelter of her own embrace. Something tugged at the edges of her consciousness, sticky and insistent.

From a distance of miles and ages, voices murmured. Gradually they drew near enough to identify: of course . . . Barbara and Frank . . . and Marge.

"There's no feeling of a *presence* at all," someone was saying. "I get a few vague impressions, and that could just be Lee Ann. There's grief and pain . . . a little fear." Marge's usually forthright voice hesitated, cast about for words. "And some of the

246

usual . . . um . . . feelings about growing up."

What absolute crap. Carrie opened her eyes and reached deep for her reserves of strength and patience. "Well," she said lightly, "at least we know what we *don't* have." Frank and Barbara answered her with rueful smiles, but Marge remained tight-wound and fretful, mulling over private failure. Her glance brushed Carrie only lightly, but the feel of it lingered, like spidersilk encountered in the dark.

The dispirited band faltered its way down the stairs and into the kitchen; under hard-edged fluorescent light their shadowy endeavors retreated in disarray. "I can't believe we didn't find *anything*," Barbara said, and she sighed, for the third time. Frank, to his credit, refrained from pointing out the irony in lamenting the *lack* of a ghost. The postmortem looped and circled endlessly in frustration. Nerves jangling, twitchy with reaction, Carrie dispensed tea without sympathy and bit back impatient rejoinders.

She clattered a handful of spoons onto the table. "If there's nothing wrong with the house," she said harshly, "I guess it means both Lee Ann and I are candidates for therapy."

"Not necessarily." Barbara rushed in to soothe, then stopped in bleak consternation, without any idea of what to say next. "Maybe," she offered lamely, "there's something only Lee Ann is sensitive to." Pleased with her idea, she gathered momentum. "Somebody, maybe, who died young. A girl her own age?"

Marge sniffed eloquently. "That wouldn't explain why Carrie's seen things too." She sat lumpishly, frowning into the aromatic steam of her mug; if looks could kill, Carrie would have lost yet another teacup.

"You were picking up some impressions," Barbara, the voice of optimism, put in. "And we don't *know* that they were from Carrie and Lee Ann. It could be someone else—something left from someone who lived here before."

Marge made a muffled noise that could have been the swallowing of a pungent retort. "Sure it could," she said acerbically. "But it was still just background noise—like static. The kind of thing that's in every house." She turned slightly to meet her hostess's eyes. "I'm sorry, Carrie. But there's no sense of anything *active* at all. The house feels . . . ordinary."

CHAPTER XX

Frank coaxed the car into sputtering life and eased it away from the curb. "I guess that does it," he said heavily. "If the house is normal, then the problem must be with Lee Ann."

Barbara sat forward precariously, leaning crossed arms on the seatback between Marge and Frank. "Ordinary is *not* the word for that place," she said emphatically. "There's something wrong in there— I've felt it myself!"

Marge looked back over her shoulder at the house, her square homely face wrinkled in tired and well-worn lines. "I never said there wasn't anything wrong," she reminded them. "As a matter of fact, going through that house was like wading in mud— a sort of sick, disgusting feeling."

Barbara's mouth popped open and stayed that way. "You didn't *say* that!" she sputtered. "Why didn't you say that?"

"Because there wasn't anything *to* say," Marge muttered crossly. "It was just a feeling, that's all." Under Barbara's indignant stare, she continued defensively. "We were looking for a spirit, a presence . . . a ghost, if you will. But there was nothing like that, nothing that could explain the experiences Carrie and Lee Ann have had. And if I couldn't tell her something useful, I wasn't going to say anything. After all," she returned Barbara's glare, "the idea was to help, not just to scare her worse."

"I don't understand it, Marge." Chastened, Barbara shook her head pensively, propping her chin on folded arms. "It doesn't make sense. But there's something wrong in the house. And it's more than just a bad feeling. They've had strange things going on ever since they moved in."

Frank's eyes didn't move from the roadway, but his hands tightened on the steering wheel. "Barbara, this doesn't make sense. It was your idea to bring Marge in for an expert opinion, and now you're refusing to accept it, just because it isn't what you want to hear." His voice was flat and very calm. "Let's face it, everything that's happened in the house has centered around Lee Ann. And we're chasing around in circles looking for a supernatural explanation because none of us wants to admit that the child is . . . disturbed."

Barbara's voice wavered very slightly before she controlled it. "Maybe I'm being unrealistic. But I don't believe we have the whole answer. Not yet." She drew herself up very straight on the edge of the back seat. "For one thing, I *know* what I felt in that house—more than once, several times."

"More than once? But not all the time?" Marge twisted sideways against the encumbering seatbelt and raised her voice to be heard above the car's laboring engine.

"No. Just a few times." Barbara tilted her head to one side consideringly. "And that's strange, isn't it? I mean, either a house is haunted, or it's not." Her laugh was raw, strung tight with nerves. "There's no such thing as a part-time ghost." Further discussion was cut off as Frank shifted gears abruptly and swung the car around a corner, sending her sprawling sideways.

Marge clutched at a handle above the door and

nodded serenely, face furrowed in thought. "That is unusual."

"That's probably because it's not a ghost at all," interjected Frank, more vehemently. "We're dealing with poltergeist phenomena, directly caused by Lee Ann! You explained it to Carrie yourself, Barbara."

"But the poltergeist theory doesn't account for the things her mother saw . . . or the feelings I had." Barbara levered herself upright and took a firmer grasp on the seat edge.

Frank's face was bleak. "If the kid can throw coffee mugs around and move the furniture without touching it, why couldn't she project a shadow on the wall?"

"I've never heard of that happening." Barbara examined the new possibility, her forehead corrugated in concentration.

"And these feelings you've had—"

"Not just me!" she snapped defensively. "There's Carrie and Lee Ann, and Penny says the place gives her the creeps a lot of the time."

Marge turned her head attentively, but neither of them noticed as Frank continued: "What could be more likely to cause a 'wrong' feeling in a house than an emotionally disturbed child?"

Barbara's mouth shut with an almost audible click.

In the face of her distress, Frank's voice was gentle. "I'm not doubting your word at all, Barbara. Or Carrie's. And I understand your feelings. Maybe better than you think." His voice came through deeper and roughened, like something torn. "Given a choice between a ghost and psychosis, I'd far rather have the ghost." He cleared his throat painfully. "But I don't think we've got that choice. Don't you see? If it were a ghost—a real spirit or just a 'recording'—Marge would have sensed it."

They pulled up to the curb in front of Marge's

251

apartment, where the car sputtered with relief and died. Frank switched it off and then sat motionless, holding his shoulders as square and upright as the headstone on a grave. "We've eliminated those possibilities, Barbara. Much as we all hate to admit it, we've run out of answers."

In the passenger seat, Marge emerged from thoughtful silence and dropped a typically succinct comment into the dead conversation. "There is one other possibility we haven't considered," she began.

Two faces turned to her sharply.

"That it's something intelligent . . . and it's avoiding us."

By then it had begun to snow, tugging an isolating blanket around the house, muffling street sounds to a distant murmur. Beyond the kitchen window, the back yard billowed away like clouds, glowing with soft sourceless snowlight. Carrie set the tea things in the sink and stood looking out, unable to think of a good reason for doing anything else.

At length she spoke to herself sternly and clicked on the overhead light, filling the room with cold fluorescent glare and turning the windows to icy black mirrors. More out of habit than hunger, she began to fix dinner, rattling pans to drive away the stillness.

The evening stretched away into infinity. Carrie ate doggedly and did the dishes, her pale reflection in the steamy window mimicking her actions. She forced herself to take up a pile of hated mending and sat sewing on buttons as if doing penance. In the corner the old television set flickered with a comforting illusion of companionship.

At nine she stretched, put aside her needle and thread, and decided to indulge herself with an hour or so of reading in bed. It was still snowing lightly as she made her rounds through the quiet house, checking doors and windows. As she passed through the living room, she picked up the top book from Marge's stack and carried it upstairs with her.

The snow had turned to sleet, whispering along the sills and scratching at the bedroom window like tiny claws. Carrie drew thick curtains against the dark and undressed quickly, cold fingers fumbling with buttons. In the dim lamplight, the reflection of her body swam whitely across the mirror's dim and wavy glass. She pulled a froth of nightgown over her head, silken folds cascading like a shiver down the length of her body.

Her hand brushed Marge's book and dropped beside it to clutch the edge of the dressertop. *I don't care what Marge says. I know what I saw and heard. What both of us saw and heard.* She frowned, turning inward to pursue an idea that had eluded her before. Neither of them had ever had experiences like this before—not in the apartment. Not even after Matt's death. *Doesn't that prove there's nothing wrong with us? That there's really something in the house?*

Carrie raised her head slowly and met her own stark gaze in the mirror, eyes shadowed and bruised-looking. *Why couldn't Barbara be right? Maybe for some reason we're specially tuned in to it—like they said about the radio receiver. After all, it's our house.*

Without thinking, she slipped a housecoat around rigid shoulders. *And she's my daughter. So maybe it has to be my responsibility. Maybe it's something Marge can't do for me.*

She opened the door, half expecting a gleam of acknowledging light from Lee Ann's room, but the space across the hall lay gray and silent. With no real idea of what she would do, Carrie slipped across the threshold and stood quietly, mingling with the swarming shadows.

The cold this time was a delicate snare, creeping

253

up almost imperceptibly and tightening around her in an immobilizing grasp. Beneath the velvety robe, she could feel the satiny stuff of her gown lying along her body like a layer of frost. Her nipples rose unbidden, knotted against the chill. Eyes widening in the dark, she crossed her arms against her chest in a parody of a comforting embrace.

What now? Suppressing the urge to flee, Carrie huddled into her heavy wrapper, hands busily rubbing warmth into her upper arms. What had Marge said? *Try to put everything out of my mind . . . make it blank. Just sort of . . . open myself up.*

Carrie closed her eyes, concentrated, produced a sort of blank screen, which wavered and gave way to a tumble of thoughts and images. *What is it supposed to feel like? How will I know?* She frowned and stilled herself again, maintaining a mental dike against the insistent flood. *There has to be something. There's nothing wrong with my mind . . . nothing wrong with Lee Ann.*

She waited. Her feet grew numb, her fingers thickened with the cold. Nothing happened. Ragged breaths went deeper and deeper, struggling to fill her lungs. Her body felt distant, light and floating, hollow with fear. Did something move—real or imagined—in the blackness she had spread out for it? She gasped dizzily, prickling back to awareness of the sapping, breathless cold.

Damn it, if there's something there, let me know. What do you want? Damn you, what do you want? She tilted her head defiantly, closed her eyes, and *willed.*

The obscene cold retreated before her onslaught. Darkness coiled inside her head, and—*There*—just for a moment—*there*—she almost had it. For the briefest of seconds, she groped outward in the blackness, and seemed to reach . . . touch . . . something

Something that was aware of her. Something that knew she was there.

Inside her chest, her heart lurched and stuttered sickly. The tenuous contact evaporated, curled away like mist, and the bed hit her in the back of the knees. Carrie sat down abruptly. *When had she moved?*

Nausea touched the base of her throat as her body forced itself to reacquaintance, pulse drumming thickly in her ears, heartbeat shifting restlessly in its cage of bone.

We were right. But the thought had little meaning. Her head was swimming, unable to put ideas together. Tiny explosions of light burst before her eyes and she slumped sideways, lying limp and resistless beneath the weight of the avid, swollen air.

Darkness thickened before her eyes and hummed in her ears. There was someone there. Someone. Eyes on her . . . watching . . . coming closer. Carrie shifted weakly. In a warding-off gesture she flung out a hand that fell helplessly to the bed. She couldn't breathe. Fretful, she tugged at the sash of her robe and pulled it open with fingers that trembled. Under the flimsy nightgown, her body was slick with sweat. The room felt . . . full.

In the next room, incredibly distant, the phone rang. Carrie jerked spasmodically, as with the jolting shock of a misstep on a staircase. In automatic response, she swung her legs over the side of Lee Ann's bed and made her way unsteadily through the darkness. The familiar hallway looped and swung around her dizzily, receding endlessly like a house of mirrors.

The man jerked too, swarming backward with a shock that left him breathless. That had been close. He licked dry lips and waited, pausing to light a cigarette, cupping his hands automatically around

255

the flare of the match even though there was really no one to see, no one to object. *Not what he had expected*. But still he'd stayed in control; overcoming his initial disappointment, playing her along just like the girl. He licked his lips again. *If the phone hadn't rung . . .*

It might have been rather fun at that. Perhaps his tastes were maturing.

Carrie dropped heavily to the bed in her room, fumbling the phone to her ear. "Hello?"

Frank's commonplace voice steadied her like a dash of ice water. "I woke you up," he said apologetically.

It took her a moment to remember what she was supposed to say. "No. No, I was awake."

"Didn't sound like it." He cleared his throat and continued awkwardly. "I just wanted to see if you were okay."

Balanced on the blade-edge between triumph and terror, Carrie struggled to order her thoughts. Could she tell him what had happened? What, after all, really *had* happened? Nothing, she decided, that could be coherently explained or described. "I'm fine" was all she finally said.

Frank bore on relentlessly. "I was a little worried about you being by yourself."

His clumsy concern tugged at the edge of her confidence. Deeply touched and bone-tired, Carrie resisted an almost overwhelming desire to blurt out her confused and disjointed tale. "I'm fine," she repeated perversely.

The phone in her hand hissed and faded into near silence; in panic, Carrie tightened her grip as though on a lifeline. "Frank? Are you there? Frank?"

The receiver emitted enigmatic electronic sounds Frank's voice emerged seconds later, as though it had just now found its way through the crackling web. "Carrie? Can you hear me?"

"Yes," she breathed out in relief.

The static abated, leaving his voice as clear as though he were standing beside her. "I'm sorry about today."

"It was worth a try," she said, trying hard for a tone of lightness. "And it's not your fault it didn't work."

"It should have, though. We were talking about it after we left. . . ."

"And what did you decide?" she asked tartly. "That we're just a couple of neurotics?"

The silence that ensued lasted only a few seconds, but it gave Carrie more than enough time to regret her acerbic tone. She slumped tiredly onto the edge of the bed, beginning to mutter an apology; then came bolt upright, clutching the receiver hard, as sharp yellow light flared behind her. Across the small stretch of landing, the doorway to Lee Ann's room shone like a beacon.

Frank's reassuring tones sounded faintly in her ear, as if through a veil of static; but this time the buzzing that blanketed his voice was in her head.

"Frank?" Strained through her rigid throat, her own voice was thin and almost inaudible. She wondered if he could hear her. "Frank!"

"Carrie? Are you all right?"

She drooped against the headboard, hitching breath into depleted lungs. "Yes. No. Frank," she said desperately, "we're not crazy. There really is something in the house." She drew her cold feet up and tucked them under the hem of the heavy robe. "I went into Lee Ann's room and tried . . . what Marge did."

"You *what?*" His voice was a howl of outrage.

"I had to. Don't you see? It's my house, and she's my daughter. And maybe for some reason we're the

257

only ones who can get in touch with this—whatever it is."

"Carrie . . ."

"Look," she interrupted, "the house sat vacant for years, but Barbara told me she never heard any stories about it being haunted. And Lee Ann and I never had any funny experiences in the apartment, even though that was where we lived when . . . when Matt died." Some disassociated part of her mind noted in passing that the words were becoming easier to say. She drew a deep breath and plunged on. "Do you see? If this was an ordinary haunting, Marge should have felt something. If Lee Ann and I were just crazy or neurotic or in shock, then things should have started happening before—in the apartment."

She reached out defiantly and turned on her own bedside lamp, deadening the invasive glow from the corridor. "It's as though nothing could happen until we came to the house. Like it was waiting for us."

"Oh God." Frank's hushed exhalation was almost a groan. "Carrie, what did you do?"

"I told you. I went into Lee Ann's room and tried what Marge told me she did . . . just being open and sort of . . . receptive."

"And you got something?"

She hesitated, searching for the right words. "I *think* so," she said carefully. "It was just for a second, but it was so *real*. Overwhelmingly real. There was someone there, and I just *knew*—without seeing or hearing or touching. I *knew*." She didn't mention the feelings that came after, the smothering weight and the lethargic, swooning blackness; already she was putting them out of her mind, letting them become unreal.

She heard his indrawn breath over the phone and hastened back to the parts she could tell, letting her words tumble faster, beseechingly. "And the light in that room came on again. By itself. Just now."

"Carrie, maybe you should call the police." His voice sharpened with alarm.

"And what?" She strove for a tone of lightness but without great success. "Ask them to come arrest a ghost?"

"Just have them come and look the place over. I don't like what's going on around there."

"Frank, the doors are locked and it's perfectly quiet. Whatever it was in Lee Ann's room, it *wasn't* a burglar."

"Then what was it?"

There was an extended silence before she answered, very quietly. "I don't know."

He muttered something that should have been unpronounceable and was probably unprintable. "Carrie, I don't think you should stay there by yourself tonight. Why don't you go over to the Burnetts'? I can call Barbara—"

Her objection was a shrill squeak. "I can't call someone at this hour and go running around in the snow! Besides, what would I tell them? That I'm afraid of the dark?"

"Barbara would understand."

And what about tomorrow? And the night after that . . . and the night after that? "No, Frank. It's just out of the question."

"Then I'm coming over there!"

Carrie huffed an exasperated sigh. "Frank, this is ridiculous. It's late, and it's snowing."

"The snow has stopped," he said offhandedly. "Would you be afraid to come downstairs and let me in?"

"No, of course not!" she denied indignantly.

"Then I'll be there in about twenty minutes," he said, and hung up on her sputtered protest.

Despite her exclamations of bravado, Carrie stayed huddled on the bed, reluctant to leave the comforting circle of lamplight. Not until she heard Frank's car

259

crunch across the gravel drive did she fly barefoot across the landing and down the stairs. He came through the kitchen door, stamping feet, shaking snow, and inquiring about coffee. Carrie shivered from cold and relief, and admired the way the house settled around him in ersatz domesticity. She measured coffee into the filter, then sent him upstairs for her forgotten slippers.

Over cooling cups of coffee, much later, Carrie's story stumbled to a halt. "That's all that really happened," she said defensively. And yawned.

He grinned at her cheerfully. "That's enough to have had *me* hiding under the bed," he said.

"My hero." She grinned back reluctantly. And yawned again.

"Why don't you try to get some sleep? I'll sit up down here," he offered good-naturedly. "Or sleep on the couch. Although I'd like to look into Lee Ann's room first, if you don't mind."

"Not at all." She looked at him humbly. "I don't really want to go up there by myself right now."

Upstairs, the bar of light from Lee Ann's room lay like a flung gauntlet across the hallway. Frank strode through the striped shadows into the doorway and stopped in shock and surprise, whistling softly between his teeth. "Cold," he said.

Behind him, Carrie nodded dumbly and stood on tiptoe, trying to see over his shoulder. When he moved into the room, she followed, staying close to the door and watching as he prowled slowly around. The overhead light was thin and arid, less a defense against the dark than a pallid conspirator. It reduced the room to a two-dimensional false front, behind which anything might lurk.

At the front dormer Frank stopped, examining the window, bending down to the floor. "There's a slight draft, but not that bad," he explained. "And the heat registers are open."

Carrie sipped tentatively at the icy air, loath to take it into her lungs. She crossed her arms tightly across her upper body. "I don't think this is exactly an ordinary cold."

"No," he shook his head, agreeing despite himself. "I don't think so."

"Do you feel anything else? Anything . . . wrong?"

He moved across to the windowed end wall, frowning abstractedly. "I'm no psychic," he said. "The room seemed perfectly ordinary this afternoon. To Marge as well as me. But right now I feel really uneasy." He glanced around the room, then smiled wryly. "It may just be the power of suggestion, but I don't think I'd want to sleep in here."

Carrie released a jerky breath and smiled at him gratefully. "I wasn't imagining things, Frank. I really wasn't."

His downcast face was in shadow as he turned, facing her across Lee Ann's narrow bed. The pretty ruffled coverlet lay between them like a field of flowers. "No, Carrie, I don't believe you were." His breathing was shallow, as reluctant as hers. His hands clenched and unclenched nervously.

Carrie began to shiver. With apparent effort, Frank wrenched himself into motion, extending a hand and leading her hurriedly toward the door.

"For one thing," he said flippantly, "your imagination didn't turn the light on." He smacked at the switch as they passed, and the darkness took possession once again.

"That doesn't prove a thing, of course," Carrie gabbled nervously. "I could have switched it on myself."

"But you didn't." At the door to her room, he drew her into his arms and held her silently. Telling herself it was just for a moment, she leaned against him, eyes shut, feeling a more-than-physical warmth rise languorously to enfold her. When he finally bent his head to hers, Carrie met his mouth eagerly, shaken by a feverish rush that engulfed her like an alien tide.

The loosened sash of her robe fell away and his hands slipped gently across her silken-clad body. Together they reentered the magic circle of lamplight that lay around her bed, their embrace first tentative, then increasingly urgent . . . and the viscid golden light trapped the moment in amber.

CHAPTER XXI

Carrie fidgeted and sneaked a look at the big round clock above her head. Almost four. They'd spent the entire afternoon in this depressing room somewhere in the courthouse basement, poring over antiquated records, looking for information that might not even exist. She sneezed, turned a page, and reached for a tissue from her depleted stock. "I don't believe how dusty these old books are. They must not have been used for years."

Across the table, Barbara examined her grimy hands and nodded glumly. "I can't imagine why anyone would want one of them. It's not exactly light bedtime reading."

"They're valuable civic records," said Marge, plunking yet another oversized volume down in the middle of the scarred old table.

Barbara groaned; the middle-aged woman at the clerk's desk lifted her head and peered inquiringly at them over the counter. Carrie resisted an urge to giggle; wound tight with sleeplessness and roller-coaster emotion, she knew that laughter would too easily turn to hysterical tears.

She and Frank had spent the previous Sunday

morning deep in discussion, over the breakfast buffet at a nearby restaurant. "We're not hiding," he had reminded her with superb dignity as he reached for a blueberry muffin. "Think of it as a strategic retreat."

They had, indeed, left the house in such haste it was almost flight. Waking slowly, drugged with belated sleep and the warm comfort of someone's arms, Carrie had jolted suddenly to wide-eyed awareness and the realization that Lee Ann could come home at any time. "It isn't really *likely*, of course," she assured him soothingly, prodding ribs and watching for signs of consciousness. "I've never known Lee Ann to come home from a sleepover before noon." Frank, wrapped snugly in all the bedclothes, appeared to be in no need of assurance; he opened one eye and closed it again, showing no trace of nervousness and only a few signs of life. Carrie filed away the fact that he was not, apparently, a morning person.

Finally upright and more or less awake, he had resisted her efforts to send him home. "I knew you wouldn't respect me in the morning," he complained piteously. And Carrie, laughing, gave up and agreed to go out for breakfast, leaving a note for Lee Ann.

They heaped plates at the buffet and retired to the farthest corner of the restaurant, anonymous amid the bustling Sunday after-church crowd. Carrie attacked eggs and bacon with unexpected appetite, eyes on her plate, rebuilding defenses bit by bit. Midnight visitations seemed vastly out of place in the matter-of-fact morning, but she could no longer push the subject into invisibility or insignificance. It had become too all-consuming for that.

Finally they faced each other, almost shyly, across the littered table. "You don't think I'm crazy, then?" she asked wonderingly. "You really don't." This time it was a statement, encouraged by the support and kindness in his eyes.

Frank shook his head decisively. "No. Neither does Barbara. Or Marge." He chased a last bit of scrambled egg around with his fork and speared it triumphantly. "Like I said, we were talking about it. . . ." He popped the bite into his mouth and chewed.

"And?" prodded Carrie impatiently.

"And we came up with some possibilities," he continued cautiously. "Just because Marge didn't sense anything doesn't mean it's a total dead end. She said so herself."

Carrie looked at him over the rim of her coffee cup, noting idly that the hand that held it was shaking. "I hadn't realized how much I was depending on Marge," she said. "And when she didn't find anything . . ." Her eyes brimmed suddenly, but she didn't look away. "I don't think there could be anything worse than doubting your own sanity."

The last of his own misgivings fled as he watched her determined effort to quell self-pity. He covered her hand with his, trying to decide what he could say . . . and how much.

"To begin with," he began, "it could be that all this is an extension, somehow, of the poltergeist."

Her mouth hardened, but her eyes met his candidly, matching his effort at openness. "You mean Lee Ann could cause all of that?" Carrie cocked her head to one side, frowning. "Playing tricks with light and shadow instead of moving objects?"

He nodded. "I know you don't like the idea, but we have to at least consider it."

"You said there was another possibility."

"It could be that your visitor is . . . limited . . . in time as well as space."

She seized on the idea immediately. "You mean it can only appear at certain times? That could explain why Marge didn't feel anything—she was there at the wrong time."

He could find at least one flaw in each premise, but he fervently hoped she wouldn't. He didn't want to have to tell her about Marge's last idea. Finally she nodded, satisfied, and he realized that he had been holding his breath.

"We talked once before about doing some research on the house. It'll be boring, but I think that's our next logical step." His voice was decisive, filling the spaces where logic gapped. "Marge will be invaluable there. She's been a library aide for several years now, and she'll know exactly what to do." He took her hand again. "We'll help, Carrie. I told you— you're not all by yourself anymore."

The conversation faltered then, silence ballooning almost palpable between them. An overly cheerful waitress refilled their cups and Frank busied himself with paper packets of sugar. The midmorning crowd was filtering away gradually, leaving them alone in their corner.

By mutual consent they'd discussed everything except the previous night. Still it stretched between them—something to hold on to. And there seemed to be no real need for words.

The house was empty when they returned, and Carrie gratefully discarded the explanation she had prepared for Lee Ann, happy that it wasn't needed. They said a decorous goodbye at the door, and she watched Frank walk away, slowly, down the front walk. On a sudden impulse she poised at the edge of the porch. "Yes," she called after him, and watched him turn, puzzled, eyebrows at the hairline.

"I still respect you in the morning."

His answering laugh was warm and loving.

Now another thick ledger lay on the vast table like a challenge, closed tight as an oyster on its pearls of knowledge. Barbara looked at it dubiously and brushed back a lock of hair, leaving a smudge of dust across her forehead. "Why couldn't there have been a nice neat family Bible in your attic?" she grumbled.

"We don't have an attic," Carrie pointed out. "The bedrooms are right under the eaves." She rubbed gritty fingers together, turned a page, and continued scanning the barely legible records. "It wouldn't help anyway," she continued reasonably. "This isn't some ancestral mansion that's been in the same family for hundreds of years. It's probably had dozens of owners."

Barbara sighed, pulled the next big book toward her, and began to scan through it determinedly. "This isn't the way it happens in gothic novels," she lamented.

"No, but it makes a lot better sense," commented Marge, relishing her role as intrepid guide in the dusty wilderness of courthouse archives. "We already found out that the house was built in 1936; now we go through the property transfers to find the names of all the different owners."

"Then what?" asked Carrie, intrigued in spite of herself. The superbly well-organized Marge had laid out their regimen like a battle plan. And perhaps, after all, that's what it was.

"Then we look up birth and death records for those families," explained Marge. "That will give us dates, so we can go to the newspaper's files and look for obituaries or stories with more information."

Barbara sneezed and turned another page. "I found one!" she said excitedly. Reaching for the pad and pencil in front of her, she began to scribble. "This is a 1947 sale; there can't be too many more owners after that, can there? Mrs. Markwell owned the house for at least thirty years, I'm sure."

Both Marge and Carrie agreed with her, soothingly, leaving their own reservations unspoken, though at this point the hunt looked endless.

The days clattered past in a kind of noisy limbo of office routine, demands of home and housework, and time snatched from both for seemingly endless research. Carrie's two free weekdays and many of her Saturday hours disappeared in the labyrinths of library stacks and courthouse archives.

Nights came, always too soon and too dark, the moon as it waned reduced to a lightless sliver in overcast skies. Carrie's optimism waned with it, as the search produced endless lists and bits of information but no useful results. The house's history seemed as unblemished as the average owner could possibly wish. Had it not been for the unflagging support of her friends, the investigation would soon have ground to an unproductive halt. And despite her frustration and disappointment, Carrie was amused by her seemingly unreasonable desire to discover some blot on her home's reputation.

Her search was moving now on its own momentum without the frantic urgency of midnight fears. The nights were as quiet as they were dark, swathed in a velvet that swallowed light and sound. Nevertheless, Carrie continued to wake routinely sometime near three A.M., responding to an inner alarm like the one that woke her every morning just before the clock buzzed. But through the weeks, nothing moved in the silent house.

This Saturday found her settled in still another courthouse cubbyhole, where the surroundings were almost as disheartening as the task, with chipped linoleum and dirty walls of institutional green, and uncomfortable chairs drawn up to a battered table. Frank sat beside her, growling menacingly at an uncooperative ledger; Barbara had been dispatched to ransack the newspaper's back files; and Marge, who had loyally continued to turn up for every excursion, was across the table with her nose in still another book.

Frank sneezed and loosed a volley of invective at the handwriting of some forgotten scribe. "I can't figure out why they didn't use typewriters," he told the yellowing page in a tone of acrimony.

"The pages of these big ledgers are too big to go in a typewriter," Marge pointed out sensibly.

"Then they should have used smaller books," he said, with a logic that was irrefutable, if a few years too late.

Hours later, Frank brought the car to a panting halt in Carrie's driveway. The passenger-side door opened halfway with a rusty scream and Carrie emerged, clutching the day's sheaf of notes and wondering tiredly what she was going to fix for dinner. Somewhere en route from the courthouse he had accepted an invitation, and although she wasn't quite sure how that had happened, it did seem only fair to provide the meal.

They were investigating the contents of the freezer when Barbara showed up, with her own contribution from the newspaper files.

"I found clippings about three of the former owners, including two obituaries," she said, "but I don't think it's anything helpful." She produced a handful of smudgy copies and spread them out on the dining-room table. "This guy"—she pointed— "got elected an officer of the Rotary club; but he was barely middle-aged then, and his family was young. It doesn't seem likely that any of them would have died. He's still in the phone book, even."

She shuffled papers and laid two more copies on top. "Here are the obituaries. One was a young child—the daughter of a couple who owned the place in 1947. It doesn't say whether she died at home or not. And the other one we already knew about—Mrs. Markwell. She owned the house when she died, but she didn't die *in* it."

Frank and Carrie passed the papers back and forth, examining them glumly. Extracting a note pad from her purse, Barbara frowned at its burden of unintelligible scratches. "I couldn't find anything at all about two of the families who lived there. And there were absolutely no murders, disappearances, mysterious deaths, or screams in the night." Her mouth drooped. "It's really very disappointing."

Carrie sighed. "How about a cookie?" she asked. "Consolation for all that hard work." Barbara munched, stowing her notepad and patting the papers into a neater pile, busy as a chipmunk. "On the brighter side," she noted, "I *did* find a hint of scandal."

It took all the energy Carrie could muster to raise her eyebrows and look interested. "Oh?" she said, around her own mouthful.

"Turns out that I went to high school with one of the women who works in the file department; she said there were some rumors about Mrs. Markwell's son. He was a schoolteacher, and it seems he was fired—or forced to resign. No details, but he left his job under a cloud, and apparently moved away right after that."

"But he didn't die?"

"No," admitted Barbara. And they each had another cookie.

Carrie and Frank were still talking at the dinner table when something went "thunk" just above their heads. Frank looked up with interest, half expecting plaster to rain down in his plate.

270

Carrie didn't even raise her head. "Lee Ann throws things when she gets mad," she explained, and waved her fork in a world-weary gesture. "Sometimes she even uses her hands."

Upstairs Lee Ann slammed the closet door. *At least she won't give me any static about going out tonight. They'll be glad to be alone, I'm sure.*

She had come in to find Barbara and Frank huddled with her mother in deep conversation, which had stopped as soon as she walked in. *Discussing me and all my problems, I guess. Hypocrites.*

Frank, of course, had stayed for dinner. *All this time I thought he was my friend. And he was just using me to get close to Mom.* She pulled a sweater out of the dresser and kicked the drawer shut. *And she can't wait to line up a replacement for Dad. Lose one and go on to the next, is that the way it works? At least for some people.*

But not for me. Lee Ann faced herself in the mirror and tears of self-pity sprang to her eyes. *I can't forget him, no matter what.*

Another series of thuds echoed down from overhead; a fugitive Pandora came slinking down the stairs and took shelter beneath the table, watching hopefully for dropped scraps. In short order the cat was followed by her owner. Smartly dressed in faded jeans and an oversized sweater, Lee Ann hovered in the doorway, poised for flight, quick and airy as a hummingbird. "I'm going out, Mom," she said unnecessarily.

"Where are you going?"

"Skating."

"Who with?"

The young face closed like shutters. "Danny," she muttered. "And some kids from school."

271

Carrie frowned. "You didn't tell me you had a date."

"It's not a date. Not like *yours*, anyway." The girl's glance was meaningful, her tone insolent. Carrie flushed despite herself.

"What time will you be back?"

Lee Ann spun lightly on the balls of her feet and headed for the door. "I don't know exactly," she threw back over her shoulder. Hand on the doorknob, she paused, mouth pinched, brows raised archly. "But I'm sure it will be late enough."

It was almost midnight before Frank left—early enough, as it turned out. An hour afterward, Carrie was still awake, sitting at the small bedroom table that served as a desk, poring once more over the impressive collection of notes and photocopies that lay spread out before her. She shoved Pandora, who was trying to take a nap in the middle of the yellow legal pad aside and looked again at the clock, alternating between fury and worry at her daughter's lateness. Her head had begun to ache. Surely Lee Ann would be home soon. It was more than half an hour past her curfew already.

Carrie began to gather papers and shove them into drawers, bundling all evidence of the research out of sight. Lee Ann didn't need to know about all this. Not yet . . . not until they found an answer. If they ever did.

The wastebasket under her desk overflowed, so Carrie wadded up one last copy and threw it at the wall. She turned out the desk lamp and began to prepare for bed. *Lee Ann will be home any minute . . . leave a light on for her.* Across the hall, she reached around the frame of the door to her daughter's room and, for once, turned on the light. Typical adolescent mess blazed into view—schoolbooks open on the desk, clothes strewn across the unmade bed, hairbrush and cosmetics on the pretty wicker table. And at the dresser . . . one small snapshot curled smugly against the mirror. Minus the cracked glass and cheap dimestore frame, a too-familiar photo grinned at her with Matt's face.

Something chased her through her dreams that night. And at some point it caught her.

Carrie came awake with a pulse-thudding spasm as if she'd dreamed of falling. The room was cold and very, very dark; the moon had set, the stars were veiled, and all the lights in the world had died.

She lay very still, gathering fragments of herself, pulling at memories, taking inventory. Saturday night. *That's right, we spent the day doing research at the courthouse. Frank and I. And the evening . . .*

What time is it? I can't see the clock.

In the hall outside her door, something creaked. Lee Ann? Carrie sat up, *listening*, straining to see, groping in the darkness with another, unacknowledged sense.

No, wait. She's home. I heard her come in, just after I went to bed. I remember.

The noise came again, tentatively, stretching like black wings in the shadows, rasping at the silence with its talons. Carrie's heart stuttered, gathering itself for a frantic leap. *Lee Ann's room. It's in Lee Ann's room.*

She slid—slithered—across the edge of the bed, and brought herself upright on nerveless legs, gripping the bedpost with fingers that were cold as bone. Knees locked, she walked stiff-legged across the room like someone on stilts, pulse beating and surging, blood thundering in her ears. Around her the darkness glittered with illusory not-light.

And a tiny furry body came hurtling toward her.

"Pandora!" It was a cliché from a bad suspense film. The little cat went flying past, into Carrie's room and onto her bed, burrowing into the disarrayed bedclothes. Carrie sagged with relief and almost burst into hysterical laughter. She retreated gratefully from the black-limned doorway, sank onto the edge of the bed and reached for the cat.

Across the hall, in her daughter's room, the noises began again.

Perhaps there is a limit to fear, some saturation point beyond which the mind simply refuses to go. For whatever reason, Carrie moved this time almost easily, a puppet with a string that drew her steadily toward the door and into the yawning darkness of the hall.

She paused on the threshold of Lee Ann's room gasping at the sudden shock of cold. Her daughter was in bed. The noises had ceased. Carrie leaned forward as though against a physical barrier, and turned her head haltingly, half expecting to hear rigid muscles creak. The floor beside the desk was littered with books and papers knocked down by the cat in her flight. On the dresser an old doll lay sprawled obscenely.

Nothing was visibly wrong. But something in the room swelled and *billowed*, like a curtain in the wind. On the bed Lee Ann moved restlessly, making small wordless effort-sounds.

The room grew, if possible, even colder.

In a moment, something would happen. Something.

Bedsprings creaked. Lee Ann gasped and arched head back, arms flung up across the pillow.

An inarticulate sound that might have been a sob battered its way through Carrie's clenched throat.

Across the room her daughter pressed deeply into the bedclothes, flinging her head from side to side against the pillow. "No," she whimpered. But

274

slowly, very slowly, she drew her knees up and apart.

Carrie, watching, was certain that she would be sick. She pressed knotted hands against her mouth, hard, bringing the coppery taste of blood welling from the inside of her lip. This was real. This was . . . ohgod . . . really happening.

"Lee Ann!" she whispered. Then again, more loudly, "Lee Ann!"

The bed creaked heavily, sagged and rebounded; Lee Ann surged upright, sending blankets tumbling. Eyes vague and shadowed, she looked at her mother with no sign of recognition. Her mouth was soft and blurred, as though from rough kisses. Despite the room's chill, her skin glistened moistly; the childish sleep-shirt lay open at her throat and clung damply down her body. Through the light knit fabric her taut nipples were clearly visible.

Carrie's courage had utterly failed; in its place rose sheer animal instinct, raw and primal, pushing her forward with the maternal imperative to protect the young.

She hurled herself against the barrier of obscene cold, onto the bed, arms outstretched, making her own body a shelter and protection. Her daughter sat passive and motionless while Carrie tugged the nightshirt down across her knees and drew the blankets up around them both . . . fragile refuge against bad dreams and bogeymen.

"It's cold," said Lee Ann. "Mommy." And she began to cry.

CHAPTER XXII

At first it didn't seem like light at all, merely a lessening of the darkness. But gradually pale grayness drifted like vapor through the windows, and identifiable objects began to emerge from the gloom. Carrie blinked groggily with eyelids rough as sandpaper. The morning had been very long in coming.

Lee Ann, exhausted, lay diagonally across the bed, taking up the greatest possible amount of space for one small body. Her breathing was regular, her face calm; but one hand remained twined fast in the sash of her mother's robe. Carrie huddled beside her in one free corner, feet drawn up like a child who fears monsters under the bed. Her head ached from its uncomfortable angle against the headboard; but the discomfort had been welcome during the night, when she had been afraid to sleep.

Now, with the room lightening, she dared to stretch, slowly and cautiously so as not to disturb Lee Ann. She touched her daughter's hair softly and wondered what they would do.

With no appetite for breakfast, Carrie simply sat over coffee, thoughts bumping painfully over old worries like a record needle stuck in a groove. *Am I wasting valuable time hunting ghosts when what I should be looking for is a good psychiatrist?* Typically, she was slow and deliberate in forming opinions, but once she did, her convictions were usually unshakable. It had taken her a long time to admit that there was something wrong in her house, and now she wanted to cling to that belief; for despite the lack of real, concrete evidence, the only alternative was far more frightening.

Lee Ann appeared much earlier than usual, looking disgustingly normal and demanding breakfast in stentorian tones. Amazed, Carrie watched her daughter down orange juice, bacon, and a stack of waffles that would have served a small village. Anyone but her mother might not have noticed that her hands were trembling.

Now Lee Ann had retreated to her room, and Carrie wondered idly at the instinct that still sought refuge in a place that had held so much terror. Following her own instinct, she reached for the phone.

"I'm sorry I woke you up," she said insincerely. At her ear Frank's disembodied voice mumbled something polite and probably equally insincere.

She drew an uneven breath and forced words through a throat that felt like a sieve. "Last night . . ."

At the other end of the line Frank came immediately alert. "What happened?"

She told him, flatly, simply, words falling in the blunt cadence of dripping water that could wear away stone. "So I'm going to talk to Keith again about finding her a shrink. I don't have any other choice."

"I'm sorry, Carrie." His voice sounded as tired as hers. "Keith will know someone. . . . I think there's a woman therapist in town who is supposed to be very good with children."

277

"I'm probably going to put the house up for sale, too." She sighed. "I still believe there's something wrong here—something that's not just in Lee Ann's mind. But there doesn't seem to be anything I can do about it. And I can't afford to gamble with my daughter's sanity."

"No, of course not. But look, Carrie, there may be one other possibility. If you're going to the Burnetts' to see Keith, let's talk to Barbara too."

"We're out of coffee," mourned Barbara, peering forlornly into the canister. "But I can make tea. Or cocoa." She stood on tiptoe to grope about in the cabinet. "How about cocoa? And cookies. If the kids haven't eaten them all."

"Sounds good," said Carrie, who was wandering aimlessly around the kitchen, jangling with nerves. "I don't think I need any more caffeine. As it is, I may never sleep again."

Standing over the steaming cocoa, wielding a wooden spoon, Barbara looked unnervingly like one of the stereotypical witches from *Macbeth*. But her nod was sympathetic. "There may still be some things we can do." She motioned with her head at the corner cabinet. "Get cups out, will you, Frank?

"We've got plenty of time to talk," she continued, pouring cocoa. "The girls won't be back from the mall for at least an hour." She set a heaping plate of cookies in the middle of the table. Jeremy appeared like a genie from a bottle, extracted a chocolate-chip bribe, and was dispatched toward the toy box with a pat on his well-padded fanny.

By the time he reappeared, Barbara had heard most of Carrie's story. She leaned backward in her chair, cheeks puffed in a soundless whistle, even as she headed Jeremy off with another cookie. "Whew," she said.

278

She drained the last of her cocoa, set the cup down, and gazed into it, frowning, as though she expected to read a message in the dregs. "Okay." She looked up decisively. "We've still got two possibilities, and I don't see why we shouldn't follow up on both of them."

Across the table, Frank and Carrie looked at each other, astonished at this entirely novel concept. Barbara ignored them blithely. "Therapy is probably a good idea," she continued. "Lee Ann's going to need help dealing with all this. Probably more so if it *isn't* all in her head."

"I'd like to think it isn't," responded Carrie drily. "But as ghosthunters we seem to have run into a dead end."

"There may still be something we can do about the house, too."

"I'm open to suggestions." Nervous energy dwindling, Carrie rested her cheek on her hand and realized how very tired she was. "A ceiling at three A.M. is not a pretty sight," she said.

They spent almost another hour around the table, making plans and more cocoa; all three of them looked up in surprise when Penny and Lee Ann came breezing in.

"Are you checking up on me?" asked Lee Ann, with just enough sarcasm to make her point but not enough to call down parental wrath in public. "Here I am, where I said I'd be!" She twirled lightly, arms flung out. "With who I said I'd be!"

"Whom." Carrie's mouth made the correction automatically, while her mind was still pondering the youthful resilience that left her daughter pink-cheeked and bright-eyed, without a trace of last night's horror. "And no, I'm not checking up on you. I'm here to talk to Barbara."

"And Frank?" the girl asked, too sweetly.

"And Frank." Carrie suppressed irritation and kept her own voice level and reasonable. "I want to see Keith for a bit, too, when he gets back. Then we can go home and have dinner."

Lee Ann, like Pandora, couldn't stand to be left out of anything. She motioned to Penny, pulled out a chair, and reached for a cookie, displaying every intention of settling in with the adults.

Carrie headed her off with those five little words that act on a teenager like garlic on a vampire. "Have you done your homework?" she asked.

Her daughter looked sullen. "No," she admitted. The two girls assumed a veneer of complete indifference and went off upstairs, snagging another fistful of cookies on the way out.

Sleep that night was thick and deep—and clogged with dreams that pulled at Lee Ann like quicksand, inexorable and treacherous. But in the narrow hours between night and morning she struggled awake, gasping and dry-mouthed beneath the avid weight. Her flannel gown, twisted and pulled awry, tangled her like bonds. She whimpered, confused, wakefulness still entwined with the disjointed remnants of dream; aware only of the intense aching, the *pressure*, that held her, building and building to a tingling peak. And then let her go.

Face hot against the cold air, harshly conscious of the blanket's rough wool against her skin, she lay still, eyes squeezed very tight. Gradually her breathing slowed and her racing heart began to settle down to its normal rhythm. Lee Ann straightened bedclothes, tugged at her gown, eradicating traces . . . everywhere but in her mind. Drowsiness stole back on her like a stalking cat, and she smiled into the darkness.

*   *   *

The man shuddered with his own release and was gone.

When the alarm went off, Carrie jolted out of deep slumber, disoriented, feeling as guilty as a sentry who has slept on duty. "It's a good thing they don't court-martial mothers," she told herself, sitting muzzily on the edge of the bed.

Monday morning. Time to fix breakfast, get Lee Ann off to school, get herself to the office. In comparison with the events of the weekend, a nice normal workday ought to look good; but Carrie had trouble summoning energy, much less enthusiasm, to deal with it. Like everything else in her life, priorities had all gone topsy-turvy, leaving the routine of daily life in second place to the exigencies of nightmare.

Over breakfast, Lee Ann was pallid and quiet, unnaturally subdued. Carrie hovered, serving waffles and sausage, feeling herself too-late watchful, and worrying about the answers to questions she was afraid to ask.

They dressed in their separate bedrooms and met again in the downstairs hall. "Do you need any money for lunch . . . or anything?"

Lee Ann shook her head and avoided her mother's eyes, standing on tiptoe to watch out the high window for the schoolbus.

"You don't look like you're feeling well. Are you all right?"

Thin shoulders lifted and fell almost imperceptibly under the thick quilted coat.

Carrie's stomach hollowed. "Did anything . . . did you . . . not sleep well?"

The girl's head turned only slightly, brow and

281

cheekbone outlined sharply against the dark wood of the door. Her face was pallid and bleak as wind-scoured bone.

"It was just a dream . . . I guess."

If this was a nightmare, it was one from which there was no waking. Carrie moved through the office day like a sleepwalker, dealing routinely with calls and correspondence, constantly fighting the weak tears that threatened to overwhelm her. Half an hour into what should have been her lunch break, still at her desk, she leaned her head on her hands, full of misgivings. Was she doing the right thing? Did she have any other options?

The endless tumble of her thoughts was maddening. Carrie reached for the phone before she could change her mind. There had to be an *end* to all this.

The voice at the other end this time was warm and pleasant, rather deep for a woman's. Despite her lofty degree and busy practice, the psychiatrist Keith had recommended unhurriedly took the time to talk and answer questions. Carrie hung up feeling somewhat more hopeful. She'd set things in motion; now she had to decide how to tell Lee Ann what she'd done.

It turned out just about as badly as Carrie had expected. "I made a doctor's appointment for you today," she said casually, over dinner.

Lee Ann frowned. "I'm not sick."

"Different kind of doctor. It's a lady; I got her name from Penny's dad. I thought . . ." Carrie hunted for words, following the approach Dr. Kerrick had suggested. "Well, all this has been really upsetting for you, and I thought . . ." A thunderhead of suspicion gathered in her daughter's eyes.

You thought, Lee Ann mimicked to herself sarcastically. Well, let me tell you, Mom, you've got no idea what's going on. She hugged her private knowledge to herself: one of the only things they couldn't touch. She almost smiled.

Across the table, her mother babbled on, oblivious. 'I thought it would be a good idea for you to talk to a counselor.'

A shrink. So that's it: they think I'm crazy. That's why all the phone calls, all of them getting me out of the way so they can decide what to do with me. Lee Ann pushed away from the table with a violent motion that rocked it on its heavy base. *What are they going to do with me? They've decided I'm crazy, and now I can never make them understand.*

She wheeled, grasping the back of her chair with clawed fingers, making it a barricade between herself and her mother. "There isn't anything wrong with me!"

"No, honey. But there *is* something wrong with the situation . . . with the house. I don't know what, but there is."

"And you're trying to blame it on me; you have right from the beginning. But it's your fault, don't you understand that? None of this would have happened, except for you."

Overhead, the kitchen light gave an absurd little *tink* and went out. They both jumped.

"See?" shrieked Lee Ann.

Carrie didn't . . . not at all. And her initial hope sagged downward into numb desperation.

"I have to keep looking," she told Frank tiredly. 'At this point I don't have much hope of really finding anything, but I have to try."

Carrie had spent the last two days of the week finding her own way through the newspaper's back files, still looking for some person or event that might lie at the root of the nightmare. Finally running out of names to research, she had been reduced to reading her way cover-to-cover through old dusty files and newer microfiche records, searching for something—anything—that might provoke recognition. Marge, doing volunteer duty at the library, had pledged to find anything that resource had to offer, and Barbara was going busily about her tasks, preparing to carry out their plans for tomorrow. Frank, attending to his own job demands, nevertheless called nightly to obtain a progress report and offer general support.

"I made an appointment with the therapist, too," she told him now, "and Lee Ann had a fit. I knew she would; but I had to do it. She's . . . still having the dreams."

He made a muffled noise which Carrie interpreted as sympathy; she strongly suspected that he was eating a sandwich as they talked. Finally he gulped, and an intelligible comment emerged. "It's going to be hard, I know; but I think Keith and Barbara were right. No matter what the cause is, the result is the same: Lee Ann's under terrible stress, and she needs help."

"I know. And at least I can feel like I'm doing *something*. Everything else has turned out to be a blind alley."

Frank took another bite of whatever he was eating and mumbled at her. "Speaking of which—did you find anything at the newspaper today?"

"Dust."

"I take it the day was unproductive."

"You take it right." She sighed in frustration. "At this point I'm pinning all my hopes on Barbara's other idea. Maybe it will work, even if we can't address our ghost by name."

"I hope so, Carrie. We'll do everything we can."

"My only other alternative is to sell the house. I

284

don't want to do it, but I may have to. If nothing else works."

"We'll know tomorrow, I guess."

But even tomorrow wasn't soon enough.

With a rhythm that had become ordinary and familiar, Carrie woke into darkness. It was just after three A.M., she knew, without even looking at the clock. The house was quiet. Carrie lay still, listening, then rolled over gratefully and began to drift back into slumber. A car went by on the street outside.

And across the hall in Lee Ann's room, something stirred.

The sounds might have been ordinary night noises—faint rustle and almost inaudible sob—but Carrie's body responded instantly, sickly, before her mind could even acknowledge what it heard. She lurched upward, whimpering her own fear, hagridden by the even greater fear for her daughter.

A few steps across the bedroom and then into the silent hall. At the threshold of Lee Ann's room now, and something loomed in the blackness, flying at her, rushing toward her face. Carrie flinched, eyes shut; flung up her arms . . . and encountered only yielding softness. The pillow plopped gently at her feet and lay inert, an inanimate puff of feathers and fabric.

The pillow? Lee Ann's pillow? Carrie stared down at it uncomprehending. And the noises began again.

Her daughter lay pressed against the sheets, hair fanned out across their whiteness like something spilled. The prim cotton gown had been unbuttoned at her throat, and its ruffled hem was pulled up around her waist. Carrie pressed a hand against her mouth and gulped against rising nausea.

Lee Ann's hands, flung up above her head, twined and knotted around the posts of the bed; her bent legs

285

were spread wide. And the bed was moving rhythmically.

The girl whimpered, then stiffened, head flung back, legs jerking spasmodically. Sound wrung its way from the grip of nightmare; a low and guttural utterance that might have been pain or pleasure . . . or both. And Carrie knew for certain that it didn't come from her daughter's throat.

"Lee Ann." Her own whisper was strengthless unable to drive back the demons that preyed on her daughter in sleep. She dragged air into laboring lungs, forced a desperate cry: "Lee Ann . . . wake up!"

The girl's head turned, very slowly, and she faced her mother with eyes that were dark-rimmed and lightless.

"I'm awake," she said.

It is a siege, Carrie thought, stirring oatmeal as though it were boiling oil to be poured over the battlements. Right now, in the twentieth century, in a little frame cottage without even a single turret. But however nebulous the opponent, the battle was all too real.

Breakfast was almost normal. Almost. Lee Ann came downstairs very late, taking shameless advantage of Saturday morning. Tousle-haired and heavy-eyed, she drooped over the table, chin in hand pretending to read the paper.

How much did she remember? Carrie dithered around the kitchen, starting questions she never finished, making tentative gestures of concern that were recalled in midair. Lee Ann, oblivious, only wrinkled her nose at the oatmeal with a theatrical shudder. "This stuff is disgusting. Why can't you ever buy ordinary cereal?" Having registered the obligatory complaints, however, she managed to suppress distaste long enough to down the entire bowlful, a batch of sausages, and several glasses of juice.

Carrie only watched, incredulous, and wished it were as easy for those of her own vintage to throw off the effects of sleeplessness and horror. She felt as though she had been pulled through a clothes wringer.

"Are you . . . all right?" she finally asked. Her concerns were too huge, too portentous, to fit in such an inane phrase. But she understood instinctively that too-close questioning would only push her daughter away—and that any step could take her much too near the edge of a precipice.

Lee Ann nodded, mouth full, politely answering the surface question and disregarding the implications beneath. Ignorance was a game they both had played.

Now the girl wriggled out of her chair, stacked her dishes in the sink, and scooped up Pandora, who had been lying under the table, waiting patiently for sausage scraps.

"I'm going over to Penny's." The girl rubbed the little cat under its chin, and loud purring filled the spaces where human conversation flagged.

"Don't forget you're sleeping over there tonight."

Lee Ann barely paused on her way out of the room. Over her shoulder she cast her mother a bored look full of too-sophisticated knowledge. "Oh, don't worry . . . I'll be out of your way."

It was a siege, all right. But Carrie had to give up her vague hope that some camaraderie, at least, might come of it. Far from improving her relationship with her daughter, the nightmare seemed to be pushing them farther apart.

Barbara's face was grim. Along with Keith and

287

Frank, she was unloading things from the station wagon, ready for their planned assault on Carrie's house. She hefted a large dark blue binder, full of loose-leaf pages that appeared to be handwritten, and handed it to Frank. "Take this in, will you? And this?" She hung a canvas tote bag on his arm, and he vanished obediently.

"I don't think Lee Ann should be in the house at night," she told Carrie decisively, returning to their original subject. Her forehead corrugated in concern. "With any luck, this will take care of it," she said. "But until we know for sure—and that may take several days—I'd like Lee Ann to stay with us."

She raised a hand to forestall Carrie, who was opening her mouth to voice a polite protest. "Just at night. And just temporarily. It's the only way to make sure she's safe. She simply can't stay here at night."

Keith nodded. "I'm sorry we didn't think of it before. It's an obvious step to take. I guess we just didn't expect things to get this bad."

They had spent most of the early evening around the fireplace in Carrie's living room, explaining what they intended to do. "It's a cleansing," Barbara had told her. "Not that different from a Church exorcism, really. We use water and salt, the symbol of earth; and burning incense, for air and fire . . . bringing all the natural elements of the earth to drive out something unnatural."

Carrie had nodded politely and clamped a tight lid on her misgivings. If there was any other choice, she couldn't imagine what it was.

Now utter darkness had drawn in around the house. Carrie drew the curtains over windows that had become shallow black mirrors. Barbara began setting out white candles, carefully, in saucers to catch dripping wax. Only one lamp was lit, and Keith, in an armchair beside it, was paging through the book, occasionally clicking open the binder rings to remove a required page. The others would be joining them soon: Louise and Mark and a woman Carrie hadn't met. But not Marge, to Carrie's surprise.

"Marge is a psychic, not a witch," Frank had explained. "If things had gone a little differently, we might have had another session with her tonight. She was game to try again, especially if we got a handle on your ghost's identity—a name, an event, anything—to give her a lead. But under the circumstances, she thought it would be more useful to try something else instead."

Something else . . . like magic? Carrie's thought had been sour; unable to exclude the impossible, she was reluctantly forced to admit the improbable.

Footsteps shuffled across the porch. Louise and Mark? Or the other member—what was her name— Janet? Carrie reached the foyer just as the door opened to admit a blast of cold air. And Lee Ann.

Color high, eyes glittering, the girl faced her across the tiny expanse. "Forgot my toothbrush." She smirked; but the lacerating glance she flung at Frank clearly suggested other, cruder reasons for her invasion.

Penny stepped across the threshold just behind her friend, flapping her hands in a semaphore of helpless explanatory gestures. Barbara's daughter understood that the arranged sleepover was more than a social visit, and she took her charge seriously. Carrie spared a moment to nod at her reassuringly.

By now Lee Ann's eyes had flicked past her mother, into the dim-lit living room, searching with entirely unbecoming fanaticism for some evidence of sin, or at least impropriety. What she found was apparently not at all what she'd expected.

"Let's get your toothbrush," Penny urged, making an abortive movement as though she might resort to physical restraint. She shuffled sideways, trying to get in front of her friend. "Come on!"

But Lee Ann stepped forward, craning. "What are you doing?" she asked.

No one had an immediate answer—at least not one they wanted to give her. The silence stretched out, long and guilty. It was Barbara, of course, who finally stepped forward, gesturing the two girls into the room.

The explanation she gave Lee Ann was a shortened and simplified version of their earlier discussions with Carrie. In the middle of it all, Louise and Mark came in with a thin, dark woman. They seemed to take in the situation at a glance and sat down silently, waiting.

"So what we're doing basically," Barbara wound up, "is like an exorcism from the church—to cast out the 'visitor' and cleanse the house."

Lee Ann's reaction was something not one of them could have foreseen.

"You can't! Oh God, you can't do that!" The girl's voice was shrill with strain. The room absorbed it, uncaring, leaving a hollow stillness as tense and fragile as the surface of a bubble. The silence surged . . . and across the makeshift circle a candle *snapped*, with a small wet sound like breaking bone. Galvanized, Lee Ann whirled and began picking up candles and saucers with frantic energy, piling them haphazardly on the coffee table. A saucer clattered to the floor and broke.

"Lee Ann, it's all right." Carrie laid her hand on her daughter's arm in gentle restraint. "Really, honey, what can it hurt?"

"He'll go to hell . . . won't he?"

Barbara's mouth rounded in a silent *Ahhh* of understanding. "We can't know that, Lee Ann. I guess he'll go where he deserves to go; but it will be because of whatever he did when he was alive. Not

290

because of you."

"No!" The girl pulled away, hard; staggered and turned to face them like an animal at bay; the last two candles, forgotten in her hands, drooped meltingly, writhed and knotted, twisting like white snakes against her fingers. Lee Ann thrust them away from her with a wordless cry, shaking her hands in revulsion. Behind her a log on the dying fire dropped with a crack and swirl of embers.

"You can't!" It was a shriek, almost of agony. She whipped her head around wildly, desperate to find comprehension in any one of the alien adult faces.

"It's Daddy. Don't you understand? It's Daddy!"

CHAPTER XXIII

Everything *narrowed* around her, and Carrie focused all her attention on not being sick. Sounds and voices receded into meaninglessness. A rushing in her ears blanketed normal hearing; vision swam and grayed. Hands grasped her upper arms roughly, deposited her in a chair and pushed her head down. She gulped air gratefully, listening to distant hubbub with no sense of involvement. Everything could just go on without her for a while.

Chaos and sickness waned after a time, and Carrie pushed herself resolutely upright from her undignified posture. Frank brought her a glass of water and brushed awkwardly at the limp strands of hair that clung damply to her forehead. The room was not as full as it had been. Carrie closed her eyes again, wondering idly where everyone had gone but without the energy to ask. She assumed hazily that someone would tell her whatever she needed to know.

"You okay?" Barbara hitched her chair closer and peered at Carrie inquiringly. "I sent Janet on home, and Louise and Mark took the girls back to our place."

Carrie drew in a breath that trembled; tears scalded their way upward and overflowed the corners of her eyes. She couldn't make her voice work, but there was nothing to say anyway.

"I don't think you should be by yourself tonight." Barbara's expression was typically kind and concerned. "Why don't you come home with us? Always room for one more."

Frank looked up from where he sat on the floor beside Carrie's chair. "Or I could stay with you."

A vestige of color rose in her drained face, but the look Carrie turned to him was anguished. "I think . . . I'd rather be out of the house," she managed.

They left the place like refugees, gathering up books and belongings, taking a small overnight bag for Carrie. She looked back, just once, and wondered what she was shutting in when she closed the door.

Oh God. The thought leaped and gibbered in the darkness at the back of her mind. *What if Lee Ann is right?*

Her mind circled with treadmill hopelessness through a long and restless night; the sleep that overcame her finally, near dawn, was shallow and fitful, full of dreams that made insomnia look good by comparison.

In the leaden morning she sat over a steaming cup of coffee, certain that her stomach would rebel at anything more substantial. The teenagers were still in bed upstairs, and Keith had gone blearily down to supervise the smaller children in the recreation room. Barbara was going about her chores in matter-of-fact fashion, providing a silent companionship more comforting than words. When the phone rang, she plucked it up casually and listened for a moment; her back went rigid. "It's Marge," she hissed, one hand muffling the receiver. "She's found something!"

293

Carrie straightened, dully willing to hope, even against all the evidence.

Barbara tipped her head, cradling the phone which was buzzing at her insistently. "That sounds right," she said. "That sounds exactly right." The phone crackled and sputtered, and Barbara nodded several times as though the speaker on the other end could see her. "Well, we can find out more this week, when the offices are open. I'll call you. Yes." She nodded again and rolled her eyes at Carrie eloquently. "This is important, Marge. Thank you. Thanks a lot!"

She hung up the phone, called down the stairwell to Keith and spun back to Carrie, eyes alight with excitement. "She found him! Your ghost! It's got to be."

"What? What? Tell me!" Carrie bumped her mug, which sloshed coffee, and mopped absently at it with a napkin.

"One of the other volunteers at the library is a retired schoolteacher, and she knew Paul Markwell. You remember, I told you Mrs. Markwell had a son who was involved in some sort of scandal. All very hush-hush, of course . . ."

"So what about him?"

"Well, apparently nothing was ever proved—he wasn't arrested or anything—but he was accused of child molesting."

They looked at each other for an endless frozen moment. Carrie drew in a long whistling breath and leaned forward, stunned, putting her elbow down in a puddle of cold coffee.

"What's going on?" Keith appeared from the basement regions, hair on end, still in his bathrobe. Carrie dabbed ineffectually at her sleeve and left Barbara to answer him.

"We've found the ghost!"

His reaction was gratifying—an open-mouthed

294

double take that would have done any ham actor proud. "No kidding?"

"We don't have all the details, but I'm sure this is it." She took pity on Keith, who looked stupefied, and poured him a cup of coffee while she talked. "Marge found out that Paul Markwell was accused of molesting two young girls—students in his class."

Keith's eyes came all the way open, and he began taking in coffee and information simultaneously. "What happened to him?"

"We don't know; it was all hushed up. Remember, this was twenty years ago, and no one talked about things like that."

"We'll have to find out," Carrie put in. "To be really sure."

Barbara nodded at her understandingly. "Of course we will. Marge said he left town right after the scandal broke . . . moved somewhere down south, they thought. That's why we didn't find a death record for him: he died somewhere else."

In the wake of a jolt of caffeine, Keith's mental processes finally came to life. He frowned. "Not to throw ice water on a beautiful theory, but why would he be haunting Carrie's house?"

Barbara looked momentarily taken aback. "Well, he lived there with his mother for a long time; he was thirtyish when all this happened. So that's probably the place he remembers as home."

Keith looked unconvinced.

"And there were some other rumors . . . nothing that was proven, you understand." Barbara gave Carrie an apologetic glance. "About neighborhood children. In the house."

They spent most of the afternoon chewing over possibilities and repeating the story to Frank, who just happened to drop in.

"So it looks like we've found the source of the problem," Barbara told him. "But we still have to decide what we're going to do about it."

Keith looked at her in surprise. "We finish what we started last night, of course," he said. "Why not?"

Carrie nodded positively. Of course they would. It had been practically their last hope, hadn't it?

They all looked at Barbara, who demurred. "What about Lee Ann?" she asked. "She's on the ragged edge as it is, and I'm a little afraid of what could happen."

"Nothing will happen. Why should it?" Carrie almost stuttered, anxious. "Once I tell her it's not . . . not her father."

"Telling her doesn't mean she'll believe it." Barbara gnawed at a fingernail pensively, something she almost never did.

"When you get right down to it, all we really have is a piece of twenty-year-old gossip, after all," Keith agreed glumly.

"So we need to find out more. Then I can tell her the whole story, not just gossip." Carrie spoke confidently enough, but her spirits dropped with a sickening rollercoaster lurch. What *would* Lee Ann say? What was she going to think? The others looked at the table in lengthening silence, and the morning's promise began to unravel.

It was Frank who finally offered a solution both simple and elegant. "When we do have more to go on, why not have Penny and Danny tell her? I'll bet she'd believe it then," he suggested, with an exaggeratedly sly grin.

Keith grinned back admiringly. "And you're the one of us who doesn't have kids!"

"I remember what it was like being one," said Frank modestly.

*   *   *

The girl was gone. The dormer room was empty, her bed was empty; but still the man returned, drawn like a moth to flame. A flame that was treacherous, like everything else; ready to burn him up if he didn't handle it just right. The girl knew. She felt it too. He knew she did.

That's how he knew she wasn't gone for good. She'd be back. They always came back. Fascinated by him . . . by the things he did to them. Oh yes, she'd be back.

Monday morning was gray and rainy and should have been depressing, but Carrie felt surprisingly optimistic. With Lee Ann gone, the night had been quiet and undisturbed, and she had awakened to a sense of hope and well-being. Now she could make plans again . . . now she could move forward. Over breakfast she had to restrain an irresponsible impulse to call the office and plead illness, take the day off and join Barbara in a research effort that finally was getting someplace.

Her three days stuck at a desk were even worse than normal; Carrie poked resentfully at typewriter keys, chafing at the dismal routine and wondering what vital progress was being made elsewhere, without her.

The answer, it seemed, was little or none. Barbara called every night with an update, but had almost nothing to report. "Schools," she told Carrie in disgust, "are incredibly coy about giving out information. I had trouble even getting anyone to admit Paul Markwell ever worked there. They did finally give me the date he was hired, and the date of his . . . resignation, but that was all."

"Good grief," said Carrie faintly, turning over the jumble in the freezer in search of dinner ingredients. "You wouldn't think it would matter after twenty years."

"Well, it was better than the school board," said Barbara resignedly. "They wouldn't talk to me at all."

"Maybe we should have expected that." Carrie ripped open a package of frozen carrots and dropped them into boiling water, thinking unkind things about bureaucrats.

"After that I went to the newspaper office—I'll bet they're getting sick of us by now—and looked at the back files for that time period. I didn't find anything, but then I didn't really expect to. I also looked up old Mrs. Markwell's obituary. Lots of times they give cities of residence for out-of-town survivors."

"That was a great idea!"

"Unfortunately, it didn't help." Barbara sighed. "They listed Paul as a survivor, but there wasn't any more information. Maybe he didn't want people in his hometown to know where he was."

"Understandable, I guess." Lee Ann would be returning for dinner soon, before going back to the Burnetts' for the night. Carrie pulled out a package of hamburger and stood looking at it, unable to keep her mind on casseroles. They couldn't have come so far only to hit another dead end. She had to have something to tell Lee Ann—something solid, something real. And soon.

Somehow she kept the disappointment from showing in her voice. "Do you have any other ideas? Something I can do while I'm off tomorrow and Friday?" Over the phone, when no one could see her face, it was easy to sound brisk and optimistic and capable.

Barbara's own energetic tone was revitalizing. "I think our next step is to find out where he went when he left town, then see what we can turn up there."

So there was still another avenue out of the maze. "Okay," said Carrie. "Any ideas how I can do that?"

"The easiest might be to find out which nursing

home Mrs. Markwell was in. It should have records of next of kin."

"Of course! I should have thought of that." Carrie noticed that she was still holding the package of hamburger; laying it on the counter, she began to assemble other ingredients. "Or the real-estate agent who sold me the house might know; wouldn't she have needed permission from all the heirs before the property was sold?"

"That's an idea. Why don't you follow up on that? Then either Marge or I will check on the nursing home." Barbara, as usual, was ticking off organizational steps. "Split the work," she said.

"Will do," answered Carrie. "I'd better go now; Lee Ann will be home any minute. Thanks, Barbara. Maybe we'll get this mess resolved, and I can take my daughter back."

"No problem." Barbara dismissed Carrie's apologetic manner breezily. "With five kids of my own, I hardly even notice one more."

The real-estate agent, having already sold Carrie the house, tended to be lax about returning phone calls. For two days, Carrie hovered near the phone, jumping at each shrill summons like a teenager waiting for a prom invitation.

On this ring it was Barbara calling, not a computerized sales pitch. "We found it!" she announced jubilantly.

Carrie pulled one of the old wooden chairs away from the table and sat down. "Honest?"

"Some small town in Mississippi—I have it written down here." Barbara was babbling with excitement. "Marge is on her phone now, browbeating the police department into looking up any records they might have on Paul Markwell."

"Will they really tell her?" After so much disap-

299

pointment, Carrie could hardly dare to hope.

"In a small town they may not be as hung up on rules and regulations," Barbara pointed out, although the observation was probably more hope than certainty. She chuckled. "Besides, at this point Marge is absolutely not going to take no for an answer. She said if necessary she'd bully her lawyer into calling them and making official noises."

Carrie was duly impressed. She was even more overwhelmed when she was called back an hour later from the Burnetts' house, Marge on one extension and Barbara on another, both talking at once. "It's him!" caroled Barbara.

"No question about it," acceded Marge.

The chair was still pulled up to the counter beneath the phone. Carrie sat down again. "Really?"

"Really!" "Absolutely." The two voices collided in midair, tangled, sorted themselves out.

"Tell her about it, Marge," urged Barbara graciously. "You were the one who talked to them."

"Maybe in a small town it's harder to cover things up," said Marge in preface. "But anyhow, this time he didn't get away with it. He apparently pled guilty to . . . let's see, where are my notes? . . . two counts of 'unlawful transaction with a minor.' He was sentenced to fifteen years, and sent to the state prison psychiatric facility."

"So he died in prison." Carrie's voice was somber.

"I guess so. We don't have all the details yet, but they're sending me copies of some of the paperwork."

"So we'll have something definite to show Lee Ann," Barbara chimed in. "Or Penny can show her," she corrected.

The next week's mail brought the fat manila envelope that would be, Carrie was certain, their passport out of nightmare. The sheriff's clerk, true to her promise, had sent copies from Paul Markwell's file, including the arrest record and documents from the court proceedings that had sent him to prison.

When her daughter came home from school, Carrie knew at once that the Burnett teenagers had also done their part. Lee Ann was thoughtful and uncertain but willing at least to listen. "Penny says whatever is in our house, it isn't my dad." She flung the statement down like a gauntlet, and her eyes, for the first time in a very long while, held some rekindling of hope. "Danny says so too."

Carrie nodded soberly and let her read the contents of the envelope. "He lived here," she explained. "Paul Markwell. It was his mother's house."

"And you think it's him. Still in the house."

"Doesn't it seem more likely? Think about it—the kinds of feelings we've had. And the . . . the things that have happened."

Lee Ann shuffled through the papers again, refusing to meet her mother's eyes. Carrie leaned forward, with an illogical sense that physical closeness might somehow help bridge the emotional gap. "This can't have anything to do with your father."

Lee Ann laid the papers back on the table with a very controlled gesture and tidied the stack. "So what are you going to do?" she asked.

"Barbara and . . . her group are going to do a sort of blessing for the house. Like they started to before. To protect us, and get rid of . . . anything evil."

Lee Ann looked down at her hands, clasped tightly in her lap as though they were the only things she had left to hold on to. "What if we're wrong?" The question was quiet, not argumentative; and with the use of the word "we" Lee Ann had finally included herself with the rest of them.

Carrie hoped that relief and jubilation didn't show too plainly on her face. "We're not wrong, honey. I'm sure we're not."

301

*   *   *

The week trudged slowly toward its end, unremarkable and uneventful. On Saturday night Danny called for Lee Ann, to go on their first officially sanctioned date since the beginning of the new year. Circumstances had forced Carrie to take a more relaxed view of a relationship that was, at least, normal and human.

Long after the teenagers were out of sight, she continued to stand at the window, apprehensively watching the darkness gather and wondering what would come with it. The plans the others had made with such confidence had no depth or reality for her, and very little comfort. When she turned back into the lighted living room, it looked as shallow as a stage set waiting for the next scene to be played out.

What did she think they were really going to accomplish? Could a primitive ritual still have power today . . . when even the ponderous majesty of the Church had turned its back on magic and mysticism . . . in a century that interpreted demons as products of the mind rather than possessors of the soul?

They arrived in cars and not on broomsticks, crunching mundanely over the driveway gravel; still in her limbo of uncertainty and disbelief, Carrie went out to greet her friends. While the others bustled and carried, Frank drew her aside into an undemanding embrace. She stood with him for a time, leaning against the fender of the car, not quite ready to go inside, drawing needed warmth and comfort from his presence. Stealing a sidewise glance at his face, at the rough-hewn profile turned up to the sky, Carrie thought she could envy him the sureness of a belief she didn't share.

The breeze shifted and cold grass rustled like a sigh. Carrie pulled her head deeper into her collar and turned her own face up to the cathedral darkness. Under the remote mysterious gaze of the crescent moon, framed in a Gothic arch of trees, she began to feel, dimly, an echo of the old religion's reverence. Wasn't it possible that what they called magic was just another manifestation of God? Another aspect of the infinite?

Carrie willed herself to suspension of disbelief and went inside, carrying the feeling carefully like a candle that might be extinguished by thoughtless movement. Taking her place with the little group, she followed along as Barbara led them through the house, sprinkling each room with saltwater and tracing protective symbols at windows and doors. Returning to the living room, she paced with them through a rite that shared so many elements with her former faith—a cup of water and a billowing censer, a chalice of wine—but within a circle drawn invisibly with a willow wand. A synthesis of symbols, engaging all the senses in one focused effort.

Within the blossoming ring of candlelight, now they all stood silent, gathering themselves for one final effort. Carrie stood awkwardly with them, uncertain about her part, about what they would do. For the most part their ritual had seemed surprisingly ordinary, almost familiar. Until now.

"Paul Markwell," said Barbara suddenly, and Carrie jumped. "Paul Markwell," she said again, in a perfectly ordinary voice as though she were addressing another member of the group. But nothing else was ordinary. The room around them had faded away, leaving their tiny group stranded on an island of light in a place that was no longer completely real. Carrie wavered, unwilling to accept the evidence of her senses, and groped for Frank's hand, for the reassuring anchor of someone else's touch.

"This was your place once, but it is no longer,"

continued Barbara, her voice building to a tone of command. "You must leave this house and those who now inhabit it. Leave this place: we consign your spirit to the place which has been ordained for you."

Is this all? Is it really going to be this easy? Carrie's eyes passed over the rapt faces around her, looking for some sign, some indication, some idea of what would happen next. It didn't occur to her that none of them knew either.

Silence grew and filled the spaces between them; Carrie could feel it like a barrier between her and Frank. *What now? Surely we're supposed to do something* more.

Across the circle, Louise gasped and clutched at Mark, pointing. Behind Barbara, just beyond the edges of the circle, the air had begun to shimmer like heat waves above a pavement. There was no color, not even a shape, just a place where reality *bent* and time shifted slightly awry. Carrie blinked, blinked again; trying to focus on something that wasn't quite there.

Cold. It was so cold, and the candles had begun to gutter. Across their makeshift boundary of light, the darkness seemed to coil and thicken hungrily. Carrie stepped back involuntarily, pulling away from Frank's hand, from the group's supportive presence, to stand alone, all alone at the circle's edge.

Barbara moved calmly, stretching out one hand to Keith, the other to Mark; Louise reached for Frank, and Janet joined them at the other side. They turned, the six of them, to face the loathsome and malignant dark—a thin human line poised against something completely Other.

Afterward, Carrie told herself that what she saw was illusion, a hallucination born of stress and fear.

Barbara began to speak, in a language Carrie didn't understand, in a voice she was sure she'd never

304

heard. The words wove in and out of consciousness, pulling at her, drawing her, linking her with them like the strands of a web.

And the web became visible. Barbara's voice paused, the linked figures tensed, and cold blue light bloomed and flickered between their hands. Then her voice rose again, drawing strength from the others, drawing the light into herself, turning it into sound.

For seconds the ravening darkness seemed to pale and dwindle. Then, finding its own strength, its own terrible footing, it surged upward again, deepening against the contrast of the arcane light. And the light began to dim.

Barbara's voice faltered, ragged with exhaustion; the cords in her neck stood out with strain. Down their wavering line, hands remained clasped with white-knuckled tension; five faces mirrored her fierce effort. The chant ceased and the room was very silent, full of an effort that was all the greater for being invisible. The blackness drew itself up, pressing inward against their feeble ring of light, pitting a singular and obsessive force against the constraint of their combined wills. Carrie could feel it, pushing at her with staggering strength. With shame, she thought how much worse it must be for those who stood between her and the Visitor, and she knew, with utter certainty, that she must take her place with them.

She groped forward, numbly, on legs that almost refused the task . . . and found Frank's hand extended. Janet's fingers groped for hers on the other side, closing the circle. The final connection was made.

Something welled in Carrie then, finally whole, exultant, almost joyful; blindly, trustingly, she *opened* herself to them, with them, in a prodigal out-pouring of strength and will. Blue light bloomed again, crackling around her own fingertips.

305

Across the circle Barbara straightened and flung her head up defiantly, arms rigid, drawing on every reserve of strength the group could give. Something—something powerful—flashed among them and flung itself outward. Under its onslaught, the black air rippled like a shockwave made visible; reality shuddered at the ragged edge as the gelid shadow grayed and began to disperse, wavering out of reality like a wisp of smoke.

The room *drained*, empty of sound or movement, and the Visitor was gone. The witches, likewise drained, leaned inward, almost without volition, huddling together, holding each other. The house *filled* once more, this time with a unity of will that refused the coexistence of malignity.

The siege was over. The house felt *clean* again, possessed by no one but its rightful owners, and ready for them to take up life where it had been so terribly interrupted. Carrie's heart filled with relief and gratitude—and a welcome rebirth of hope.

CHAPTER XXIV

The man paced savagely, furious at the unexpected obstacle. *How nice for her, surrounded by friends. All of them, sticking together, getting in the way.* All of them so smug, so certain that they had slammed the door on him. And none of them had the vaguest idea what was really going on.

Stupid bitch, chasing shadows. When all along, the hunter prowled just out of reach, like a jungle cat at the edge of the campfire's light.

The next morning began like a hangover, all bright sunshine and hard-edged shadows, with no room at all for the shadow world of the previous night. *What in hell did I think I was doing?* Carrie propped her elbows on the old kitchen table and fixed her coffee cup with a sullen glare. *Magical mumbo jumbo in a suburban living room. Conjuring spirits over the coffee table. And what do I do? Join right in, and start seeing things too.* The tenuous logic of magic began to unravel in the remorseless light of day . . . but despite the aftermath of distaste, Carrie could not quite bring herself to disbelief.

Around her, the house was sunny and pleasant,

flooded with light; altogether ordinary. And it remained that way . . . serene, silent, and normal. Even at night. Even after Lee Ann came home to her own room. She and Carrie stayed poised in brittle trepidation for a time, then gradually relaxed, exhausted, and allowed themselves to remember what life had been like before the Visitor. Both of them slept undisturbed, and nothing walked at night except the cat.

It was yet another week, late in February, when the real-estate agent called Carrie at the office. "I'm so sorry, Mrs. Sutton," she burbled, "I've been out of town and just now got your message. One of the other agents in the office would have been glad to help you, if there's a problem . . . ?"

A problem. Carrie almost laughed, still giddy with relief, and started into the cover story she had prepared. "No, not at all. I had wanted to get in touch with Paul Markwell—the son of the lady who owned the house, do you remember?"

"Oh yes, of course. I had to get his permission, along with his sister's, for sale of the property." The real-estate agent paused delicately. "I don't know whether you know . . . ah . . . about the circumstances."

"Yes," Carrie assured her solemnly. "I found out through a local acquaintance—someone who knew the family—who also told me that he had died."

"Died? Why no, dear." The agent's voice was quizzical. "I had a letter from him just the other day, wanting to know about financial arrangements during his parole. There were legal questions, you understand, about his share of the estate. But I assure you, he's very much alive."

Carrie's free hand, suddenly clammy, flattened on

308

the desktop as though for greater contact with reality. *Parole. He's alive, and he's out of jail.* She bent forward sickly, leaning hard on the edge of her desk. *Then it was all real after all.*

He had been in her house. Turning on lights, opening doors. Watching them. *Oh, God. It couldn't be. . . . How could it be?* Fragmented thoughts clashed and gibbered and tried to arrange themself in some coherent pattern. But only one was really important: *He's out, and he's home. And he's after Lee Ann.*

There were times, Carrie had always thought, when life should simply come to a stop, like a freeze-frame out of a moving video. This should be one of them—now, when she needed time to *think*, time to decide what to do.

The phone in her hand was buzzing inquiringly. Carrie muttered at it—something polite and explanatory, she hoped, although she could never afterward remember what—then hung up and tried to call home. The phone buzzed at her again, over and over in the monotonous busy signal. *Well, if Lee Ann's on the phone, she must be all right.* But the queasy shaken feeling remained, leaving her sick with unreasoning panic. Carrie dropped the handset back with shaking fingers and bolted out of the office.

I've got to get home. Be with Lee Ann. Prisoned in the car, stoppered in the thickening late afternoon traffic, she hammered at the steering wheel with fists gnarled in frustration. *The police. I should have called the police.* And told them what? *This whole thing makes no sense. How could someone have gotten into my house—all those times, over and over?* It just wasn't possible. But it was the only answer. And Carrie hoped she hadn't arrived at it too late.

It seemed like hours before her house loomed up, gray and silent in the middle of the block. There was no light anywhere, not even in Lee Ann's dormer window. Carrie rattled at the door, fumbling her key into the lock with shaking hands. "Lee Ann?" Inside, the rooms were deep in shadow, and where was her daughter? "Lee Ann!"

Something moved, in the living room, in the darkness. Lee Ann—curled up in her favorite chair, in a posture that would give a yogi pause. *She's all right. Thank God.* The relief left Carrie feeling unraveled, taut muscles suddenly lax, pent breath letting go like a collapsing balloon. But almost before the breath was gone she saw the man.

Standing in the dining-room doorway just behind Lee Ann, he was sandy-haired, medium-sized, and ordinary, so ordinary that Carrie held onto hope for another wild second. Maybe he was a neighbor . . . or a salesman . . . somebody who had a right to be here. Maybe it was all right after all. But of course it wasn't.

He spoke first, his voice high-pitched and pettish, as though this were his home and Carrie the intruder. "I'm sorry you came," he said. "I didn't want to see you. If you'd just been a little later, we'd have been gone." Lee Ann flinched as he moved toward her and rested his hand on the chairback near her shoulder.

"Who are you? What are you doing here?" Carrie's own voice was shrill, and her prosaic demands were powerless.

Stupid bitch. The man looked at her calmly. His eyes were blue, a little watery, and quite mad. "I'm a friend of Lee Ann's. A special friend." He smiled, and the expression was more chilling than any scowl. "She called me here. And I came. I came to see her."

"No." Carrie rounded on him fiercely. "She didn't call you. No one called you. And we don't want you here. You have no right to be here."

He blinked, but only once; with a small gesture he

brushed her words away. "I used to live here, you see," he explained earnestly. In the slightly protuberant pale eyes and fleshy face Carrie thought she could see an echo of the boy he had been then. "I had a little workroom in the basement; I used to make toys for the kids. They always liked me."

It was so *right*, and yet so monstrous. The last dark piece fell into place, completing the pattern that Carrie's unwilling mind had tried so hard to reject. "The room upstairs, in front . . . that was your room."

The man nodded approvingly, like a teacher with an apt pupil, then moved his hand so it rested on Lee Ann's shoulder. "She sleeps there now," he said. "In my room. That was the first sign, you see."

"No!" Carrie's voice was strangled, her breathing harsh. "It wasn't a *sign*. It was . . . an accident. A coincidence. That's all. It doesn't mean anything."

The man continued to smile at her softly. *What did she know about it? What could she possibly know?* His pale eyes slid loosely around the room, and he changed the subject with a madman's abrupt logic. "I dreamed, you know. There wasn't a lot else to do. In that place."

"In prison," Carrie reminded him harshly. "Jail. Which is where you'll go again, if you do anything to us."

The threat, however remote, was her only weapon. Strung tight, Carrie watched for some faltering, some reaction to it. But he passed her words off as if they had no meaning, rambling on with no change in his empty smile. "At first they were just regular dreams," he said. "All jumbled up, just a lot of stuff that didn't make sense." His hand moved upward to rest on Lee Ann's head, stroking her hair, brushing lightly at the stray wisps at her temple. "But then they changed.

311

And it was so real. I dreamed this house again, like coming home."

He slipped his hand under Lee Ann's chin and tipped her head up gently. "I dreamed you," he said.

Ohgod, he's crazy, absolutely crazy, and there's nothing I can do. Nothing I can say will make any difference to a crazy man. Carrie's knees weakened and everything inside her went sick and hollow. Across the tiny space of the living room Lee Ann's face was paste-white and very still. The man's hand—Paul's hand—moved in an absent caress, long fingers crawling like a spider on her neck. Lee Ann shuddered, and he frowned.

Don't let him—God, don't let him. Carrie swallowed against the sour taste of nausea. *Stall, just stall. Play for time and maybe something will happen, someone will come.* But she didn't really believe it.

It was, however, the best idea that came to mind. Carrie drew her shoulders up achingly tight and forced herself to assume a calm and conversational tone. "I don't understand. What do we have to do with your dreams?"

"You were in them. She was." The man—Paul—dropped a fatuous glance downward at Lee Ann, who didn't look at him. "Then after a while, they weren't dreams anymore . . . they were real. I was really here."

The room chilled into silence. *Oh, God it can't be, it can't be real, it isn't possible.* Carrie's body felt leaden, lifeless, only the panicked heartbeat stirring, pounding like fists against the cage of her ribs. It was like that book of Barbara's—about ghosts of living people. *But surely it wasn't possible.* How could someone *dream* his way into their house . . . into their lives?

"I don't know how it happened, but it was real."

312

The man's face glazed with a reminiscent smile as he bent over Lee Ann, touching her cheek in a parody of tenderness. His eyes had a hectic shine. "I could see you. Watch you. Even touch . . ." His hand moved again, downward, idly tracing the neckline of her blouse.

Spots of scarlet appeared on Lee Ann's cheekbones, clownish against the pallor, and a scream clawed at the back of Carrie's throat. *What is he going to do?* And then, *What has he already done?*

"Let her alone!" she burst out. "Get out of our house! You don't live here anymore, you have no right to be here. Get out, or I'll call the police."

Bitch. Jealous bitch. But I'm the one who's in control now, and there's nothing you can do about it. The man's breathing accelerated nervily, ratcheting against the silence; but he continued to smile, and his lips were wet.

Carrie took two inadvertent steps forward before she saw the knife. It glittered in his hand, mesmerizing, turning to catch the light; dangling almost negligently beside his leg, where only she could see it.

The phone. Call the police. But the phone was in the kitchen, behind him. *Could I make it upstairs, to the bedroom extension?*

That thought died immediately. She couldn't run and leave Lee Ann, no matter what.

The man gave her a slow and superior smile. "It's perfectly all right," he said. "The dreams were signs too, don't you see? And then when I was here, I could leave signs for her, too." *First the lights and the bedroom door. Little things. But she noticed, and she knew. Going slowly, patiently, like always . . . never too fast, that could ruin it. Then the photo. That was the best, the final inspired touch.* After that he'd had her right in the palm of his hand. He dropped his eyes to Lee Ann once more, fingers exploring

313

delicately along her neck and collar. "And you knew all along, didn't you? Didn't you?"

"No!" Lee Ann's voice was pitched almost to inaudibility, and she surged forward, away from him, away from the invading hands and insistent voice of her own dreams. "No!"

But the man moved far faster. With catlike reflex, the hand at her neck tightened viciously and yanked her upright, pulling her out of the chair, pulling her hard against him. "Little bitch!" The other hand came up, bringing the knife to a rigid vertical, trembling with tension, level with Lee Ann's eyes.

"After all that, you shut me out. You and your friends. With your candles and your incense and your stupid chanting." Over the girl's head his eyes met Carrie's. "I don't know how you did it, how you knew," he raged, a patch of froth forming like a canker at the corner of his mouth. "All I had were my dreams, and you took them away."

He wrenched at Lee Ann, almost tugging her off her feet. *Little bitch!* "And you let her do it!" His bared teeth were set in a rictus of anger and pain. *Cheap little tease, just like all the rest of them.* "But not anymore. I'm not going to let you do that to me." Frenzied, he waved the knife in a shallow arc before her eyes and brought it to rest against her neck.

White-lipped, Lee Ann strained backward against him, feet slipping on the polished floor, her fingers twining around his pinioning arm, and her neck twisting away—away from the knife. The man smiled, pleased; his hand at her neck loosened and drifted downward, inside her blouse, roughly fondling her breasts. A button popped and rolled across the floor.

The girl whimpered, a small animal sound, and drew up her hands, pushing ineffectually at his arm. The knife shifted, just a little, and she froze, a thin

314

trickle of red running down her neck. The man tightened his grip, pulling her close; his hand moved lower, to her groin, pressing her to him, rubbing against her from behind, swelling with a foretaste of gratification.

"She's going to come with me now," he said, smoothing his voice over roughening breath. *It's going to be the way I say, the way I want, for a change.* He clamped his arm like a bar around Lee Ann's waist and swung around, propelling her toward the front door and the darkness outside. In her ear his voice was very soft. "It's going to be just the way the dreams showed me."

Carrie swayed forward again, reflexively, but there was the knife, cold steel against her daughter's neck, sharp, so sharp. And there was nothing she could say or do, nothing that would stop it. Nothing that would stop him.

The knife gleamed, filling her vision, riveting her panicked attention, leaving no room for anything but its deadly threat. Then behind the struggling pair there was an answering gleam—a glint of eye, a shiny button. Something moved, very quietly, in the darkness of the dining room, and a tall form detached itself from the surrounding shadows.

Frank! Moving faster than his normal easygoing manner would suggest, he swung a tire iron through a whistling arc and brought it down heavily across the back of Paul's head.

Markwell lurched forward, arms still around Lee Ann, and dropped like a stone, bearing her to the floor with his weight. The girl screamed just once and immediately after began to sob in great tearing gulps, scrabbling hysterically at the floor, nails scraping ineffectually, fingers tangling in the fringe of the rug.

Carrie lunged forward and dropped to her knees,

315

encircling her frantic daughter. Frank twined his fingers in the man's shabby sweater and dragged at the limp form, pulling it away; then he sprawled on the floor beside them, trying to enfold them both with arms that didn't seem quite long enough.

"I tried to call," he explained to Carrie. "But I couldn't get through, so I decided to drop in."

Carrie swallowed a lump that felt like a bird's nest in her throat and nodded. "You're always welcome," she told him.

CHAPTER XXV

"Do you ever feel like you run a refugee camp?" she asked Barbara later, over restorative coffee; after the police and the ambulance had come and gone, after the impersonal questions had been answered, and a kindly young technician had given Lee Ann a sedative. They'd put her to bed on Barbara's couch, in the midst of all the activity, and she'd gone to sleep holding Danny's hand.

Carrie slumped in a chair at the table, allowing herself to unwind and hoping that she wouldn't unravel. "I've never been so scared in my life," she began again. "If Frank hadn't come along . . ." Her voice choked off and she pressed a fist against her mouth, trying hard not to give way to tears.

"We have Marge to thank; if she hadn't phoned me . . ."

"Marge?"

Frank nodded, still grim and thin-lipped with reaction. "Someone from the prison remembered, and they sent her notice that he was being released." He ran a hand across his forehead as though he could wipe away his own thoughts. "I tried to call you, and when I couldn't get through . . ."

It took a minute for that to sink in. Very slowly, Carrie came upright in her chair, hands pressed hard

317

against the table's surface. *"Being* released?" she croaked. "When? You mean he just now got out?"

"Uh-huh," affirmed Frank. "Earlier this week. Monday or Tuesday, I think Marge said."

"But . . ." Carrie sputtered, once, and stopped, completely at a loss. "Then he couldn't have been in my house . . . before."

At the counter, Barbara wrinkled her brow, putting together sandwiches and pieces of their story at the same time. "Maybe we were right after all: Paul Markwell was our ghost. . . ."

"Except he wasn't dead. . . ."

"Seems like a proper ghost really *ought* to be dead first," grumbled Frank. "It's downright indecent."

The smile that flickered across Carrie's face was little more than a ghost itself, but Frank noticed it with pleasure and relief.

Barbara set a plate of sandwiches on the table and sat down across from them, cupping her chin in her hands. "It was one of the things we talked about, remember? Ghosts who turned out to be apparitions of living people."

Carrie drew a shaky breath, remembering. "He said . . . he said he dreamed us." She shivered, drawing her shoulders up tightly and taking a hard grip on the hot mug of coffee. "And then somehow the dreams were real. He was really there. Watching us. And doing things, like turning on lights, opening doors—trying to communicate. Trying to . . . get through . . . to Lee Ann."

"Ugh!" Barbara made a face.

Keith, beside her, leaned back in his chair with a low whistle. "A man obsessed with young girls, cooped up in prison with no outlet for his feelings . . ."

"And then Lee Ann happened along." Frank frowned, working out the implications. "Another young girl, this time actually living in his house." I

318

was only an echo of Carrie's own thought, but the words, finally spoken aloud, made her feel that icy feet had walked up her spine. "That was the link he needed . . . to come home."

Home. Right now it was the saddest word Carrie had ever heard. She began to shiver again, curiously bereft; leaning for warmth into the comforting circle of Frank's arms.

Spring came, like a surprise visitor, bringing flowers. Along with the greening plants, a For Sale sign blossomed in Carrie's front yard.

"I just can't live here anymore," she explained to Frank, and shot a quick look at Lee Ann who, along with Penny and Danny, was sitting across the table from them. In the past weeks, the girl had come to a quiet acceptance of Frank, poignantly aware that she might well owe him her life. The shared ordeal had brought them together, all of them, finally, in some deep and unspoken way.

"*We* can't live here anymore," Carrie corrected herself. They had tried, she and Lee Ann, sleeping together in the other front bedroom, or downstairs on the pull-out couch. But the house was too full of nightmares that had come true, and if the rooms were no longer haunted, nevertheless their dreams remained full of ghosts.

Lee Ann turned her head, listening, and nodded heartfelt agreement. Settling back in her chair, she stared meaningfully at Frank.

Who looked back, fidgeting, then dropped his eyes to the table. "Umm," he said. "You know, if you're going to be looking for a new place to live anyway . . . I think my place is plenty large enough for three."

Carrie, who probably should have expected something of the sort, nevertheless would have expected

319

the offer to be made in more private circumstances. She actually blushed. Glancing sideways, she gave him a quick promising smile, then turned her attention back to Lee Ann, who was watching her smugly. There must be something she was missing here.

Three young faces beamed at her across the table, pleased with themselves for having made such a splendid arrangement. "It's not very far from here," Lee Ann informed her. She grasped Danny's hand firmly and swiveled her head to smile at both her friends. "I can still go to my same school," she said.